The
Dark
Side
of
the
Dream

Alejandro
Grattan-Domínguez

THE DARK SIDE OF THE DREAM

Published by EgretBooks.com
Laredo, Texas

$16.95 US

Front Cover Original Art: © 2012, Xill Fessenden

Book Design: Mike Riley, ajijiccomputing.com

Library of Congress Control Number: 2012947972
The Dark Side of the Dream / Grattan-Dominguez, Alejandro —
Revised Ed. 2012.

Printed in U.S.A.

ISBN 978-1-4812558-1-3

EgretBooks.com, 2163 Lima Loop, PMB 071-409, Laredo, TX 78045, www.egretbooks.com
EgretBooks.com Is A Member Of The Independent Book Publishers Association, 1020 Manhattan Beach Blvd, Suite 204, Manhattan Beach, CA, 90266, www.ibpa-online.org

—READER AND MEDIA REACTION—

* "It explores the uniqueness of the Mexican-American experience, yet this historical novel places it within the context of universal human dilemmas – sure to be an award-winning film." – Public Broadcasting System (PBS) – USA

* "A terrific first novel . . . the stirring saga of a Mexican family in the US during the 40s and early 50s will remind readers of Steinbeck's classic 'The Grapes of Wrath'." The Alameda (Ca.) Journal – USA

* "It brings you to tears and instills terror . . . a panoramic and absolutely gripping historical novel." The Calgary Sun – Canada

* "The delight of a great read is not forgotten, and like Steinbeck's 'The Grapes of Wrath,' the story sings without preaching." Guadalajara Reporter – Mexico

* "With a riveting narrative and lean but lyrical prose, the novel is a profoundly moving epic about immigrants from Mexico who came to Texas shortly after the US entered WWII." – Texas Review of Books – USA

* "A monumental historical novel. Marvelously vivid portrait of both the tragedy and triumph of one Mexican family in the US." Booklist – USA

* "The author deals not in simplistic black and whites, but in the world of grays, which is, of course, where the truth usually resides." – El Paso Herald – USA

* "Filled with many complex characters . . . dozens of scenes of great emotional power… much wry humor. A historical novel that stays in one's mind long after it has been read." – MRTA – Mexico

* "The author has a refreshing contempt for stereotypes. Impartially, he heaps scorn on cultural chauvinists at both ends of the spectrum. . . at home with both the Mexican and American sides of his heritage." – Beyond Borders – Mexico

Now in 1400 libraries in the US and Canada

This book is dedicated to the many previous generations of Mexican-Americans who labored, sacrificed, fought and endured to make the United States a better place for those of us who have followed after them.

In Loving Memory
Of my Irish-American father,
Who gave me his love of books;
My Mexican mother,
Who gave me her love of Mexico;
And my brother Tom,
Who gave me his lust for life.

Other novels by Alejandro Grattan-Dominguez:

Whereabouts Unknown 2005

Only Once in a Lifetime 2004

Against All Odds 2003

Hollywood & Vine 2003

The Stuff of Dreams 2003

Breaking Even 1997

With the exception of the late Captain Gabriel Navarrete, the former commander of "E Company," 141st Regimentof the 6th Infantry Division, a division later famous as The Texas Volunteers during WWII, all characters in this historical novel are fictitious.

THE DARK SIDE OF THE DREAM

It is said that throughout all of the sky, only the great eagle can freely roam. For to the truly brave, the entire world is his home.

— Ovid

In the Libyan fable it is told that once an eagle, stricken with a dart, said when he saw the fashion of the shaft, "With our own feathers, not by other hands, are we now smitten."

— Aeschylus

PREFACE

During the early part of the 20th century, Mexico underwent a tumultuous social and economic revolution that was to have a deep and long-lasting effect on the United States. In the wake of that revolution's shattered dreams the first of the Mexican migrations arrived, driven by the mythical promise of *El Norte*.

The United States was on the brink of the First World War, and the song its citizens would soon be singing was called "Over There." Before that war was won, more than five million Americans had indeed been sent "over there," thus leaving the country with a desperate need for domestic manpower.

Heeding the call, Mexico sent north some half-million workers to help make the world, in President Woodrow Wilson's unforgettable words, "safe for democracy." This initial migration was unique in two ways: first, it was greatly welcomed by the American people and their government; further, it gravitated to that section of the United States that had once belonged to the ancestors of those Mexicans now returning to it.

Mexican labor began to help mine the ore, till the soil, maintain the railroads and make the guns, all vital to the war effort. Yet this labor force was consistently mistreated — and almost always by the same type of Americans who over the course of the next half-century were to most fervently court cheap Mexican labor during times of national crisis.

Unlike other laboring minorities, however, the Mexican, his fighting nature recently forged in the crucible of the Mexican Revolution, now came forward to demand his share of the democracy being won on the blood-soaked fields of France. In New Mexico and Colorado, viciously exploited Mexican mine workers went on strike. Within hours, the mine owners brought about what they called a "negotiated settlement," leaving twenty-two Mexican men, women and children dead.

The incident gave the U. S. public a rather bad taste in its mouth, and by way of overcoming it, most Americans simply elected to ignore both the tragedy, as well as the "foreigners" it had left dead.

With the First World War finally won, the United States ushered in the era of the "Golden 20s." Yet for Mexican-Americans — who had worked, fought and died to make the 20s so golden — it became a period of benign neglect. Prosperity was in. Those of Mexican ancestry were out.

Then came the Wall Street Crash of 1929, and nowhere were the aftershocks of the Crash more severely felt than in Mexico, with the peso so fatally tied to the dollar. Now came the most disastrous economic period in Mexican history, thus setting the stage for the next monumental migration to the United States.

With nearly a quarter of its population in a state of starvation, the eyes of the Mexican people again turned northward. Within one year after the Great Crash, more than a million and a half Mexicans would venture across the border.

This time they came not by invitation, or even in search of a better life, but simply in the hope of staying alive. But soon realizing that conditions were little better in the fabled *El Norte*, many returned to Mexico. If they were fated to starve to death, many felt it best to die on their own soil.

Those who left voluntarily returned to Mexico with their dignity intact — for many opportunistic politicians in the U.S. now were blaming this last wave of immigrants for the Depression itself, conveniently ignoring that the migration had not even begun until after the Wall Street crash. Xenophobia spread across the United States like a virulent disease.

Massive deportation measures were established, and tens of thousands of Mexicans were rounded up like common criminals to be entrained south in cattle cars. Thousands of American citizens of Mexican ancestry, some with roots in the U. S. that dated back for a full century, were likewise deported. Many of these Mexicans had fought as Dough Boys in France, but they were also shoved into the cattle cars, despite having been promised that naturalization would be their ultimate reward for serving in the U.S. military.

The Depression deepened, and for several years the border was unusually quiet, as Mexico began to pick up the pieces of its own shattered economy. That recovery would gain speed with a federal decree, the full import of which would remain largely unfelt in the United States for another forty years.

Nationalizing its oil industry, the Mexican government quickly sent packing the American oil cartels as if *they* were the illegal aliens. The American response was, surprisingly, quite restrained, made so perhaps by alarming events around the world that soon would set the stage for the next great Mexican migration.

The Japanese attack on Pearl Harbor came just as the United States was emerging from the worst economic depression in its history, only to hurl it into another world war that would eventually cost more, in terms of men, money and material, than any other in all of recorded history.

Yet as with every previous war, fighting men would have to be fed and supplied. Hence, the call went out once again to America's neighbor to the south. But this time, Mexicans were not so interested in chancing yet another humiliation, or, even worse, suffering a military defeat at the hands of a foreign enemy of the United States' own choosing.

The U. S., desperate for farming and factory labor, soon developed an enlightened and humane program for the importation of Mexican workers. Swayed by the stirring words and progressive programs of President Franklin D. Roosevelt, the Mexican people felt for the first time a common bond with the United States. Responding to the president's plea, they returned by the hundreds of thousands to again help settle an issue that the U.S. thought had been determined with the winning of the First World War.

The period 1941-1945 is considered as one of the finest in American history. An American president later would give some credit for it to the Mexican immigrants of that famous epoch; justifiably so, for on the home-front, Mexican labor helped till the soil in a manner which astonished our allies and confounded our enemies, while overseas, men of Mexican blood would become, in ratio to their numbers, one of the ethnic groups most highly decorated for valor under fire.

Set against this tumultuous historical background, *The Dark Side of the Dream* is the story of the Salazar brothers, who, with their families, come to the United States from northern Mexico shortly after the attack at Pearl Harbor. The novel is a chronicle of what they came searching for, and what they finally found. Yet the story is but a single variation of one which has been experienced tens of millions of times before—for America is, as we are so proud of reminding the world, a country that has been continuously replenished by those who were, in the immortal phrase on the Statue of Liberty, "yearning to be free."

We are truly a nation of immigrants, and therein lies part of what has helped make the United States one of the great nations of the world.

PART ONE

CHAPTER 1

In the first fragile light of that cold December morning, Miguel Salazar stood at the foot of his grandfather's bed and watched as the old man struggled for breath in his tortured sleep. Miguel waited, hoping each gasp would be the last one.

He hated himself for harboring such a thought. Yet Miguel knew that if the old man broke from his coma long enough to issue his final command to the others in the family, that deathbed mandate would surely shatter Miguel's most cherished dream.

Sinking to his knees on the hard earthen floor of the small adobe-walled room that stank of rotten eggs, the stench of his grandfather's stomach cancer, Miguel glanced up at the crudely carved crucifix hanging over the back of the rickety wooden bed.

"Dear God, forgive me for asking this, but if now is my grandfather's final hour, please take him before he awakens," he murmured. "Let me keep my dream, dear Lord."

The object of Miguel's dream was named Lupita Palacios, and since he'd been old enough to envision his future, he had felt they were destined to marry someday. But fate sometimes had to be coaxed.

Lupita was the only daughter of the prosperous farmer who owned the fifty hectares adjoining the Salazar farm—five acres of starving soil that barely managed to feed Miguel and his family. Lupita's father considered Miguel a decent, hard-working young man who might someday carve a niche for himself. But for a long time Miguel had been painfully aware that Señor Palacios hoped his pretty daughter might make a more advantageous marriage.

Over the past several months, however, Miguel and Lupita had slowly worn down his resistance. Only the previous Sunday, he had at last granted them his permission to marry.

"But only, my children, after you both have reached the age of eighteen. Then you shall have, if not my enthusiastic support, at least my consent," Señor Palacios had glumly decreed.

1

But as Miguel and Lupita were now only sixteen, their triumph was tinged with disappointment. Two years. An eternity!

That Sunday, December 7, 1941, was a day Miguel would later remember for another reason. He had trudged home to tell his family the bittersweet news, but only his grandfather was there to hear it. The old man was listening to a radio broadcast as Miguel walked into the foul-smelling bedroom.

"Grandfather, Señor Palacios has finally agreed to let me marry Lupita — but only after we wait for two years. I think the old goat hopes that in the meantime Lupita will find somebody even richer than himself."

Miguel had barely blurted this out when his grandfather waved him to be silent. Then the old man fitfully murmured that he had himself made a decision that morning. Hearing what that decision was, Miguel stood mute, stunned, blinking back his tears, as his grandfather slowly lapsed back into semi-consciousness.

Miguel had been given a temporary reprieve.

But now, a few days later, as the early morning light sliced higher through the splintered shutters of the old man's bedroom, he finally opened his eyes. For a long moment, he stared blankly at the bare, straw-streaked adobe walls. Then his ravaged features tightened over the bones of his face, and his watery gray eyes suddenly seemed to snap into focus.

Miguel knew his reprieve had come to an end.

He rose from his knees and watched as his grandfather's gaze came to rest on the large calendar nailed to the wall nearest the bed. The old man had written much of the history of his illness on that calendar. But after he had become too sick to get up, the scribbled medical notations had abruptly terminated. The last two unmarked months seemed mute but eloquent evidence of Sebastián Salazar's impending death.

"Good morning, Miguelito," Sebastián muttered, his voice but a distant echo of his once brusque baritone.

Miguel cautiously laid his hand across the old man's forehead and gently stroked it. He had come to sit on the edge of the bed, and with his face only a few feet from his grandfather's mouth, the stench almost overpowered him.

"Grandfather, you are finally awake again," Miguel managed to murmur. The old man chuckled softly. Miguel winced. His grandfather's teeth had decayed long before the rest of his body.

2

"In my present condition, that is not such a great consolation," Sebastián said with a dark smile. "Now tell me, boy, what is the exact date today?"

Miguel glanced toward the calendar, which was vividly illustrated with a drawing of an Aztec warrior and a voluptuous maiden standing near the top of a snow-capped mountain. He had often fantasized that the two magnificent figures were noble ancestors of his. Then he noticed something else.

"Grandfather, I forgot," Miguel exclaimed. "Today is the ninth of December. Your birthday!"

The old man grasped Miguel's hand, and the sudden strength in his grip startled the boy.

"Yes… and a fine day to start for the other side of that mountain," Sebastián wheezed, nodding toward the calendar. He knew of Miguel's fascination with the illustration. "Hurry, bring the family to me…important to tell them."

Miguel's parents had gone to early Mass at a cathedral about a mile away from the Salazar farm—the oldest church in Chihuahua City, indeed the most ancient in all of northern Mexico. Over the past three centuries, it had become encrusted with hundreds of legends, like barnacles on a ship. A few of them, his grandfather had told him, were actually true.

Sebastian's favorite was the story of the sorrowful sentry. It had happened back in the most desperate days of the Revolution, when the rebel leader Pancho Villa had once sneaked into the church. No one knew why the blasphemous Villa had chosen to do so, but the story went that the sentry he had left behind to guard the door had laid aside his rifle. As Villa and a few of his officers came out of the church, the soldier was strumming a guitar.

The officers insisted that the sentry be shot on the spot. But Villa needed every able-bodied man he had, and instead ordered that the fingers of the soldier's guitar-strumming hand be hacked off. Villa was, however, a practical man, and allowed the soldier to keep the one finger he would need to pull the trigger of a rifle. Later, according to the legend, the former guitarist would become one of the many heroes of the Revolution.

Miguel often wondered what lesson his grandfather had meant to impart by telling him the story. Now the moral seemed clear.

Life was neither predictable nor fair. But one did the best he could with what he had.

The church stood like a fortress in the center of the city, and, as always, when Miguel walked into the cathedral, he felt himself deeply stirred, though not for any religious reason.

Like his grandfather, Miguel was contemptuous of the sanctimonious local priests, who sometimes sold their spiritual services at prices poor people could ill afford.

Instead, what stirred Miguel was the history of the ancient cathedral as it related to his own family. Here, he and his two brothers had received their First Communion, and here both his parents and all four of his grandparents had exchanged their marriage vows—and in this same church, Miguel still hoped to someday marry Lupita Palacios.

The Mass had just ended. Miguel stood waiting like a sentinel in the granite-stoned foyer of the temple. As his parents and younger brother, Santiago, emerged from the musty innards of the massive building, his father sensed why he had come to speak to him.

"Find your Uncle Francisco," he quietly commanded. Then his somber tone went sour. "Then go to see if your brother Raúl can spare his family an hour of his precious time this morning."

Miguel needed no further instruction. He knew he could find his Uncle Francisco at the main produce market, trying to sell what little surplus the family farm had yielded the previous week. As for Raúl, he could surely be found at the Hotel Victoria, already on the prowl for early-rising American tourists. Miguel had never understood what service his handsome older brother provided his tourist clients, though it struck him as strange that most were older women.

The main *abastos* market sat a few blocks behind the church, on a cobblestone street pitched slightly uphill. It had rained hard the night before, and there was a large pool of water at the base of the street. Hopping across the pool in five quick strides, Miguel started up the incline, hurrying past dozens of small canvas-topped produce stalls.

Up near the crest of the hill, Miguel's Uncle Francisco saw the boy approach and waved. As Miguel climbed closer, a sight he had noticed many times before somehow seemed sadder than ever. Most of the stalls were manned by old people; yet their produce was fresh. In contrast, Miguel's uncle, a handsome and vigorous man in his early forties, attended to the Salazar stand, where the carrots were gnarled and bent, the lettuce black at its base, the onions yellowish and soft. Francisco's wife Juanita was at this moment scrubbing a batch of shriveled squash and cucumbers with water in a futile effort to make them look better.

Miguel quietly told his uncle why he had come. Then he greeted his young cousin, Alejandro, sitting off to one side reading a comic book. Francisco quickly began to shutter up the stand.

"Put away your book, Alejandro," Francisco said to his son.

"Do I have to go, Papá?"

"This might be the last time you see your grandfather alive."

Fifteen minutes later, Miguel hurried into the dimly lit bar of the Hotel Victoria. His older brother, Raúl, was at the far end of the ornately-furnished room. There was a woman with him, but Miguel could not see her face. He could see, however, that they were both drinking tequila.

"Papá wants you to come home." Miguel had stopped some ten feet away from the table, reluctant to come any closer. Raúl looked annoyed.

"What's wrong now?" he asked, leaning across the table to light the woman's cigarette.

"Grandfather has something to say to the family."

Raúl brushed a piece of lint off his sports jacket and smiled at his companion. "I'll go a little later."

"Later he might not be alive," Miguel muttered.

Raúl's expression went grim. Crushing out his cigarette, he rose from the table. "I'll be back in a while, Señora," he said to the woman in badly broken English.

"But, Raúl darling, we were going sightseeing this morning," the woman mildly protested. "That was why we got up so early, wasn't it?"

"Later, mi querida," Raúl murmured, starting away from the table.

As the woman swiveled around in her chair, Miguel saw her face for the first time. She was a horse-faced Anglo woman whom he thought looked old enough to be Raúl's grandmother.

"But, Raúl, darling, I don't really have that much time!"

"Neither does my grandfather," Raúl called back.

Half an hour later the entire family was gathered around Sebastián Salazar's bed, as he haltingly disclosed the decision he had reached the previous Sunday after hearing that the Japanese had bombed Pearl Harbor.

"A long war now commence… the United States… need many men, strong arms, take the place of those who become soldiers. A new country, a new culture… hard. But the American president is a great and good man… when war over, he will remember those who helped his country to win it."

The old man began to cough, hacking sounds so severe that Miguel gritted his teeth and moved away from the bed. Blood formed around his grandfather's lips. The two women in the room hurried forward to make him more comfortable.

Sebastián's declaration had come in garbled, fitful spurts. Noting its cost, the others stood stunned. From the far corner of the crowded little room, Miguel watched the sad spectacle of a human life unfold to its full length. He felt devastated by the looming specter of his grandfather's impending death, yet disappointed that the old man still had the strength to continue.

Already the garbled words were coming again.

"So today, completion of my sixty-fourth year, I decide to be done with my life…when a man sick this bad, the Good Lord sometimes lets him go when he wants," Sebastián whispered, his eyes holding on like hooks to Miguel's father's, José Luis's, eyes. "But whether I die today or next week, I want you, José Luis, to sell our farm for whatever you can get. Money, you use to take entire family to… United States."

There it was. Miguel shuddered. The fateful declaration. In the gloomy silence that followed, his father exchanged a furtive glance with his brother Francisco. Both men seemed to be waiting for the other to speak. José Luis spoke first.

"Forgive me, Papá, but is it right that you will yourself to die before God is ready to take you… "

The slight spark in Sebastián's eyes went cold with what seemed disappointment. Miguel's eyes widened with wonderment, and for one exultant moment he believed his father, José Luis, might dare, just this once, to disobey his own father.

"José Luis. My first-born son, always so wary of the unknown," Sebastián muttered, as if reading an epitaph. "But this time you must lead others… And if any refuse to go, their share of the farm shall go to you. For only with your effort can the family find a better life."

Miguel's father made no reply but stood in silence at the foot of the bed. Sebastián uttered a quiet curse and turned to the youngest of his descendants, Miguel's cousin Alejandro. He weakly beckoned the boy forward. Miguel let drop the arm he had draped around the boy's shoulder, wondering why his nine-year-old cousin had been singled out at such a crucial moment.

"You, Alejandro, the youngest of the Salazars," the old man muttered in a barely audible whisper. "Yet, if you the only one with courage to obey me…to you the money must go. And perhaps one day you will not have to stand at the foot of your own father's bed to explain why you failed to improve the fortunes of your family."

Alejandro's eyes had filled with tears. He turned back toward his father, Francisco, and saw by the expression on his family's faces that his grandfather's words had seemed to stain them with shame.

Francisco came forward, his compact muscular body seemingly charged with late-found resolve. "If this wish is your last command, Papá, it is as good as done. When the farm is sold, I will go north with my wife and son. Of course, I cannot speak for the others."

Miguel felt his throat tighten. If his courageous Uncle Francisco had given in so easily, what hope was there that his more timid and obedient father might stand firm?

"But, Papá, this is all speculation," José Luis muttered in a defeated tone. "What if we can find but little work in the United States?"

Miguel's older brother, Raúl, spoke for the first time. "No, with the world at war and all the Americans rushing off to get killed, there should be many opportunities for those of us smart enough to stay out of somebody else's fight."

Miguel grimaced. His older brother looked as if he already wanted to start packing. Miguel glanced at his grandfather. The old man's emaciated face was wreathed with a small smile of satisfaction. Miguel knew why. The ploy with his young cousin had worked.

Sebastián turned toward José Luis. "You ask what if there is little work in the north?" the old man murmured. "There will be work…but if not, have I raised a bunch of *burros* who would remain at a well that no longer has water?"

"But, Papá, why do we have to sell the farm? Could we not rent it out, so that it is here when we return?" José Luis asked.

Sebastián's features quivered with irritation. "Our soil has been almost dead for last two years, and only most expensive fertilizer brings back to life…so do not return until you have saved five-thousand dollars. Enough to buy a business or a farm strong enough to carry all of you on its shoulders."

José Luis sighed and finally nodded. "I promise you this, Papá: when such a sum is saved, I and my family shall return to Chihuahua almost that very same day."

The pact had been made. The family would soon be on its way to el Norte.

Now, summoning forth as much sentiment as his reserved nature and wasted condition would allow, Sebastián beckoned them closer, one by one, to say goodbye.

When it came Miguel's turn to bid his grandfather farewell, he tried to choke back his disappointment.

"I have always loved you, Grandfather," Miguel whispered. "I will never forget you, and one day I will make you proud of me."

Sebastián Salazar died within the next hour, having hung on long enough to issue his final command. Yet even as Miguel's eyes went soft with grief, his resolve began to harden.

Death had finally staked its claim on his grandfather's life, but Miguel vowed he would not allow it to vanquish his dream.

The news of the old man's death spread quickly. The house and veranda soon filled with mourners. Milling through the crowd, Miguel wondered whether his own death would draw even a fraction of such a gathering. He mused about what the inscription on his tombstone might say. "Here is buried Miguel Domingo Salazar… ¿Y a mí, que?" So what?

But such a sorry inscription would certainly not be on his grandfather's gravestone. Miguel had never seen his family so emotional. Many Mexicans believed that the tears of family and friends made the road to Heaven easier to walk for the deceased. Miguel did not share in this belief. Like his grandfather, he thought the strongest emotions were best kept tightly controlled.

After the old man's body was taken to be prepared for burial, Miguel followed his mother and his Aunt Juanita into the kitchen where the two women began to make the evening meal. The aroma of rice, beans and goat meat was a relief from the stench that still befouled the other side of the house.

José Luis wandered in and sat down next to a blood-stained butcher's block. Miguel felt his stomach muscles clench. He had hoped to first enlist his mother's support before having to confront his father.

Warming his hands over a sputtering fire, Miguel set his plan in motion.

"Señor Palacios has given me his consent to marry Lupita."

"Yes, so you already informed us, Miguel," José Luis muttered, vaguely annoyed. He took a sip of the steaming coffee his wife had set on the block for him.

"That will not be for another two years," Miguel's mother said. Graciela Salazar had guessed what was on the boy's mind.

"That is true, Mamá. But if I go north with the rest of you, I will lose Lupita," Miguel said, pouring himself a cup of coffee, grateful that he had something to do with his hands. Wringing them would be bad form, he thought.

"So, Papá, I ask your permission to stay. I can quit school and get a real job, and maybe Señor Palacios will allow me to sleep in his stable."

"No! I will not have a son of mine sleep in a shed that was built for horses," José Luis abruptly announced. "We are poor, but we are proud—and not to be led around like horses!"

Miguel stared at his father. It seemed his sudden show of anger was aimed more at the far, now vacant, end of the house than at him.

"But more important," José Luis exclaimed, "we must respect your grandfather's last wishes."

"And my wishes, Papá? Are they not worth any respect from anybody?"

"Be silent, muchacho," José Luis exclaimed, rising so abruptly that his coffee cup fell to the hard-packed earthen floor and shattered. "You have yet to do anything worthwhile with your life. Why should your wishes be more important than those of your grandfather?"

Miguel stared down at the ground, as José Luis, looking troubled and vaguely contrite, quietly left the room. Miguel glanced over at his mother and Aunt Juanita. They seemed embarrassed. He knelt down and began to gather up the broken pieces of the coffee cup. My father is right, he thought. What have I ever done to earn anyone's respect?

He knew that in his father's eyes, he was simply the son in the muddled middle of his progeny. José Luis's youngest, Santiago, was regarded the smartest; Raúl, the oldest, was easily the handsomest and certainly the most enterprising.

Dropping the coffee-cup pieces into a garbage barrel, Miguel made a silent vow. *Someday, by God, he would show all of them!*

CHAPTER 2

Miguel's father was at the wheel of their old produce truck when the accident happened. Tired and tense, José Luis had spent the previous week haggling with the few buyers still interested in the Salazar farm, none willing to pay more than a fraction of the two thousand dollars it was still worth.

José Luis reluctantly took the best offer, four-hundred dollars, then pushed the family into making ready for the two-hundred-and-thirty-mile trek to the Texas border, a journey now made more hazardous by heavy rainstorms.

Just prior to the accident, Miguel was thinking about his father and his Uncle Francisco. His uncle sat huddled alongside him in the rear of the tarp-covered truck. Miguel's two brothers, Raúl and Santiago, crouched nearby, trying to sleep.

Young Alejandro was up front with his mother Juanita and Miguel's parents. It was raining in sweeping, heavy sheets, the night freezing cold.

The dramatic difference between his father and uncle had always fascinated Miguel. His father was quiet, careful and rather homely; his uncle, fun-loving, adventuresome and handsome enough to have been compared to Chihuahua's favorite celebrity, Anthony Quinn, who ten years earlier had ventured all the way to Hollywood to become an actor.

Miguel knew that his father and uncle respected each other, yet was aware of the unspoken resentment that existed between the two. His father had been the more diligent son, but on those rare occasions when his grandfather Sebastián had ladled out affection, Francisco always received the larger share. Such slights had left Miguel's father a pessimistic, rather guarded man. Yet Francisco also had reason to be resentful. Being the younger brother, his opinions had never carried the same weight as José Luis's with Miguel's grandfather.

"Are you glad we're going to the United States?" Miguel quietly asked his uncle.

"I have been searching for something for many years, and only recently did I realize that I would never find it in Chihuahua — but perhaps north of the border... "

"I wish I felt the same, uncle. But I already found what I want and now I might lose it."

Francisco chuckled. "Or you just might find something better. In any case, you should always remember that old saying, 'Life is what happens to us while we are out making other plans.'"

At that very moment, as if on cue, Miguel felt the truck groan as it twisted around a sharp curve, then heard the grinding sound of the brakes. He did not know that the two-lane highway had suddenly disappeared under a mass of water strewn with large rocks. Then he heard an eerie sucking sound.

"The brakes are locked! I can't stop!" Miguel's father shouted from the cab of the truck. "Dear God! Everybody hang on!"

Miguel instinctively reached in the dark for his brother Santiago. Then, with one arm snaring the boy's shoulder, he grabbed hold of the metal frame that held the tarp in place and planted his feet firmly on the rolling bed of the truck. A wild thought bolted through his brain: so this is how it's all to end.

The truck was veering sideways. Miguel felt his footing give way and heard Raúl scream a curse. Then a voice knifed through the turmoil.

"Move to my side! We're going to tip over!" yelled Francisco. A split second later, Miguel's head was jarred by what felt like an explosion. His body crashed against the bottom of the truck. Water was already engulfing him. He gagged as the brackish liquid filled his mouth.

Jerking his head out from the water, Miguel clambered to his feet. His first thought was for his younger brother. Then, in the sudden quiet, he heard Santiago cry out. Reaching toward the sound, Miguel took the boy's arm, and together they waded toward the rear of the truck. Raúl was already there and had worked open the canvas covering. The water had already reached his waist and rising swiftly.

"Lift Santiago out first," Francisco commanded.

Chaotic seconds later, they were safely on higher ground. The truck was flat on its side, having tumbled into a narrow ditch, and was now sinking fast into the water.

Miguel stood watching it, frozen, dazed as Raúl, still cursing, pulled a waterlogged suitcase from the rear of the truck and saw that his uncle had carried Santiago to the top of the ditch. A wave of relief swept over Miguel, but it was short-lived.

"Help us... we can't get out," José Luis weakly pleaded.

Miguel watched his uncle and his older brother stumble forward. Then something snapped into focus, and he hurried toward the cab where the rest of the family was trapped.

Francisco started to climb up to the driver's side of the cab, which had sunk halfway into the water.

"Let me do it, uncle! I'll pass them down to you," Miguel exclaimed, pulling him aside. Then Miguel began to haul himself up along the undercarriage. The wet, greasy metal was hard to grasp, but in a few moments he reached what was now the top of the truck. There, balancing his body off to one side of the door, he finally pried it open.

In thirty seconds, Miguel had pulled out his father first, then his mother, and finally young Alejandro. They seemed badly shaken but uninjured. Miguel gently passed them on down, one by one, to the outstretched arms of his uncle and his older brother. Then he lowered himself once more into the cab.

Blinded by the darkness, he groped around for his Aunt Juanita, who, on the far side of the cab, had caught the full, brutal brunt of the impact. Now, with the water well over his head, Miguel's hands became his eyes. In the black void, he finally found her arm, felt himself go limp with fear when he thought she was pinned to the door. She had been under the water for more than a minute. In another minute, she would surely drown. Then Miguel's fingers told him something that, had he not been underwater, might have made him smile. It was not her arm that was caught, but only her coat sleeve. Ripping it free, he quickly shifted his body, placed his feet up against the closed window, and slowly pushed Juanita toward the open door above him.

As Miguel climbed out after her, he saw his uncle's expectant expression crumple. Juanita seemed already dead.

Then, as Francisco, Raúl and José Luis carried her to higher ground, Miguel waded back to the bed of the truck where he tore loose several of the long wooden stakes that supported the canvas cover. Carrying them, along with a piece of the tarpaulin, up to a small rise, he began to construct a makeshift shelter.

Raúl came to help. They worked silently in the rain that now had nearly made them blind.

"You did great, Miguel. No one else could have gotten her out of there alive!" Raúl yelled, making Miguel's chest surge with pride.

When the shelter was finished, Juanita was placed inside, and Francisco and Miguel crawled into it. With another burst of thunder, Francisco saw Juanita's face. He grinned and quietly said, "Thank you, Miguel." Turning to the others crouched near the edge of the flapping cover, he said, "She's still alive."

For how long? Miguel thought. The accident had hit hardest the weakest of them. Several miscarriages had long since left Juanita's body brittle and worn-out. Miguel placed his tattered overcoat gently over her almost lifeless body, then crawled to the edge of the shelter and stared down toward the road. It was almost midnight, and he knew very few people would still be out at such an hour and in such a storm.

The family had left Chihuahua City early that morning, expecting to reach the town where they were told they could find lodging for the night before sundown. But two blowouts and a temperamental radiator had seriously slowed them down. The town they had hoped to reach by nightfall was still more than forty miles away. There would be no more traffic on the road that night.

"We will have to wait till morning, and by then..." He left his thought unfinished, though obviously the others had reached the same conclusion. Staring toward the darkened highway, he silently cursed his Aunt Juanita's fate. Except for her son, she had never had much luck.

Lightning suddenly crackled high overhead. Miguel saw that the surrounding countryside was filled with little more than prickly cactus plants, spear-tipped mesquite brush and jagged rock formations. A Spanish explorer had once written that in the desert of northern Mexico, nature had virtually armed itself for war. Now, there was little left that anyone could do or say. They could only wait and pray in the darkness that enveloped them like a black shroud.

Half an hour later, another streak of lightning bolted across the sky, and in its phosphorescent wake, Miguel saw three men approaching from a nearby ravine. A long-bladed machete hung from each man's hand like a curved tentacle.

As the three men drew closer, Miguel took Alejandro's shivering hand in his. José Luis, Francisco and Raúl edged out from under the wind-torn tarp and waited. Miguel's mother remained behind, Juanita's limp body cradled in her arms.

The three blunt-faced men angled closer. Then two of them split off in small, measured steps. Miguel thought their movements stealthy as those of a scorpion. The tallest of the trio, however, kept a slow but steady pace until he had come to within ten feet of the shelter.

In the glare of another flash of lightning, the tall man glanced down at the capsized truck, then peered into the tarp-covered shelter where Juanita still lay unconscious. He turned and beckoned his companions closer.

Miguel guided Alejandro back under the tarp, and exchanged a long glance with his Uncle Francisco. Both were thinking the same thing. They were four against three, but were unarmed. If they could take the machete away from the man closest to them, they might have a fighting chance.

As Miguel girded himself, the strangers began to speak among themselves, a quiet, singsong dialect that made them sound like small children. Miguel smiled and slowly came to his feet.

"It's all right. They won't harm us," he said. "They're Tarahumara Indians."

Miguel had heard many stories from his grandfather about this legendary tribe of Indians, who considered paper money worthless, and only bartered with what they crafted or harvested themselves. The Tarahumaras were also famous for their stamina, and could run for several hours a day in hot pursuit of game.

The tall Indian eased to the edge of the shelter and then removed his straw hat and crawled into the shelter, his gracious gesture seeming, under the circumstances, almost comical. The Salazars crouched down and waited.

The Indian bent over to listen to Juanita's heartbeat, and then gently lifted her eyelids. Turning back, he called out to his companions.

The two men raised their machetes and began to hack away at a large mesquite bush. While this was going on, the tall Indian crawled out of the shelter, and in a mangled mixture of Spanish, pantomime and his own language, he delivered his diagnosis.

"I think he says she will dead by daylight if she is not helped very soon. His village is in the hills, only a mile from here," Miguel said. "He and his friends saw the lights and heard the crash. No one in the village can save someone so badly injured."

"So what the hell do we do?" Francisco angrily asked, coming to his feet. "Sit here and pray that a doctor happens by before she dies?"

The word 'doctor' had apparently been understood by the Indian. He repeated it twice, and went on speaking.

Miguel, who had once befriended a Tarahumara boy, relayed as best he could the message to the others. "There is a doctor in a town five kilometers west of here, where—"

"Doctor, doctor!" the Tarahumara said, following the gist of Miguel's translation.

"Well, any plan is better than none," Francisco growled, nodding to the Indian. The tall man smiled solemnly, and took a bit of a medicinal herb from a pouch that hung from his waist. Ducking back under the tarp, he carefully placed it in Juanita's mouth. Miguel had no idea what it was, but figured it could not make her condition any worse.

In another few minutes, the Indians had Juanita strapped to a litter and wrapped up with what remained of the tarpaulin. Then the tall Indian took up the front of the litter, his two companions the rear, and off they went at a brisk pace.

Trailing behind them, Miguel thought the procession looked like a funeral cortege. Several scenes played out in his imagination. He saw his Aunt Juanita surviving the ordeal, and the entire family, chastened by her near-fatal accident, returning to Chihuahua. He and Lupita would marry soon thereafter, and name their first son Sebastián after his grandfather, in honor of the man whose love and guidance Miguel had already started to miss.

It was a hopeful scenario that would help him to keep moving over the next five rock-strewn kilometers.

They arrived shortly after daybreak, and as they came trudging into the town, Miguel thought his family looked like the remnants of a badly beaten army. But the Indians, who had refused all help in carrying the litter, seemed as if they had spent the night sleeping in their own village.

The town sat on a plateau, its rust-colored streets running off into the infinity of a cobalt-blue horizon. It reminded Miguel of a photograph he had once seen of a Tibetan village high in the Himalayas.

The town's only medical clinic, a small, bare, three-room structure was staffed by an elderly doctor and his granddaughter, who served as his nurse. When the doctor saw that Juanita was unconscious, he decided to examine her first, ahead of the other patients already lined up outside his door.

"A fracture of the right forearm," the old doctor finally concluded. "Contusions to her ribs and a badly bruised spleen. I am amazed she lived through the trip all the way from the highway."

"The Indians gave her something," Miguel explained. "I don't know what it was."

"Probably peyote," the old man said, smiling. "The Tarahumaras use it for everything from killing pain to stimulating their sex drive. But whatever it was, it must have helped her. She should recover within a week."

Francisco's haggard features split into a wide smile. Leaving Juanita resting comfortably, he and Miguel went outside to tell the others the good news. Miguel's mother, Graciela, immediately pulled the family together with her pudgy arms, and led them in a short prayer of praise to a merciful God.

Francisco turned toward the three Indians. They too had waited to learn the fate of the young woman they had carried for most of the night toward an uncertain destiny.

As Francisco approached them, Miguel noticed that his uncle had tears in his eyes. But before he could count out the money he had taken from his pocket, the Indians smiled and began to back away. The news that the young woman would recover, they seemed to say, was their best reward.

Then with a wave, the three Indians set off at a trot, headed east toward the sun, which had earlier ushered in a gloriously clear day.

CHAPTER 3

An hour later, after they had eaten breakfast at a two-table café, Miguel, Jose Luis and Francisco found the only mechanic in town who owned a tow truck. The rest of the family remained behind in the little boarding house the old doctor had recommended. Miguel felt proud he had been asked to come along. He hoped that his actions of the night before had prompted the invitation. He was still intent on changing his father's mind about continuing on to the border.

Miguel also liked being around his Uncle Francisco. He loved to hear him expound on his favorite theories, and tell his tall tales. His uncle, he thought, could have talked the Romans into taking Christ down off the cross.

But Francisco might well have been a mute for all the impression he made on the surly mechanic. Having a tow truck made him an important man, and prominence had not improved his personality. In a harsh voice, the burly mechanic informed them that he neither needed nor wanted the work the Salazars had to offer. "Too far to go for too little money," he growled. "Besides, I already have a week's worth of work in my shop right now."

"You don't understand," Francisco exclaimed. "If we don't get our truck out of that ditch, the water will ruin the motor!"

"That is your problem, Señor," the mechanic shot back before turning away to yell at his two teenaged helpers. Miguel glanced over at his uncle whose hands were now balled into fists. He started toward the stoutly built mechanic.

"But I can make it your problem, as well," Francisco murmured with a chilling smile.

Miguel held his breath and waited for the brawl to begin. But the tow-truck owner was either braver than he appeared or more dense than he looked, for now he simply ignored the threat and went back to berating his young assistants. It was not until Miguel's father doubled the initial offer that the husky mechanic finally agreed to drive out to the El Paso highway the following morning.

About mid-afternoon, while the others still slept, Miguel accompanied his father and uncle over to the cantina across the muddy, rutted road from the boarding house.

Inside were several shabbily dressed, disgruntled-looking men. The Salazars had just taken a table and ordered a round of soft drinks when a lanky gringo sauntered into the foul-smelling, packed-dirt floor bar. With a good-natured swagger, the man called out his order in near-perfect Spanish. Tequila, the best brand the bartender could offer. Then he turned and looked intently around the large room. After a moment he aimed his eyes in the direction of Miguel's table.

"You boys don't look like part of this here local talent," the broad- shouldered man said, smiling.

"No, we're from Chihuahua City," Francisco replied.

"Ain't bound for the border, looking for work, are you?"

The surprised smiles coming from both José Luis and Francisco seemed all the answer the tall man needed.

"Well, this is your lucky day," he continued. "You see, I'm down here recruiting labor for a few of the biggest farms in Texas. Work pays forty cents an hour, and provides decent food and housing for every worker and his family. How does that sound to you boys?"

It sounded terrible to Miguel. He still hoped his dream of returning home might come true.

"It sounds too good to be true," Francisco ventured with a cautious smile.

The gringo chuckled and tossed down the rest of his tequila.

"Yeah, under ordinary conditions, it might be. But it's now wartime in Texas. Entire country's soon gonna be desperate for farm labor. Soldiers can't fight on empty stomachs, so the work should last for the full duration of the war... and Mexican labor could make a difference in who wins it."

Miguel's father and uncle were beaming. The Texan had just confirmed much of what their father had told them on his deathbed. Miguel ruefully wondered: why couldn't the old man just for once have been wrong?

The gringo pulled from his pocket a large wad of money, and with a wide smile said, "Well, I got me a nice big bus that'll be bound for the border within the next hour or so. When it goes, I'd sure like to have you boys on board."

The Texan peeled a few dollars from his money clip and laid them on the table. "Meanwhile, your soda pop comes free, courtesy of your new employer."

Miguel looked over at his uncle, who had arisen from the table to politely explain why it would be impossible for them to accept the man's kind offer immediately. They were, however, most interested in finding good paying work. The gringo looked disappointed.

"Hey, no big deal," the Texan muttered. "I'll be back here within a week for another busload of workers, and hope to see you boys then."

As the Texan strode out of the bar, José Luis and Francisco sat staring at each other. "Can you believe it, brother?" Francisco quietly marveled. "Our bad luck of last night has turned into good luck today!"

Miguel frowned. His own luck had just gotten worse. He sat silently as his father and uncle began to revise their plans. José Luis and his family would travel on to El Paso as soon as the truck could be repaired. Francisco and the others would follow as soon as Juanita was able to travel. Besides, she would be more comfortable riding in the labor contractor's bus.

But best of all, they now had the promise of good-paying jobs. Forty cents an hour! "And even if the wage proves only half of that, what the hell," Francisco argued enthusiastically, "we can still make more in a day than a farm worker here in Mexico makes in a week!"

Miguel smiled for the first time. When his grandfather had set the family's goal at five thousand dollars, Miguel had thought that the old man might as well have said a million.

"And with all of us working," José Luis added, "we might be returning much sooner than we thought!"

To celebrate such a prospect, Miguel ordered another Coca-Cola, and wished he had a shot of the gringo's fine tequila to go with it.

Early that evening, the family walked over to the clinic to check on the condition of its only patient. Miguel thought his Aunt Juanita still looked like baggage that had been very carelessly handled. But her broken arm had been set, her ribs taped, and she was now conscious. Francisco wasted no time in telling her of the incredible events and mysterious strangers of the night before. Juanita's first response was to break into tears. Francisco seemed annoyed by her reaction.

"Forgive me, Pancho," she uttered, reaching for his hand. "I have caused all of you so much trouble."

Miguel, standing back near the door, could not squelch a smile. His Aunt Juanita was the one person in the family who had always remained impervious to his uncle's flair for the dramatic. Now, in the awkward silence, José Luis tenderly took her outstretched hand to tell her of the friendly Texan they had met that afternoon, and of the good wage and inexpensive housing he had promised them. Graciela quickly corrected him.

"No, José Luis, our family will not stay in a labor camp! I shall find an apartment in El Paso big enough for all of us," she declared, gently brushing her hand across Juanita's forehead. "The apartment will be waiting for you, my dear, when you arrive."

Juanita's soft brown eyes shimmered with hope. Like the others, she had harbored grave misgivings about the move to los Estados Unidos. She tried to smile. "Perhaps the accident was not so unfortunate...maybe my injury had brought us a little luck."

Poor Aunt Juanita, Miguel thought. Nothing had ever come easy to her.

By now the visit had sapped much of her strength. The family was filing out of the bare, windowless room when she softly voiced a request.

"Francisco, would you allow Alejandro to stay a little longer? He can read to me until I fall asleep."

Francisco flashed a smile. Alejandro needed no further encouragement. Brushing past his father, the boy swiftly settled in the room's only chair and took from inside his coat a tattered newspaper. Miguel knew what was coming next.

He felt a special fondness for his young cousin. There was almost always something somber in the eyes of the nine-year-old boy, that came, Miguel thought, from something deeper than mere deprivation. Perhaps the boy had realized that his father did not truly love his sickly mother. The rest of the family had known this for a long time.

Alejandro began to read the newspaper to his mother, a ritual of sorts that always made the boy feel proud that he had surpassed his mother, who could not read or write. Listening to him now, Juanita's eyes began to glow, as if she was savoring the living proof that her marriage had not been completely without compensation.

Miguel watched from the hallway. The night before, he had saved them both from drowning. Now, for some reason he could not fathom, he felt forever responsible for them. The thought made him happy. It lightened, if only a little, the guilt he still harbored for having wished his grandfather dead before he could issue his final command.

Early the following morning, the mechanic loaded every tool he might conceivably need into his tow truck and then brusquely ordered Miguel's family to climb in. Francisco and Alejandro had come to see them off.

"You are sure, Pancho, that I am doing the right thing in going on to El Paso?" José Luis yelled over the roaring motor of the truck.

Francisco grasped José Luis's hand in his. It was the most affection Miguel had ever seen his uncle display openly.

"José Luis, for as long as I can remember, you have always done the right thing…and even when I sometimes hated it, I always respected you for doing so."

Miguel felt a lump rise in his throat. He was thinking of all the precious years that had been wasted between the two brothers. He wanted them to say more to each other, but already the mechanic had ground his vehicle into gear. As the truck began to roll down the dirt road, Miguel waved back at Francisco, with a troubled look.

Eight days later, Francisco, Juanita and Alejandro were finally again bound for the border. They did not know that the contractor's bus was headed for Laredo, rather than El Paso.

Later, when Miguel's father found out, he was furious. The gringo had obviously played a cruel trick on them! Miguel thought, however, that the mix-up which sent Francisco and his family hundreds of miles away might have been simply a misunderstanding, because, to the contractor, the "border' could have included any number of towns in Texas, not just El Paso.

What Miguel did not realize was that he and his family would never again see his Uncle Francisco or his Aunt Juanita — and that by the time he finally was reunited with his cousin Alejandro, several years would go by and many battles would have been fought by both of them in the far-off corners of the world.

CHAPTER 4

Miguel's grandfather had always been fascinated by the history of El Paso, a city he had once visited in 1930. But he would have scarcely recognized the El Paso of 1942.

In the late 1800's, it had been the last stop for many of the most notorious desperadoes of the Old West, where a dispute could still be legally decided in favor of whoever had the fastest gun. Later, cotton, cattle, and copper, as well as the once-famed Seventh Cavalry—whose remnants still roosted quietly just north of the city at Old Fort Bliss— would restore the city's tarnished image.

Now, only a few weeks after the American president whom Sebastián Salazar had so much admired had gone before the U.S. Congress to demand a declaration of war against Japan, the border city was becoming a boomtown.

Fort Bliss soon changed from a colorful old stockade into one of the largest training centers in the entire country. An Army Air Corps base, Biggs Field, abruptly arose out of the desert like a mirage, to be used in training many of the airmen who would later play an important part in the American counterattack in the Pacific.

The war effort quickly became El Paso's primary business, as the city swelled to twice its former size. Eventually, more than one hundred thousand people, many who had hardly heard of the place, would be drawn to this border town grown boisterous with newfound purpose.

Miguel and his family were among those new arrivals, and as their battered produce truck finally crossed the long bridge that spanned the Rio Grande River, their luck soon changed, exactly as Miguel's grandfather had predicted.

It got worse.

They quickly discovered there was very little farm work around El Paso, and December was hardly the best time to find it. Miguel's mother, however, did find a large six-room apartment; big enough, she thought, for the entire family when they were finally reunited. She was, however, staggered by the rent—forty dollars a month, a fortune for a family who arrived with less than a hundred and sixty dollars.

Graciela counted out the money in precious pesos and paid the Anglo landlord. Miguel's mother, by nature an optimist, was convinced that the family's luck would soon change for the better. A few days later, it did.

José Luis found work in an icehouse, replacing a young man who had just enlisted in the Army Air Corps. The icehouse was within walking distance of the apartment, which sat on the top floor of a three-story tenement, whose roof quickly became Miguel's favorite place. From its south side, he could see the bruised buildings and cardboard hovels that angled down toward the edge of the river.

This blighted part of the city was called the Second Ward, where most of the newly-arrived Mexicans chose to encamp; their hopes still colored with caution, they had obviously thought it prudent to inch their way into the United States only a few feet at a time.

The barrio was crescent-shaped, bound on the south by the looping curve of the Rio Grande, on the north by the main highway which led west to Los Angeles, east to Dallas. At the westernmost edge of the Second Ward, the barrio narrowed to a needlepoint, ending at the Union Train Depot. Just beyond were the refineries and factories, now operating non-stop because of the war effort, belching black smoke twenty- four hours a day.

What Miguel disliked most about the barrio was its almost total lack of greenery. In an area that ran some five miles long and a mile wide, there were few large trees. Down by the river, however, there was a string of scrawny mesquite, and on the first day he arrived in El Paso, Miguel walked over to it, soon to become an almost daily habit, for whenever he peered across the river, he usually felt less **homesick.**

Two weeks after Miguel's family first crossed the Rio Grande, a letter arrived general delivery from his Uncle Francisco, confirming what they had feared. Francisco, along with his wife and son, had ended up hundreds of miles away. They had come into Texas far to the southeast of El Paso to finally end up near a little town called Mission.

The farm work paid less than promised and was brutally hard. The housing was rotten, the food almost as bad. The family farm back in Chihuahua, Francisco wrote, had fed them far better.

Yet Francisco had written that in spite of this, he was happy. He had found something in south Texas he had been looking for most of his life.

Months later, Miguel was still wondering what it was his uncle had found. He had himself found little in the United States. Earlier he had enrolled in the barrio's only high school, but his wretched understanding of English soon relegated him to the rear of the classroom where the teacher kept the dunces.

Miguel's first job was even worse. He had been hired as a bus-boy/assistant dishwasher in a fancy restaurant, but it paid him only thirteen cents an hour for a shift that went from six in the afternoon till midnight, seven days a week. School was depressing, his job exhausting.

One night Miguel fell asleep on his feet and toppled over into a sink filled with soapy dishwater. The Mexicans working in the kitchen thought his swan dive hilarious and offered to teach him how to swim. His Anglo employer was not so amused. Miguel was fired that same evening.

Shortly after his debacle in the dishwater, Miguel got the last letter he would ever receive from Lupita Palacios. The marriage engagement was off. She had met another boy, one her father thought was ideal marriage material. He was the son of the owner of a movie theater.

Miguel ruefully remembered that he and Lupita had attended many a matinee in that same theater. Rereading the letter, he felt his feet sliding out from under him. But her decision was one he would not contest. Too proud to plead, he vowed instead to quickly forget Lupita, though for a long time afterward he carried her letter in the breast pocket of his favorite jacket where it lay like a stone against his heart.

A short while after he received Lupita's letter, he got a job working behind the concession stand at a downtown movie house that played only Mexican films. The hours were long, but often when business was slack, he would watch stars like Pedro Infante, Maria Felix and Jorge Negrete performing brave and dramatic deeds.

But best of all, his job allowed him to take off Friday nights and all day Sunday. Both days quickly became very important, each allowing him to give vent to different and often warring elements in his personality.

Every Friday night there was a dance at the Teen Canteen in the basement of the only Baptist church in the barrio. On any other day or night the church was almost deserted. Competing with the Catholic Church in an area made up entirely of Mexicans was a foolhardy venture; in desperation the pastor had made the place available for the teen dances, wishfully thinking that those who came to dance on Friday would return to worship on Sunday — but they rarely did so.

But on Friday nights the place was always packed. Miguel would usually arrive rather late, having stopped along the way to fortify himself with a couple of beers. He came hoping to find among the dozens of pretty girls someone like Lupita Palacios. But he was a less than graceful dancer and a worse conversationalist, and often when he ventured across the crowded room to ask a girl to dance, he had to make the trip back across the floor alone.

But the music was good, usually Latino-style jitterbug, and Miguel liked to watch the bodies hurtling through the air. He also liked to study the people who came to the dances, intrigued by the way they invariably broke up into groups, each suspicious of the other.

There was, however, one group that was greatly respected by everyone: the young Mexican-American servicemen, who wore their army uniforms like a badge of honor and carried themselves with a dignity which belied their years.

Miguel had noticed that few soldiers were ever refused a dance, and seldom was any servicemen involved in the fights, which invariably erupted behind the church just after the dance had broken up. It was thought unpatriotic to start trouble with a soldier; also, given their rigorous physical training, downright dangerous.

Sundays were Miguel's day for fighting.

A boys' club had been created by some of the businessmen in the barrio, and though it was shabby and poorly equipped, it had something that immediately attracted Miguel's attention: a boxing ring. There wasn't a boy his age that could stay in the ring with him for more than a round or two. Even using cumbersome sixteen-ounce gloves, he had knocked out more than a score of opponents and had finally been asked to take on some of the older and more experienced boxers. He had at last begun to earn the respect he so desperately craved. But except for Fridays and Sundays, it was a grindingly dull six months that slowly passed out of his life.

Those six months had been, however, a momentous period for his family's adopted country. Trying to improve his English, Miguel often read the morning newspaper to them at breakfast, and was especially proud that a military unit comprised of many men from his own barrio had won a reputation for great proficiency and courage under the most arduous of training conditions.

The unit, called "E Company," was part of the 141st Regiment of the 36th Infantry Division, a fighting force later to become famous as the "Texas Volunteers."

By the middle of 1943 Miguel and his family had settled into a tedious routine that was rattled only by his older brother Raúl. Now twenty-three, and kept clear of the wartime draft because of flat feet, Raúl had become an open sore on his father's back.

José Luis had never forgiven Raúl for not having taken a regular job when they had first arrived in El Paso. Instead, Raúl had established a numbers game in the barrio and augmented his income by meeting occasionally with lonely, middle-aged Anglo women. To José Luis, both of Raúl's schemes were heartless and immoral.

Listening to their savage arguments, Miguel often thought his father would rather see Raúl killed in the war than continue to disgrace a family whose only asset, in José Luis's opinion, was its honor.

Their quarrels would often start in one room, then roam throughout the shabby, sparsely furnished apartment, their voices bouncing off the thin walls. Invariably they would end only when Raúl climbed out the window onto the fire escape and slipped down to the street.

More than Raúl's manner of making a living festered inside his father. José Luis was a proud man, and it galled him to take orders from his much younger Anglo supervisor at the icehouse. In Chihuahua, his father had been the only person José Luis had ever allowed to tell him what to do, and even Sebastián had always couched his command in the form of a request or suggestion.

At the icehouse, the young supervisor never even bothered to address him by his proper name. It was, "Joe, do this," and "Joey, do that." José Luis would cringe every time he heard anybody call him by either name. It seemed to diminish his stature; indeed, he could almost feel himself growing smaller. In Mexico, people treated him with respect, regarding him a diligent and honorable man.

José Luis felt he was still the same man, but his inner qualities had somehow failed to register with most of the Anglos at the icehouse. They teased him about his thick accent and old-fashioned manners and the tamales he brought in his lunch pail, and they made fun of the way he quietly muttered a prayer of thanks before he ate and always made the Sign of the Cross after he'd finished his noonday meal.

Hearing their jibes, José Luis would pretend he couldn't quite understand what was being said to him. In the beginning, he had hoped to win their trust and friendship by working harder than anybody else in the plant. He was first to arrive for work and last to leave. But this only seemed to provoke greater contempt.

"Hey, Joey, you trying to win the war single-handed, are ya?" they had taunted. "Lighten up, pinto bean. You're making the rest of us look bad!"

The strain soon began to tell. Often when José walked home in the afternoon, the insults he had heard that day still rang in his ears. But, by God, if he couldn't earn the respect of his co-workers, he vowed that he would certainly command it from his family.

Yet as the weeks turned to months, they, too, seemed to grow distant—even his wife, Graciela. She had a knack for friendship which he had never possessed, and before long she became the *padrina* to many of the children born to her fellow-tenants in the apartment house, her advice continually sought, even by people who had lived in the United States for many years. But very few people sought José Luis's counsel, least of all his eldest son Raúl.

What hurt José Luis the most was that Graciela had obviously grown fond of living in El Paso, and was no longer enthusiastic about returning to Mexico. José Luis took this as a personal insult. Their intimate moments grew fewer and less passionate. Often when they were alone together, he would simply sit reading his Chihuahua City newspaper, lost in a quiet reverie.

It was not that easy for Miguel to escape the grind of his own daily existence. Now nearly eighteen, he worked full-time as a stock- boy in the catacombs of the city's largest department store.

Reputed to be the finest store anywhere west of Dallas and east of Los Angeles, it was a handsome structure of seven stories with an interior of highly polished hardwood floors, chrome fixtures, and chandeliers. Its clientele was equally impressive. Mostly up-per-middle class, they lived in Kern Place, a prestigious residen-tial section on a large bluff overlooking the city.

The store's female customers rarely came down from their lofty perch without dressing in their finest clothes. They would often spend hours in the store without making a purchase. Shopping was considered a serious occasion, and the hushed, somber mood inside the store was much like that of a cathedral.

Miguel had gotten the job through the efforts of his only friend, Alfonso López, who had been working there for the past several months. Alfonso had flunked out of high school in his sophomore year, as had Miguel.

Miguel's younger brother, eleven-year-old Santiago, was the only one with a gift for scholarship. The boy was making excellent grades, learning to speak fluent English even faster than Raúl, whose line of work back in Chihuahua City had given him a head start.

It was Santiago who proudly wrote regularly to his Uncle Fran-cisco and carefully preserved what few letters were sent in return. To Miguel, those letters were a window opening into another world; yet he had never figured out what his Uncle Francisco had found in the Rio Grande Valley of south Texas that was so special.

CHAPTER 5

A dream had been born the day Sebastián took Francisco to his first bullfight. He was only ten-years old, yet it was a moment he never forgot. For the next few years, the boy spent his every spare second out behind the family corral, practicing his moves and footwork with a series of friends he had talked into playing the part of the bull. And always, when he made a graceful pass with his burlap cape, he would remember the raucous roar of the bull-ring, the sweetest sound the boy had ever heard.

He was soon fighting some of the young bulls at the ranch of one of his father's friends and hoping that later he could go to Mexico City and train to become a full-fledged matador.

But with the family struggling to stay alive in the blast furnace of the Revolution that was Chihuahua City in 1913, the loss of an able-bodied boy was a luxury Sebastián Salazar could ill afford.

"Pancho, you show both skill and courage in fighting these young bulls," his father had told him. "But for the time being, your future will have to be here on the farm, and not at the Plaza de Toros in Mexico City. Besides, even a good bullfighter rarely lives much longer than a bad soldier."

Francisco took the disappointing news with a grim smile. He had already demonstrated what he most wanted to prove, both to himself and to his father. He had courage and one day the great man he felt he was destined to be would arrive at his door. All he would need then was the right place and the right time—and most important of all, the right cause.

Francisco had found that cause near the little town of Mission, Texas, the final destination of the long journey that had brought him across the barren desert of northern Mexico and into the fertile fields of the Rio Grande Valley.

He and his family had arrived in Mission early one Sunday morning. Noting the name of the town, Francisco had smiled. It was, he thought, a favorable omen.

But it was only as he walked through the large migrant camp, which sat a few miles outside the town, that his long-awaited destiny became obvious to him.

Texas, as was most of the United States, still struggling to climb out of the Great Depression. But here, on one of the largest farms in the state, the battle appeared to have been both won and lost. Francisco had seen poverty, disease and malnutrition before but never in such pitiless contrast to such affluence.

Although the migrant camp looked like a leper colony, gleaming tractors, expensive cars, and barns bloated with ripe produce were in evidence everywhere.

The migrant workers who had harvested the crops that filled those barns milled listlessly through the camp, as if walking in their sleep, a surprise that stunned him like a blow to the back of his head.

Like his father, he had admired almost everything about the United States. The Land of Opportunity! But what he saw now in that migrant camp seemed the dark side of the American Dream: the brutal price a forgotten people were paying so that others more fortunate could realize the dream.

Francisco had finally discovered what his mission in life was to be. He had been brought to the Rio Grande Valley of Texas to change the way things were done. Somehow he would better the way these migrant workers were treated, fed, housed and paid. He would see to it that the table was someday properly set for these poor people who labored and lived and died on some of the richest farming land in the world.

"Juanita, I have found my place and time," he had quietly said. But neither his wife nor Alejandro, both utterly exhausted by the long and arduous trip, had the slightest idea of what Francisco meant.

They also did not know that their journey had only just begun.

Over the weeks and months that followed, Francisco slowly came to realize that his initial impressions had been somewhat erroneous. In actuality, the plight of the farm worker in south Texas was much worse than he had first imagined.

The migrant camp outside Mission, along with the five others that he, Juanita, and his son Alejandro had lived in since they arrived in Texas, were quagmires of filth and disease. Dysentery, rickets, measles, whooping cough, influenza, small pox, shingles, as well as a half-dozen other maladies, were so prevalent as to constitute a minor epidemic.

Yet these were the hidden plagues, apparent only to the workers affected by them: the families and friends of the ill, the dying, the maimed and the malnourished.

But to Francisco, what seemed almost as crippling was the apathy and fear which had settled into the bone marrow of most of the workers he had met: apathy, because virtually none of them believed their situation could ever be improved; fear, of the formidable strength and position of the owners and managers of the farms on which they worked.

There was, however, another debilitating element that had affected even Francisco himself: a strangely perverse sense of patriotism. The United States was now engaged in a global war that threatened never to be won. American forces had suffered crushing defeats in the Pacific, as well as horrendous shipping losses in the North Atlantic. In Europe, France—together with a string of smaller democracies—had fallen before Hitler's Panzer tanks and dive bombers like a line of wobbly dominos. It seemed England would surely be next.

Hence, it hardly seemed appropriate for Francisco to protest now. Yet he had never forgotten something he had once read about overcoming injustice: *If not now, when? If not here, where?*

The first meeting was held one Sunday night in a shack on the very edge of the migrant camp. The dwelling was large enough to house three families, but for the past week only Francisco's family had lived there. The other occupants had recently returned in despair to Mexico.

Francisco invited seven men to the meeting, but only two showed up. Neither seemed suited for the struggle which lie ahead—both men in their sixties and long dogged by frail health and faded hopes.

The smaller man was Paco González, "Old Paquito" to his many friends. Paquito was proud that he had seen service in the American army during the First World War. His fighting days, however, now seemed far behind him.

The other man was a courtly-looking black, Thomas Jefferson Jones. Francisco had decided earlier that Jones might be the more important to his cause. The black man had read many articles and pamphlets about Saul Alinsky and Harry Bridges and had patiently tried to answer the many questions Francisco had asked about the two famous labor leaders and their methods and tactics.

Alinsky had gained fame as the organizer of the stock-yard workers in Chicago, Bridges having done the same with the longshoremen in San Francisco.

Old Paquito and Jones had joined Francisco around the kerosene lamp which sat on a three-legged table in the center of the crudely furnished shack. In the far corner and next to an open window, Juanita and Alejandro were sitting on a cot. Outside the window was a badly polluted irrigation ditch, its stench almost overpowering.

The night was hot and humid, and Juanita had left the window open. She had grown used to the foul smell, but the brutal humidity she had never experienced before. She found the air hard to breathe and had lost much of her energy. What distressed her was the effect the weather had on her hair. She had always considered it her best feature, but now it hung damp and lifeless.

Francisco had just repeated the eloquent injunction he had already decided would be the catchphrase of the movement.

"Yes, I know there are a thousand reasons why it cannot be done. But we must at least try... for if not now, when? And if not here, where?"

"You're forgetting something, Frank," the black man said quietly. "All them other labor groups was created mainly by white folks and for white folks. There ain't never been nothing put together by people like us. Poor whites least got their color going for 'em. All we got is our hands."

"What also you do not see, Francisco," Paquito added, "is Mexicans can be deported. I live here many years, even fight for Los Estados Unidos, but this is still not my country. The first time I make trouble, I am a foreigner and nothing else."

"So?" Francisco asked, smiling. "Alinsky is a Jew whose family came from Europe. Bridges is an Irishman who—"

"You're missing the point, Frank," Jones muttered. "They both are white men in a white man's country."

"Also you miss something else," Paquito said, solemnly rolling a cigarette. "Already, many of the growers and their foremen know how you feel. You complain to their faces too many times. A mistake, my friend. Because the day is coming when they no longer hire you. Then where will you be? I tell you: back in Mexico, or dead."

The three men went on quietly talking. Off in the far corner of the darkened room, Alejandro had been trying to study a schoolbook, but hearing the word dead, he looked up. The same word also affected Juanita, and she suddenly drew him closer to her. Alejandro's gaze slowly returned to his book.

In the few short months since they arrived in Texas, he had attended three schools, as his family had moved from one camp to another. To most children his age, school was a bothersome chore, but to him, it was the only place where for a few fleeting hours, he could feel almost normal. It was also the only place where he had ever come to like an Anglo, for though his English was still badly fractured, his teachers had been kind and encouraging.

"You're a smart little boy, Alejandro," more than one teacher had told him, and a few of them had gone out of their way to repeat this in front of his mother. It had made him feel very proud.

Now a car horn honked outside. The sound was not from a Model-A Ford, the only car he had ever seen a migrant worker drive. This sound was from a much newer car, and the only people who drove such cars were the bosses.

"Hey, Salazar, come out here!" a voice boomed from the darkness. "And bring your organizing pals with you."

Francisco rose and walked to the doorway, now bathed in the glare of the car's headlights.

"What do you want?" Francisco called out, shading his eyes.

"Just some congenial company, that's all," the voice replied. "So why don't you and your friends come along for a little ride?"

Both Paquito and Jones had risen from the table, their faces drawn with apprehension. Francisco glanced over at Juanita and Alejandro and gave them a reassuring smile. He turned back into the blazing light.

"We're a little tired, Señor... and we have a big day of work tomorrow out in —"

"Yeah, we're a little tired, too," the voice interjected. "So let's get moving, huh?"

Francisco's eyes hardened. "Why do you want me to go with you?"

"Because if you don't, we'll have to conduct our business in front of your wife and the boy."

A long moment passed before Francisco replied. "Okay...but leave my friends alone. They only came to see how my son is doing in school."

"Naw, we need 'em as witnesses, just in case you later try to make up some silly stories about us. So now come on, huh?"

Francisco reluctantly beckoned both Jones and Paquito forward. This was the first time he had ever placed friends of his in serious jeopardy, and the realization showed in his grimly etched features.

A few moments later, Francisco and the others were herded into a Cadillac sedan by three men he had never seen before. Two of the men had pistols strapped to their belts.

Before the Cadillac rolled to a stop behind a deserted railroad siding, Francisco knew why the men had come for him. The "ride" had lasted less than three minutes.

"Please, let my friends go now, eh?" he murmured, as he was hauled out of the car. "This is my problem, not theirs."

The blunt-faced man who had earlier done all the talking peered back into the car, glaring at Paquito and Jones.

"Yeah, maybe you're right, Salazar. Snake with no head ain't a snake no more," he said with a contemptuous frown. "Besides, these two old farts don't look like they'd be able to survive much more'n a kick in the head. So we'll just let 'em watch, huh?"

"Is that what you plan to do, kick me in the head?" Francisco asked, trying to smile.

The blunt-faced man grinned. "Naw, what's about to happen to you is what they call an 'industrial accident.' You know, where you catch your hand in something or other."

Out of the corner of his eye, Francisco saw one of the men take an axe handle from the trunk of the car. Then someone else drew forth a pistol.

Fifteen minutes later, Alejandro heard a car pull to a stop out in front of the shack. From the moment his father had been taken away, he and his mother had been on their knees, praying for his safe return. Now he rose and cautiously moved toward the door.

In the moonlight, Alejandro saw the back door of the car open, but it was several seconds before anyone came out of it. Then Jones emerged into view and reached back to gently help Francisco from the car. Paquito followed them into the shack. The large sedan began to snake its way out of the camp.

At first, Alejandro thought his father was drunk. But when Francisco was finally brought into the light, the boy saw that his father's hands were bruised and bleeding. Juanita began to quietly weep, and went for a pail of water and some rags. The others laid Francisco down on the cot. No one said a word.

When Juanita had cleared the blood off his hands, the sight of his injuries stunned her into silence. She stopped crying, her anguish replaced by rage.

Both of Francisco's hands looked as if several of their bones had been broken. Alejandro seemed in a daze as he knelt down to cradle his father's head in his arms.

When Francisco regained a little strength, he glanced over and saw that Paquito and Jones were still in the shack. This surprised him. He had thought that the events of the evening had forever frightened the little Mexican and the old black man away.

"I'm okay," Francisco whispered. "Thanks for getting me back…but better you leave before you get deeper involved in all this."

Jones and Paquito nodded, yet made no immediate move toward the door.

"Well, what are you waiting for?" Francisco quietly asked.

Jones's weathered features slowly formed a smile. "We're waiting for you to tell us when the next meeting gonna be."

Juanita's eyes flashed with anger. "Señor Jones—and you, Paquito! You will forget these meetings and instead start thinking how my man can go on earning a living with these broken hands of his!"

"We take a collection," Paquito softly declared. "And we will keep taking it up until Francisco's hands have healed. Your husband, Señora Juanita, has more friends than he thinks."

Francisco slowly straightened up. He sat staring at his mangled hands for a moment; then, despite the pain that still raged through his entire body, he smiled. His broken bones had succeeded where his lofty slogans had failed.

CHAPTER 6

Some two blocks from their apartment, they began to split away from each other, José Luis off toward the icehouse, Santiago to his grade school, Miguel on to his job at the department store. Raúl, however, had already reached his own place of business.

"So try not to work too hard, eh?" he called out, parking himself at one of the tables of the outdoor café, which served as his office. "Easy habit to get into, but damned difficult to break!"

Ordering a café con leche, Raúl spent the next few minutes happily making lewd comments to some of the young women hurrying by on their way to work. Most of them smiled. Raúl was considered one of the few good catches left in the now-depleted barrio.

Miguel waved his older brother a cheerless goodbye. He had grown to resent that Raúl earned more money than he did, yet seemed to work far fewer hours. This struck Miguel as worse than unfair, yet somehow very American.

The matter weighed heavily on him, and by the time he reached the department store, he was more than ten minutes late. Cursing himself, Miguel broke into a trot. But as he rushed past one of the store's display windows, something brought him to sudden stop.

Standing among several demurely smiling dummies dressed in the swankiest feminine fashions of 1943, was one male figure, wearing only a skimpy brassiere.

Dashing into the store, Miguel quickly sneaked into the rear of the display window. He waited for a few people to pass by outside, then grabbed at the male manikin like a mugger, grabbing it by its throat and arm. Pulling the dummy from the display case, he started across the store with it.

Several customers, watching Miguel maneuver the brassiere-clad figure through the already crowded store, stared at him with slightly stricken expressions.

Then Miguel saw that he and his silent companion had also been seen by his supervisor. Harold Metcalfe, a balding, bland-faced man, took out his pocket watch, glanced at the time, and began to jerk the watch around by its chain.

But as Miguel took a fast turn into the store's main stockroom, his mind was on something else. Moments earlier, he had noticed that Lorena Calderón, standing behind her notions' counter, had smiled at him.

He still remembered what he had thought the first time they met. She was the most beautiful woman he had ever seen, with a glamorous mystique he had never before encountered anywhere outside of a movie screen.

Her black hair, cut in a pageboy, perfectly framed her finely chiseled features and thickly lashed green eyes. Her skin had the look of beige-colored satin. She was tall for a Mexican, but there was nothing skimpy about her figure.

Miguel thought Lorena Calderón was a worthy match for the most gorgeous film stars he had ever seen. The only drawback was that she was some three years older than he was. The afternoon he had met Lorena, Miguel came home from the department store and burned his last letter from Lupita Palacios.

The stockroom was humming with activity. Miguel quickly parked the dummy in one corner, placing its face toward the wall. Then he struggled into his work apron. It was precisely when his arms were momentarily caught that a cardboard box came flying at his head, thrown by his friend Alfonso López, a sly-looking little Mexican built along the lines of a fireplug.

"Hey, better hide in there. Old Man Metcalfe knows you're late again!"

"Yeah, I know," Miguel muttered, having barely ducked out of the way of the flying box. "I saw him outside swinging his watch around like it was a club."

Alfonso chortled. "And if you don't start getting to work on time, someday he's going to brain you with it."

Miguel frowned. Although Alfonso was about a month younger than Miguel, he considered himself wiser to the ways of the gringo because he was born in the United States; hence almost everything he said sounded like fatherly advice. Miguel didn't like getting such advice from anyone but his own father.

Taking his place alongside the other Mexicans working next to a conveyor, Miguel whispered, "I really try to be on time, Alfonso. But for some reason, it takes me longer now to get ready for work. I don't know why, but—"

"I know why," Alfonso interjected. "Since the day you met Lorena Calderón, you spend an hour every morning just combing your crummy-looking hair."

The monotonous clank of the conveyor was broken by a ripple of laughter. Miguel turned away from the others. Alfonso's remark had nicked a nerve. Everyone knew how proud Miguel was of his thick, wavy hair. It was, he thought, the only handsome thing about his head. He considered his cheekbones too high, his nose too broad, his jaw too square.

"So what can I do, Alfonso?" Miguel quietly asked. 'You know the way I feel about Lorena.

Alfonso bared a snaggle-toothed grin. "Well, first you start by taking a very cold shower!"

The room rippled again with laughter, but it ceased as abruptly as a radio suddenly clicked off. Many of the Mexicans stared down at their work with renewed interest.

"Well, Salazar, nice of you to join us this morning," Harold Metcalfe growled, having crept up behind Miguel. "Now, assuming you can spare us the time, we need three dozen of the new sweatshirts up in sporting goods right away!"

Miguel nodded. He could almost feel the supervisor's breath on the back of his neck. Metcalfe stood, bouncing from one foot to another, then strode out of the stockroom.

Miguel turned away from the conveyor, and, opening up a large box, he began to take out some sweatshirts.

"Miguel, you better ask Lorena for a date," Alfonso whispered. "Now, while you're still working here."

Miguel had just had the same thought.

"Go ask her on your way upstairs," Alfonso badgered. "Who knows, she might even say yes! In my great and colorful life, I have seen stranger things happen."

"Yes, so have I, and you are one of them," Miguel muttered, closing back the box. He started for the door.

Alfonso flashed his teeth again. "Bet you a taco you turn chicken again."

Miguel peered back over the stack of sweatshirts he was carrying. "No, make it a real bet. The best dinner in the best place in town," Miguel challenged and walked out of the room.

Sauntering over to the door, Alfonso winked back at the other workers. But he wasn't all that crazy about taking such a large sum from his friend. Since the day he and Miguel had flunked out of high school and found each other loitering around the football field afterward, both too embarrassed to be seen leaving the grounds before the final bell, they had been the best of pals. But that didn't keep them from bickering with each other. The other Mexicans in the stockroom called them "the old married couple."

Out on the department store's main floor, and some fifty feet away from Lorena's notions' counter, Miguel's legs felt as if they'd begun to move through quicksand. At the far end of her long counter, a hatchet-faced old woman was sniffing various perfumes.

Miguel was grateful for the diversion; it gave him time to go over his speech again. He had memorized a suave line of patter from a Mexican movie he had seen the week before. But the exact words eluded him. His heart was now racing so fast that if anybody had asked him to simply spell out his own last name, he would have been at a loss for letters.

Finally, Lorena finally noticed him. Excusing herself from her customer, she started toward him, obviously unaware of what her sensuously swaying hips were doing to Miguel's crippled concentration.

"Good morning," she said, in a voice that sounded like a symphony to his ears.

"Good morning, Señorita Calderón," Miguel said, as if she were the last person he expected to see standing behind her own counter.

"Did you want to see me about something?" Lorena asked, bringing her swaying hips to a full stop. "Or are you just hiding out from Metcalfe again?"

"Hey, I'm not scared of him! Just wanted to say hello, that's all," Miguel stammered before leaning down to pick up the sweatshirts he had dropped. Noting his nervousness, Lorena smiled sympathetically.

At the other side of the room, and partially hidden behind the door of the stockroom, Alfonso was also smiling. Stroking his wispy mustache, he turned back to the other workers.

"Hey, anybody know the most expensive place in town to eat?"

The stockroom immediately filled with blank expressions. The Mexicans obviously were no experts on such matters; yet even if they were, Alfonso knew the chances of any of them getting served there were next to nil. About the same chance, he thought, that Miguel had of getting a date with a woman as classy as Lorena Calderón.

But when Alfonso turned back toward the notions' counter, his lopsided smile warped into a grimace. Lorena was nodding at Miguel in an alarmingly way.

"Yes, Miguel, a Saturday-night picture show sounds very nice. But this coming weekend I have to—"

"Saturday night!" Miguel interjected, feeling rather dazed that she had accepted so easily. "Seven o'clock, and I'll be right on time, okay?"

Lorena chuckled. "That sounds fine. Do you know where I live?"

Miguel nodded uneasily. He had followed Lorena home from work the first day he had met her.

"Well, then I'll see you at my house next Saturday night," she murmured, touching his hand lightly as if he might be running a temperature. Miguel mustered an uncertain smile and backed away from the counter.

But in turning away from Lorena, he suddenly found himself face to face with Metcalfe.

"Now why aren't you up in sporting goods with those sweatshirts?" his supervisor snarled.

"Oh, the sweat shirts? Sure, they're right here, Mister Metcalfe!" Miguel stammered, somewhat startled to see them still in his arms.

"I can see that," Metcalfe growled, running one hand through what was left of his sandy-colored hair. "But this is the notions' department, Salazar, not sporting goods. One way you can tell the difference is there are no dumbbells down here...or weren't until a moment ago!"

Pausing to catch his breath, Metcalfe saw that Lorena was staring at Miguel with ill-disguised concern. This seemed to make him angrier.

"Oh, I swear, Salazar, you haven't got the brains God gave those dummies in the window... and don't think I didn't notice that little prank you played with one of them this morning. Now move, boy!"

Miguel flushed with embarrassment and strode toward a nearby elevator. Metcalfe followed after him, apparently determined to rag him all the way to the sporting goods department.

When Miguel finally returned to the stockroom, Alfonso was standing behind the door, trying to keep a smirk off his face. Miguel stopped just outside the door.

"You're the one who dressed up that dummy so crazy this morning, aren't you?" he asked with quiet menace. Alfonso smiled sheepishly. "Don't be confusing things. What did Lorena say?"

Miguel grinned. "She said yes. Saturday night, seven o'clock. You lost the bet," he said and then shoved open the door so wide that Alfonso went crashing back into a canyon of cardboard.

CHAPTER 7

Failure had become Miguel's main stock in trade. He had flunked out of high school, lost Lupita Palacios, and been fired from his busboy job. Now he was probably headed, he thought, for a similar fate at the department store.

"Maybe I ought to put a 'going out of business' sign on my head," Miguel had once grimly joked to Alfonso.

His upcoming date with Lorena now took on greater significance. If he could successfully court the most coveted woman in the barrio, it would bring him a status he had long yearned for, but never been able to achieve.

Miguel was like a gambler, trying to recoup his losses with one final roll of the dice. His success with Lorena depended, however, on his being able to lure his older brother into a trap. It would not be easy. Raúl was an expert at evading traps. Many young women in the Second Ward had attempted to lure him into marriage but had little more to show for their efforts than the loss of their virginity.

Miguel was thinking of all this when Raúl walked into the apartment. Graciela had just carried in a steaming platter of rice from the kitchen.

"Nothing for me, Mamacita," Raúl murmured. "I'm only here to kill a little time until I meet some friends later for supper."

Draping his six-foot body across a threadbare sofa, Raúl began to thumb through the *Life* magazine he had carried in with him. The rest of the family quietly started their meal.

"Hey, look at this," Raúl exclaimed, referring to an article in the magazine. "Some clown here is getting rich selling worms to the government that he's been growing in his own back yard."

Raúl's remark register only with his youngest brother, Santiago.

"Are they also buying cockroaches?" he inquired. "We sure have plenty of those around here."

"Santiago," José Luis growled. "This family does not speak of worms or cockroaches at the supper table."

José Luis went on serving out portions from the platters Graciela continued to bring in from the kitchen. Miguel, sensing an opening, spoke for the first time.

"Just a little rice, Papá. I have a problem that has killed my appetite."

"Say, what do we run here, a restaurant?" José Luis irritably asked, his serving spoon suspended in the air. "You think you order only what you want, then get up and leave any time it pleases you?"

With his question claiming no response, José Luis now clasped his hands in prayer. The blessing ended with the request that the Good Lord help his family raise as soon as possible the five-thousand dollars needed for their return to Chihuahua City. José Luis had not forgotten the promise he had made to his dying father.

It was a vow that Raúl had never taken very seriously. As soon as José Luis said the blessing and made his plea, Raúl reopened his magazine. "Yeah, sure seems like everybody's making a killing on this war but yours truly," he quietly groaned.

The war was also on José Luis's mind. The barrio had been drained of most of its able-bodied men, leaving José Luis with workers either too young or too old to handle the hurtling hundred-pound blocks of ice; in the last several months, his back-breaking job had become a dangerous one, as well.

José Luis carefully wiped clean his eye glasses. "Listen to me, big shot. Forget this fortune that you so clearly are not making. Instead, consider yourself lucky you sit here with a magazine in your hands and not overseas with a rifle in your arms..."

"Now, José Luis," Graciela quickly cautioned, "it is not Raúl's fault the army would not take him because of his flat feet."

"No, Graciela, but it is his fault he still refuses to find honest work and goes on with disreputable companions and dishonest ideas."

The battle had started again. It amazed Miguel that his father and Raúl could not be in the same room for more than five minutes without getting into an argument. One could almost set a watch by it, and Raúl now stood up from the sofa to do exactly that.

"Well, I'm meeting some of those people you think are so terrible for supper tonight, so I better get going," he muttered, walking over to kiss Graciela goodbye.

Time to spring the trap, Miguel thought. The words he had carefully rehearsed blurted out.

"If I cannot get ten dollars by Saturday night, I will forever be a disgrace to this family."

His short speech made an impression, though not in the way he wished. His mother and father, along with Raúl, intently peered at him as if he were half-drunk. They knew that his only vice was a fondness for cheap wine.

"Ten dollars in American money?" his mother finally asked.

Miguel nodded grimly. "Yes, Mamá. I have to buy a suit before this Saturday night."

Miguel shot a glance at his younger brother, who was sitting at the other end of the table. Santiago smiled. He seemed a well-trained actor awaiting his cue.

Their father's surprise had by now melted into amused curiosity. "Miguel, did somebody die, that you need a suit to go to their funeral, or what?" José Luis gently inquired.

"No, but if I don't get the suit, I might die myself... You see, Papá, this Saturday night, I have a date with a lady who could change my entire life."

José Luis frowned. He hated overblown statements, a commodity his son Raúl seemed to specialize in. Yet, the news that Miguel had found another young woman sounded good. Both José Luis and Graciela had suffered with him through his previous romantic disappointment. The news also sounded interesting to Raúl. Tossing aside his magazine, he positioned himself directly behind Miguel.

"Hey, this new girlfriend of yours must be very special to make you trade in your sweatshirt for a suit," Raúl ventured. "I would personally like to meet any girl who has worked such a miracle."

Miguel could not see Raúl's face but knew his older brother was smiling. "Forget it, Raúl," Miguel exclaimed. "You already have most of the girls in the barrio roped into your corral."

"Brother, when you get a little older," Raúl replied, laying a hand on Miguel's shoulder, "you'll realize that it's a wise man that always makes room for one more."

Miguel smiled. He knew that the general topic of females could always put Raúl into a more relaxed mood. Now was the moment to lure him closer to the trap. Miguel nodded slightly in the direction of his younger brother.

"Hey, Raúl, maybe Miguel could borrow your new suit for just one night, huh?" Santiago casually inquired. "If the family can save ten dollars, that means we get back to Mexico just that much sooner, right?"

"Santiago speaks the truth, Raúl," José Luis declared, beaming with pleasure, as he always did on those rare occasions when his younger sons gained an advantage over their older brother. José Luis also had seen the trap and hoped Raúl would fall into it.

"Forget it, Miguel," Raul said, beginning to comb his hair. "I got a date myself this Saturday night," "Besides, my suit pants would be a little long for you, anyway."

"Mamá could alter them," Santiago suggested, smiling. He had rehearsed his lines well.

"Hey, Santiago," Raúl bristled, "you sure got a lot of big ideas for such a little kid!" Raúl didn't know that Miguel had provided Santiago with these same ideas.

The discussion, as far as Raúl was concerned, seemed headed in the wrong direction. After all, what was his was his. It was everything else that was negotiable.

"But, Raúl, Mamá could change your new suit to fit Miguel," Santiago coolly continued. "Then later that night, she lets the pants out again—"

Before Santiago could expound further, Raúl threw his comb at him. With the comb still ricocheting around the room, Graciela stepped into the melee, her voice and manner that of a referee who has decided to stop a one-sided boxing match.

"Stop this foolishness right now!"

When it was quiet again, Graciela issued her verdict.

"This coming Saturday night, I will shorten Raúl's suit pants to fit Miguel. Then he will return home early to change into something of his own. By that time he will already have made an impression on his new girlfriend, and the suit will no longer matter."

Graciela paused to make sure she still had her family's undivided attention. "Then I shall let the pants out for Raúl, who afterward can go out on his own date...and that way, we will all get back to Mexico ten dollars sooner."

Graciela had a flair for the dramatic and had spoken as if reading an important announcement. Now, awash with admiring looks from everyone but Raúl, she blushed with pleasure.

"Graciela, you are truly worth your weight in gold," José Luis murmured, his eyes soft with loving admiration.

"Well, remember that, José Luis, the next time I ask you for ten dollars myself," Graciela remarked, taking up his plate to reheat his supper.

Raúl tossed the magazine aside and said, "As usual, four against one. I'm leaving to go find better odds that that!" and started out of the apartment.

When the door had closed behind him, Miguel smiled and extended his hand to Santiago. "You remembered everything. Raúl couldn't shake you."

"Ah, it was easy. Raúl's not nearly as smart as he thinks he is," Santiago said, grinning. "And someday, that might get us all into a lot of trouble."

CHAPTER 8

September 10, 1943: One day after the day that was to mark a major change in the course of the war in Europe. But at seven-thirty that morning, most of the people in the Second Ward had not yet heard the momentous news.

As Miguel walked to work that morning, he paused to look at the alligators in the plaza. Few people seemed to know where the sloe-eyed creatures had come from, yet there they were, penned up in a pond in the center of a city, which was itself in the middle of a desert.

Gazing at the creatures, Miguel chuckled. The reptiles reminded him of his older brother, cunning and unpredictable. Raúl always strove to do the unexpected and usually succeeded. Miguel still carried the emotional scars of two such surprises.

The first had occurred only a few months after they had arrived from Chihuahua.

"Miguel, my boy, it is nothing short of a social disgrace that at the age of sixteen, you are still a virgin," Raúl had declared. And with his usual enterprising spirit, he had vowed to remedy this embarrassing situation.

For the deflowering ceremony, Raúl promised Miguel a beautiful young prostitute. Raúl claimed he had already tested her expertise and could personally vouch for her skill. He guaranteed Miguel it would be an experience he would never forget.

His brother had spoken the truth, for even now, almost two years later, Miguel still vividly remembered every horrific detail.

It had been raining hard that night in Juárez. By the time Miguel and Raúl crossed the long bridge that led from El Paso to the Mexican city, the dirt road leading to the prostitute's hotel was awash with muddy debris. The battered old building keeled heavily to one side, like a drunk about to collapse in the street, Miguel thought, as he dragged his feet through the freezing slush that blanketed the twisting street.

Reaching the hotel, Miguel followed his brother up a crumbling staircase. In the dim light, he noticed that the hotel had no lobby. Not an encouraging sign. He suddenly felt the urge to bolt back to the bridge.

Then, overcoming the impulse, Miguel prayed he would not disgrace himself by wetting his pants before he had even gotten the chance to take them off.

After they had climbed to the third floor he saw that there was but one room. Beyond its partially closed door, he could see a candle flickering in the darkness.

"How are you feeling?" Raúl whispered.

"Horny," Miguel lied.

Then he took in a large gulp of stale air and positioned himself behind Raúl.

"Consuelo, it's me, Raúl Salazar," Raul said, tapping on the door.

A voice that sounded very close by quietly growled, "Is the boy with you?"

Miguel shuddered. The voice seemed that of someone even older than the hotel.

Raúl loudly cleared his throat. "Yes and very anxious to meet you."

The door flew open. A tiny woman stood framed in the doorway, the flickering candle dancing behind her. She sent out a strangled shriek of laughter, and then her hands flung forward like tentacles to wrap themselves around Miguel's wrists with the strength of what seemed to Miguel a sea monster.

But jerking away from her clawing, grasping hands, Miguel stumbled backwards and fell to the wooden floor. The woman, still cackling with laughter, bent over him. Miguel could no longer see her, but he could feel her hands dangling over his face, her fingers running across his cheeks like centipedes.

Finally struggling to his feet, he stumbled down the stairs, the sound of the old woman's screams and Raúl's laughter exploding in his ears.

When he hit the street, Miguel ran for more than a mile and did not stop till he reached the international bridge. There another ignominy awaited him. He did not have the three-cent toll charge, and was forced to borrow it from an American customs officer.

The alligators had begun slowly slithering into the shade, for even this early in the morning it was already hot enough to indicate that another West Texas scorcher was on its way.

As Miguel wiped the sweat from his brow, he noticed a large truck stop alongside the plaza.

"Extra! Extra!" two young boys yelled, jumping from the truck to go milling through a fast-forming crowd. Miguel paid little attention to the commotion. Having just relived his first sexual catastrophe, he was now remembering its more successful sequel.

"Yeah, it was a pretty lousy joke, Miguel. But maybe I can make it up to you," Raúl had said, trying to convince him of his reformed intentions. It had not been difficult.

Raúl had planned, however, yet another surprise.

This time the girl was indeed young and pretty, the hotel room nicely furnished and even adorned with red roses. It also sheltered three people too many. Raúl, along with two of his friends, had hidden behind a wardrobe bureau in one corner of the small room, only a few feet from the bottom edge of the bed.

The preliminaries went smoothly enough. Then the lovemaking turned serious. The room was filled with the noise of Miguel's body slapping against the young woman's. The bed springs groaned, as if straining under the weight of a couple of elephants. Miguel's impassioned protestations, the dialogue of which he had memorized from a third-rate Mexican movie, seemed almost as loud.

For the first few minutes, Raúl and his accomplices were able to contain their mirth—until the urgent sounds coming from the bed proved too much for them.

The laughter from behind the bureau had reached percussive proportions. Yet Miguel remained oblivious to everything but the fire raging through his lean, muscular body.

Then it happened.

Miguel's unseen audience, no longer able to control its riotous laughter, suddenly tumbled forward. The massive bureau keeled over, and with a thunderous blast crashed down across the lower edge of the bed.

Miguel and the girl were sent flying a full foot off the bed as rear its legs splintered into small pieces. When the lovers returned from their brief flight, they were lying at a severe angle, yet still locked in sexual embrace.

So this is what an orgasm with a woman feels like, Miguel had happily concluded.

Later, Raúl and his friends would express amazement that he had not seemed to notice the disturbance. Instead, when the young girl had first screamed with surprise, Miguel had thought he had brought her to the peak of sexual excitement. That had been more than enough to trigger his brain-rattling completion.

Afterwards, sitting in a bar with Raúl and his two friends, Miguel glowed with male pride. He had won the admiration of them all, even the young woman, who had joined them for a drink.

"Miguel, you were nothing short of heroic," Raúl said, "like in those war movies, where the American pilots come through all that heavy flak and machine-gun fire to still hit their target. I tell you, to witness it was a fucking inspirational experience!"

Miguel smiled. He had successfully completed his maiden voyage.

He was savoring this memory when he saw something that abruptly yanked him back from the past. One of the newspaper boys had come close enough for him to read the headline. "ALLIES LAND AT SALERNO!"

Miguel had no idea where Salerno was, but he could see that the news of the landing had set off a celebration. Women were crying, men were yelling, and everywhere people were embracing, as many of them began to shake hands with a few Mexican-American servicemen there in the plaza waiting for a bus.

For a long moment Miguel intently studied the faces of those so joyously congratulating the soldiers, faces filled with admiration, gratitude and respect.

A troubling notion came to him as he realized that he would give almost anything to earn such admiration—even fight to defend a country he had never grown to like, much less love.

The thought amazed him.

CHAPTER 9

Punching in his timecard that morning, Miguel quietly cursed himself. On this, the most important Saturday of his entire life, he was late for work again.

"Fifteen minutes late, huh, Salazar?"

Alfonso's smirk was moving along behind a cart full of manikins. Darting to the far side of the cart, Miguel quickly fell in step with his friend, using the cart as a cover of sorts.

"Hey, Alfonso, you have to broadcast my arrival every morning?" Miguel hissed. He wanted to sound more menacing, but he had just spotted Lorena Calderón across the already crowded store. She had waved to him in what he sensed was a very special way. Alfonso had not yet seen her.

"Take it easy, Miguel. I was just yoking," Alfonso said, parodying as he sometimes did his own thick accent. "But hey, did you hear the radio broadcast this morning?"

"I heard it from the newsboys. The American Army has landed at Salerno, eh?" Miguel muttered, glancing back toward the notions' counter. Lorena was smiling at him.

Noting this, Alfonso's own smile went sour. "So, what picture show are you taking her to tonight?"

Miguel's expression knotted. The choice of a movie was the one thing he had not yet determined in an otherwise carefully planned campaign.

"I cannot chose,'María Candelaria' or the Negrete show at the Colón. It costs a little less."

"Don't be a monkey about money," Alfonso cautioned, happily shifting into his role as Miguel's principal advisor. "Spend the extra money. I have already seen 'Maria Candelaria' and guarantee you it will make Lorena cry like a baby. Once you have a woman in tears, anything is possible!"

By now they had made it halfway across the store. Miguel was breathing almost normally again. Metcalfe's glistening dome was nowhere in sight.

"Well, maybe you are right, ugly," Miguel shot back with some asperity. Did Alfonso know everything about everything? "But I have heard is that getting a woman to laugh, not cry, is the faster way to her heart."

"Hey, who the hell is talking about getting to Lorena's *heart*?" Alfonso replied, frowning.

Miguel suddenly felt the entire conversation unworthy of further effort. Alfonso did not understand how he really felt about Lorena, and half a dozen poets could not have explained it to him.

"Okay, Miguel, what's your plan for before and after the show?" Alfonso asked, already vicariously enjoying the evening.

"Well, I will have just enough money to pay for five songs before the show, then maybe afterward to buy her a little supper at—"

"Ay, Miguel, first you act like a monkey about money, now you are a complete tonto about time!"

Alfonso brought his dummy delivery to an abrupt stop. "Listen, can't you see that by the time you leave the movie, the night will be running out?"

Miguel nodded uncertainly. "Forget the supper, eh?"

"Sure," Alfonso shot back. "Yeah, because at this late part of the evening, you don't want to feed her stomach, you want to stir her blood—and for the same money you spend on food, you could take her out dancing. Get her heart pumping, man!"

By now Miguel's own blood was pumping. Aware that he'd become a stationary target for his supervisor, he had been bouncing from foot to foot, trying to urge Alfonso to complete their journey to the stockroom. But Miguel knew that once his friend started dispensing advice, he could remain rooted to the same spot for hours.

Nervously glancing around, Miguel broke from behind the cart and hurried the last few steps into the stockroom. Once inside, he stopped to wait for Alfonso.

"But I don't dance so good," Miguel muttered, rather reluctantly picking up the conversation. "I am better at eating than dancing."

Alfonso looked like a man about to make a noble sacrifice. Miguel knew that look and had come to distrust what usually followed it.

"Okay, my friend," Alfonso said, heaving an oversized sigh. "I will teach you how to dance and romance at the same time, even if I have to miss my lunch to perform such a miracle."

Miguel warily backed away. "Are you helping me because you are my best friend... or do you have another reason?"

Suddenly, it seemed they had become strangers.

"I had not thought of it before, but yes, I have another reason...for if even with all my help, you still fail with Lorena. Then when it comes my turn with her, I will at least know what not to do...and just because I am an ugly little man, do not think I will always be content to be nothing more than the best friend of the guy who gets the girl. Life is not the movies, Miguel."

With that, Alfonso hurried away with his cart full of manikins. Watching him go, Miguel made a vow: he would never again call his friend ugly.

A full hour would pass, however, before Miguel could force himself to apologize. Extending his hand to Alfonso, who was on the other side of the conveyor, Miguel whispered, "Forgive me, Alfonso...and I promise never to call you ugly again."

A big smile unzipped across Alfonso's wide face as he shook Miguel's hand. "But you have to wait an hour before saying you're sorry?"

Miguel grimaced, wondering whether his apology had been worth the effort. Alfonso chose to interpret Miguel's sour expression as a sure sign of sincere contrition.

"Because we just lost an hour we could have spent in dancing, and I got this funny feeling you will need all the practice you can get."

Alfonso was right. By three o'clock that afternoon, even after he had sacrificed his lunch and rest break, Alfonso had been unable to teach Miguel to dance any better than a donkey.

"No, Miguel, come forward with your left leg," Alfonso pleaded as he continued to coax him through the basic steps of the rhumba. "No, the left leg! That's the one on the other side of the right one, remember?"

Alfonso rolled his eyes upward, and in that moment he noticed that only the manikins were still smiling. He tried to catch his partner's attention. But Miguel, still glaring down at his feet as if they were his implacable enemy, continued to shuffle around. Then he noticed another pair of feet standing directly in front of him, wearing two-tone oxfords that he instantly recognized.

"Well, Salazar, it seems you dance about as well as you work," Metcalfe murmured, looking as if the exhibition had given him gas pains. "But the party's over now. When you punch out this afternoon, take your timecard up to Personnel. They'll have a severance check for you."

A stifling silence fell over the room. Even the conveyor had momentarily gone dead. Miguel could not think of a thing to say, nor even where to fix his gaze. The other Mexicans were staring down at the floor. Miguel felt as if he were standing in a crowd at his own funeral.

"Please forgive me, Mister Metcalfe. This will never happen again, if you could just..."

Miguel's voice trailed off. He was not quite able to beg to keep a job he had always hated.

Firing Miguel, however, had provided Metcalfe with a little pleasure. Picking on the muscular young Mexican had been one of the few enjoyable things left to him in a management career that had gone dead in the water many years before.

"Well, Salazar, for once you're right," Metcalfe quietly declared. "It certainly won't happen again. Not at this store, at least."

Metcalfe started for the door. Reaching it, he turned to point a finger in Alfonso's direction.

"And you're next, little man, unless you start shaping up awfully damn quick!"

Metcalfe straightened the knot of his hand-painted necktie and bolted out of the room.

Miguel trudged back to take his place alongside the other workers at the conveyor that Alfonso had set in motion again with a well-placed kick. Miguel noticed that his co-workers had edged away from him, as if he now carried a communicable disease.

CHAPTER 10

An hour later, Lorena heard the news that Miguel had been fired and went immediately to Metcalfe's office. He was enjoying his mid-afternoon snack, but Lorena's questioning soon spoiled his appetite.

"Okay, so the boy was wrong, Harold. But did you have to make an even bigger mistake by firing him?"

"But if I let him get away with only a warning again, how's that going to make me look with all the other workers?" Metcalfe grumbled, staring at the sandwich in his hand.

Lorena's presence in his cramped office appeared to disconcert him. Sitting down next to his desk, she crossed her legs and leaned closer. Metcalfe began to perspire. He could barely keep from glancing at her shapely, bronze-burnished legs, now near enough for him to touch.

Noting his discomfort, Lorena smiled.

"I'll tell you exactly how that's going to make you look, Harold," she muttered in a husky voice. "Like a man who's big enough to change his mind...a man fair enough to give somebody a second chance...and you know there aren't many executives that big in this entire store—men who have never come to appreciate your own efforts."

An undecided look came over Metcalfe's pink face. He did not really appreciate Lorena citing his stagnant career to prove her point. What he did like was the new and intimate tone in her voice.

"You're a real Joan of Arc, aren't you?" he murmured, chuckling. "Hell, we can't say 'boo' to any of your people around here without you jumping onto your high horse."

Lorena had to chuckle. The comparison with the most famous woman in French history was more flattering than most of the others she had heard about herself in the three years she had worked in the store.

Those three years suddenly flashed through her mind. From the first day she had been hired as a sales trainee, she had been on the lookout for any signs of discrimination against her people. But in doing so, she had often made a fool of herself.

The first incident came when a young Mexican janitor was accused of stealing supplies out of the stockroom. Lorena was so upset she wrote a letter to the president of the store himself. Later, the old gentleman called her to his office to show her the confession the young janitor had signed. Lorena was mortified but hardly discouraged.

However, the president was impressed by her spirit, and agreed not to file formal charges against the young Mexican and instead simply fired him.

Lorena had better luck with her next cause. An elderly night watchman had been slightly wounded when he had chased a burglar out of the store and onto the street. But since he had been shot outside the premises of the store, the company was not inclined to pay for his medical expenses.

Again, Lorena had written a letter, arguing that the store was penalizing the old Mexican simply because he had taken his guard duties so seriously. This time the president agreed, and corrective measures immediately were taken.

Other incidents soon followed. But within a year after Lorena had come to the store, several of its executives had branded her a troublemaker and suggested that she be fired. Instead, the old man, after personally looking into the matter, had promoted her.

He was not wealthy by accident, and his shrewd eye had noted that the sales in the notions' department had increased since Lorena had joined its staff. The old man, Homer Jacobs by name, knew why. Lorena had a sweet-faced beauty that was the best possible advertisement for the store's beauty products. Her skin, hair and makeup were flawless; many a sale had been made after she casually implied to a patron that she was her own best customer.

Success had built a protective shell around her, but she had never overcome the fear that it could still be pierced at any moment. Lately, Lorena had tried to become, if not more tactful, at least more clever.

"And you're also overlooking one other thing, Harold."

"Which is what, pray tell?" he inquired with a smug smile.

"Miguel Salazar is strong as a bull. You'll have to hire two people to replace him—and there goes your budget."

Metcalfe seemed stuck for an answer. Opening up his sandwich bag, he peered into it, as if thinking he might find a solution inside the sack.

"Besides, Miguel will soon be of draft age anyway," Lorena continued, "and then probably out of your life for good. But meanwhile, Harold, find him something more interesting to do. He's way too smart just to be a stock boy."

"That's rich, Lorena," Metcalfe stammered, his mouth filled with half a sandwich. "First I fire him because he can't handle the simplest job in the store; now you want me to hire him back in an even more responsible position. Oh, that's smart all right."

"Maybe it's both rich and smart. They go together, don't they?" she replied, letting the implication fall where it may. "But if Miguel does better in a more responsible job, guess who'd get credit for having made a brilliant move? And you know how our president likes to think that this store is the salvation of every single Mexican who works here."

Lorena stood up, and, with a cryptic smile into which almost anything could be read, she said, "If you do this for the Salazar boy, I'll take it as a personal favor—and I'm famous for returning favors."

Saying that, she pointed her finger down at him, made a funny clicking sound, and walked out of the office.

Metcalfe leaned back in his chair and made a clicking sound of his own. Lorena Calderón would soon be in his debt.

At five-thirty that same afternoon, Miguel punched out his time card. He had not said a word to anyone since his encounter with Metcalfe a few hours earlier. His gloom was contagious. Even Alfonso, standing behind Miguel in the time-clock line, was unusually somber.

Metcalfe suddenly materialized. "I'll take that time card, Salazar."

Miguel handed him the card, then watched with amazement as Metcalfe placed it back in its rack.

"But I'll be counting the days, boy, until they draft you into the army. Meanwhile, next Monday morning, I'm reassigning you upstairs to sporting goods. Demonstrating our weightlifting equipment should, I trust, place no strain on your brain."

Metcalfe reluctantly released a small smile and strode away, leaving in his wake several befuddled Mexicans.

"Wow, Miguel," Alfonso muttered, whistling softly with pure wonder and ill-disguised envy. "As the gringos like to say, you just went from the outhouse to the penthouse."

Miguel grinned. He knew who had been responsible for this short but surprising journey. Only one Mexican in the store could have talked Metcalfe into changing his mind. "Well, Alfonso, it's only for about another month. I'll be counting the days myself."

"Yeah, but when it comes my turn to get drafted, I'll enlist before they can grab me," Alfonso muttered, still dazed by Miguel's good fortune. Alfonso had worked in the store longer than Miguel, and was considered the better worker. It didn't seem fair. Still, if anyone had managed to climb out of the company's catacombs before he did, Alfonso was happy it had been his best friend. 'Yeah, I'm going to try to get in with that Mexican rifle company. Even the gringos say that our guys are some of the toughest bastards in the whole American Army."

"My father brags about them all the time," Miguel replied with hardly a ripple of pride, though by now the Mexican-American rifle-company had distinguished itself in the landing at Salerno.

Months earlier, it had also been a cause for celebration in the barrio when Mexico itself had declared war on the Axis Powers, and had put its men where its declaration was. The first military unit formed was a full squadron of Mexican fighter pilots and crews, later to become famous as the "Flying Aztecs," who had by now flown hundreds of combat missions in the South Pacific.

But this was now late Saturday afternoon, and Miguel was only a few hours away from launching a major campaign of his own.

The late afternoon newspaper reports that Allied forces had broken past the German positions at Salerno and were now racing north toward Rome had refueled the joyous celebration like gasoline poured over a fire.

Later, however, these reports would prove to have been premature.

But for now, amidst a swirling rush of excited people, Miguel caught sight of Lorena Calderón. Watching as she quickly broke from the crowd and started south toward the barrio, he decided to ask if he could walk her home.

But he had gone no more than a few yards when he stopped. Earlier, he had conjured up several topics of conversation for their date that night, subjects he hoped might interest her. But to waste them now, he decided, would be foolish.

Instead, he decided to simply follow her. He loved the way her hips swayed when she walked. Trailing at a discreet distance behind her, he began to sum up all the things he knew about her — and abruptly realized that he knew very little. He was aware that Lorena had no brothers or sisters and that her mother had died when she was only fifteen. A few months later, her father's mind started to slip, and he lost his job. Lorena had been forced to quit high school and take a job to support them. Lately, her father had grown worse. He now roamed around the barrio reciting radio jingles to himself.

There were other things Miguel knew, but didn't like to dwell upon, though they were facts he could not ignore.

Lorena held a responsible position at the department store, a job that paid her more than three times his own salary. He was also aware that she was a far more cultured person than the average young woman in the barrio. Even more impressive in Miguel's eyes, she was buying the little house where she and her father had made a home. In the Second Ward there were not many Mexicans who had ever qualified for a home mortgage.

Hence, he had often wondered what someone like himself could offer Lorena, and with so little to offer, what chance of winning her did he really have? Late at night, the obvious answer to that question had weighed on him like a hundred-pound sack of cement.

He didn't know was that for the past several months, she had also been under a great deal of pressure. She had committed herself to a romantic course of action, which she hoped might finally provide her with an avenue of escape from the barrio. When it had proven to be a dead-end street, she was emotionally crushed.

Then, as if in proof of the bromide that disaster comes in pairs, her father's condition grew much worse. Lately, she'd had to employ an old woman to look after him while she was at work, an expense Lorena could ill afford. But her father had fallen into the

65

habit of roaming away from the house, sometimes ending up many miles north of the barrio.

His memory had failed him. Twice he was picked up by the police but was unable to tell them his name or where he lived. After the last incident Lorena made a little name tag for him and wept as she fastened it around his neck like a dog collar.

Now, walking home that afternoon from work, she looked as if there was a much greater weight hanging around her own neck.

CHAPTER 11

Miguel's mother took a few more straight pins from her mouth and stuck them through the cuff of one leg of the pants he was wearing. Standing in front of a full-length mirror, Miguel caught a glimpse of himself. Even in Raúl's new suit, he didn't like the way he looked.

"Miguel, I still cannot understand," Graciela mumbled, taking another pin from her mouth. "First you were fired. Then a few hours later you were hired back and given a better job. This makes no sense to me."

Miguel frowned. He was not eager for the subject to become the evening's main topic of conversation.

"It was because of this lady at the store," he muttered. "Lorena Calderón is always sticking up for somebody."

Graciela still looked confused. "I need more pins," she said, slowly getting to her feet. She had been troubled for years by a heart murmur, and her condition was not helped by her fondness for fattening foods.

"Santiago, come help me find them. You know how my eyes get this late in the day."

"Don't you know where they are?" Santiago asked from the far corner of the room where he was standing on his head. He had read that this exercise helped a person to think more clearly and, as of late, had been testing out the theory.

José Luis disliked the theory and the question. Looking over from the windowsill where he was sitting, José Luis said, "If your mother knew where they were, Santiago, she would not need your help. And if you continue to stand on your head, you will end up with refried beans for brains."

Santiago reluctantly brought the room back into proper perspective and went after his mother. When they were both out of the room, José Luis walked up behind Miguel, who was still avoiding his image in the mirror.

Graciela called in from the bedroom. "Well, I still think Señor Metcalfe must have a better reason for hiring you back."

"Sure he did," Miguel exclaimed. "With me gone, who else does he have to pick on?"

No answer came from the other room. Miguel knew his mother must be frowning. So did José Luis.

"Miguel," he whispered. "Don't tell your mother any more about this Metcalfe man. You know how she loves to think everybody in this country is an angel, that El Paso is Paradise itself. We leave her with her illusions, eh?"

Miguel nodded. Chuckling, José Luis fished a dollar bill from his pocket. "Get Norberto to serenade your new girlfriend with a few of the old songs. But don't tell your mother I gave you the money, eh?"

Graciela and Santiago returned to the living room. José Luis gave Miguel a wink and went back to the window and the cool breeze from the river. Graciela stood studying her tailoring project for a moment, then noticed that José Luis was staring intently off into the distance.

Miguel also noticed. He had often seen him staring out across the river. The sight always made Miguel sad. His father sometimes seemed like a child who, torn from the arms of its mother, would never be truly happy until they were finally reunited. Miguel understood this better than anyone else in the family.

Graciela turned back to him. She reached into the pocket of her apron and took out a half-dollar. "Here," she said quietly. "Buy your friend an extra Coca-Cola tonight. But say nothing to your father. I don't want him to accuse me of delaying our return back to Chihuahua by even so much as fifty cents."

Squelching a smile, Miguel nodded. As his mother knelt to continue placing her pins, he turned to examine his baggy image in the mirror for the first time — and suddenly laughed out loud. The others seemed startled by the outburst, but Miguel offered no explanation.

"People who laugh out loud over nothing," Santiago finally said, looking up from his headstand, "are usually sent to a place far, far away."

Santiago's words would prove prophetic.

Old Norberto had curvature of the spine so severe that for many years he had been unable to walk. Yet in still managing to eke out a living for himself and his retarded sister, he had won the admiration of the entire barrio. Late every afternoon, his sister would ease him onto a wooden plank bolted to a small wagon. Then she would pull him down near the river to a small plaza and leave him there. Taking up his crudely made guitar, Norberto would begin to sing the old Mexican songs he had learned as a boy. Soon people would begin pulling him from one group to the next — making him a strolling musician of sorts.

At the end of the night, there was usually some friend who would tow him home. In more than thirty years, the old musician had never been stranded or robbed. Even the thieves who roamed the banks of the river at night knew enough to grant him safe passage.

"Hola, *Don* Norberto," Miguel respectfully greeted the old man, who was fine-tuning his guitar. The crowd in the little park had thinned out, with a welcome stillness in the air at this time of early evening.

Norberto smiled. He was, Miguel thought, a striking-looking man. His hair and neatly trimmed beard were almost white, but full and lustrous, and his mustache curled down perfectly at each end. But it was the old man's eyes that had always commanded Miguel's attention, eyes that were clear and kind and younger-looking than the rest of him. It seemed a cruel caprice that such a noble-looking head was mounted on such a badly broken body.

"Ah, it is you, Miguelito," the old man said. "I did not recognize you in such a handsome suit of clothing. It is a funeral you are going to—"

"*Don* Norberto, exactly what my father asked me when I told him how much I needed a suit."

"How is your father?"

"Fine," Miguel answered, rather anxious to get on with the business at hand.

"Your father works too much hard," the old man quietly commented. "And those hundred-pound blocks of ice can kill a man just as sure as a bullet."

"I know," Miguel said, embarrassed he had nothing more to say on the subject. "Anyway, he wanted me to ask you to play a few of the old songs, and he gives you this dollar with his best respects."

Taking the money, the old man looked confused, though not in a troubled way. "So, Miguel, do I sing these songs to him, or for you — or maybe just to myself?"

"Don Norberto," he replied, lowering his voice in hope of impressing him with the seriousness of the situation, "This is the most important night of my life."

"I will listen most carefully," Norberto said, trying to look suitably impressed.

"Can you accompany me over to the house of Señorita Calderón, and later provide us with music to Dominguez's cafe, a distance of five songs, for the price of two dollars?"

Trying not to smile, the old man handed Miguel the rope to his wagon. "Lead the way, my young friend. With my songs and your sincerity, nothing shall stand in our way."

By the time Miguel had towed the wagon to within one block of Lorena's house, the barrio had burst forth with the unmistakable sounds of a Saturday night. Horns were honking and music came from almost every window and doorway. What seemed a thousand conversations rent the air like the insistent droning of bees, raising a racket that always startled the Anglos driving through the Second Ward on their way to Juárez. But to the Mexicans, these were sweet sounds, signaling as they did that all was well on their own little stretch of American soil. They had survived another week.

Miguel's zero hour of seven o'clock was only a minute away when he decided to add further ammunition to his arsenal. Advising Norberto that he'd be right back, Miguel wove across a crowded street and went into a flower shop.

Flowers were an extravagance he couldn't afford, but by now he wanted to have something in his hand when he arrived at Lorena's doorstep.

Purchasing a small bouquet of daisies, he was about to leave the shop when he noticed a man and woman sitting out under a tree in the tiny patio-cafe behind the shop. The woman had her back to him, but something about her seemed familiar. Miguel had never seen the man before. He wondered what could have lured an Anglo so deep inside the barrio.

He noticed that the young Anglo was about the same age as his brother Raúl, and was dressed in a beautiful suit that made the one Miguel had on look like a laundry bag. The young blond-haired Anglo was even more handsome than his suit. But what really caught Miguel's eye was the expression on the stranger's face. Whatever was being said at the table was causing the young man considerable embarrassment.

Then the man, apparently sensing Miguel's interest, abruptly turned to face him. They eyed each other for a moment across a distance of some twenty feet. Then the woman turned around, as if to see what had distracted her companion.

Lorena Calderón's expression seemed like a single frame from a motion picture that by itself unveiled the full nature of a relationship. She was in love with the young Anglo.

Over the last year, their romance had grown in fits and spurts, always cloaked in total secrecy. She and the young Anglo had first seen each other over the previous Christmas holiday, when the young man had walked into the store on his way up to his grandfather's office on the seventh floor.

At that time, Lorena had no idea that the good-looking young man was related to the elderly gentleman who was the sole owner of the store in which she worked. She had been struck by how handsome he was, and they had smiled shyly at each other. A few days later she received a note asking her if she would join him after work for coffee at a small restaurant a few blocks from the store.

She had long harbored a theory that blond, blue-eyed men were dull, passive, and condescending. Philip Jacobs was to prove her wrong. He spoke amusingly and confidently about many things and seemed to regard her as his equal in every way.

This was a dramatic change from most of the men she had dated in the barrio, who either were totally tongue-tied in her presence or tried to immediately dominate her. Friendship with a young man like Philip Jacobs seemed a promising prospect.

He was home from college for the holidays, and over the course of an hour's conversation, he mentioned that he was a pre-law student at Southern Methodist University in Dallas. He hoped to become a lawyer, though his grand-father wanted him to eventually take over the reins at the department store, but he doubted he could ever be happy simply "moving merchandise."

She had laughed at the way he'd described his family's business, telling him it was a rotten phrase to use for both his grandfather's work, as well as her own.

Later that same night, he had taken her to the swankiest restaurant in Juárez for dinner. Afterwards they saw each other every night until he returned to college.

Back in school he wrote her several letters, professing his love. To Lorena love meant marriage—but to the young scion of one of the wealthiest families in West Texas it apparently meant something else. When he came back for the summer vacation, he seemed in little hurry to announce their engagement. Desperate, she threatened to break off their relationship.

When that didn't prod him into making a commitment, she used her one remaining weapon. Their try at sex, however, had been an unmitigated disaster. Lorena had traded away her virginity for little more than a bad case of heartburn.

Now, he had happened to drop back into her life on the very night Miguel had come calling for her.

Watching them, Miguel felt as if he were sliding across the tile floor of the flower shop, unable to stop, headed for the edge of an abyss. He had had a similar feeling many months before, when he had read Lupita Palacios's last letter. Remembering that sensation, Miguel hated himself for again reacting in the same way.

Staring down at the flower bouquet in his hand, he felt gripped by an overwhelming desire to push himself back in time. He saw himself still standing across the street. But too late to erase the moment. Lorena had seen him.

She mustered up a brittle smile and waved. Miguel felt his throat tighten. He could barely swallow. But he could think, and he wondered: had she forgotten their date? That was terrible enough, but the obvious alternative seemed even worse. She had not forgotten the date but rather had decided to break it at the last moment.

With a hint of a nervous shudder, she turned back to her companion. This was Miguel's chance to flee. A moment later, before she could glance back, he and his bouquet of daisies had disappeared.

Walking away, he seized on the one explanation that would let him hold onto whatever remained of his pride. The answer was simple. Lorena had not forgotten their date, but instead had simply gone over to the flower shop for a moment, perhaps to buy a carnation for her hair. There she had run into an old boyfriend.

But now that she knew Miguel had come for her, she would soon hurry home. Later, the matter would be too trivial to mention.

This feeble conviction lasted only until he crossed the street. His problem now was how to save face with his friend Norberto, but all he could think to say was that his plans had changed. Tossing his bouquet into a garbage can, he took up the wagon rope and began to pull the old man back toward the plaza.

They made the two-block journey in silence. Leaving his friend at the plaza, Miguel spent the next hour trudging aimlessly through the barrio. Then, with the instinct of a homing pigeon, he started over the long bridge leading into Mexico—something he shared with only his father. Whenever José Luis was lonely or troubled, he would often cross the bridge to Juárez. There, he would sit listening to the mournful music of the mariachis as they sang their sad songs of lost love and vanquished dreams.

But Miguel had not come to Juárez to listen to music, but to get drunk, try to forget Lorena and hunt down the same young whore his brother Raúl had found for him many months before. But though he went from one bar to another, the little prostitute was hard to find, mainly because he could not even recall her name. The name he could remember was Lorena Calderon, the one he now wanted most to forget.

A few hours later, he came back across the bridge. The barrio was dark as a tomb, with even the little food stands and souvenir stalls that catered to carousers returning late from Juárez had been shuttered for the night.

Miguel trudged toward the little plaza where his fateful romantic misadventure had begun. Remembering how he had told Old Norberto that this was an evening that would change the course of his life, he cursed himself for having been a sentimental fool.

The plaza seemed deserted. But as he drew closer to the bandstand, he saw a young soldier and a girl standing in the shadows just below it. The girl was clinging to the soldier as if she never wanted him to leave her side.

Miguel politely nodded but quickly veered away, not wanting to break the spell of their intimacy. Somewhere off in the night, a radio was playing a love song, one he had always loved; yet now, as he listened to its lyrics, he decided that it was full of false words and treacherous sentiments.

The song ended, but its lyrics lingered on. He started to walk again. At the edge of the plaza, Miguel noticed something that slowly brought his painful reverie to an end. He had seen it a hundred times before without ever giving it a second thought. Stamped at the bottom of the recruitment poster were the words UNCLE SAM WANTS YOU!

Peering at the poster, he said to himself, *"Well, Uncle Sam, it seems like you're the only one who does."* He had been right all along. This was a night that would change the course of his life.

CHAPTER 12

The early morning sunlight had just nicked the tip of the majestic mountain that stands like a sentinel over the city of El Paso. Down below, the barrio had not yet shaken from its slumber. Only a milkman and a paperboy could be seen moving through the gauzed, reddish light. The paperboy, catching sight of someone standing in a third-story window, waved up and then hurried on.

An hour later, Miguel was still at the same window. Behind him, his father and two brothers had gathered uneasily around the dining room table. Graciela was in the kitchen, preparing their breakfast.

"Well, you better straighten out your son, José Luis," Graciela murmured from the kitchen. "Miguel is too young to be making such a serious decision."

From the tremulous tone in her voice, they knew she was on the verge of tears. José Luis hesitated. Already he was aware that the matter was more complicated than she thought.

Miguel turned away from the window, and with an expression stripped of all emotion, he quietly repeated himself. "Believe me, Papá, this is probably the only smart thing I've ever done—because in another thirty-four days, I'll be eighteen and get drafted for sure. But if I enlist now, they might let me join up with the rifle company with guys from our own barrio. Better, I think, to fight alongside my own people than with complete strangers who dislike us almost as much as they do the Germans."

"Miguel, be sensible," Graciela urged, as she brought in a platter of refried beans to the table. "Even when you become eighteen, perhaps the draft board will not call you right away. Maybe—"

"No, Graciela," José Luis softly interjected. "Miguel is a Mexican and in good health. He will be among the first to be called." By now José Luis had grown accustomed to seeing young men from the barrio placed at the top of the draft list.

Miguel was not surprised by his father's stoic attitude. He was, however, rather startled by Raúl's reaction. Raúl seemed almost as upset as Graciela. Miguel suspected the real reason. Raúl was torn with guilt. Miguel was going away to fight and perhaps die in the service of a country that had been far kinder to Raúl than it had ever been to Miguel. Yet Raúl felt no loyalty to the United States. The outcome of the war mattered to him only insofar as it affected his own safety and success.

Raúl had considered this a smart attitude, but at this moment he didn't seem so proud of himself.

"Dammit, Miguel, can't you just sit tight for a little while longer?" Raúl stammered. "Hell, the way things are going now, the war could be over in another six months. Why get yourself killed for nothing? Volunteering is worse than crazy. It's stupid!"

Miguel chuckled. His brother Santiago had been right when he'd said that Raúl was not quite as smart as he liked to pretend.

"Raúl, I know you do not follow the news of the war too closely, but men who enlist are not the only ones who get killed. You think a bullet cares who it hits? But if I enlist, I can always say that I had the courage to volunteer."

'Yeah, but *dead* men can't talk," Raúl muttered. He looked defeated. Miguel had checkmated his opposition.

Silence fell over the family. Only Santiago seemed to approve of the plan. Miguel knew why. His younger brother had been ridiculed by his classmates because Raúl, though of prime draft age, had still managed to avoid the war. That Miguel had decided to enlist made Santiago secretly proud.

But now, noticing that the others looked as if they were already attending Miguel's funeral, Santiago was stabbed with remorse. "Miguel, why the rush?" Santiago contritely murmured. "Wait, see how you feel in a week or —"

Miguel batted the question away and turned toward his father. "I will never go back to the department store—so if you won't sign my enlistment papers, I'll just hang around here until I get drafted. But sooner or later, I'm going into the army," Miguel said, walking into the bedroom he shared with Santiago, slamming the door behind him.

For a long moment, the others remained frozen figures in a still-life painting. José Luis turned and peered out the window. When he finally spoke, there was a hint of pride in his voice.

"Our son is no longer a boy, is he, Graciela?"

Graciela's eyes went blank. She knew she had lost one of the most important arguments of her life.

"And alongside his people overseas," José Luis quietly continued, "he will have a better chance of coming home someday. It is his life at stake, not ours. And each man should have the right to protect it as he thinks best."

Graciela had moved to José Luis's side to put her arms around him. But for the first time in as long as she could remember, his powerful arms brought her no consolation.

From across the room, Raúl was somberly watching. When his mother began to softly cry, he abruptly rose from the table and walked toward Miguel's bedroom.

Miguel had changed out of Raúl's suit and back into khakis and a sweatshirt. Carefully placing the suit on a hanger, he handed it to Raúl a moment after he entered the room.

"Sorry I didn't get the suit back to you last night. Guess I forgot all about our agreement."

Raúl chuckled. "Forget it. The girl I was with last night likes me much better with my clothes off, anyway."

Miguel began to sort through his collection of tattered clothing, most of which had once belonged to either his father or his older brother. Except for a few sweatshirts, he had never bought anything new for himself.

Raúl stood watching Miguel as he rummaged through the clothing. "Your date was with Lorena, right?"

Miguel jerked several shirts and a battered leather jacket from the closet. "You guessed the way I talked you out of your new suit, huh?"

Raúl frowned. "No, you and Santiago were too slick for me last night. Yesterday afternoon, I bumped into Alfonso López. Your funny little friend gave me the full lowdown."

"Alfonso is much funnier when he keeps his mouth shut," Miguel muttered as he pulled a small cardboard suitcase from underneath the bed. "Anyway, what does it matter? I got stood up."

A smile broke across Raúl's face. "So *that's* the reason you're running away," he exclaimed. "But, Miguel, getting stood up by Lorena Calderón could have happened to anybody. Hell, even me! Don't you know she's been in love for years with some Anglo asshole? His grandfather owns the store you work in, and you didn't know about it!"

Miguel had not known this, but was now aware that Raúl had accidentally explained something else. Miguel often wondered why his older brother had never made a move on a woman many people considered the most beautiful in the entire barrio.

"Anyway, here's the lowdown, kid," Raúl continued. "It seems this guy's parents split their pants when they found out their sonny boy was going with Lorena. The last thing they wanted was some brown fox from the barrio for a daughter-in-law. The big blowout came a few months ago. But the poor little rich kid still comes sniffing around every now and then, and when he does, Lorena lays out her scent again. I'll bet that's what happened last night."

Miguel thought that was *exactly* what had happened the previous night. Walking slowly over to the window, he sat down on the sill and stared in the direction of Lorena's house.

"Thanks, Raúl. Makes me feel a little better. See, it's not just what happened last night. I think my whole life has stood me up. One broken date after another... and I have run out of places to turn. We can't go back to Mexico yet, but I can't stay here anymore. Maybe I'll find a place for myself in the army."

Miguel came away from the window, and unlatching the suitcase, he began piling his clothes into it. There would be no turning back now.

When Raúl finally spoke, he seemed more solemn than Miguel had ever seen him. "I know how you feel. You see, I am also looking for something. Now, you won't believe it, but I want to someday get involved with something that has a little dignity to it. I am sick of taking money from rich women and poor people who cannot afford to gamble on the numbers. And if I ever get my chance, whatever I find, part of it will be yours when you come home from the war. And if you don't believe that, you have even less respect for me than I think you do."

Miguel believed his brother. Raúl had always been generous with whatever he had. Remembering many past instances of his generosity, Miguel felt tears well up in his eyes. Raúl had been a good brother. Looking up, he saw that Raúl was nearly in tears himself. A moment later, they fell into an awkward embrace.

Only weeks afterward would it dawn on Miguel that Raúl had cleverly reversed their roles in the final moment they had been alone together. Raúl had made it seem that it was he, not Miguel, who was about to so courageously march off to war.

Lying on his bunk one night in training camp, Miguel would remember that moment and smile. His brother was one slick Mexican who would undoutably make it big one day — if somebody didn't *kill* him first.

CHAPTER 13

When the Second World War began, there were more than two-and-a-half million people of Mexican descent living in the United States, eighty-five percent of whom resided in five states: Texas, New Mexico, Arizona, Colorado and California. One-third of these people were eligible for the wartime draft.

But in early 1941, an order had already been issued by the commander of the 36th Infantry Division that a new unit be formed, comprised of only Hispanic-Americans. That edict included both officers and enlisted men.

Whether the order was discriminatory cannot be easily judged. What is indisputable is that it later gave rise to what became one of the most highly decorated fighting outfits in American history.

The new unit, called E Company, became part of the 141st Regiment of the 36th Division, a division later known as the Texas Volunteers. The all-Hispanic rifle company quickly drew recruits from every part of the Southwest, including many men who had long been members of the National Guard in their home states.

The rifle company became noted for its excellence in every field of training endeavor. The one remaining question had been how well it would do in combat—a question resoundingly settled when the Texas Volunteers had stormed the Italian beach at Salerno.

Some two weeks after that landing, Miguel arrived at the division's training center. Camp Bowie sat out in the middle of Texas, many miles away from a single city of any size. The camp had been named after the inventor of the famous hunting knife, Jim Bowie, one of the legendary heroes of the Alamo. Miguel found it ironic that the camp named after one of the defenders of the Alamo was now filled with Mexicans.

More surprising was the arrival about a week later of his friend, Alfonso López. His reason for enlisting had not been patriotism. In Miguel's absence, he had become Metcalfe's new whipping boy, who had been insulted by Miguel's abrupt departure and had taken his fury out on Alfonso. After three days of non-stop abuse, Alfonso had decided to enlist, certain that even the army could be no worse than the department store. Within twenty-four hours after his arrival at Camp Bowie, Alfonso realized that he had made biggest mistake of his life.

"Man, Miguel," Alfonso muttered one night at mess hall. "I knew the Army would be tough, that I could maybe get myself killed. What I didn't know is it would be my own guys, not the enemy, who would do it!"

Over the next month, the roles they had previously assumed with each other were completely reversed. Miguel became the undisputed leader, and without his constant help and encouragement, his little friend would never have made it through the camp's arduous training program.

For Miguel, the physical rigors of the program were the easiest part. He was six feet tall, weighed more than one-hundred and eighty pounds, had enormous strength in his shoulders and arms, and was blessed with excellent hand-to-eye coordination. His reflexes had tested out in the top one-percent of the entire camp. All this, in combination with an almost reckless form of courage, quickly took him to the top of his training class.

Then there was the matter of motivation.

The Hispanic recruits were shown a series of films entitled "WHY WE FIGHT." The series minced neither words nor intentions: Hitler was a mass murderer, posing as a political messiah; Tojo a snake, pretending to be the savior of the Far East; Mussolini, a pathological clown and almost as vicious as his two more demonic partners.

The message hammered home by the film series was that all three of these maniacs were hell bent on the destruction of democracy and everything it meant to most Americans.

But many of the Latino recruits had seen little of that democracy in action and hence did not understand exactly what in the social and political fabric of American life they were defending. Most Mexicans had enlisted not to defend democracy, but rather to achieve what to them was a more important purpose: to be accepted as true Americans.

Miguel's motive was both different and more complex. He had enlisted in the infantry to prove himself a man, and because the training was rather easy for him, he quickly came to love the service, though he had not found a home in the Army, as many men before and after him had. Instead, he found an avenue of escape, a release from all that had held him back, as well as the terrible awareness of what he sensed he could never become.

Ten long weeks later, Miguel and Alfonso completed basic training, now full-fledged privates in the United States Army. They were given a one-week furlough before shipping out for Italy, where their division was engaged in some of the most ferocious fighting of the war.

The week in El Paso passed like a prison sentence, straining Miguel in ways the training program had never done. He was uneasy with the way his father and brothers treated him as if he were a returning hero. He had proven himself only in mock battle. It embarrassed him that they seemed unable to distinguish between that and actual combat.

Even worse was his mother's reaction. The war had seemed vaguely remote to her until she first saw him in his uniform. From that moment on, it seemed she was crying, praying, or trying to pump more food into him.

Somehow the seven days passed. Miguel had served his sentence and was on his way to war.

The Union Train Station that morning was filled with other families seeing their young men off, and most of the women were as emotional now as Miguel's mother had been over the previous week. But as the moment of his final departure drew closer, Graciela became almost serene. Placing a medal of the Virgin of Guadalupe around his neck, she turned away, not wanting him to see the tears in her eyes.

Miguel was the only one who was not crying. Raúl came forward to embrace him. "Remember, Miguel, what I said before you left for the training camp," Raúl muttered in a choked voice. "If I have any luck while you are away, half of it will be here waiting for you the day you come home."

Miguel grinned and turned to his younger brother. "I'll be expecting good things from you, Santiago," Miguel said, drawing the boy closer. "So don't be a *pendejo* like me. You stay in school, and one day you'll be the one we will all be the proudest of, eh?"

"I won't let you down, Miguel," Santiago murmured, trying hard to smile.

Miguel leaned down to kiss Santiago, and then slowly walked over to his father. José Luis was standing off to one side, still holding Miguel's army duffel bag in his hand. He had insisted on carrying it all the way from the apartment and now looked as if he never wanted to let it go.

José Luis had said very little on the long walk to the station. It seemed he knew that his voice would falter if he tried to speak. Miguel, aware of the pact his father had made with his emotions, silently embraced him and gently took the bag from his hand.

"Don't worry, Papá. I'll be back," Miguel whispered. "I hear it's only the good guys who get killed."

The train began to move. Climbing on board, Miguel waved back to his family and smiled. But as the train slowly pulled out of the station, taking with it many of the best of the border town's barrio, his mood grew somber.

Already he was imagining the long journey ahead—a trip that would take him by train to New York's Staten Island, from there by troop transport across the Atlantic Ocean and the Mediterranean Sea, and finally to the hills of southern Italy, where the men of E Company were desperately awaiting replacements.

CHAPTER 14

About a month after Miguel's departure, his family was rocked by another event. It happened not in El Paso nor in Italy, but in a migrant shack just outside the town of Mission, Texas.

Francisco's son Alejandro hated the shack and never more than now that he had sensed what was happening inside it. Several times that night he had run away, but, like a colt breaking free from its corral, then missing its mother, he had always roamed back to the cardboard hovel.

Inside the shack, a few old women were softly chanting a prayer as they went about applying cold compresses to the feverish body of Alejandro's mother. The women would occasionally glance up at a tattered picture of the Virgin of Guadalupe, tacked to the tarpaper wall behind the bed. Alejandro noticed that afterward, the women would usually turn to glare at a tiny photograph of his father on an orange crate next to the head of the bed.

The day before, when his mother had first grown feverish, she had begun to scratch at her face. Alejandro was grateful that her hands were now being held by his Uncle Pedro, his mother's only brother, who had recently joined the family from Chihuahua City.

As the chanting continued, a strange thing happened. Juanita's eyes opened, glistening with a fervid expression. A serene smile came over her face. The years seemed to fall from it like ancient scabs.

Many of the migrant workers packed along the far wall of the shack softly cried out in surprise. Juanita was again as pretty as she had ever been, and her words, when they finally came, sounded strong and firm.

"Please tell Francisco to hurry."

Alejandro's uncle nodded happily, a wave of graying hair falling across his oak stump of a face. "Yes, my little sister. Any minute now, Francisco will be home!"

Alejandro, standing in the shadows at the other end of the shack, felt his chest swell with relief. His mother had regained consciousness. For a fleeting second, his spirits soared.

Then a female voice from just outside the door muttered, "What Juanita needs is not a man, but a miracle. Her husband, she has done without for many years."

The woman's words slithered across the silence like a snake striking everyone in its path. But before anyone could rebut her brutal appraisal, the migrants were startled by a strange noise.

It sounded like a branch being pulled loose from a dead tree, and as the nerve-grating noise subsided, Juanita's body stiffened. She grasped her brother's hand more tightly.

"Alejandrito? Where is my little boy?"

Pedro turned to the others. "Bring the boy to his mother."

A man's voice came from the far end of the shack. "No, Pedro, not good the boy should watch his mother die. Better he remember her the way she was—"

Pedro's eyes flashed with anger. Gently breaking from his sister's grasp, he rose to his full height. Alejandro's uncle was not a tall man, but his arms and shoulders were thickly muscled from years of backbreaking work. Few men in the camp did not fear and respect his strength.

"Nobody is going to die," Pedro muttered. "So I say it just one more time. Bring the boy to his mother."

No one had paid much attention to Alejandro that night, but now everyone seemed to know exactly where he was. He was quickly ushered toward the bed.

Coming into the light thrown by a candle sitting on the crate next to his mother, he looked like a frightened animal.

Juanita saw the fear in his face. Mustering what was left of her strength, she took his hand. Peering deep into his brown eyes, she smiled that secret smile which had always been his and his alone.

"I want my little man to read for me," Juanita said.

Alejandro's face flushed with pleasure. Of all the things his mother might have said or done at that exact moment, nothing could have more greatly reassured him. He was especially proud that he could now read and write English even better than in his native language.

As he reached under the bed for the newspapers he always kept there, he heard a commotion from outside the shack. Several people moved clear of the door to make way for a late arrival.

His father had finally come home.

Francisco slowly approached. He waited for Alejandro to abandon his spot on the bed, then sat down and took Juanita's sweltering hands in his. Alejandro moved back into the shadows.

For several seconds, Francisco seemed too stunned to speak. So he simply smiled, a big beautiful grin that even now made Juanita remember what she had thought the very first time she had met him. When Francisco Salazar smiled, it seemed nothing short of a forecast of fair weather and fine crops.

"Well, Juanita," Francisco finally murmured, feigning a light-hearted tone of voice. "I have been trying to get back here since yesterday afternoon. But first the car broke down. So we fixed it. Then it ran out of gas, which was not so easy to fix because nobody had any money. So I had to hitchhike, and thirteen rides later, here I am. I could have got here faster on a burro."

Juanita tried to smile. She wanted to tell the husband she had never been able to please that she understood. But her voice brought forth only a faint gurgling noise, no more audible than the sound of softly boiling water. The deep lines and wrinkles returned to her face, and once again she looked like the mother of the twenty-nine-year-old woman she actually was.

Francisco was suddenly gripped by the thought: if he could only continue to talk and keep from showing the fear he felt in his heart, her condition might somehow stabilize.

He doggedly went on with the one-sided conversation. But the effort was too late. Francisco had not bothered to speak to his wife at such length since they had first come to Texas. He had wasted two full years.

"So anyway, Juanita, the trip was a long one. We were coming back all the way from Uvalde, where I went to recruit some farm workers. But by the time I got there, most of them already had gone north to catch the cantaloupe crop. I should have known they would be moving, but I forgot. So maybe it's me that is a burro, eh?"

Juanita tried again to smile. But a moment later, the branch-breaking sound came once more as a spasm swept gently across her face, leaving its features finally at peace. She had died much as she had lived, trying to cause as little fuss as possible.

Several people began to weep. Even Alejandro's Uncle Pedro started to cry. He had stood like a sentry on the other side of the bed and now knelt to bury his face in the sweat-soaked bedding. Listening to his uncle's muffled sobs, Alejandro placed his hands over his ears and drifted to the far side of the shack.

Lifting aside a piece of tar paper, he stared up into the starless sky, trying to find the North Star his uncle had once pointed out to him. But a dark mist hung over the camp, and he could see nothing.

Yet he thought that if he could only concentrate hard enough on something, anything, he might be able to ignore his mother's death out of existence.

His father knew better. Getting to his feet, Francisco noticed some tiny vials on the windowsill, next to the coffee can that Juanita had always kept filled with wild flowers. "Why was I not told she had no more medicine?" he muttered, staring dumbly at the empty vials.

An old woman answered. "What she suffered from, no medicine could cure."

She was standing so close to him that her voice startled him. He turned away from her accusing face. But many of the faces that filled the shack bore similar expressions. A man hidden in the shadows at the other end of the room broke the silence.

"You are wrong, old woman. The right medicine and a good doctor could have saved her. She died from nothing more than the influenza."

Another voice came from the darkness. "Yes, but who had money for medicine or a doctor?"

One last voice, as if completing a chant, said, "Juanita needed more than a doctor. She needed a husband. But what she had was a man who cared more for a cause than for his own wife."

The words fell on Francisco like blows from a hammer. Strangling back a sob, he lurched out of the house, drunk with grief.

Watching his father stumble out, a strange calm came over Alejandro. Walking back to the bed, he took his mother's lifeless hands in his. The room began to swell with the mournful sound of the rosary.

He gripped his mother's hands more tightly and silently cursed the fates that had taken the brightest light of his young life. But most of all, he cursed his father.

CHAPTER 15

Some five thousand miles away, ill fate would soon befall another Salazar.

A week before Miguel enlisted,the Allies had landed at Salerno and were soon advancing up the lower length of Italy toward their ultimate goal: The Eternal City of Rome.

The American Fifth Army, which contained elements of the Texas Volunteer Division, had led the offensive. But in early January of 1944, the assault ground to a halt.

Several things transpired at the same time, and in combination dealt the American forces a stunning counter punch. The Italian terrain had grown much steeper. Mules were needed to haul supplies up to the front lines, as well as to carry casualties down from the mountains.

The enemy had regrouped around their Gustav Line, a natural barrier of defense, which ran between two large rivers, the Garaglino and the Rápido. The Germans held the high ground, and from their base at Monte Cassino, were shelling the American troops below with shattering accuracy.

Then the Italian winter, with its driving sheets of rain, made a swamp of the entire sector. Hundreds of American Sherman tanks sat stalled alongside washed-out roads. Yet the Allied advance had to continue, for the longer it stalled, the stronger the German army would become. Its southern forces had been severely jolted by the landing at Salerno, and entire divisions from the north now raced to their rescue.

It was vital that the impasse at Monte Cassino be broken. Beyond lay the open fields of the Liri Valley, the gateway to Rome, and once into that valley, the American tanks could finally make felt their superior numbers.

But for now, in the dead of winter, the war in Italy had come down to that most basic element in any army: the foot soldier. It was now his war to either win or lose.

The Texas Volunteers had been in the vanguard of the Allied offensive since Salerno, and by the time the Fifth Army had liberated the city of Naples, Miguel's Hispanic-American rifle company had proven itself to both friend and foe.

From here on, however, the Allied advance would be measured not in miles, but in blood-soaked yards. In places like San Pietro, almost every yard gained came at the price of another American casualty.

By the time the 36th Division reached the Rápido River, Miguel and Alfonso had become battle-scarred soldiers. Miguel bore the heavier load. Because of his strength and expert marksmanship, he became the BAR man for his unit. The Browning Automatic Rifle, a lightweight machine gun, packed a meaner punch than any other weapon the company carried.

The weather turned even colder, as the impasse in the fighting froze, along with everything else. Many American officers thought they were on the verge of losing the war in Italy. Desperate measures were needed if the Fifth Army was to avoid a debacle like the British had suffered at Dunkirk.

One such measure would soon materialize.

In mid-January of 1944, the men of E Company were ordered to form a small squad and cross the Rápido River to determine the feasibility of a subsequent crossing by their entire company. French forces had crossed the Rápido in another sector, encountering only token resistance. The commander of the American Fifth Army, stung by the success of the French, demanded that his own troops repeat the maneuver.

On January 17th, some twenty-five men from E Company, led by Lieutenant Gabriel Navarrete, forded the raging waters of the Rápido and soon discovered that the other side was heavily fortified over a long stretch of terrain. The Germans had laid barbed wire and felled trees along the riverbank. Beyond loomed machine gun emplacements and a force Navarrete estimated at more than three thousand men.

The reconnaissance squad barely made it back across the river. One soldier was killed, several others wounded, including Navarrete himself. Reporting to Regimental Headquarters, the lieutenant informed his superior officers of what he had seen. It was insane, the lieutenant declared, for a single rifle company to attack such a large enemy force. The assault called for nothing less than a full battalion.

The warning fell on deaf ears and closed minds. The regimental officers argued that they were only following instructions from divisional headquarters. Nothing could be done to alter the mandate. The officers did manage, however, to make one decision, ordering the commander of E Company to check himself into a field hospital—as good a way as any to silence the outspoken young officer, they probably thought.

But though weak and unsteady on his feet, Navarrete chose not to obey the order. Instead, to avoid what he considered the senseless slaughter of his men, he decided to go over the head of his immediate superior.

At battalion headquarters, he again declared that the proposed crossing by a single already badly mangled rifle company was nothing short of suicide. The battalion commander, Major Buckley, countered irrelevantly that the Mexican-American officer had grown too close to his men, which was clouding his judgment.

The young officer conceded that he had known many of his men long before the war and gone to high school with several of them. Yet this did not alter the present reality. The mission was a murderous trap, and much of whatever blood was shed would be on the Major's own hands, Navarrete bluntly asserted.

The senior officer had heard enough. Curtly dismissing Navarrete, he ordered him directly to the hospital. Some hours later, the Major reconsidered and added a few more men to the mission. As luck, or the lack of it, soon proved, even a few *thousand* more men were not enough.

The southern edge of the Rapido River was littered with empty ammunition cases and bloodstained rubber boats, remnants of the disastrous reconnaissance mission of a few days before. Now, the men of E Company had bivouacked about a hundred yards inland from the riverbank as they awaited the news from battalion headquarters that would determine their own fate.

With Lieutenant Navarrete in the hospital, command of his rifle company had passed down to two staff sergeants. One of them was named Frank Casillas.

Miguel, Casillas's newly-appointed driver, had been alerted that the sergeant was leaving for battalion headquarters to plead the company's case one last time. Like Navarrete, Casillas realized the futility of their mission. The entire company also knew it. But for the past fifteen minutes, Miguel had managed to block the matter from his mind. He was writing a letter home, and as always, was careful to make no mention of anything that might upset his family. In such letters, truth was invariably his first omission.

The rain and sleet had stopped, but the air was still bitterly cold. Alfonso was huddled a few feet away from Miguel, his teeth chattering softly as he cleaned his rifle.

"You clean your rifle, Alfonso, more than you brush your teeth," Miguel muttered, his mind still thousands of miles away.

A few soldiers sitting nearby snickered.

"Hey, my teeth don't keep me alive, this rifle does," Alfonso protested, twisting his weapon around to peer down its barrel.

"Oh, yeah?" a soldier muttered. "Let's see you try to eat K-rations without chewing them first."

Alfonso shrugged and ran a finger across his teeth. They had been hurting him for weeks, but since every other part of his body also hurt, he had not thought about his teeth till now.

"That's right," Alfonso growled. "And what happens if they all fall out?"

The same young soldier piped up again. "Well, you can always sip soup through a straw. Only they don't serve us soup very often, do they?"

Alfonso grimaced. Just one more damned thing to think about, he mused. An older soldier sardonically smiled. He had been with the rifle company since Salerno and was amazed that Alfonso was still alive.

"Hey, forget it, little man. "If Sergeant Casillas can't get that crossing order changed, you won't live long enough to eat lunch tomorrow anyway."

The soldiers standing nearby chewed on the older man's remark. Then, spotting a mail truck sloshing its way up toward them, they hurriedly stumbled down toward it. Sealing his letter, Miguel started for the truck. Alfonso reluctantly followed after him.

"So what did you write your parents?" Alfonso glumly asked. 'Dear Folks, you won't believe how pretty the Italian countryside is this time of year and how the food is almost as good as I got at home.' "

"You're right," Miguel admitted. "And I also wrote them that I like it over here so much I have decided to stay in the army after the war."

Alfonso stepped dead in the ankle-deep mud. "What, you mean *permanent*?"

Miguel nodded. Alfonso stared at him with disbelief. "Hey, you completely crazy?"

"Totally," Miguel said, smiling. "That's why I think it'll work out."

The mail truck had pulled into the encampment. An orderly climbed out and, standing on its running board, he began barking out the names on the letters in his hand, passing down the mail. After a few other names had been called out, he said: "Private Miguel Salazar!"

Miguel took the letter, gave the orderly the one he had written, and started away through the crowd of soldiers. Alfonso trailed after him, wearing the same disinterested mask he always wore at mail call. His aged parents could neither read nor write. He had received only one letter in all the time he had been in the army, a dunning notice from their landlord.

Miguel beckoned him closer. "Come on, let's read this together. It's from my brother Santiago. Unlike me, he always writes the truth."

"Ah, getting a letter from your own brother is no better than getting a date with your sister," Alfonso groused, moving closer.

The letter was brimming with bad news.

Miguel's Aunt Juanita had died. Details were vague, Santiago wrote, but apparently she had suffered from nothing more than a simple case of the flu.

Miguel knew better. Years earlier, when he pulled her from what could have been a watery grave, he felt he had not really saved her life, but only prolonged it slightly.

The second half of the letter shook him far worse.

His father's shoulder had been crushed in an accident at the icehouse. He had permanently lost the use of his right arm. Miguel remembered old Norberto telling him, the night he had hired the crippled little man to serenade Lorena Calderón, to look out for his father's health. Yet there was nothing Miguel or his father could have done to circumvent the mishap. The war had stripped the barrio of almost all its younger, able-bodied men, leaving José Luis dependent on co-workers who simply did not have the strength to handle the hundred-pound blocks of ice. The man who caused the accident was sixty-three-years old.

Refolding the letter, Miguel put it into the inner pocket of his long woolen coat. Turning away from Alfonso, he stared off into the darkening forest. He was not the only member of his family, he realized, who had been fighting a war.

CHAPTER 16

"Private Salazar, down here on the double!"

Miguel saw Sergeant Casillas striding toward a bullet-riddled jeep. Scrambling to his feet, he hurried to join him. Casillas was on his way to battalion headquarters.

It lay less than ten miles away, yet the trip took more than an hour. Neither man said a word the entire way. Miguel was busy weaving in and around bombed-out roads and hairpin turns to bother with any chitchat. There were also enemy snipers still in the area. Despite this, he felt a strange sense of security. He was in the company of the soldier he most admired.

Sergeant Casillas was the reason Miguel had decided to make a career of the army. Now in co-command of E Company, Frank Casillas had been Miguel's ideal almost from the time he joined the outfit. It had not taken Miguel long to piece together the sergeant's history.

Casillas was a professional soldier, having enlisted in the army at the Old Presidio in San Francisco in 1935. The previous year, Casillas had slowly wandered west from his hometown of El Paso in search of work.

As the Depression deepened, he had stood in sullen bread lines all over the southwestern part of the United States, fought in hobo camps for scraps of horse meat, and more than once had been brutally beaten by desperate men for nothing more than the shoes on his feet.

Finally reaching San Francisco, he realized he had come a long way only to see more of the same. Things were no better in the fabled Golden State than they had been in the barren desert of West Texas. A few days later, Casillas enlisted in the army. A full year of sleeping in parks and railroad yards, forced to beg or steal for his every meal, had taken from him a large piece of his self- respect.

Casillas was a natural-born soldier. He would later tell Miguel that the army was the best thing that had ever happened to him. His first post was to the Philippines; later, when E Company was formed, he transferred to the new unit. Two days after the landing at Salerno he won a Silver Star for bravery and was promoted to staff sergeant.

Casillas was not a handsome man, but a strong jaw line and cleft chin gave his features a formidable cast. Miguel thought the sergeant looked tough enough to strike a match off his face. But what Miguel admired most about him was his attitude. He neither feared nor hated the Germans. Emotion was for amateurs, and Casillas prided himself on being a professional.

But Miguel knew only what the sergeant had chosen to tell him, as well as the few scraps of information he had been able to pick up from some of Casillas's fellow sergeants. There was, however, much about his life that Casillas had never told anyone; things that embarrassed him, or caused deep wounds which had never properly healed. The problems had started even before his birth.

The Casillas family owned a small general store in Parral, along the extreme southern edge of the state of Chihuahua. When the Mexican Revolution broke out, all property holders were considered the enemy by the revolutionaries. Villa's men repeatedly looted the store, and one night they burned it to the ground.

Casillas's grandfather, broken in spirit, as well as financially, took his son and pregnant daughter-in-law away from Parral that very night, bound for the Texas border, more than three hundred miles away. The five-week trip in a mule-driven wagon finished what the Revolution started. By the time they reached El Paso, the old man's health had crumbled. He would live only another year.

Frank Casillas was born a few months after the family arrived, a stroke of luck which automatically made the boy an American citizen. His father was also lucky. He found steady work as a cabinetmaker, and by 1920 he had managed to save enough money to open up his own shop. It was an instant success.

Young Frank became something of an oddity among the Mexican families of south El Paso: he was an only child because of his mother's inability to ever conceive again. Lacking brothers or sisters, the boy grew especially close to his father, a fun-loving, affectionate man. But when Casillas had just turned twelve, his world would collapse. His father, still only in his late thirties, suffered a severe stroke that left him almost totally paralyzed.

Devastated by his father's illness, Casillas spent every free moment at his bedside, reading to him from comic books, feeding and bathing him. Young Frank became his father's nurse and was constantly on the lookout for any improvement in his condition.

Ironically, soon after his father had made a partial recovery, a second stroke paralyzed him again. Then the process was repeated. The third stroke killed him. To the boy, it was if his father had died three times.

From that day forward Casillas never again looked at the world in quite the same optimistic way. His mother took the loss in an even worse fashion. Still a pretty woman in her mid-thirties, she became obsessed with losing her looks, and began spending more money than she could afford on cosmetics and new clothes. What troubled Frank even more was her newfound habit of hanging out in some of the barrio's sleazier *cantinas*.

Later, Casillas would realize that the death of his father had caused his mother's mind to slip. But at the time, he had more immediate problems.

An important one was the ex-prize fighter his mother brought home with her one night: a tall, good-looking Mexican with a sticky smile and darting eyes. Julio Rojas was some seven years younger than Frank's mother. The boy took an immediate dislike to him.

Two weeks later, his mother and the former boxer were married. Rojas moved into the house as if he owned it and was soon selling off many of the ornately-carved pieces which the boy's father had made. When Frank registered a mild complaint, his new stepfather took him out behind the house.

The boy expected a whipping, but nothing like the one he got. Rojas smiled and beckoned him closer, then fired his fists into Frank's stomach and kidneys. Falling hard to the ground, he blacked out. When he came to a few moments later, his stepfather was still smiling. This was to be the first of many such beatings— and always served up with a smile.

Much later, Casillas would learn that there was a name for such people. His revenge, however, came much sooner. He had discovered baseball and quickly exhibited a real talent for the game. A stocky youngster, he could pull the ball with power. Best of all, baseball was a harmless way of releasing his anger. He was also good in school, but when his father's savings were exhausted, he was forced to quit and take a job delivering newspapers.

Rojas, dreaming of a comeback as a fighter, refused to find any other kind of work, and would often sharpen his skills on Frank. But not wanting to leave any marks on the boy's face, he was careful never to hit him above the shoulders.

Some time later, Frank had injured himself slightly sliding into second base. The trainer, trying to treat the skin-burn, asked Frank to remove the shirt of his uniform. When he hesitated, the man carefully peeled it off. The other players were dumbfounded by what they saw, and as they stood staring at the purple bruises on the upper part of his body, Frank quietly began to cry with shame. His teammates knew of his situation at home and didn't have to ask how he had come by the bruises.

The next night, several of those same players caught Julio Rojas coming out of a barrio bar. Alone, neither of the teenagers would have been a match for him, but as a pack, they gave him a beating worse than any he had ever suffered in a boxing ring. A week would go by before the former fighter could walk straight.

Frank did not learn of the incident until the following morning when his mother came into his room. With vacant eyes and a sad smile, she said, "Frankie, honey, you have to find another place to live."

He didn't argue. The time had come for him to leave. He barely knew his mother anymore, and what he knew of his stepfather he detested.

At age sixteen, Frank Casillas was on his own. What surprised him was how much he liked it. He quickly got himself a better job, found a furnished room, and over the next few years still managed to find a little time for sandlot baseball. Then came the Great Depression, and just about everyone's life, including his, went much darker. For Frank Casillas, that darkness began to lighten only several years later when he joined the United States Army.

CHAPTER 17

Now Casillas was on his way to protest an army order as senseless as any he had ever seen in almost ten years of military service. He was headed for a palatial villa, until recently the property of an elderly baron. Only a few weeks before, when he had spotted the approaching columns of the American Fifth Army, the old man had fled to his Fascist friends in the north. Captured by Italian partisans now fighting on the side of the Allies, the aging aristocrat pleaded his case. After listening courteously, his captors offered him a cigarette, a glass of wine, and gently placed a blindfold over his eyes.

The baron's villa was now battalion headquarters. When Casillas and Miguel arrived, soldiers were carting away most of its furniture. Major Buckley stood in the doorway of the villa's library, now his office, glumly watching the soldiers strip the adjacent foyer. Noting Casillas's presence, Buckley waved him forward.

"Well, to the victor belongs the spoils, right, Sergeant? Only in this case it ain't the enemy who's done me in, but my own goddamned chain of command. All this is going over to the colonel's headquarters. War is hell, huh?"

Chuckling, the blustery-faced man ushered Casillas into his office. Another group of soldiers was hauling paintings and artifacts from it and in the confusion Miguel stood at the doorway unnoticed to overhear what followed.

"Okay, Sergeant, I can guess why you're here. But you could have saved yourself the trip. Like I told Lieutenant Navarrete before, and like I'm gonna tell you now, if we don't get across that Rápido River pretty quick, this entire division will soon be going home in a pine box!"

Casillas looked unimpressed. "Major, I want it on the record that you are aware that my men could be outnumbered on this mission by as much as twenty to one," Casillas quietly replied.

"Oh, now, who the hell told you those were the odds on this upcoming game?" the major sputtered.

"Sir, that's what our recon detail reported — and if you're the only officer in this division who's not aware of that report, I respectfully suggest such neglect might come under the category of gross dereliction of duty."

Military procedure was one of the many things Casillas knew well, and for a fleeting second, Miguel thought that it might make a difference. Casillas's remark had also made an impression on the major.

Stepping behind his desk, the major seemed to realize that Casillas had introduced an element, which later might look incriminating on a War Department report.

"Sergeant, if crossing that river is so impossible, how come the French fucking frogs have already done it?"

"Sir, the French crossed in battalion strength. They were also lucky. But you're asking my men to cross with less than one-tenth that force, which means we're going to need a lot more luck — and even you may have noticed, sir, that my company has not been so lucky lately."

"Sergeant, I understand how you feel, but that doesn't justify insubordination," Buckley barked, trying to recover the initiative. "And, of course, I am aware of the condition of your company. But as the colonel has said many times, those boys in E Company are some of the toughest who ever put on a uniform. That's why they were *chosen*, for God's sake. Hell, Sergeant, they ought to consider this mission an honor!"

Casillas smiled contemptuously. "Let somebody else have the honor this time. My company has already won more decorations than some entire regiments. We've earned a rest, Major. That or give us a hell of a lot more men."

Buckley didn't answer. Instead, he took a single sheet of paper from the top drawer of his desk and handed it to Casillas.

"You're discussing this with the wrong man, soldier. The colonel himself signed the order."

Casillas suddenly felt very foolish. It had been stupid to think he could change the Army's mind about anything. Buckley, sensing victory, quickly added, "But the colonel did tell me that when we finally get to Rome, he's gonna grant a seventy-two-hour pass to your entire company!"

"By that time, Major, there may not be a company anymore," the sergeant murmured, staring down at the order in his hands.

Only now did Buckley notice that Casillas's hands were heavily bandaged. "Hell fire, Sergeant, you're already in pretty sorry shape! I ought to order you into a hospital, like I did Lieutenant Navarrete. Let you sit out this next game, so to speak—"

Casillas recoiled as if he had just detected a foul odor. "No, Major, it's not going to be that easy for either one of us to get out of this."

Tossing the order on Buckley's desk, Casillas gave him a stiff salute and started away. Miguel stood watching the major for a moment. The officer stared down at the order and prodded it a few times with the tip of his swagger stick. To Miguel, it seemed the gesture of a man warding off a poisonous spider.

CHAPTER 18

Night had fallen, and a heavy mist hung over the encampment, the eerie silence broken only by the sound of a harmonica played by a young soldier, who, along with the other men of E Company, was intently watching the set of headlights drawing closer.

Miguel brought the battered jeep to a stop. Casillas slowly stood up and waited for the soldiers to approach. He studied the faces of these men whose fate he now held in his injured hands. He had thought earlier about making a speech to his exhausted band of brothers; now he realized that to attempt to justify the suicidal command would only lower him in the eyes of his men. So he simply made the Sign of the Cross and quietly said, *"Bueno, compañeros, que Dios nos acompañe."* May God be with us.

Miguel had never heard Casillas speak in Spanish before. Nor had he ever heard him invoke the name of the Lord. Casillas had once told him that he considered it presumptuous to pray for one's well-being. God had more important matters on His mind.

The sergeant came off the jeep and strode toward his command tent. "All noncoms and squad leaders, come with me. The rest of you go over your equipment. We cross the Rápido at zero-five-hundred."

Miguel watched Casillas disappear into the tent, then turned and nodded to Alfonso. They trudged over to get their weapons and started down to where their own squad was already forming.

"Hey, what's the big deal about the Rápido River?" Alfonso asked. "Hell, it's just another river. Like the old Rio Grande you and me crossed so many times before!"

Miguel smiled sadly. "Alfonso, you are either much braver than I ever thought—or even crazier."

Yet Alfonso had asked a question that stayed with Miguel for the rest of the night. Lying in his bedroll on the frozen ground, staring up into a starless sky, he wondered how bloody the ford-ing of the river would be. Any worse than the death and destruction he had already witnessed? Sights and sounds swirled in the fog that lay over the camp like a shroud—the starving families roasting parts of dead dogs and cats; his fellow soldiers screaming in anguished surprise as they reached for an arm or leg that was no longer connected to their body; others seriously wounded by flying fragments of teeth and bone from the bodies of their own compatriots torn to shreds by grenades, the gaunt, hollow-eyed young Italian girls—some no more than twelve-years old—offering their emaciated little bodies to the Americans in return for a half-bar of chocolate.

The men of E Company had freely given the chocolate, but their generosity and compassion had brought them no relief. Now perhaps the indelible images would all end in death. For the men of E Company, the war in southern Italy had narrowed down to one impossible mission: the crossing of the Rápido River.

As he walked down to the river that next morning, Miguel felt no fear of death, though he hoped if it came, it would be quick. What he feared was disgrace. If this was his company's final battle, he wanted it to be their finest hour.

It was still dark when the soldiers reached the river. They would attempt the crossing several hundred yards away from where the reconnaissance party had earlier encountered the large German force—a flanking maneuver Casillas hoped would allow the rifle company to secure a perimeter on one side of the enemy and thus enable a much larger contingent of American soldiers to later cross the river with greater safety. This larger force was now being assembled. Casillas had been promised it would soon be following his own unit.

The loading of the boats went quietly and efficiently, and at exactly five o'clock on the morning of January 21, 1944, Sergeant Frank Casillas looked toward the sky and said a silent prayer. He waited for a small cloud to pass in front of the moon, and then gave his armada of rubber rafts the signal to cast away.

For the first few minutes the crossing went well. But about halfway across the river the Rápido suddenly started to live up to its name. The small rafts were caught in a swift, swirling current. All available paddles put to the water. But the current was so strong, the rafts were being pulled down river, and toward a larger concentration of the enemy.

As dawn began to push aside the darkness, the rafts cleared the rapids and headed for the far bank. Moments later, the fog commenced to lift—and within another thirty seconds, the small armada of rafts became visible before the German guns.

Yet for several seconds, the Germans did not fire a single shot. They seemed stunned that such a minuscule number of men would attempt an assault against their own vastly superior force. In the lull before the battle began, a few soldiers gallantly called out to the approaching boats.

"Turn back," the voices shouted. "Turn back before it is too late." The Germans had realized what the American senior officers refused to even consider. The mission had suicide written all over it.

But the men of E Company kept coming, though by now they knew they had lost their most important weapon: the element of surprise. As the first boats reached the bank of the river, a huge searchlight flashed on. Then two other lights came alive, snaring the flotilla in a blinding glare. With the light came the clatter of machine-gun fire and the heavy thud of German mortars.

Caught in a crosscurrent of gunfire, Miguel and his compatriots moved in the one direction they could. But as quickly as they dug in, the holes filled with water.

The blazing explosions and blinding lights gripped Miguel like a nightmare. In his mind, the battle seemed drained of all color but red, white and black, and the red was the color of blood.

By the time he had waded ashore, the riverbank was already drenched in gore. Crawling, stumbling, he made it to a large fallen tree. In a crevice, he set up his BAR and began firing furiously, blasting out the nearest searchlight. Then he blew out a second one, and had just turned his BAR barrel toward the third light when he was startled and almost hit by short, staccato bursts of machine-gun fire, coming from just twenty feet beyond the felled tree.

Without waiting to shift his body or properly aim, he turned his weapon toward the spurting flashes of flame. A few seconds later the machine-gun nest went dead.

A third searchlight now swung around to ensnare the last incoming raft, as German guns began ripping the men to shreds as they came off the raft. Miguel let out an anguished curse. He had made a tragic mistake, he felt, in not taking out the searchlight when he'd had the chance.

Wheeling around, he blasted out the light, and then with the tree for cover, inched his way toward the only two survivors from the raft. They were lying wounded past the end of the tree, ten feet out in the open. He paused, waiting for the machine-gun fire to abate; realizing there would be no respite, he broke from his cover.

Crawling on his stomach, he made it over to his fallen comrades. Both men had lost the lower part of their legs. Grabbing them by their belts, he dragged them through a hailstorm of lead, back to some safety behind the fallen tree.

But in rescuing the men, he had dropped his BAR, and before he could recover it, several Germans bolted from around the far end of the felled tree. Pushing the two wounded men to one side, he turned to find himself facing more than a half-dozen German guns. Still several yards away from his own gun, he took out his knife, and fought his way back to his BAR and then blasted away at the shadows darting and dashing all around him.

What seemed a lifetime later, he felt his body explode. Everything was in slow motion as dreamlike, darkened figures danced in every direction—a deadly yet graceful ballet.

Miguel's mind began to drift. He was outside his body and saw himself dragging soldiers down toward the water. Then he felt himself floating, his legs no longer connected to the rest of him.

Images from his past floated through his mind—his grandfather, his parents, Lupita, Lorena, a little dog he had once had as a boy: pieces of time in the mosaic of his life. He had no idea how long or how far he floated, for by the time the raft finally drifted back to the other side of the river, he was as near death as most of the men in his boat.

Lieutenant Gabriel Navarrete was lying in a battalion hospital when he learned that of the original attacking force of more than one hundred and fifty, only twenty-three had survived. Hearing the news, Navarrete quietly dressed, slipped out of the hospital and went looking for Major Buckley, intending to add that officer's name to the battle's casualty list.

Navarrete was as deadly serious now as he had been on another morning a few months earlier when he and his men had forced a large German unit to surrender. But when Navarrete asked its commander to hand over his weapon, the officer had spat in his face. He would not surrender his Luger to anyone but an American officer. Navarrete was at the time only a sergeant.

Calmly stepping back, he fired off two short bursts, first blasting the officer's pistol from its holster, then grazing his face with a second shot. Again Navarrete politely asked the officer to hand over his weapon. This time the German fell to his knees, grabbed his pistol, and came crawling forward with it. Later, the incident had been gleefully circulated throughout the entire division.

Now several soldiers in that same division knew that Navarrete had gone gunning for one of their own officers. But the news of the rifle company's disaster had become common knowledge by then, and Major Buckley had been quickly transferred by General Walton Walker.

The general had not known of the ill-fated order and was deeply incensed that it had been given. In convincing Navarrete to call off his vendetta the general assured him that there would be a complete investigation by the War Department. That investigation would be a long time in coming, but for the moment there was still a war to be won.

Eventually, E Company was brought back up to full strength, and months later it had fought all the way to the banks of another river, one of the last great natural barriers that lay between Miguel's comrades and Berlin itself.

Crossing the Rhine at Wissenbourg, the rifle company proudly planted the flag of the Lone Star State of Texas on German soil. Later, other elements of the Texas Volunteers captured the celebrated Field Marshall von Runstedt, as well as took prisoner Hermann Goering, once the second most powerful man in the now fast-crumbling Third Reich.

But for Miguel, the war was over after the Battle of the Rápido River. His right knee and hipbone had been shattered, as had his hopes of making a career for himself in the United States Army.

Another dream had turned to dust.

CHAPTER 19

The journey from West Texas to southern Italy had taken less than a month, the return trip, almost a year. But now Miguel's train was at last racing across the great desert of the American Southwest that once belonged to his native country. Home was less than a hundred miles away, and Miguel was remembering all the sights he had seen from the windows of so many medical wards.

From Italy, he was flown to an army hospital in England and, several months later, finally back to the United States. In Los Angeles, army orthopedic surgeons were able to get him back on his feet for the first time—his knee rebuilt with hard plastic, the bones in his nearly shattered hip anchored with steel bars.

But more had been built up than just his body. He had completed high school through army correspondence courses, and on the advice of his friend Frank Casillas, since promoted to captain, Miguel had become a naturalized United States citizen. Casillas had written that naturalization would put Miguel in a better position to claim his disability and GI-Bill benefits, and, as always, he had deferred to the judgment of his former commander. But Miguel felt that he would always be a Mexican—no mere piece of paper could ever change that.

Now, the immense, barren stretches of open desert gradually gave way to the long ridge of green farmland that ran alongside the Rio Grande River. Spotting the river he had crossed so many times, Miguel smiled. He was almost home.

At the other end of the Pullman coach, some half-dozen Mexican-American soldiers stood draped around a young private who was playing a guitar, all happily mangling the song they were singing. An air-corps sergeant went weaving past Miguel, carrying an armful of fresh supplies for the men at the far end of the coach. He looked about three-quarters drunk and appeared determined to finish the job. Staring dumbly down at Miguel, he offered him a bottle of beer.

"Here, Private, this fixes the blackest of the blues!"

"No, thanks, Sergeant. I'm okay," Miguel said with a stiff smile.

"Hey, I'll say you're okay," the airman barked, noticing the battle ribbons and the Purple Heart medal on Miguel's uniform, as well as the cane he held in his hand.

"Yeah, that bum leg of yours should get you a disability pension, and all those battle ribbons will pull in plenty of pretty viejas to help you spend it. Hell, you're looking good, man!"

Miguel was not so certain of that, but before he could respond, the sergeant was already stumbling back toward his companions, who still sounded as if they were singing several different songs at the same time.

An elderly, black porter came into the car and called out: "Alright, men, we're coming into El Paso. But them traveling further east best to stay on board — I'm too old and too tired to go hunting you down when we pull out, you hear?" The soldiers smiled and went on dismantling the song, as the train slowed down to pull into the station.

Miguel had come to the end of a fifteen-thousand-mile journey. Girding himself, he took hold of an overhead railing with the crook of his cane and hoisted up his body. But as he reached for his duffel bag, the porter's hand got there first.

"Thank you, sir," Miguel said with a surprised smile. The old porter studied Miguel's battle ribbons for a moment.

"No, thank *you*, soldier," the black man quietly said. Then, for the first time in many miles, the porter smiled. It had been a long, loud trip from Los Angeles, and the noisiest part had not yet abated.

Most of the disembarking servicemen came off the train to be greeted by family and friends who were lined up alongside the track. Up near the station a platform had been hammered together, and around it a few hundred people stood waiting.

When Miguel finally came off the train, many of them suddenly surged toward him. He turned around, half-expecting to see that the commotion had been caused by someone else.

Miguel's youngest brother, Santiago, reached him first. Then he was quickly engulfed in the embrace of his entire family. Dozens of people he had never seen before were jubilantly shaking his hand. The black porter, caught up in the contagion, suddenly felt remiss in not offering his own hand, and did so.

Then, amidst all the clamor and confusion, Miguel saw something that brought tears to his eyes. His father looked ten years older than when he had last seen him and seemed to carry his withered arm like a weight that strained at his soul. Yet both men, as if by instant accord, pretended to ignore the other's disability, and gave themselves over to the elation sweeping through the crowd.

A mariachi band struck up "The Eyes of Texas." As Miguel limped closer to a makeshift platform, he noticed that his friend Norberto, perched on his own platform, was playing with the band. Miguel waved to the crippled old man, though no sooner had he raised his arm than several people lowered it to shake his hand.

Others were yelling his name and cheering, but only his brother Raúl was able to overcome the noise long enough to introduce Miguel to a tall, rugged, wide-smiling man by the name of Wade Donahue.

The crowd swept Miguel closer to the reception stand. But as he shuffled forward, he recognized another face in the crowd—and suddenly he could no longer hear the raucous noise all around him.

Lorena Calderón was standing alone, back near the rear doors of the station, smiling in that way Miguel had never forgotten. But as he limped forward, he noticed that an aura of sadness seemed to surround her. She looked as if she had also fought some important battles and had lost, as he had, more than she had won. They waved at each other.

Then people whom Miguel had never seen before greeted him like an old friend and helped him up the steps and onto the platform. A fat, flustered little man hurried to shake Miguel's hand and ushered him to a place of honor. Struggling with the buttons of his ill-fitting suit, the fat man strode to the edge of the platform, carrying a large plaque in his pudgy hands. The band stopped in mid-note. The crowd quickly quieted.

"Thank you, my good friends, thank you!" the little man said, looking disappointed that his presence had elicited no applause. "It is my great honor as your hard-working councilman to welcome home our barrio's most famous son, Private Miguel Salazar!"

A roar rose from the crowd, which by now included many of the servicemen who had just returned home with Miguel. The little politician, encouraged by the crowd's reaction, continued to

chatter for another few seconds, before, with ill-disguised reluctance, he turned the ceremony over to a man seated nearby.

"To make the presentation itself, Antonio Vargas, the first president of El Paso's chapter of the GI Forum, and also a highly-
decorated veteran!"

A large, crater-faced man climbed unsteadily to his feet. Vargas
had been seriously wounded in the war and carried himself as if
some pieces of his body no longer properly fit him. He was about
thirty but looked more like forty, something Miguel had seen
many times before. The war had done this to many men.

Vargas glanced over at Miguel. Then, with a vaguely contemptuous smile, he took the plaque from the politician and turned to
the crowd.

"Councilman Soto has asked me to read the official commenda-
tion on this plaque from the city of El Paso," Vargas muttered before laying it aside to take a piece of paper from his pocket. "But
with respect to our city's 'hard working' officials, I want to read
you something that is the real reason we are here today."

Miguel flinched. He sensed what Vargas was about to do.

"I have copied this from the congressional citation," Vargas proclaimed, adjusting a pair of spectacles over his eyes. "And I now
read it to you word for word."

As the crowd quieted down, Miguel stared at the cane in his
hand. What was coming next, he thought, would be one of the
best but most embarrassing moments of his life.

In rapid fashion, Vargas began to read the citation. "On the
morning of January 21, 1944, in an amphibious assault across the
Rapido River in southern Italy, Private Miguel Salazar single-
handedly wiped out three enemy machine-gun emplacements.
Later, though wounded, he fought off more than a squad of enemy soldiers as his comrades tried to get back to their own side of
the river. Then, with the battle hopelessly lost, Private Salazar,
now even more seriously wounded, still managed to help some of
his compatriots back into the rubber rafts that eventually carried
several of them to safety. Hence, for heroism above and beyond
the call of duty, and for his gallant concern for his fellow soldiers,
Private Miguel Salazar is hereby awarded our nation's highest
military decoration, the Medal of Honor. Done so by Special Act
of the Congress of the United States of America."

Having completed the reading of the citation, Vargas carefully put it into his breast pocket. He had read it in a rather flat tone, as if thinking that by underplaying its powerful words, he might lend more dignity to the occasion. But he had been too solemn, for now the crowd stood hushed and uncertain. Only after Vargas took off his glasses to wipe his eyes, and then beckon Miguel forward did the crowd finally explode.

Miguel stood alone at the edge of the platform, as wave after wave of unleashed emotion came surging forth. He looked back toward his father and smiled, as if sharing with him the applause. His father had also paid a precious price for the Allied victory in Europe. The icehouse in El Paso had, in its way, been as dangerous as a war zone.

As the crowd quieted down, it was Miguel's turn to surprise the more than two hundred people who had come to welcome him home.

"Thank you, Señor Vargas, for reading that citation as fast as you did," Miguel said, his voice steady as steel. "But if I had known I was going to have to make a speech, I might have stayed on the other side of the Rápido River."

Most of the crowd laughed. But those few who had known Miguel before the war were struck silent by his measured manner. He had not realized he had said something funny and now waited for the laughter to die away.

"Getting a medal is a strange thing," he continued. "I don't think I earned this great honor, but at the same time I believe that every soldier who fought overseas deserves a medal, no matter what he did. Being there was enough. When I was in a hospital in California, I read that all men feel great fear when going into battle, and maybe the only difference between a hero and coward is the direction in which he runs. I was just lucky my own fear took me in the right direction."

There were people in the crowd whom he had by now recognized. Yet they were staring at him as if they had never seen him before. Pausing, he glanced off to one side. Lorena still stood in the shadows under the station's archway, and she, too, seemed unsure, as if wondering whether the man making this speech could be the same boy she remembered from the department store.

Smiling, Miguel decided to stop while he was still ahead. "I thank you for the honor you have shown me and my fellow soldiers who came in with me today. But now, with your permission, I think we would just like to head in the direction of our homes. *Gracias!"*

Turning away from the crowd, he dutifully shook hands with the dignitaries as the band struck up a Mexican *corrida.* The throng of people began to reluctantly troop back toward the station.

It took Miguel several seconds to climb down from the platform, and only then did he notice that Lorena had disappeared. He felt his legs go lifeless. Had she ever really been there? Or had her presence been another one of his illusions?

But in glancing back at the train that had brought him home, he saw something he knew was no mirage. Six flag-draped coffins had been taken from the train and were sitting on large baggage wagons. Mexican families stood nearby, their bodies bent with grief, already looking, he mused, like the pallbearers they would soon become.

CHAPTER 20

By the time the family finished their meal, most of the local events of the past year, both large and small, had been hurriedly introduced, like talkative acquaintances who had been invited to the homecoming celebration only to keep the conversation from going dead.

Santiago was in high school now, making excellent grades in every subject but Spanish, a fact Raúl found hilarious but one that deeply disturbed their father. Yet Santiago simply could not bring himself to study something he felt he was born knowing. Graciela had a job stitching nylon parachutes, though with the war almost over, she expected to be let go almost any day. José Luis had received a small disability settlement from his former employer and had been exploring how best to invest it, once the family moved back to Mexico. That return trip would be, he hoped, within the next year.

"And we have written to your Uncle Francisco, asking him to allow us to take Alejandro with us," José Luis said, glancing at Graciela.

"Yes, with the boy's mother now long dead and buried, what life can he have there with his father, who is always going from place to place?" Graciela asked, taking some serving plates back to the kitchen.

"And the work Francisco is doing is very dangerous." José Luis continued, as he sipped his beer. "Alejandro wrote us a few months ago that his father had been thrown into jail. Before that, he was beaten up and had to go to a hospital. In a way—and may God forgive me for saying this—I am almost glad Juanita did not live long enough to see what has happened to her family."

"How does Alejandro get by? How does he live?" Miguel somberly asked.

"He works, what else?" José Luis murmured. "Luckily, he has grown close to Juanita's brother. Pedro looks after him as best he can. But still…"

Graciela's voice came from the kitchen. "Your brother Raúl has also been sending the boy a little money now and then."

Miguel glanced at Raúl and smiled. "Is Alejandro still in school?"

"No, Miguel," Santiago interjected. "Seventh grade is as far as he got. Too bad, because he was doing pretty good."

"So you see, Miguel, all the more reason for him to come with us back to Chihuahua," José Luis concluded. "There, we can put him into school again. Then afterwards maybe he, if nobody else, will want to work with me in whatever little business I decide to buy." There was a subtle note of accusation in José Luis's voice.

Now, with most of the dinner dishes cleared away and the general topics of conversation utterly exhausted, a stiff silence hung over the table. Miguel noticed a veil of sorts drop over his mother's face. As the long lull continued, she seemed to grow more anxious. Rising from the table, she went to the kitchen and began to wash the dishes.

"Santiago, come to help me. Leave the others to their business," Graciela called from the kitchen. Santiago rose with a moan, but Miguel thought his younger brother seemed vaguely relieved to have been called away from the table.

José Luis abruptly lurched off to get more beer. Miguel glanced around the room, hoping to discover something different about it that might give him a chance to reopen the conversation. "Is that little white sofa new, Mamá?" he asked. "Or has the beer already hit me?"

"Raúl bought it for us," Graciela replied in a cautious voice. Miguel heard the door of the cooler slam shut. His father had found more beer and now returned to the table to refill Miguel's glass, as well as his own. Taking a sip of the beer, Miguel's attention drifted toward the living room. Raúl was sitting on the sofa he had bought, quietly smoking a cigarette. He had said very little during the entire meal.

"So what's been happening with you, Raúl?" Miguel asked. "You've been as slick as some guy who struck gold but doesn't want all his creditors to know about it."

Raúl grinned and slowly ground out his cigarette.

"I've struck something almost as good as gold...but I've been waiting for the others to tell you their news. Now I'll tell you mine."

Raúl rose and started for the dinner table. But before he could reach it, José Luis suddenly got up, and taking along his bottle of beer, walked over to the window and looked outside. By now the day had almost died, tinting the barrio in soft pastels.

Raúl, noting his father's departure, pushed a frown from his face. He sat down in the chair his father had vacated and looked at Miguel straight in the eye. "About three months ago, I got a job with Wade Donahue's construction company," Raúl said with quiet urgency. "He's the tall, tough-looking gent I introduced you to at the train station. Anyway, I'm in a terrific new thing called public relations, which is—"

"I know what it is, Raúl. But what's it got to do with a construction company?" Miguel asked. Leave it to his older brother, he thought, to be making good money at a job that wasn't really necessary.

"Raúl's job is perfect for him," José Luis muttered, still staring out the window. "He is good at talking people into buying things they cannot afford."

"Ah, that's the old-fashioned way of thinking, Papá," Raúl complained with an anemic smile. "You see, Miguel, with a construction company, public relations is simply the way we get people to understand that their interests and ours are one and the same thing. Get it?"

"Like advertising?" Miguel asked, as Graciela refilled his coffee cup. He looked up at her and smiled, but she had already turned her eyes away.

"The jerks from advertising can come up with a little icing on the cake," Raúl persisted. "But it's the soldiers like me who have to hit the street to sell the cake itself. And that's where the battle is won or lost!"

Miguel still had no idea what Raúl was talking about.

"Anyway, to make a short story longer," Raúl grinned, "Donahue has set this company up to make good low-cost housing for the veterans here in the barrio. But we really haven't kicked it off yet. Donahue's just been waiting for you to get home..."

Miguel chuckled. His brother was like a crab, always approaching everything from an angle.

"Donahue wants me to buy a house?"

Raúl bolted from his chair and began to pace around the table. "Oh, Sweet Mother of God, you think I'm telling you all this just to sell you one little goddamned house? Hey, get this through your battle-bruised brain: Donahue wants you to be one of the top guys in our company! He wants to use the slogan 'Veterans Helping Veterans,' and what better veteran could he get than the most famous one in the barrio!"

What was the catch? Miguel wondered. He turned toward his father, but José Luis still had his back to the room.

Raúl suddenly seemed off stride. "But, hey, Miguel, if you can't see the potential in all this, maybe he made a mistake in wanting you to join the company. But after he saw the way you handled yourself today at the train station, he told me he is completely convinced you're the right Joe for the job."

Miguel flashed a blank smile. The army had taught him to always expect the unexpected, yet Raúl had surprised him in a way that left him momentarily speechless. Miguel again turned to his father. "This sounds too good to be true, eh?"

Draining his bottle of beer, José Luis tilted his head in the direction of the table. Miguel thought his father seemed to be pushing himself toward something and was annoyed it was taking so much beer to get there.

"All of Raúl's ideas are too good to be true," José Luis muttered, and then went silent. Miguel felt disappointed. His father had offered no specific reasons.

"Okay, so what's the hitch, Raúl?" Miguel brusquely inquired, feeling somewhat proud that he had not already spread his legs like an old whore over in Juárez. He had noticed that his mother and Santiago had come back into the living room to sit in what seemed a neutral corner.

Raúl parked himself at the table again. "Hey, you know the problem with most Mexicans in this country?" he asked Miguel. "They are always suspicious of good luck! Oh, but now, bad luck they invite right in like an old and trusted friend. But this is superstitious bullshit!"

Raúl sighed and leaned across the table. "Listen to me. Donahue will start you out at a hundred and fifty dollars a week—about *three times* what the average *able-bodied* man can make in this barrio—and he's offering both of us a little piece of the profits. Can you afford to walk away from such a deal?"

Miguel sat digesting what he had heard as if it were a sweet-tasting meal, but one that might contain unknown ingredients. Then Raúl posed a question Miguel had already asked himself.

"Have you not earned the right to a little good luck?"

Graciela now spoke up, her voice soft as a prayer. "Miguel, your father and I...we think you should use your GI Bill to go to a good trade school. So when we return to Chihuahua, you can get a decent job."

Raúl spun around in his chair. "Listen, Mamá, nothing will give Miguel the chance to make more money than he can right now with the construction company! Besides, how many opportunities does my father think there are back in his beloved Mexico for a poor guy who can barely walk and doesn't have even a highschool education?"

José Luis turned away from the window. In the late afternoon shadows, Miguel could barely see his face. When he spoke, his voice seemed strangely disembodied.

"You forget, Raúl, that we are still Mexicans, and that we came here only because your grandfather thought it was the only way we could survive. But now there is good work again in Mexico. Real work, not this funny business that one does only with the mouth... And also you don't remember that a boy becomes a man by helping others, not just himself. Selfishness is not strength."

"But what better way to help other people than with this low-cost housing program?" Raúl asked with a patronizing smile. "What else can most of us do, Papá? Discover a cure for pneumonia? Open up an orphanage? What would you suggest?"

José Luis could not muster an answer.

A subtle shift now took place. It reminded Miguel of the changes of command he had witnessed in the army. The change was always welcome if it brought in a leader who knew the terrain and the enemy better than his predecessor. This change of command in the family had been brewing for the past few years. Now it had come, and everyone seemed to know it.

José Luis suddenly clutched his shirt pocket, found it empty, and muttered something about his tobacco pouch. He walked across the living room, stiff-backed and staring straight ahead as if the room had filled with strangers. He went into his bedroom, softly closing the door behind him.

Graciela rose from her chair and turned on a lamp. Miguel noticed that she had tears in her eyes.

"I am sorry, Mamá," he said gently. "But I think Raúl is right about this job."

Graciela turned toward the bedroom. It seemed she was trying to reach past its wall. "If you understood your father a little better, you would know that he agrees with you. But since his accident, everything has been so hard."

She looked back at Miguel, yet it seemed her words were aimed at Raúl. "Your father, for all the faults some people think he has, brought this family through many difficult moments. We should never forget and always be grateful for that."

Miguel gazed at his mother. Her words sounded like a eulogy she might have spoken at his father's funeral. Graciela hurriedly put on her coat.

"Well, I once vowed to the Blessed Virgin that the day you came home safe, I would go to thank her. I hope she will forgive me that we had our supper first. Santiago, you come with me. Leave your brothers to their business."

Santiago rolled his eyes. "Terrific, everybody but me got to tell Miguel everything!"

Miguel had to laugh. His younger brother was the one member of the family who still seemed the same. "We'll have a good long talk later, Santiago. Just the two of us, okay?"

Santiago paused by the door. "I have a lot to tell you."

Miguel chuckled. "I knew that would be the one thing I could count on."

Watching his mother and Santiago leave, Miguel shifted his weight. He had been seated in the same chair since he'd first come into the apartment; it now felt permanently attached to him. Rising unsteadily to his feet, he limped over to the window. Raúl followed him.

Down below, Graciela and Santiago were crossing the street, heading toward the spires of a small church.

Raúl nervously lit a cigarette. "I have to go see somebody myself," he muttered. "But I doubt she is also a virgin."

"Even if she is, you'll soon take care of that. Who is she; anybody I know?" Miguel felt a knot form in his stomach. He had sensed the answer.

"You remember Lorena Calderón?" Raúl snorted, putting another match to his already lighted cigarette.

"I recall that name," he murmured with a half-smile. "She was at the train station today."

"Sure, I invited her. You see, she finally got dumped by her boyfriend, who later married some rich bitch from his own social set. So, a few months ago, I ran into her...and well, we've been dating ever since."

Miguel tried to keep his expression blank. "Let me have one of your cigarettes."

Raúl seemed surprised. "You on the weed now?"

"I'll try anything once," Miguel said. "Are you serious about her?"

"I'm certainly serious about taking her to bed! But she's a tough little nut to crack. No, to tell you the truth, I really don't know how I feel about her...which I guess already takes her to the top of the class, huh?"

Miguel frowned and laid aside the cigarette. "You go keep your date. I'll see if I can cheer up the old man."

"Miguel, I love that old fool in my own way as much as you do. But it's our future, not his past that we have to think about now."

Miguel felt his bad knee tighten up. "Yeah, but I don't want to win anything if he has to lose something. I'll think about the job, okay?" Raúl grinned, patted Miguel on the shoulder and started away. When the sound of his footsteps faded away, Miguel knocked lightly on the door of his father's bedroom.

"Are you okay, Papá?"

José Luis's muted voice came through the door. "Yes, I am just resting. You go visit your friends. Go see Alfonso."

"Alfonso is still in a hospital back in Virginia. But hey, maybe we can take a little walk. Work off some of the beer, eh?"

"I'll be all right, Miguel." The voice sounded cold.

Limping away, Miguel paused in the middle of the now deserted room. A sudden wave of sadness came over him. Perhaps he had come home expecting a little too much. Putting on his service jacket, he quietly let himself out of the apartment and shuffled down the dimly lit hallway. He needed a drink, something stronger than beer.

Like a military dirigible that had served its purpose, the city of El Paso was shrinking back to its pre-war size. But Juárez, whose economy was anchored by the perennial pillars of free-flowing sex and cheap liquor, still boomed unabated.

Miguel had taken cab across the bridge to have a few shots of tequila in clubs now packed with former American servicemen. Their talk bored and distracted him.

"Hey, I'm telling you, soldier!" one drunken veteran bellowed in Miguel's face, "The average Jap soldier was a better, more resourceful fighter than anything the fucking famous Third Reich ever threw up against us!"

Nodding blankly, Miguel paid for his drink.

Back in El Paso, he began to walk through the nearly deserted streets of the downtown area. The army doctors had told him to stay off his feet as much as possible. Yet he couldn't afford to take cabs for the rest of his life, even if he had more than eight hundred dollars in mustering out pay in his pocket. There had not been many things to buy in a military hospital.

About an hour later, he found himself standing in front of a tattered recruitment poster, not the same one he had seen the night he decided to enlist in the army, but its image and message were the same. Staring down at it, he thought ruefully, *Okay, Uncle Sam, what's next on the program?*

He had not walked more than fifty away from the poster when he found his answer. His brother Santiago was parading along with a small group of boys. With their baggy pants and coats that hung almost to their knees, they looked like a tiny army of circus clowns.

"Hey, Santiago," Miguel called out.

"Miguel! Wow, I didn't expect to see you on the street tonight," Santiago stammered, eyes wide with surprise.

"Well, I just wanted to see what you guys had done to the old neighborhood,"

Santiago and his friends brought their march to an abrupt halt. Miguel noticed that the boys were staring at the battle ribbons on his service jacket.

"Hey, this is my brother Miguel," Santiago proudly proclaimed. "The hero who shot up all the Nazis!"

Miguel frowned. "You boys are not out looking for a fight yourselves?" Somewhere along the line, he had picked up his former commander's manner of speaking. Captain Casillas could make almost everything he said sound vaguely like a threat. The boys shook their heads emphatically.

"And what's with these crazy outfits you're wearing?"

Santiago smiled sheepishly. "Oh, just what all us barrio boys wear these days. You know, to be different from the gringos."

"Does Papá know you dress this way?"

Santiago looked down at his clothes as if they had suddenly started to smell. Miguel smiled. His younger brother was changed more than he had thought.

"Yeah, I get it. Almost, anyway. But I don't think our father is going to get it at all," Miguel said. "So if you don't want to get ambushed, I'd stay as far away…"

Miguel had seen something down the street. The others looked off in the same direction but saw nothing out of the ordinary.

"What is it, Miguel?" Santiago asked, grateful for the diversion, whatever it was.

"Something that was in town the night I decided to enlist," Miguel replied. "You guys stay out of trouble."

As he limped away, Santiago and his friends ambled over to the doorway of the drug store, furtively counting the change they had to buy a pack of cigarettes.

A half-block away, Miguel glanced up at the marquee over the movie house. It was the same theatre where he once worked. The marquee read: MARÍA CANDELARIA—Brought back by Popular Demand!

It was the film Miguel had once intended to see with Lorena Calderón. Remembering that night, he smiled wistfully, and buying a ticket, limped into the theatre.

CHAPTER 21

Wade Donahue rose from the far end of the table and passed out cigars to the nine men who already worked for him, as well as to the man he hoped would soon be joining his company.

Miguel had noticed that except for himself, Raúl, and the hired help, there didn't seem to be another Mexican within miles of the El Paso Country Club. Donahue then began to refill everyone's champagne glass. He seemed rather adroit at ceremonial gestures, but Miguel sensed that it was an acquired talent.

Ten years earlier, Donahue had been a mud-caked, oilfield roustabout and minor-league speculator who possessed all the finesse of a junkyard dog. But several hard-bitten years later, one of Donahue's tiny fields struck oil. He made enough money to buy a small construction company that swiftly grew bigger eating off the wartime building boom. Along the way he smoothed off the rough edges of his personality so successfully that people now meeting him for the first time never guessed the long, rutted roads he had traveled.

The champagne and expensive cigars were premature. Miguel had still not decided to join Donahue's company. Not so many years before, Donahue might have banged his fist on the table and demanded a decision. Now, he simply smiled and raised his glass in Miguel's direction.

"Well, young fella, we're kicking off the new company at the big banquet tomorrow night, and we'd sure like to have you on our team. But if you truly think you can do better someplace else, I guess we gotta get ourselves another Mexican-American war hero."

Raúl, sitting directly across from Miguel, flashed him a nervous smile, his expression reminding Miguel of a saying he had heard in the army: Situation hopeless but not serious.

"Your offer is more than fair," Miguel said to Donahue. "But that is exactly the problem. I know nothing of the construction business. I can get by on my Medal of Honor for only so long. To-day, it bought me my lunch, but soon it will be nothing more than another little piece of metal."

This was the first objection Miguel had voiced that had meat to it, and the rangy Texan quickly took it between his teeth.

"I appreciate your concern, Miguel. But in this case, I think you're dead wrong. You see, if you can do no more than simply help us convince your fellow vets in the barrio that they've come back to a better country and better housing, you'll be performing a great service you can be damned proud of—"

"Is it a better country we came back to?" Miguel softly interjected.

Donahue smiled indulgently, but a long, drawn-out lesson in sociology didn't seem to be on his agenda. "Miguel, I can prove that to you without even leaving this here table."

"Yes, sir, please," Raúl stammered, wiping his brow with a linen napkin.

Donahue leaned toward Miguel and lowered his voice. "Okay, you ask any one of these here Mexican waiters when was the last time anybody from your end of town came into this country club, other than through the kitchen door."

Miguel already knew the answer. Earlier he had caught the eye of one of the waiters, a frail man in his mid-sixties, who, over the course of the long luncheon, had cautiously glanced at him more than once.

Miguel now smiled at the man, who nodded and went on with his work.

"You see, soldier, that's something you've already changed," Donahue declared.

Strange, Miguel thought, how such a major decision could sometimes be made for the slightest reason; it was now little more than the hint of fear in the elderly waiter's eyes that had settled the matter. It was an expression Miguel never wanted to see again in the eyes of a Salazar.

"Is Donahue an Irish name?"

The question seemed to surprise everyone at the table.

"Yeah, they're even allowing my kind in here these days," Donahue replied with a confused grin. "Why do you ask?"

"Curious, that's all," Miguel answered. But there had been a reason. Many years before, his grandfather had told him a story about the famous Saint Patrick's Battalion. During the Mexican-American War, those Irish-American troops had broken away from the invading U.S. Army to join ranks with the Mexican cadets who were defending Chapultepec Castle, Mexico's last unconquered citadel. Later, a grateful republic would erect a monument in their honor, and from that time on, the Irish had occupied a special place in the hearts of the Mexican people. Miguel never forgot the story.

Yet it seemed stupid, he thought to make a decision on nothing more than the nervous expression in an old man's eyes and a fragment of nearly forgotten history. But he was relying, as he always had, on his instincts; they had, after all, brought him home from the war almost in one piece.

"When do we go to work?"

Donahue bolted to his feet with a smile of relief. He had been bluffing about replacing Miguel with another man, for though the barrio was filled with war heroes, he knew that none had won a Medal of Honor.

"Soldier, we hit the beaches at the banquet tomorrow night. Then we start changing things!"

"Okay," Miguel said, shaking hands with Donahue. "But before that, there's something else I want to change. So if you will excuse me, I'm going to go buy some civilian clothes. Thank you for the lunch."

The other men at the table came to their feet, all executives who would be working with Miguel. He made it a point to shake hands with each of them. Donahue stood waiting for him to pull away from the table, and fell in with his halting gait.

"Now, you do plan to be in uniform at the banquet, right?" Donahue's smile seemed rather slim.

"Is it that important? I am tired of the color of brown."

"Listen, Miguel, if I'd won all them medals, I'd sleep in that damned uniform," Donahue said. "Anyway, just for special occasions, okay, soldier?"

"You don't call coming to work every morning a special occasion?"

Donahue laughed, grunting an obscenity. They shook hands again, and Miguel started for the door. Limping out of the building, he smiled. He and Raúl probably had been the first Mexicans to ever enter the El Paso Country Club by its front door.

CHAPTER 22

He was a tiny man with basset hound eyes that clashed with his relentless humor, and he had helped Miguel into one sports coat after another in that cheerfully chattering manner sales people often think is an effective technique.

Miguel glumly studied himself in the full-length mirror, but he was thinking about what had transpired an hour earlier. He wasn't at all sure Donahue had been right in saying that the Mexican-American veterans had returned to a changed country. He did know, however, that he had changed greatly. Three months of brutal combat and the eight months in army hospitals filled with the screams of men in too much pain to die had made him feel like a middle-aged man. The experience had also re-forged him into a hard-eyed realist.

Frank Casillas had once told him that in the mysterious ways of the world, the more a man craved something, the less likely he was to get it.

Miguel had not coveted the construction company job, and perhaps that was the exact reason why it had been given to him. Maybe this theory held true, he mused, with women as well as work.

What was obvious was that all his opposing ideas had failed. He had wanted both Lupita Palacios and Lorena Calderón almost more than life itself, but he had been little more than incidental in their own lives.

The timing of this thought could not have been more perfect as suddenly a pair of soft green eyes, bright with amusement, were reflected by the three-sided mirror along with his image.

"Can this be the same person who never wore anything but sweatshirts?"

Miguel laughed and turned to shake Lorena's hand. "Hey, I didn't think you still worked here," he said unconvincingly.

"Where else, Miguel? Not all of us get to be big shots with a new construction company," Lorena replied as her eyes drifted back toward the mirror.

"How did you know?" Miguel asked.

"Your brother Raúl called me with the news."

Miguel shook his head, and stepped closer to the mirror. "You like this sports coat?"

"I like you better in your uniform."

Miguel and the little man frowned. "That's what almost everybody thinks." He turned to the salesman. "Okay, Mister Swanson, please wrap this coat up with all the other stuff, okay?"

"Yes, sir, Mister Salazar," the little man exclaimed as he helped Miguel out of a blue blazer, who handed him some money. "Thank you, Mister Salazar," he said, scampering away with a satisfied smile.

Lorena seemed vaguely impressed. "*Mister* Salazar, huh?"

"I remember when they used to call me something else around here," Miguel muttered, getting back into his service jacket.

"And here comes the clown who used to call you those names," Lorena quietly warned. Miguel smiled. He had looked forward to this moment.

Harold Metcalfe seemed as though he had escaped out of a time warp. He didn't appear to have aged a day in the year since Miguel had last seen him. Metcalfe still looked forty-five years old and probably would until the day he died.

"Well, isn't this just dandy! The boy I've been reading about in all the newspapers. Welcome back, Salazar," he said, reluctantly extending a pampered-looking hand in Miguel's direction.

"Good to be back," Miguel replied, flagging down Metcalfe's hand long enough to shake it.

Metcalfe flashed a brittle smile. "So what are your plans now?"

"Harold, you have no idea of the good luck—" Lorena interjected, before Miguel cut her short.

"Just make it like I did overseas, one hour at a time."

Metcalfe's smile now looked genuine. "Well, that job up in sporting goods happens to be open again. Of course with your disability, you couldn't do much demonstrating, but I might be inclined to give you another chance at it. If you're not planning to run away again—"

Lorena did not wait for Miguel to respond. "Harold, do you really think he came home a war hero just to cart around department-store dummies for the rest of his life?" she asked with a cold smile. "Besides, he's already taken a job where he might soon be making as much as the vice-president of this entire department store."

Glaring at Lorena, Metcalfe wheeled to Miguel. "Then perhaps instead of a job, I can give you a word of advice. Don't try to go too far too fast. Lorena here can tell you how dangerous that can be. Good day."

With a sticky smile, Metcalfe moved away.

The little salesman had returned with Miguel's change. "Here we are—and per your instructions, the apparel shall be delivered to your home no later than ten tomorrow morning. Good luck to you, sir!"

Miguel tried to keep a straight face. 'Thank you, Mister Swanson, but I already got my share."

The basset-eyed salesman smiled, and pivoted to fire a frown at Lorena. He had not forgotten her remark about liking better the way Miguel looked in his uniform, a comment that might have cost him a sizable commission.

The little man drifted over toward another customer. Watching him go, Lorena quietly said, "I better get back to work myself. Will you walk me over to my counter?"

Miguel fell in step with her. But as they walked, he suddenly felt embarrassed about his halting gait, and decided to follow a few paces behind her. After a short spell of silence, he finally said, "I hope you're not going to be in trouble over what happened with Metcalfe."

"Oh, I'm on borrowed time here, anyway."

Miguel thought of pursuing the matter, but something had distracted him. Lorena was wearing a tight-fitting sweater and a woolen skirt that hugged the rest of her even more snugly. In the year since he'd last seen her, Miguel had thought many times about her perfectly sculpted body—and in his anger and punctured pride he had imagined himself brutally taking her from behind, pressing her beautifully curved buttocks so hard it took the air from her lungs.

"I bet Metcalfe still has his eye on you, huh?"

The question seemed to annoy Lorena.

"Oh, it's a long story, with probably a sad and silly ending. I like short stories, happy endings. Like yours, for instance," she muttered as they came up to her counter.

Miguel felt his face flush. She was making fun of him. "Raúl told me the two of you are dating now. What kind of an ending will that story have?"

The question surprised her. She slowly walked behind her counter. "Oh, I suppose another sad and silly one."

"Yeah, you could be right. Raúl's not rich."

Lorena's eyes went blank. She moved a few steps away from him. Miguel silently cursed himself. Throwing her old boyfriend's wealth in her face was cheap and unfair.

"I'm sorry, Lorena. I had no right to say that," he said, staring down at the cane in his hand. "It's just that after all this time, I had gotten up the nerve to ask you out again myself."

Lorena sounded a hollow laugh. 'Yes, Miguel, that would take some nerve, since you never showed up for our last date!"

Miguel slowly raised his eyes. "What the hell are you talking about?" Suddenly, he felt slightly dizzy.

Lorena was still chuckling. "I remember, even if you don't—you hurried off to join the army the week before our date, without even calling me. I waited that Saturday night until ten o'clock and finally took my father for a walk around the plaza. So you better be real sure before you dare ask me out on another date."

That was what had happened, Miguel thought with dazed wonder. It had been simply a *misunderstanding*! But because of it, he had joined the army, gone off to war, won a medal, become a cripple, and now had come home to an incredible opportunity, only to discover that the woman he still loved was going with his own brother.

Miguel didn't know whether to break out laughing or burst out crying. It was as if he had almost killed himself in scaling a mountain, only to later realize that he could have taken a detour around it. Yet the climb had been exciting, and certainly the view from the top of the mountain was better than from the bottom.

But even so, he suddenly felt like nothing more than a puppet in a marionette show. He had to admit, though, that whoever controlled the strings of his life certainly had one hell of a sense of humor.

Lorena had never seen Miguel laugh, and seemed somewhat intrigued, as well as rather concerned about the attention he had attracted. Several customers were staring at him.

"What is so funny?" she whispered. Miguel demoted his laugh to a chuckle. "It would take me a full year to explain it to you. Anyway, I suppose Raúl has asked you to the GI Forum banquet, huh?"

"Yes, I have bought a bright blue dress just for the occasion," she exclaimed, looking rather relieved.

Miguel smiled unevenly. "And you know the banquet is tomorrow night, right?"

"Yes, seven o'clock, correct?"

"At the Del Norte Hotel," Miguel added emphatically.

"Yes!" Lorena replied, annoyed by his insistent tone.

"Well, I'm just making sure that you're sure," he muttered. "I don't want my brother running off to join the army like I did."

Lorena's features knotted with confusion. But Miguel offered no further explanation. He had remembered his friend Frank Casillas once telling him there were only two beneficial states in which to leave a woman: complete bliss or total confusion.

CHAPTER 23

Most of the two hundred people crowded into the fanciest banquet hall in El Paso had never before been inside it. They had entered cautiously, as if carrying temporary entry permits that could easily be cancelled. But now, a few hours later, the free-flowing liquor and beer had shaken the sediment somewhat.

Up on the rostrum, a plaque read: The GI Forum—Dedicated to Mexican-American Servicemen Who Never Came Home from the War. Above the rostrum, a banner hovered, mysteriously covered for the moment.

Miguel and his brother Raúl, along with Antonio Vargas and various barrio notables, were seated on the dais. Below them, the room was packed with former service-men, several whom still bore the reminders of how they had won their Purple Heart decorations.

José Luis and Graciela Salazar were at a table near the dais. At the rear of the hall, Lorena Calderón sat alone in her new dark blue dress, listening as Wade Donahue was finishing his speech.

"The war is almost over now, and your record speaks for itself. You have won more medals for heroism than almost any other group in the entire history of this country. So I'd say the Mexican-American has finally earned his rightful place in this here good old United States of America!"

Polite applause rose from the room. The large crowd had come hoping for more than simplistic slogans. Toward the rear of the room, Jorge Cantú clapped along with the others, yet the harsh manner in which he brought his hands together implied something less than approval of Donahue's speech. Cantú was in a wheelchair and very drunk. He had survived the death march in Bataan, but it didn't seem he would make it safely through the banquet.

Donahue was wrapping up his long speech. "So it is with your new position in mind, a status won with the blood of your brothers, that we have formed the Lone Star Construction Company — a company carrying both the motto and pledge of 'Veterans helping Veterans.' Thank you and enjoy the evening!"

Again the tepid applause. Donahue had merely grazed the large audience but never once hit its collective heart. Antonio Vargas returned to the rostrum. "Thank you, Señor Donahue, for those encouraging words. But as we all know, it is possible to earn something and yet not always get it. Even when it has been won, like you say, with the blood of our brothers. One example: despite our record overseas, we are still denied membership in the Veterans of Foreign Wars organization, as well as the American Legion. However, I promise you that this, along with many other things, will change. That is why we have formed our own group, the GI Forum — to make sure that the sacrifices made by men like one of those we honor tonight will not have been made in vain. Now, ladies and gentlemen, please join me in once again welcoming home our barrio's most famous son, Miguel Salazar!"

This was the moment the crowd had been waiting for. Miguel slowly rose to his feet, as if on the billows of the standing ovation. But it was obvious he'd had too much to drink. Donahue shot Raúl an irritated glance. Raúl instantly got up and helped Miguel to the rostrum. The crowd quieted down.

"Thank you, Señor Vargas," Miguel softly stammered. "I have been told to talk about my wartime experiences — but there are many men in this room tonight who fought many more battles than I did. Also I have been asked to say something about the future — but what more do I know about it than you?"

The audience was ready to applaud almost anything Miguel said, but frustrated that he had not yet offered them the slightest pretext. Donahue sat glumly gauging the crowd's reaction.

"Also asked me to discuss my new job," Miguel continued, dragging his words along as if they were themselves crippled. Then the speech stopped dead. Miguel was drunk enough to have been slurring his words, but not so intoxicated that he wasn't deeply embarrassed by it. Now he stood silently praying for help. A long moment later, he got it from an unexpected source.

"Salazar," boomed a voice from the back of the room. "You don't seem to know too much about nothing, do you? So how the shit did you get yourself such a good job?"

Cantú's voice was charged with such contempt, it had carried to every corner of the large room. The crowd sat stunned. Only Miguel was still smiling. He knew help had come in the form of a challenge.

"What he says is true," Miguel said, pointing toward Cantú like a teacher singling out his brightest student. "I been wondering the same thing myself!"

The large crowd emitted a nervous laugh, which only seemed to rile Cantú even more. "Hey, big fucking hero, is that your answer?" he yelled, leaning forward in his wheelchair. "Hell, you've gotten as slick as the gringos!"

This time there was no laugh. Dozens of former soldiers, sailors and airmen abruptly came to their feet and muttered menacingly in Cantú's direction. They were proud of Miguel, and as guests at a banquet in his honor were not about to stand idle as his reputation was being publicly maligned. They also were well aware that one drunken, foul-mouthed Mexican could do their cause more harm than a dozen slick-talking gringos.

Hearing the angry swell of voices, Cantú's upper body went limp. Then, with the mortified look of a man who has just soiled himself with his own excrement, his eyes slowly filled with tears. He made no protest when a couple of men began to wheel him toward the door.

"Hey, leave that man where he is," Miguel called down from the dais. "He has earned the right to say whatever he wants!"

The men pushing the wheelchair brought it to a stop. The crowd stirred, then settled back and waited. Miguel had reclaimed their attention.

"His legs are already dead. What else do you want, his brain?" Miguel exclaimed. "And that man knows, as we all know, that I am standing up here only because of what I did overseas. But I also know that I will hold my new job with the construction company only if I can make a contribution to it...because a man cannot live forever off his military record, and for Mexicans in the United States, the time is even shorter. Our only friends from here on will be our skills."

Miguel turned abruptly away from the rostrum. The hall stood quiet for several seconds. Then there came the sound of soft clapping back near the door. It was Jorge Cantú, and this time there was nothing derisive about his applause.

Others began to clap, until at last the entire audience was up on its feet. They were applauding not only what Miguel had told them, but the manner in which he had said it. Blunt talk was something they respected.

As Miguel limped back to his chair, a cord behind the dais was pulled to uncover the large banner which hung over the speaker's platform: *The Lone Star Construction Company 'Veterans helping Veterans.'*

Noting the sign, many former servicemen began to clap again, though it seemed they were simply using the unfurling as an excuse to reclaim the festive mood of the earlier part of the evening.

A string ensemble was playing *Perfidia*, a song Miguel had requested. The tune went perfectly with the rather melancholy mood that hung over the darkened banquet room.

At the far end of the banquet hall, Captain Frank Casillas watched as many of his former comrades slowly moved around the dance floor with their wives and sweethearts. Casillas had arrived late and would not have come at all if not that the announcement in the newspapers had mentioned the drinks would be free. Now, sipping his scotch whiskey, he sat waiting for the evening's guest of honor to present himself. Casillas's deeply ingrained sense of military protocol mandated that a captain should never ask for an audience with a private.

Across the crowded room, Miguel was also waiting for somebody. Lorena was angling toward his family's table, with Raúl walking just ahead of her. Miguel noticed they were holding hands.

"Mamá, I want you to meet somebody special," Raúl said, his grin slightly dippy with drink. "I have introduced you to dozens of girls, but this lady is different. Lorena Calderón, who—"

"Yes!" Graciela beamed, warmly shaking Lorena's hand. "You are the one who once saved my Miguel his job at the department store."

Lorena laughed and instantly felt more at ease. This was a gift Graciela had, one that had made the move from Mexico much easier for her entire family. She turned and beckoned to Miguel and José Luis. Raúl winced. He had hoped to introduce Lorena to his family, one at a time.

Making the best of the situation, Raúl draped his arm around Miguel's shoulder and said to Lorena, "Ah, tonight's guest of honor, my famous brother, whom I believe you already know."

Miguel and Lorena studied each other for a long moment. He was now almost sober, and in a mellow mood.

"I like your new dress," he said with a gentle smile.

"Thank you, Private Salazar. I liked your speech," Lorena replied, holding his bemused eyes with her own. Raúl loudly cleared his throat and gestured toward his father.

"And this handsome gentleman here is my father, Don José Luis. Papá, this is—"

"I have heard of Señorita Calderón," José Luis said with a cold, knowing smile. He had heard talk around the barrio that she had made a fool of herself in trying to marry the grandson of one of the richest Anglos in El Paso.

José Luis abruptly turned, leaving Lorena's extended hand laying out like a piece of unclaimed luggage. Miguel looked away, embarrassed, and now saw for the first time that his former commander had made the party.

"Papá, there's Captain Casillas! Come on, I want you to meet him." Miguel and his father started across the room, as Raúl stalked off to get himself another drink. His father's rude behavior had infuriated him, dampening what earlier had been the best night of his life.

It had also been the best of evenings for Miguel. But now, it would grow much dimmer. As he approached his wartime commander, he noticed that though Casillas was dressed in a handsome, well-tailored suit, everything else about him no longer seemed to fit. He was out of his element, Miguel thought. Like a caged eagle.

"Hello, Captain, been a long time," Miguel exclaimed, extending his hand.

Casillas came to his feet. "Yeah, long enough for you to get rich and famous, while I just got a little older." The captain was wearing a black glove on his right hand, and awkwardly offered Miguel his other hand. "It's going to take me a long time to get used to being left-handed," Casillas explained.

"That hand of yours was pretty chewed up even before we got to the Rápido River," Miguel muttered, glancing down at Casillas's right hand.

"And I got it burned worse crossing the Rhine. The doctors think the nerves might be dead now...and if they are, so are my chances of staying in the army. But hell, things could be worse. At least I don't have to try to make my living playing baseball."

It was a short speech whose punch line usually got him a laugh. But neither Miguel nor his father liked the joke, though José Luis did admire the way Casillas masked his obvious dismay. The two men smiled, having already decided to like one another.

"I wanted you to meet my father," Miguel said.

"I am honored, Señor Salazar," Casillas murmured.

"It is my honor, Captain," José Luis declared, taking Casillas's left hand with his own. "I thank you for all you did for my son."

"That is kind of you, Señor. But my own father would have wanted to thank your son for what he did for me," Casillas said with a rueful smile. "You see, I was one of the men Miguel helped get safely back across the Rápido River."

José Luis turned proudly toward Miguel. Casillas now muttered something about them joining him for a drink and signaled to a nearby waiter. Miguel sank gratefully into a chair. His left leg felt like it had a tourniquet tied around it. José Luis nodded toward Casillas's gloved hand and said, "I hope it does not keep you out of the army, Captain. Miguel thinks you are the finest soldier he has ever known." The compliment didn't seem to register.

"Oh, I just wish I had been born left-handed, that's all," Casillas murmured.

"Yes, I was also right-handed," José Luis said softly, glancing down at his arm as if he were suddenly ashamed of it.

Casillas's features contorted. "They were shipping Mexicans your age overseas—?"

"No, Captain," Miguel interjected. "My father had an accident at the ice docks here in El Paso."

José Luis smiled, as if trying to dismiss the seriousness of his disability. "When the war took all the younger men, we were left with only the old ones, who were not as strong. It was a good cause, but we could hardly explain that to a hundred-pound block of ice."

The expected laugh didn't come. Casillas looked away, as if filing away the incident amongst an already large list of grievances.

"So the three of us have something in common, huh?" he finally declared. "We'll drink to that if I can ever get the damned waiter over here!" Casillas threw a gesture at the waiter, who was still loitering nearby.

"What have you been doing since you came home, Captain?" Miguel asked, in an awkward effort to lighten the conversation. "I heard you were on medical leave from the army."

"Waiting to see what the doctors say about my hand," Casillas said, as he watched the waiter casually meander toward their table. "In the meantime, I'm selling used junk at Jenkins Car Corral. Every jalopy guaranteed to make it at least off the lot, or your money back. I love it."

"But if nothing else works out, you can always use your GI Bill to learn another decent trade."

"A man is lucky if he can learn to do one thing really well, and I already got my quota of good luck."

The waiter arrived. A large, beefy man, he stood leaning against the back of a chair, staring disdainfully down at them. "Hello," Casillas barked, as if issuing an order.

"Good evening," the waiter replied, slightly startled.

"You can speak, huh?" Casillas asked. "Now, can you also get us another round of drinks?"

"We're about out of hard liquor," the waiter muttered, glancing at his wristwatch. He looked as if he had already waited on enough Mexicans to last him a lifetime.

"Then just make it three beers. Easy enough, huh?"

"We're also out of beer. Matter of fact, we're just about out of everything, I think."

Casillas's smile faded. "Somebody ordered you not to serve us dumb Indians any more firewater. Am I correct?"

The waiter rose to his full height, and carefully measured Casillas. "No, you're wrong there, amigo," the man grimly replied. Casillas did not, however, look very friendly. He slowly got to his feet. The heavily muscled waiter was a full six inches taller, and easily fifty pounds heavier. Miguel shot his father a warning. They were a trio of cripples who even together might prove no match for the waiter.

Casillas seemed oblivious of the short odds. "Okay, big fella, here's the program: you can take me to the man who issued the order, or we can slug it out right here, or you can, of course, just go get the goddamned drinks."

The waiter pondered his options. Then he noticed all the decorations on Miguel's uniform. "Okay, I'll see if there's anything left," he said, and lumbered away.

Casillas grinned and sat back down. But noting the expression on Miguel's face, he quickly lost his smile. "You're not feeling sorry for me, are you, soldier?"

"No, Captain, of course not," Miguel lied.

"Good," Casillas muttered. "Because that's something I reserve exclusively for myself."

Miguel's bad leg suddenly began to cramp up. Casillas seemed to be sinking away right in front of his eyes, yet there was nothing he could do to help him. He recalled how helpless he had felt watching his comrades go under the waters of the Rápido River for the last time.

"Is there anything I can do, Captain?" he asked in a daunted voice.

Casillas gulped down the remainder of his whiskey and stared into the empty glass for a moment. "Yeah, Miguel, can you go back in time and get us those replacements we always needed but nearly never received…or maybe you can explain to me why they sent out a single rifle company to cross the Rápido, when a full battalion wouldn't have been nearly enough."

Casillas peered around, as if awaiting an answer from somebody else. "Maybe there is an answer somewhere; some explanation for why one of the best rifle companies in the United States Army was sent to its slaughter like nothing more than a herd of old horses. Find me that reason, soldier, and you will have saved my life twice."

His voice had clouded with an emotion he couldn't control. Turning away, Casillas stared out toward the dance floor. Despite the late hour, it was still crowded. It seemed many of the Mexican-Americans, sensing they might never again be invited to such a fancy affair, were determined to make the evening last as long as possible.

Miguel watched as the veterans slowly wrung the night dry. The sight reminded him of the old newsreels he had seen of the marathon dances during the time of the Depression. A somber thought crossed his mind.

In the uncertain days ahead, men of his breed, tied by tradition and culture to one country but bound by blood and sacrifice to another, would need all the endurance of those courageous marathon dancers.

CHAPTER 24

There were two general delivery letters waiting for Francisco that Saturday afternoon in Weslaco. It had been more than a twenty-mile bus ride, but for the past several months he had felt himself a marked man in the little town of Mission. Even the delivery of his mail was no longer a sure thing.

"Funny how some stuff can get lost," the postmaster in Mission had casually muttered. "And always seems to involve folks who like to make trouble about one thing or another... who don't much care for these here United States, but don't wanna go home, or over to Russia, neither. Yeah, plumb funny, all right."

That same day, Francisco decided to change his mailing address to Weslaco, a town where his organizing efforts on behalf of the farm workers were not so well known. In Mission, many of the local merchants would no longer sell to him. Whenever he or Alejandro needed anything, the boy's Uncle Pedro would have to go into town to buy it.

But the town's attitude didn't bother Francisco. What troubled him was the effect it had on his son. The boy was openly scorned by many of the townspeople, who thought Francisco's activities bordered on treason. He was considered a card-carrying Communist.

Scoffing at such a notion, he often reminded people that he had never advocated anything but a fair wage and decent working conditions. If that made him a "communist," he was in good company. Franklin Roosevelt, Harry Truman and Texas's own Lyndon Johnson had often fought for the same things.

Alejandro had no idea what "communist" meant, but he could see and feel the hatred and derision when people would say, "Hey, there's the Russian commissar's son."

It was another reason for Alejandro to despise the obsession, which had never loosened its grip on his father, even after it had partially caused the death of the boy's mother.

It was about six when Francisco got back to the migrant camp, and as he walked through it, the decision he made over the return ride from Weslaco became more firm with every stride he took across the foul-smelling mud.

The shack where he had been staying for the past week sat just beyond the camp—out in a small clearing. As he came closer, Francisco noticed that the cardboard walls and thatched roof of the shack had been recently reinforced with several pieces of tin— all parts of rusty and long-discarded signs. Most were of the "Buy Victory Bonds" variety, which featured smiling blondes and grateful-looking servicemen.

Francisco felt a faint tinge of guilt. The only soldier whose welfare had ever concerned him was his nephew's. One of the two letters he had in his pocket was from Miguel.

"You got a letter from your cousin Miguel," Francisco said, walking into the shack. Alejandro was sitting on a bench in one corner of the room, polishing his only pair of shoes. His Uncle Pedro had promised to take him to a movie that night. Pedro was at the other end of the shack, tending to a kettle of beans.

Alejandro quickly set aside his work and came forward to claim the envelope. Opening it, he saw that it contained a letter and a twenty-dollar bill.

"Look, Uncle Pedro," he enthused, showing him the bill. "So I will buy the tickets tonight. You save your money."

"Then I buy the popcorn," Pedro said, smiling. "I am not a man who takes advantage of every millionaire I meet."

Alejandro walked back to the bench and began to read the letter. Francisco ambled over to taste the beans.

"These beans need something, Pedro."

"Like what?" Pedro asked. He stirred them a little faster, as if what they lacked was motion.

"How should I know?" Francisco muttered. "I'm not the cook in this family...and some people think not much of anything else."

Pedro continued to stir the pot. There was a vague hint of hostility in Francisco's voice, and Pedro had caught it. It was a feeling that had been building for the past year, from the time of Juanita's death, and Alejandro began to grow more distant toward his father and closer to his uncle.

Back in Chihuahua the boy had never been especially close to his Uncle Pedro. Juanita's older brother had been a construction worker, and his job, whenever he was lucky enough to find one, had often taken him to the far reaches of the city. There were times when Alejandro would not see him for several months.

But now it was his uncle who seemed more like his father, his father little more than a distant relative who occasionally came to visit.

"I also got a letter today," Francisco said, taking it from his hip pocket. "From your Uncle José Luis."

"Can I read it?" Alejandro asked, looking up from his own letter.

"I already read it. Your uncle wants you to come to El Paso, where you can go back to school...and then when they all return to Mexico, he wishes for you to go with them. Your Aunt Graciela still thinks it is no life for you here, and I finally agree with her."

Alejandro slowly stood up. Carefully placing his own letter back inside its envelope, he went over to his Uncle Pedro.

"What should I do?" he quietly asked his uncle.

Pedro's features furled with embarrassment. "That is for your father to decide, not me."

"Will you come with me?" Alejandro asked, averting his father's wounded expression.

"What your Uncle Pedro does is not your business," Francisco abruptly declared. "I think your mother would want this for you. I am gone most of the time, and with us moving every month or so, it has been impossible to keep you in school, or even to feed you properly. This might be best for everyone."

"For you, too, Papá?" Alejandro asked.

Francisco turned away, but not before the others saw his lower lip quiver with irritation. Pedro knew why. For the past year Francisco had been haunted by guilt; it seemed that every time he looked at his son, he thought again about the night the boy's mother had died. Alejandro's presence was a cruel reminder to him that Juanita's death was in part the result of his own callous neglect. It was also a reminder, Pedro believed, of how badly he was now neglecting his duties as a father.

"I want you to go to El Paso," Francisco said quietly, peering out of the shack's only window.

Alejandro glanced toward his uncle. "I won't go without my Uncle Pedro."

"But the invitation does not include him. Just be grateful, boy, that they have asked you to—"

"Then I'll stay here."

Francisco turned away from the window to look down at the crudely planked floor. "Why will you not listen to me anymore? I talk to many people every week who listen to me like they never have done before... but my own son is not one of them."

"I am sorry, Papá," Alejandro muttered. "But I cannot go without my Uncle Pedro."

Francisco heaved a sigh. "Well, I will not force you to go. Your mother would never forgive me. But I cannot understand why you want to stay here. No home, no school, and the only future you have without schooling is fieldwork. Is that what you want?"

"It will not be forever, Papá."

Francisco's eyes clouded with emotion. "But why should it be different for you?"

"Because when I am old enough, I will become a soldier like my cousin Miguel. Then everyone will be proud of me. Maybe even you, Papá."

Francisco nodded half-heartedly. He wanted to say something more, but the words never came and he finally walked out the door. Alejandro went to stand next to his uncle. Through the window they watched Francisco slowly trudge back toward the camp.

"Your father has always been proud of you," Pedro said, putting his arm around Alejandro. "But the sad thing is he has never been able to tell anyone what is really in his heart."

Alejandro's eyes went blank. Staring down into the pot of beans, he asked, "What picture show shall we see tonight?"

Pedro shrugged and smiled. "What a burrito you are sometimes. There is only one movie house in town, and you want to know which one to see."

Grinning, Alejandro tasted the beans. "You know what these beans really need?"

'Yes, many things we cannot afford to buy," Pedro said, chuckling. "So we will just have to again use our—"

'Yes, I know. *Imagination*, eh?"

Pedro looked down at the boy. Their eyes held for a long moment. 'You have not burned yours out by now, have you?"

"No, it works okay," Alejandro said, sprinkling a little salt into the kettle. He was thinking of the movie that night and hoped that when they walked into the theatre, no one would say anything cruel to his uncle.

CHAPTER 25

The postwar housing boom had begun, and within months would change the face of the city as drastically as the war altered it four years earlier. New low-cost tracts were coming up as fast as their concrete foundations could be poured, as veterans from El Paso's south side barrio moved into them in numbers that approached a small-scale migration.

Many years before, a young country had been pulled west with the promise of free and fertile land for every man with the courage to make the arduous and dangerous journey. Now, a grateful government was rewarding the sacrifice made by war veterans, allowing them to stake claim on a small patch of their own ground. For the Hispanic veterans, it was the American Dream come true.

Donahue's selection of Miguel Salazar was a masterstroke. Within one year, the Lone Star Construction Company had virtually cornered the marketplace. Miguel now had a private office, his own secretary, and was making double his original salary. He had even been given the lofty title of Vice-President in Charge of Community Relations.

But as he saw it, he really didn't have a job. Donahue's idea of appointing a war hero to his board of directors demanded nothing of him—his Medal of Honor had given the company a rock-ribbed reputation for honesty, which was all the average barrio veteran needed to know about it.

There was, however, one embarrassment. Neither Raúl nor Miguel had been able to talk their father into budging from the humble apartment that had been their home since they had first arrived from Chihuahua. Miguel and Raúl offered to make the payments on a new house, but their father was totally deaf on this subject. Explaining this anomaly to potential home buyers confounded even glib, smooth-talking Raúl.

Miguel didn't bother trying to explain this or anything else. His job, such as it was, allowed him to *almost* come and go as he pleased. He was, however, expected to attend every function in the barrio, regardless of its type or purpose. There, he would always make the same short speech Donahue had written for him. Whatever company business he conducted on these occasions defended on how much liquor he drank. When it was not enough, he often ended the evening on the south side of the river.

There, in the town's most disreputable and dangerous district, he would drink and listen to music, aimlessly roaming from one rundown cantina to another. He could afford to frequent much finer places but had developed an aversion to being around people he knew. Their fawning admiration had ceased to comfort him. He had coasted too long on his wartime achievements; the former soldier these people still admired was now a stranger to him.

Then one night, Miguel finally saw the young prostitute he had searched so hard for that evening years before, the night he decided to enlist in the army. She stood shaking the rain from her hair and wiping the dripping mascara from her eyes, then she glanced around the long, dimly lit cantina, gauging her prospects. Miguel was seated at the far end of the room.

As the woman cautiously walked down the long length of the bar, Miguel thought he recognized her. But as she came closer, he decided otherwise. The woman he remembered was much younger and prettier. Yet she, too, had been very short, with the same bird-like legs. He studied her with a thoughtful gaze, trying not to stare at the dark bruise on one side of her face.

The little woman, noting his gentle manner and the expensive cut of his clothing, smiled. Climbing onto the stool next to him, she took a compact from her purse to glumly study what was left of her make-up.

"Would you like a drink?" Miguel asked her in Spanish.

"Tequila, gracias."

He motioned toward the bartender.

"So what happened to your face?" he quietly asked.

"I ran into some bad luck," the woman said, freshening up her lipstick. Noticing Miguel's cane, she asked, "What happened to your leg?"

"Same story as yours," he said, grinning. "I slipped off a bar stool."

The woman laughed and gulped down her tequila. Miguel ordered her another, which disappeared just as quickly. Then she turned to stare at him in a peculiar way. "Oh, we should get along just fine. I like liars."

It seemed for a moment she had recognized Miguel. Then she shook her head, as if she had changed her mind. But now he knew for sure. She was the same prostitute who had initiated him into manhood; the young girl had said the same thing to him. I like liars. That night her comment had sounded comical; now, only sadly cynical.

Miguel was almost drunk when the woman first walked into the bar, but by daybreak he was sober. Her bruised face and attitude had destroyed his desire to drink. Yet over the course of the night they told each other many things. It saddened Miguel to realize that the longest conversation he had had with anyone since returning from the war was with a person he barely knew.

The frail-looking woman had been severely beaten a few days before by a disgruntled client. Now, she desperately wanted to find some other form of work. But she had been a prostitute since the age of sixteen. It was the only way she knew to feed herself and her young daughter.

It was nearly dawn when she finally brought up the subject Miguel had been expecting all night.

"Would you like to come home with me?" she quietly asked, averting her eyes. Miguel found her sudden show of shyness strangely appealing, though not in a sexual way.

"No, I've had too much to drink," he lied. "I wouldn't be much good for anything."

"So I'll do all the work for both of us," she murmured, gently brushing the hair back from his forehead. "Come on, I live close by, and after I get cleaned up, I'll look a lot better."

'You look fine," Miguel muttered, downing the rest of his drink.

"I'll even give you my early-bird discount."

Miguel stared into his empty glass.

"Not even for old time's sake?" she finally asked.

Their eyes held for a long moment.

"You finally remembered me, eh?"

"I didn't till about an hour ago. You were the one with that crazy, good-looking brother, no?"

Miguel chuckled. Would he always be remembered by some people for little more than being Raúl's brother?

"So what do you say, eh? Maybe we can break another bed apart."

Miguel smiled sadly. He had not been with a woman since he was wounded in the war, and was reluctant to chance the attempt now — not stone cold sober anyway. Sliding off the stool, he steadied himself with his cane and handed her a wad of money.

Wishing her luck, he dragged his right leg toward the door and heard the woman yelp with surprise. He had left her more money than she ordinarily made in a month.

Outside, the air hung hot and befouled by the open sewer that ran alongside the cantina. He stood staring at the tiny hovels on a nearby hill, wondering if the woman lived in one of them. That alone would be enough to darken anyone's horizon. He remembered that not so many years before she had been a carefree, vivacious young creature. Now, probably not yet twenty, she already seemed a burnt-out, middle-aged woman. Life was shorter than he had ever imagined.

He turned to gaze north across the slate-colored river, toward the barren, rocky mountains which cradled the city of El Paso. His eyes seemed to be searching for something as yet undefined. But the sour smell in the air and the sticky aftertaste of cheap brandy ended his reverie.

What Miguel was looking for, though he had not yet found the words to express it, was another cause like the one he had found in the mountains of southern Italy.

CHAPTER 26

"Hey, Señora Salazar! Come to the window and take a look at your son's new car!" Raúl yelled, hitting the horn of his Ford convertible. Within a few seconds almost every window fronting the street had filled with gawking faces.

Leaning out of her window, Graciela smiled but seemed embarrassed by the commotion. Raúl grinned, hit his horn again, and bounded into the building.

As Miguel and Santiago joined Graciela at the window, she motioned to her husband, who was just finishing his evening meal. "Come, José Luis, see Raúl's new car!"

"I'll see it soon enough," José Luis muttered.

Raúl charged into the apartment. Striding over to the window, he pointed down toward the street. "Some chariot, eh, Mamá? And that sweet little buggy of mine is only fifteen minutes old."

José Luis glanced up from his food. "It'll probably take you fifteen years to pay for it."

"No, Mamá," Raúl said, smiling at Graciela as if she had made the remark. "I got another big raise today."

Miguel winced. In the last few months he had seen his father's tolerance of Raúl's good luck dwindle to nothing.

"Nifty-looking ride," Santiago enthused.

"Yeah, it's real nice, Raúl," Miguel murmured, already deducting what Raúl had probably paid for the car from the figure the family still needed for the trip back to Mexico.

Raúl happily cuffed Miguel's shoulder. "Hey, you like it, go buy one for yourself! You just got the same raise I did. Mister Donahue wanted to tell you himself, but you had already left the office. Man, I wish he'd let me get away with keeping the same hours you do."

Graciela made the Sign of the Cross. "Thank God that such a wonderful man came into our lives. Now if only you and Miguel could each find a nice Mexican girl to marry, my work would be almost done."

Raúl laughed and cupped his mother's chin with his hand. "You don't get rid of us so easy, Mamá. But what we all should do is move out of this dump. With the money Miguel and I are bringing in, we could afford to buy one of our company's fancy two-story models. Four bedrooms, a double garage, even a balcony where Santiago could keep those filthy pigeons of his. What do you say, Mamá?"

Graciela's smile seemed too slight to stay in place. "It has been a little crowded since Miguel came home…like you were saying the other day, eh, José Luis?"

José Luis returned from washing and stacking his dish in the kitchen. Sitting back down, he waved a fly away from his coffee. Santiago came over to sit next to him.

"I know what you are thinking, my son. You do not want to move away from your friends and your school. But I promise you, the only time we move from here is when we return to Chihuahua. You will be happy there, Santiago. It is where our traditions are, our roots, our history, not here in this crazy country that your brother Raúl likes so much."

Santiago smiled and rose to refill his father's coffee cup. Miguel eased farther away from the table, as if backing away from an accident he knew was about to happen.

Raúl stood fuming at the far end of the table. "Do you really think, Papá, a couple of uneducated guys like me and Miguel could have done half this good down in your beloved Mexico?" Raúl's eyes hardened in a way Miguel had never seen before. He glanced over at his father. But José Luis simply went on carefully measuring sugar and milk into his coffee.

Raúl took a deep breath. "No, Papá, you can't really believe that. But you have come to dislike both me and the United States so much, it has made you blind to the truth."

José Luis sat silently stirring his coffee. Raúl strode over to the window. "You once said that all my schemes and dreams were too good to be true. But you look out this window, and tell me that brand-new car sitting down there is just another one of my illusions!"

Miguel glanced over at his mother. She had sunk down on the sofa Raúl had bought for her, as if waiting for a force she could not control to finally subside. Raúl walked back to the table and began to slowly circle it.

"And just what, Papá, were all these great traditions we had in our glorious fatherland? What, of being poor and probably doomed to die that way?" Raúl snarled. "Of having our faces stepped on by rich Mexicans like nobody has ever done to us in this country? These are the traditions you are so proud of, Papá? "And are you really so impressed that we came from a country where every law, every official was for sale, but where only the rich could afford to pay the price? Where the police are no better than rabid dogs that in any civilized country would be shot like the mad animals they are! Is that another tradition you are so proud of, Papá? Well, perhaps I am not as enlightened as—"

"Stop it, Raúl," Miguel suddenly yelled. "Stop it or I'll bash you with my cane. I swear I will!" He had limped over to the table, breathing heavily, as if the cruel words had come from his own mouth.

A stifling silence came over the room. Miguel could hear his mother quietly crying. "Listen, Papá," he finally said, "Raúl did not really mean what he said about—"

"Like hell I didn't!" Raúl shot back, though by now he had moved out of range of Miguel's cane.

José Luis rose from the table. Miguel was shocked to see that his father had angry tears in his eyes. It seemed he hated that the others now thought he could no longer defend himself against his eldest son. Yet he also looked ashamed that there was some truth in what Raúl had said about Mexico.

"Forget what Raúl and I say to each other, Miguel. We gave up on each other a long time ago. It is you who now worries me the most."

Miguel felt his body stiffen. "But why, Papá? I have a good job. I save my money. Why do you worry?"

José Luis gave Miguel a searching stare. "You have a job that pays you a very handsome salary. But can we call it a good job when it involves convincing people to buy new houses they cannot always afford and promises your company does not always keep? For months, I have been hearing stories—"

"Miguel knows nothing about all that," Raúl broke in. "Complaints are my department, and almost all of them come from buyers who bitch because they were too stupid to read their contracts."

José Luis gave Raúl a withering smile. "Yes, everybody in the barrio is stupid, including me. But in one respect, you are wrong, Raúl. I do not hate the United States, nor am I so stupid not to know it is the most powerful country in the world—but what you have accomplished here, you could have also done in Mexico—for in many ways, all that you are is a pimp for a dishonest whore."

Raúl recoiled as if he'd been slapped across the face. Struggling to control himself, he turned to Graciela. "Well, Mamá, you just found the extra room you needed. I'll send somebody over to pick up all my things," he muttered, walking out of the apartment, slamming the door hard behind him.

The Salazars, Miguel thought, were now a family of four. In the smothering silence that followed, José Luis gently put his good arm on Miguel's shoulder.

"What worries me, Miguel, is that your job is turning you into a drunkard. I already lost one son. I do not want to lose another."

Miguel felt his eyes sting with tears. He turned to his younger brother. "Come on, Santiago, let's see how your pigeons are doing." José Luis followed Miguel to the door. He seemed shaken that their conversation had so abruptly ended.

After the door had closed behind his two younger sons José Luis wandered aimlessly around the room and then sank down on the sill next to the window. He felt a chilling sense of emptiness and was grateful when Graciela came to his side. Together, they watched as the last light of late afternoon danced off the Rio Grande River.

When José Luis finally spoke, it seemed his entire life was slowly passing before his eyes as surely as was the river a half-mile away.

"I have never had the gift, Graciela, for understanding the people who mattered most to me. First my father, my brother Francisco, now my son Raúl. Maybe even Miguel."

Graciela brought her hand to rest on his crippled arm. "No, mi vida, what happened with you and Raúl is not your fault. And what has happened between us is the fault of no one. That is perhaps the saddest part of all."

From the roof of the apartment house Miguel watched the lights of the bridge come on, brilliantly etching the long span of steel against the darkening sky. Turning away, he went to help Santiago lay out some feed and water for the homing pigeons he kept in a cage alongside the southern edge of the roof.

Graciela came into view, and with the light almost gone she began to take down a batch of clothing, which hung on a makeshift line. Miguel and Santiago went to help her.

"Your father is going through a bad time," she finally murmured, her voice not much louder than the wind.

Miguel's features settled into a sardonic expression. "Of course, he's the only one who's got problems, eh?"

"It is worse with your father. He does not feel like a man any longer...not even in my arms, anymore—and he has it in his mind he will never again feel like one until we return to Mexico."

She seemed to want to say more, but the words already uttered apparently had come at too painful a price. Tears welled in her eyes. Stuffing the last of the clothing into a straw basket, she handed it to Santiago. He stared into the basket for a moment. "I don't want to go back to Mexico. My father thinks it's the answer to everything. But he can be wrong, just like anyone else, can't he, Mamá?"

Graciela had been asked to criticize her husband in front of his sons, and this her upbringing obviously would not allow her to do. Miguel felt sorry for her.

He turned toward the purple mountains, far to the south of the river. "Yes, Santiago, our father can sometimes be wrong," Miguel said softly. "But he can also be right. Sometimes I have wished we were back in Chihuahua. Far enough away from always having to play the hero. Even far enough away from somebody who will never love—"

Graciela took Miguel's hand. "Your brother's friend, Lorena Calderón?"

Miguel looked away. Santiago discreetly drifted over to his pigeons. Graciela turned back to Miguel. "Have you told them about your feelings?"

Miguel mustered a smile. "What could I say? Is it their fault they are attracted to each other? No, the fault is mine. I came home from the war understanding too little but still expecting too much."

159

Graciela could not comprehend what it was Miguel did not understand. She did know that he wanted to be left alone. Calling Santiago, she started for the door that led back down into the apartment house.

Miguel turned toward the bridge. Beyond it, the lights of Mexico shone seductively in the distance.

CHAPTER 27

The tourist traps had been shuttered for the night, its main drag taking on the melancholy look of a carnival that had just closed. But Miguel had not come to Juárez to attend the carnival. Instead, he had ventured across the river to make some decisions.

Yet many drinks and a few hours later, the solution to his problem still evaded him. But in crossing back over the long bridge, he noticed something that suddenly brought his dilemma into sharper focus.

Beneath the bridge, a Mexican boy stood shivering in muddy water that came up to his waist. The boy was a beggar, though an enterprising one. He held a long pole, at the end of which was affixed a cardboard cone; the tool of his trade.

Miguel looked down at the boy and waved him closer so as to toss coins in his direction. The little beggar moved swiftly through the water. Maneuvering his pole with great dexterity, he managed to catch every coin. Miguel smiled, and gave him a salute. The boy, who looked no more than ten-years old, grinned and raised his lance in silent tribute.

He and Miguel had often conducted such financial transactions. The boy started for the far bank of the river, apparently having made enough money to call it a night.

From the edge of the bridge, Miguel watched him trudge out of the water, and pause to count his earnings. How much had the boy made that night? He probably made less in a month, Miguel figured, than he himself spent on a single night's worth of liquor. His grandfather Sebastian had been right. Life was unfair. Yet as Miguel watched the lad stumble up toward a tar paper shack, he felt strangely envious of him.

Fate had dealt the boy a bad hand, yet the beggar was playing as best he could the cards that had come his way. Miguel had been given far better cards and now realized just how badly he had played them.

He remembered the GI Forum banquet of more than a year before, and his own words of warning that night. "No man can live for long on nothing more than a medal." Yet this was exactly what he had done since he came home from the war. In all this time he had learned nothing about the construction business, missing out on a marvelous opportunity, and in doing so, he had ceased to grow.

But why, he wondered, had he not even tried? Was it that dark sense of fatalism, so common to Mexicans living in the United States, that made him believe that good fortune, so blindly bestowed, could just as inexplicably disappear? Perhaps Raúl had spoken the truth when he'd said that most Mexican-Americans distrusted good luck.

Yet even when Miguel tried, the result had gone sour. The one great achievement of his life had been forever tarnished, sadly enough by the man he admired most. The Battle of the Rápido River had been a senseless suicide mission, Captain Casillas had said. Miguel and his gallant Mexican-American compatriots apparently had been used as no more than cannon fodder to embellish the reputation of high-ranking Anglo officers. The night Captain Casillas had first suggested this, Miguel did not want to believe it. But over the course of a year the notion had grown inside his brain like a malignant tumor.

Well, to hell with the United States of America and everything it stood for. It had cruelly used him. Now he would return the favor. He would learn all he could about the construction business. Then, in another year, when he had saved enough for his family to return to Chihuahua, he would use that knowledge to open up a small construction company of his own down in Mexico.

Perhaps his cousin, Alejandro, would come to work with him, maybe even become his partner someday. Miguel had not forgotten his sense of responsibility for the boy, and over the past year he had sent him a little money almost every week.

Lorena. Miguel knew that during the last several months, Raúl had simply been toying with her, showing no inclination of wanting to marry her. Well, he did want to marry her. Tomorrow morning, he would walk into the department store and propose— and even if she turned him down, he would have the satisfaction of knowing he'd had the courage to ask her. No different, he guessed, than when he volunteered for the army instead of waiting to be drafted.

Raúl would be, of course, deeply incensed. But that no longer mattered. He had lived long enough in the swirling current of his older brother's oversized ambitions.

CHAPTER 28

"Miguel Salazar?" the uniformed man asked.

"What's the trouble?" Miguel warily inquired. It was a mailman he had never seen before, and an Anglo at that.

"Special delivery from Washington, D.C. Sign here."

Miguel signed the postman's pad and softly shut the door. His parents exchanged a nervous glance. Nobody in the family had ever received a letter by special delivery, and from the look on their faces, one would have thought it a warrant for their arrest.

After reading the letter Miguel tried to explain it to them. But there was much about it he did not understand himself. "I have to go see Captain Casillas," he muttered, trying to smile. No sense worrying his parents. They had enough troubles of their own.

The wide boulevard was a few miles north of the barrio, in an area that had once been the most prestigious residential section of the city. Some thirty-five years earlier, General "Black Jack" Pershing had led the famed Seventh Cavalry down this same boulevard, bound for Mexico in search of its marauding rebel leader, Pancho Villa, who had amused himself north of the border once too often.

Later, the thoroughfare had been the site of the large parade for the city's returning Doughboys from the fighting fields of France. Then had come the Great Depression, and the majestic old homes had fallen one by one as the street slowly sunk into commercial use.

Jenkins Car Corral sat positioned between two of the stately mansions that remained on the boulevard. In such company, the car lot's fluttering pink pennants seemed in poor taste. Hanging high overhead was a tattered banner: "The Home of Oldies But Goodies" The motley collection of pre-war heaps hunkered around the lot confirmed only the first half of Jenkins's boast.

Alejandro Grattan-Domínguez

The owner himself was a flabby fellow, at the moment sitting inside his sales office, glumly sucking a Coca-Cola as he watched how his salesman would handle the Mexican-looking cripple who had just limped onto the lot.

Miguel had come to show Frank Casillas the letter he had just received from the War Department. But finding his former commander in such shabby surroundings, he gave in to an impulse, and decided to buy a car. Any car, just so Casillas could collect a commission. Miguel, who had once been Casillas's driver, could no longer operate a car, but this seemed unimportant at the moment.

"What about that Nash over there, Captain?" Miguel asked, pointing to the latest model on the lot.

"Hah, not even worth shooting," Casillas replied, lighting up a cigarette.

"What about the DeSoto?" The car didn't look as if it could make it off the lot without being either pulled or pushed.

"Oh, hell, that one died even before the war," Casillas shot back, tossing his cigarette away. "Come on, Miguel, stop the baby talk. You didn't come here to buy a car, did you?"

Miguel winced. He should have known better than to try to fool his wartime mentor. Casillas looked away, as if to ascertain the exact whereabouts of his employer, and moved further away from the office.

"Hey, this Dodge has some equipment I think you'll like," he said, in a voice loud enough for his boss to hear.

Getting into the Dodge, Casillas motioned for Miguel to join him and then reached under the seat to pull out a half-empty pint of brandy. Pouring a slug into the bottle cap, he furtively gulped it down, and then poured another for Miguel, who did the same.

"A pint of poison once a day keeps the world away, huh?"

Miguel flashed a rueful grin. "I should really be feeling fine. All I do for the construction company is just drink with customers almost every night."

Casillas snorted. "Wish to hell I was paid for drinking. By now, I'd be a millionaire."

As Casillas poured out another slug, Miguel noticed that Jenkins had come to his feet, and was peering in their direction.

"Captain, you're right, I didn't come here to buy a car, I got this letter from the War Department—"

166

"I got the same letter," Casillas said, stowing away his bottle. "Well, okay, let's fire up this old bitch, see how you like the sound of her."

Casillas started the engine, and over the sound of its sputtering valves, he wryly observed, "Like a couple of cats copulating inside a cement mixer, huh?"

Miguel nodded impatiently. "Captain, what you told me that night at the banquet about what really happened at the Rápido River, now is our chance to set things straight."

"Sure, if *that's* what you want to do. The army board of inquiry arrives at Fort Bliss next week," Casillas muttered, gunning the engine.

Miguel felt his palms go moist. He was seeing what he thought was a new side to his former commander. "But if so many men in our company were sacrificed for nothing, it's the least we can do to testify about—"

"Come on, let's see if we can catch those cats in the act!" Casillas had already climbed from the car and was hoisting up its hood. Miguel got out of the car, and only now noticed that Casillas's right hand was still encased in black leather. For a moment, the two men simply stood staring down at the car's clanking motor. Then their eyes met.

"I can't testify, Miguel," Casillas finally said. "I'm due for another medical evaluation in a few weeks. But the doctors will never let me back into the army if they've heard that I spilled my guts in front of the inquiry board—and without the army, my prospects are lower than whale shit, as you've probably already noticed."

Miguel remembered the night of the banquet and the ravaged look in Casillas's eyes as he relived the Battle of the Rápido River. Now his former commander seemed to be engaged in another struggle. Reaching up, Casillas took the hood and slammed it shut with a thunderous bang.

The blast startled the fat man. Coming out of his office, he cruised slowly toward them.

Casillas looked back at Miguel. "You better think twice about going up before that board yourself. It could cost you that fancy job of yours—because your company, hell, even your family, will not be too happy to see a Medal of Honor winner shovel shit all over the battle that won it for him."

Casillas flashed a rueful smile. "So you see, soldier, life is not so simple for any of us. Here comes than mean old world again."

Miguel felt his body sag. He leaned back against the car for a long moment. Only the night before, there on the bridge, everything had become so clear to him. Now he was not so sure anymore about anything. Glancing up at the fluttering pennants, a somber thought crossed his mind. Both he and Casillas, like the battered cars on the lot, had probably passed their prime.

"Say hello to your father for me, will you?" Casillas said. Miguel broke from his thoughts. Clapping on a bleak smile, he shook Casillas's left hand, and limped away.

He had just climbed back into the taxicab that had brought him when he heard Jenkins call out to Casillas.

"Well, hell, Captain Marvel, you can't even sell an automobile to a fucking cripple!"

"Hey, I could have sold him any junker on this lot if I had wanted to," Casillas yelled back.

"Then great day in the morning, why the hell didn't you want to?" the fat man sputtered.

"Because he's a friend of mine," Casillas snarled.

Hearing this, Miguel wondered if Casillas's half-empty bottle of brandy would be enough to see him through the day. His former commander would now, Miguel decided, have to be classified as Missing in Action.

"Get me downtown quick," Miguel quietly said to the cab driver. "I seem to be running out of time."

CHAPTER 29

Harold Metcalfe had been timing their conversation. He had never seen the Mexican before, though when the man first entered the store, Metcalfe had been reminded of somebody else, someone he still disliked.

Raúl had been standing next to Lorena's notions' counter for ten minutes, quietly presenting his proposal of marriage.

"But, Raúl, if you have such wonderful prospects," Lorena wryly interjected, "why don't you marry a movie star?"

Raúl winced. He was not crazy about sharp-tongued Mexican women. "I don't want a movie star. What I want is Mexican sales-girl. If I wanted to marry a film star, I'd go to Hollywood."

'But why me?" Lorena asked, lowering her voice. "You've never even said you like me, much less love me enough to marry me."

"What the hell does love have to do with anything? Far as I'm concerned, that's just another four-letter word," Raúl exclaimed. "All that matters is that I'll take damn good care of you. You're a classy woman. You deserve the best."

"And that's where you come in, I suppose?" Lorena murmured, unable to strip the sarcasm from her voice. Then her eyes went wide with surprise.

Metcalfe was standing at the end of her counter. How long has the bastard been there? she wondered.

"Now, Lorena, you know my rule about socializing during business hours," Metcalfe said with a sticky smile.

"Yes, Mister Metcalfe, my friend was just leaving," Lorena stammered. She seemed rather grateful for the intrusion.

Metcalfe's expression became friendlier, but she knew that was only because she had remembered to address him formally. Since her demotion of more than a year before — one Metcalfe had personally engineered because of her lack of romantic interest in him — Lorena had lost many of her previous prerogatives.

"So you're Metcalfe," Raúl suddenly exclaimed. "The guy who used to give my brother Miguel such a tough time!"

Raúl's frustration had shifted over with the swiftness of an electrical current. He started toward Metcalfe.

"I would have sworn it was the other way around, but I never argue with a customer," Metcalfe replied. "Are you shopping for anything special today, Mister Salazar?"

"Yeah, as a matter of fact," Raúl growled. He stopped only a few feet away from Lorena's supervisor. "I came here shopping for a wife."

"Pardon me," Metcalfe said in a less steady voice. "Shopping for... a wife?"

Smiling, Raúl gestured back toward Lorena. "Is that the best model you have in stock?"

"Well, if your taste runs in that direction." Metcalfe had the queasy look of someone being forced into a dangerous game whose rules he didn't quite understand.

"Oh! Is she a bit too dark for you?" Raúl politely inquired.

Metcalfe lost his smile. "Oh, no, all I meant was that, well, you're still a young man, and marriage is after all a very serious and responsible endeavor."

"I see what you mean," Raúl replied with an ambiguous grin. "Maybe I ought to wait till I can halfway afford to bring a bunch of little brown beggars into the world, huh?"

Metcalfe felt his skin crawl back to the edge of his receding hairline. He glanced in the direction of the store's security guard. Then he remembered that the store had recently begun to cater to middle-class Mexicans. Raúl, dressed in a tailored pinstripe woolen suit that Metcalfe knew must have cost four times what he had paid for his own, seemed exactly that sort of Mexican.

Tugging at the cuffs of his starched shirt, Metcalfe began to back away. "Remember what I said, Lorena."

Watching him walk away, Raúl quietly said, "Well, I won't press you any further, Lorena. I just thought that together we could really go places—and then stick it to all the pompous piss ants who tried to keep us from getting there."

Lorena looked off in Metcalfe's direction and smiled. Raúl had just said exactly the right thing at precisely the proper moment.

"But, Raúl, what about your father? He doesn't like me very much."

"Forget my father," Raúl said, grinning. He was almost sure she was now seriously considering his proposal. "He and my family are moving back down to Mexico anyway."

"Okay, but what about my father?" Lorena asked. "I cannot so easily forget him, can I?"

Raúl's voice was strangely adamant. "Your father will live with us. I could afford to put him in a nursing home, but I know what it feels like to have somebody you love dump you like so much garbage."

Hearing this, Lorena's eyes went moist. Raúl, looking rather stunned, leaned across the counter to pass her his handkerchief. "What the hell did I say wrong?"

"You surprised me," she murmured, dabbing her eyes. "Saying such a sweet thing about my father."

Raúl chuckled. "Hey, people have called me a bastard, but nobody yet has ever called me a *heartless* bastard."

"Then till death do us part, huh?" she softly asked.

"Or some shyster lawyer does it first," he said with a crooked smile. "So we'll get married tonight up in New Mexico where they've got no waiting period. Then we'll take a cabin up in the mountains. I already told my boss I needed some time off for a honeymoon."

"You were that sure I would say yes?" Lorena said, handing him back his handkerchief. Raúl started to answer, then simply smiled. He leaned across the counter and gave her a hurried kiss. "I'll pick you up at your house no later than six o'clock."

Watching him walk away, she was overwhelmed by mixed feelings. She had just changed the course of her life, though as yet she had no idea why she had done so. She did know that if Metcalfe had not come along, she probably would have turned down Raúl's proposal. Even stranger, she had agreed to marry a man she didn't love; one whom, in many ways, she barely knew.

CHAPTER 30

Lorena had hoped to have a serious conversation with Raúl while they drove the forty-five miles to Las Cruces, New Mexico, where they were to be married.

Raúl had, however, brought along a small thermos of martinis, and before they had even cleared the El Paso city limits, he was already acting like a schoolboy playing hooky for the first time.

Earlier, Lorena had just barely had time to change into her best dress and arrange for someone to look after her father before Raúl arrived to pick her up. Now she had many things to discuss with him, things any young woman hurtling headlong into marriage would have wanted to settle.

But Raúl seemed more interested in demonstrating his command of trivia. Only later did she realize he was simply trying to calm his nerves.

"…Okay, next question: in what picture show did Humphrey Bogart say to the girl, 'Here's looking at you, kid?'"

"Raúl, please! I haven't been able to answer any of these crazy questions."

"Here's an easy one," he exclaimed, taking a slug from the thermos. Lorena glanced at the speedometer. Raúl was pushing his new Ford convertible faster than seventy-five miles an hour.

"The motors for the PT boats were made by what car company?"

Lorena suddenly was smiling. Raúl had coaxed her into taking a few swallows from the thermos, and because she rarely drank, the alcohol had just jump-started her own motor.

"I don't know, Raúl, Packard?"

Raúl's expression soured. "How did you know that?"

Lorena suddenly felt apologetic. "I just guessed. Lucky, huh?"

"Sure you didn't read that somewhere and made a goddamned point of remembering it?"

"No, honest, I just guessed, that's all," she protested, wondering what in the world she had said to upset him.

Raúl relaxed. "Well, that's okay then."

"Boy, that's a load off my mind," Lorena murmured, a slight glint of fire in her eyes.

Raúl chuckled and slowed down. They were coming into Las Cruces. "No, you don't get my drift, sweetheart. I got this theory that the human brain can only store so much info, and only dummies like me fill it with bullshit—but smart people like you remember only the important things!"

Lorena smiled nervously. "So you don't ever plan to remember anything important, huh?"

"No, that'll be your job," he said, laughing. "You handle the heavy stuff; I'll take care of all the silly shit."

Lorena turned away and thought: is this crazy bastard really worth marrying? But she didn't have much more time to change her mind. They had arrived in Las Cruces.

The little town was famous for its rapid marriages. No waiting period, no blood tests, and only some sign of a pulse rate. Any licensed minister could perform the ceremony, and the place was pockmarked with them.

Raúl had seen one of their signs when he remembered something. "Oh, hey, the one thing these quickie joints do require is a best man, or at least a witness. Am I right?"

Lorena stopped checking her make-up. "Raúl, you're asking me as if I do this all the time!"

"Well, hell, thought I told you to keep track of all the important stuff," Raúl muttered, wheeling the car on down the main road. He took a cigar from his breast pocket and began to anxiously puff on it.

"Shouldn't you light it first, darling?" Lorena sweetly asked.

"That's not something important," Raúl mumbled.

Five minutes later, Raúl brought the car to a stop in front of the local bus station. A few people were standing outside, their luggage parked at their feet. One of them was a young army private.

"Hey, Captain, where you headed?" Raúl called out, leaning across Lorena.

"On my way to Tucson, sir," the soldier cautiously replied.

"When does your bus leave?" Raúl asked.

The freckle-faced soldier checked his watch. "Not for another forty-five minutes. That's if it's on time."

Raúl flashed his most engaging grin. "How'd you like to make twenty dollars while you're waiting?"

The young man frowned. "Depends on what I have to do for it."

Raúl seemed stymied. Lorena now spoke up for the first time. "We're getting married, and we forgot to bring along a best man. You'd be doing us a great favor."

The soldier still seemed wary. "I've never been a best man before. How good do you have to be?"

Lorena smiled. "Why don't you come along and find out?"

The soldier grinned and grabbed his duffel bag, but made no move toward the car. "How much you say?"

Raúl growled under his breath. But Lorena wasn't finished. "Thirty dollars and a large glass of champagne."

The soldier quickly started toward the car.

It was seven-thirty when they arrived back at the marriage mill, but already the elderly minister and his wife were preparing to retire for the night. Both were in their bathrobes. The minister was a pinched-faced man who seemed vaguely annoyed that his routine had been rattled by the Mexican couple now standing before him.

"Of course our rates are higher in the evening hours."

"Naturally," Raúl muttered, returning the little man's vacuous smile. After the necessary birth certificates had been inspected and the proper forms completed, the minister hurried over to the small alcove which served as his main place of business and festooned with artificial flowers, plaster angels, and other assorted trappings, all seemingly there to promote the beauty of marriage.

Raúl snickered. The props seemed more suitable to a funeral service. Lorena shot him an annoyed glance.

The minister began to recite the ceremonial words in a low, but speedy, monotone. He seemed anxious to pocket his fee and return to bed. His wife stood just behind him, stifling an occasional yawn.

Raúl and Lorena looked at each other, then back at the young soldier over near the front door. He seemed embarrassed by the unseemly speed of the ceremony. Raúl's expression knotted with irritation. He couldn't have cared less for the words, nor even their meaning; what deeply annoyed him was the minister's obvious lack of interest. Raúl had seen meat butchers in the barrio display more emotion.

He decided to capture the minister's full attention.

"...Do you, Lorena Calderón, take Raúl Salazar to be your lawful wedded husband?" the red-faced man was asking.

"I do," Lorena said quietly.

"And do you, Raúl Salazar, take Lorena Calderón to be your lawful wedded wife?" Their last names had come out sounding like "Sali-va-zar" and "Cold-iron."

Raúl grinned, but made no reply. After a long spell of utter silence, the little man looked up from the booklet. Lorena smothered a nervous flutter.

"Well, do you, Mister Salazar?" the minister asked.

Raúl feigned confusion. "I'm thinking."

Lorena quickly interceded. "I'm sorry, sir," she muttered to the minister. "He's a little tired — but I'm sure he does!"

"Well, he has to say so himself!" the little man's wife heatedly interjected.

Raúl shrugged. "Yeah, okay, I guess so." He smiled at Lorena, who finally relaxed. She had realized what he was trying to do.

The minister was already racing ahead in his prepared text. "To have and to hold, in sickness and in health—"

"Listen, can I ask a question?" Raúl abruptly inquired.

The minister and his wife rolled their eyes toward Heaven. "What?!" the man grunted.

"Exactly how sick are we talking about?" Raúl politely asked.

"Terminally!" the man's wife barked.

Raúl smiled. "Sorry. Just asking, that's all."

Someone laughed. Raúl turned and gave the young soldier a mildly scolding look. Bringing his hands to his mouth, the young man wiped the smirk from his face.

The ceremony again commenced. It had just about concluded with no further flaps, when the minister gave Raúl another opening. "You may now place the ring on your wife's hand," he mumbled, with ill-disguised relief.

Raúl and Lorena turned toward each other; both looked genuinely flustered. They had forgotten all about a ring. Then Raúl had an idea. Taking out another cigar, he peeled off the cellophane, eased the band off the cigar, and gently slid it on Lorena's finger — a perfect fit. The minister and his wife looked on with vaguely horrified expressions.

"Sorry about the cigar band, folks," Raúl muttered with an apologetic shrug. "But see, I spent all my money on a couple of bottles of good champagne. Got them right outside in my car if you people would like to have a glass with us."

Before the elderly couple could muster a coherent reply, Raúl took Lorena in his arms and kissed her. Then they heard the muffled sound of clapping. Breaking from their embrace, Raúl and Lorena turned around.

The young soldier was applauding, it seemed, both the newlyweds, as well as Raúl's performance.

That same night, they drove on to a resort town in the high country of southern New Mexico. She had never known there was such greenery so close to the barren desert and bald mountains of El Paso. Lorena had been rather disappointed by the wedding ceremony, but the setting for the honeymoon greatly pleased her. The rustic, colorfully furnished cabin sat down near a rippling creek, and in the moonlight the water could be seen dancing from the windows of the cabin.

A short while after the door had been closed, and they had another glass of champagne, Raúl began to undress his brand-new bride. Yet he did it with such casualness, Lorena quickly lost her nervousness.

They were lying on a thick rug in front of a blazing fire, and when she was nude, she averted her eyes and shyly asked, "Do you like me this way?"

Raúl studied her breasts. Then, with mock amazement, he softly said, "There's *two* of them, huh?"

Lorena giggled. She liked the nonchalant, yet expert way in which he was going about making love to her—in marked contrast to that of her former Anglo boyfriend; the one night they had tried to have sex, he had gone at it with the grim intensity of a physician engaged in exploratory surgery.

That evening was a disaster, and she had not been experienced enough to know that it was not her fault, for despite her smooth style and seductive looks, until that night, she had been a virgin. Later, she lay wondering how she could have had so many romantic ideas about sex.

Raúl, however, was bringing them all back. Years of experience at pleasing women had made him a maestro, a master violinist whose Stradivarius was the female body. Lorena had never felt such heat and desire. Before the night was over, Raúl had left her shuddering with deep pleasure.

Later, as sunlight began to slip through the curtains, she gazed thoughtfully at Raúl, who was sound asleep. He had certainly earned a rest, she thought. Suddenly, she felt a great wave of affection for him. His devil-may-care personality and irreverent sense of humor had always intrigued her. She also felt greatly attracted to his suave good looks and lithe, muscular body.

But was this truly love, or just a common case of lust? She smiled and laid her head back, remembering the lyrics of a popular song. *"But if this isn't love, it'll have to do, until the real thing comes along."*

CHAPTER 31

For the first time in several months, Miguel had arrived at his company's office before noon. Walking past the glass doors that carried the firm's motto "Veterans Helping Veterans," he made his way past several draftsmen, clerical workers, and elderly secretaries.

Many of them had never seen him in the office so early and were nursing tepid smiles. Yet there was a tense feeling in the large room that he had never seen before. When he reached the far end of the room, he stopped outside a large mahogany door and softly tapped on it.

Inside a large wood paneled office, Donahue looked up from a sheaf of papers and smiled.

"How's our vice president for community affairs doing this morning?"

Miguel grinned. That was exactly what he had come to discuss with Donahue. "Not as busy as I would like to be."

"Wish to hell I could say the same," Donahue retorted. "Listen, when's Raul getting back from his honeymoon?"

"What honeymoon?" Miguel heard himself say.

"You didn't know?" Donahue replied. "He came in early yesterday morning, to ask me if he could have a little time off. Said he planned to marry that gal he's been going around with, you know, the one at the department store."

Miguel felt his legs go limp. He eased into the office and slumped into a chair. Donahue was speaking again, but Miguel could only hear a droning sound in his ears.

"Can't blame him. She's sure one prime piece of work. But meanwhile, back at the ranch, all hell's busted loose. I need Raúl's help."

Miguel rose from the chair and limped forward. "Let me do it. Whatever it is, I'll handle it."

"No, don't think so—this trouble falls into the complaint department."

"Yes, I've been hearing about a lot of complaints lately."

Donahue's genial expression went slack. "Well, we're doing the best we can, young fella. But old Honest Abe was right when he said that you can't please all the people all the time."

"President Lincoln said you cannot fool all the people all the time," Miguel quietly replied. Seeing the surprised look on Donahue's face, he added, "I had to learn a lot of American history when I took my citizenship test. I feel like a fool myself. Been with the company for more than a year, but still can't tell the difference between a tack and a ten-penny nail."

"Oh, no more than a few decimal points," Donahue muttered, eyes drifting back to his sheaf of papers. "Really that important, as world-shaking issues go?"

"What I'm trying to say, Mister Donahue, is I'd like to learn the construction business. From the ground up. Can I start at the new building site?"

Miguel had reclaimed his full attention, but not much empathy came with it.

"Why the sudden interest?"

The question surprised Miguel. Donahue had always dealt fairly with him, and deserved an honest answer. But all Miguel could muster was a half-truth, which was, he knew, the same as a lie. "I am tired of eating off my Medal of Honor."

Donahue chewed on that answer for a moment before deciding that he liked it. "Okay, young fella. But don't try learning so much that you forget to do your own job."

Giving Donahue a mock salute, Miguel walked out. He had almost forgotten the lie he had just told. All that was hammering inside his head was that Raúl and Lorena were going to get married. Hell, probably already were! You gutless moron, Miguel muttered to himself.

Back in his own office, he drifted over to the window. Across the plaza was the department store where he and Lorena had first met. It seemed such a short while ago. But now he had run out of time. He remembered what he had thought the night he had come across the little prostitute over in Juárez. Life was shorter than he had ever thought.

"Telephone call for you. Line five, please."

Miguel reluctantly reached for the phone. He did not receive many calls at his office, and most of those were invitations to social functions he had long since grown tired of attending. The call, however, was from Alfonso Lopez's mother.

Alfonso had been transferred the week before to a military hospital in El Paso, where he was now allowed to have visitors, though only at very specific times.

"I don't care about the normal visiting hours, I'm on my way right now — thanks for calling to tell me, Señora."

Hanging up the phone, Miguel suddenly felt better. His friend Alfonso would surely be able to counsel him about the letter he had received that morning from the War Department.

Their relationship was again reverting to its original basis: Alfonso, the wise counselor; Miguel, his troubled client.

CHAPTER 32

The William Beaumont Army Hospital lies nestled against the foothills of the barren mountains that cradle the northern edge of the city of El Paso. It was a long cab drive from the downtown area, and along the way Miguel prepared himself for the worst. Alfonso's mother had said that her son's condition was still serious.

Alfonso had been wounded at the Battle of the Rápido River, but quickly recovered and was with his outfit when it later crossed the Rhine. From a hospital in England, Miguel had avidly followed the exploits of his old rifle company. He knew that in May of 1945, only a few weeks before the German surrender, his division had begun to encounter only token resistance.

The once-vaunted German army, now desperate to avoid the onrushing Russian juggernaut, was surrendering to the Americans by the tens of thousands. What little was left of the German defense in E Company's small sector was manned by recent recruits, some no more than fifteen years old.

One morning, Alfonso and his squad had stumbled across several of these would-be warriors. The young Germans seemed nearly hysterical with fear and in a state of virtual starvation. Alfonso and his comrades had finally coaxed them into surrendering. But as they slowly came forward, Alfonso made a tragic mistake. He lowered his rifle to reach for a bar of chocolate in his back pocket, intending to offer it to them.

But to the fright-crazed lads, it seemed he was reaching for the cluster of grenades hanging from the back of his belt. A short burst of fire later, Alfonso lie sprawled flat on his face. One bullet had pierced his lung; another broke through his breastbone to nick the edge of his heart. He was almost dead when his comrades finally got him to a field hospital, and for many weeks afterward his condition was critical. Even now, almost half a year later, he could barely walk.

Regular visiting hours didn't begin until four in the afternoon. But the sergeant on duty at the main gate was a Mexican American, and after listening to Miguel's story, ordered the gate-guard lifted. As the cab rolled onto the grounds of the hospital, Miguel prayed the lie he had told to get in would not prove prophetic. He'd said that Alfonso was not expected to live long enough to see another day.

Looking out the window of the slow-moving cab, he saw hundreds of former fighting men, all dressed in maroon-colored robes, slowly shuffling around a tree-lined quadrangle. But at least they can move, Miguel said to himself, recalling the many bleak months he had himself spent in one military hospital after another.

"I think it's this place here," he said to the cab driver. The car pulled to a stop.

Inside the building, the first-floor corridor was littered with patients. Most seemed too frail to be able to venture outside, yet perhaps too lonely to want to stay cooped up inside their own rooms.

"Hey, pal, what's this I hear about them little señoritas over in Juárez?" a very young man in a wheelchair asked Miguel as he walked down the hallway.

The question drew the interest of several other patients standing nearby. Miguel thought for a moment. "Well, the last lady I knew over there got so excited she broke off two of the legs on the bed. So you better be in good shape when you cross that river."

The men smiled. Miguel could not have given them a better answer. But as he came closer to the room number he had been given at the main gate, his mood changed.

A doctor had just exited from one of the rooms up ahead and stood completing a form on his clipboard. Then a gurney with a sheet-covered body was wheeled out from the same room.

"Excuse me, doctor," Miguel said hesitantly. "Is this room one-fifty-seven?" He had already seen the numbers on the door. The stern-faced black doctor turned to Miguel. "Who are you looking for?"

Miguel fought an impulse to glance at the gurney. "Corporal Alfonso López, sir."

The doctor's frown slid into a grim smile. "Well, you're in luck. That's his roommate we're taking down to the icebox. But what are you doing here, anyway? Visiting hours don't—"

"Please, Captain, just for a moment. I haven't seen him since we were together over in Italy."

"Yeah, okay," the doctor groused. "But only a few minutes. Your friend is not having one of his better days."

"Thanks," Miguel murmured, already moving past the gurney and into the room.

Inside, there were only two beds. Walking past the one that was now empty, he went on to the far end of the room. There was a man lying in the bed next to the window. For a moment, Miguel did not recognize him.

His face was emaciated, and there were flecks of gray in his thinning hair. Only when Miguel saw the snaggle-toothed smile did he know that he'd come into the right room.

"I'll bet you thought that guy under the sheet was me, huh?" Alfonso said, his voice sounding twice as old as his actual age. Miguel tried to laugh.

"If I did not know better, I'd swear you had done that to me on purpose."

Alfonso pointed to a chair. Miguel quickly pulled it up to the bed. "They'll only let me stay for a few moments. But I had to see how you're doing."

"Oh, like making love, up and down, up and down," Alfonso uttered softly. "Some days I feel like I'm going to make it; other days, well...but maybe I'll get better now that my mother can bring me some Mexican food."

It'll take more than Mexican food, Miguel thought. "Yeah, that'll sure be better than the baby food they give you in a hospital, huh?" he said with failed enthusiasm.

"Cheery-looking threads," Alfonso quietly observed, taking in the cut of Miguel's sports coat. "My mother wrote me that you are a big shot now."

"Well, at least I'm not a stock boy in a department store anymore."

"You ever see that old bastard Metcalfe anymore?"

"Yeah, still the same old jerk, playing the same old games. He even offered me that sporting goods job again. I felt like stepping on his face, but it would have just made him look better."

Alfonso chuckled. "And that gorgeous girl at the store, what happened to her?"

"She's getting married to my brother, Raúl," Miguel muttered.

A hoarse laugh came from Alfonso. "So now you get to play the part of the best friend of the guy who gets the girl, eh?"

A nurse had just come into the room. She nodded to Miguel, as if to indicate that his visiting time had ended, and then stripped the other bed of its sheets. Miguel stood to take his leave.

"Listen, Alfonso, you know that the Army has started an investigation into what happened at the Rápido River?"

"What's to investigate? We got the hell beat out of us."

'But they're trying to figure out why only one rifle company was sent out, and why us, and not some other—"

"What are these guys, deaf and dumb? We got the ticket to cross that river because we were the only ones with any chance of making it. Don't these guys know we were one of the best damned outfits in the best damned army in the world?"

There was now a small spark in Alfonso's eyes. "Yeah, Alfonso, they can't take that away from us, can they?"

Miguel suddenly felt an emotion welling up inside him that he wasn't sure he could control. Giving Alfonso a mock salute, he started for the door.

"I'll be back tomorrow, okay?"

"But you wanted to ask me something?"

Miguel stopped at the door, but did not turn back. "Oh, just if there is anything special you want me to bring you."

Alfonso looked over at the middle-aged nurse. "Yeah, see if you can sneak in some tequila, and a sexy *vieja* who won't mind doing most of the work."

Managing a laugh, Miguel walked out of the room.

As he limped back down the corridor, past men who had still not recovered from a war that had been over for several months, Miguel's thoughts drifted back in time. He was remembering the faces of many of his compatriots who had been severely wounded in the service of their adopted country.

For those who recovered, it was probably the memory of their great achievement that pulled them through. The distinguished record of Company E was now forever etched in history.

Why then, Miguel wondered, should he involve himself in any investigation, no matter how well-intentioned, that might serve to tarnish that record?

Outside in the cold, gusty air, he stood staring at the mountain that loomed over the hospital. He was recalling another bitterly cold morning in the mountains of southern Italy. He had been driving Frank Casillas back to a field hospital so that a doctor could look at his badly burned hand. Casillas had planned to downplay the pain ripping through his entire body, fearing the doctor might pull him out of combat.

When Miguel had asked the sergeant why, Casillas had said there were few times in a man's life when he could make a major decision that was not personally painful to him.

Miguel had just made such a decision.

CHAPTER 33

Over the next few days, Miguel went through a crash course in the construction business, asking hundreds of questions of dozens of people, noting down every answer. But since his company had almost completed the seven-house tract, most of what he learned seemed rather abstract and difficult to grasp. He wanted the chance to see, even feel with his own hands, the way a house was built from the ground up. A new project would soon be starting, and he looked forward to being there the day the first foundation was poured.

The initial warning that Miguel would never see that day arrived early the next morning. His mother was just preparing to leave for work. As she adjusted her hat, he and his father watched her from the kitchen table where they were having their second cup of coffee.

"I don't understand why you keep working, Mamá," Miguel complained. "The parachute job, now the laundry job. You know that with this last raise I got, we have —"

"I work for one reason, Miguel," Graciela interrupted, gazing into a mirror at the reflected images of Miguel and José Luis. "To make your father's dream of returning to Chihuahua come true this next year."

The matter of his mother continuing to work had been discussed and settled before, but he still picked at it like a scab that wouldn't disappear.

Graciela got into her coat and moved toward the door. "I'll be home a little late, José Luis. Your son got back from his honeymoon last night, and I think somebody from this family should congratulate him on his marriage."

José Luis looked up from the Chihuahua City paper he was reading. "Raúl is certainly to be congratulated. He has always wanted to be a gringo. Now he has wed a woman who has always wanted to marry one. They should be very happy together."

Miguel winced. His father's appraisal sounded, sadly enough, quite accurate.

There was a knock at the door. After Graciela opened it, Miguel heard someone say, "We are here to see Miguel Salazar. Is he at home?"

It was a man's voice, one Miguel had never heard before. He slowly rose from the table, grabbed his cane and limped toward the door.

"I ask a simple question, Señora. Is Miguel Salazar at home?"

The man had the hooded eyes and gaunt features of an Indian, while his companion was swarthy and built like a pit bull. Both seemed serious, Miguel thought, about settling some score with him.

"I'm Miguel Salazar. What can I do for you?"

The swarthy man suddenly seemed uneasy. "We are sorry, Se-ñor Salazar, to bother you —"

He turned away, deferring to his companion. The gaunt-faced Mexican didn't seem so polite.

"You can start by straightening out what you and your crooked company have already done to us!"

Miguel felt his body tensing up. "You want to tell me what this is all about, or did you come here just to insult me in front of my mother?"

The Indian's eyes narrowed. "It is about brand-new houses that already are falling apart — also about how we have been complain-ing for weeks to your brother, but nothing ever comes out of his mouth but *mierda*.Well, we were going to the police, but Antonio Vargas at the GI Forum asked us to see you first. He says you are an honest man. But you will have to prove that to us."

"Who is it, Graciela?" José Luis irritably called over from the kitchen.

"It's nothing, only some friends of Miguel," she warily replied. Miguel and his mother took a few steps out into the hallway. Suddenly, a sickening sensation swept over him, much like what he had experienced just before going into battle: anger, apprehen-sion, and a gouging sense of inadequacy. He stood trying to throt-tle back emotions he did not yet know how to channel.

"Listen to me, Miguel," Graciela whispered. "Go see Señor Var-gas first. You will need him behind you before you start to fight with the people at your company."

She must have heard, Miguel mused, the same rumors he had. He gave his mother a hurried kiss and called back, "I'll see you tonight, Papá."

"I'll be here," José Luis said. "And if you see that no-good brother of yours, tell him just because we hate each other doesn't mean he can't come around every now and then to argue with me."

Miguel barely heard his father's last words. He and the two strangers were already halfway down the hall. After a moment, Graciela went back in the apartment and walked over to the window.

"Look, Graciela," José Luis enthused, circling with a pencil one of the ads in his newspaper. "Here's a little printing shop for sale right in the heart of downtown Chihuahua—and for only about four-thousand dollars."

Graciela nodded vacantly as she watched Miguel and the two men down below climb into an old sedan.

"And some of those new printing machines can run almost by themselves. So maybe even I could handle one of them, eh?"

José Luis looked up to get her reaction, but she seemed not to have heard a word he had said.

Mexican-American servicemen were still being denied membership in the Veterans of Foreign Wars and the American Legion, but their own group, the GI Forum, had become the fastest growing Hispanic organization in the United States. The Forum chapter in El Paso was named after Captain Gabriel Navarrete, who had been the commander of Company E throughout most of the war. He had returned from Europe one of the most highly decorated officers in American history: two Silver Stars, one Bronze Star, the Distinguished Service Cross, and seven Purple Heart medals—all eloquent proof of his contribution to his country.

Vargas's office seemed a shrine to the heroics of Mexican Americans during the war. Plaques, pictures and citations were on every wall and involved almost every campaign—from Bataan to Bastogne, from Casablanca to Cassino, El Alemein, the Aleutians, Tarawa, Tobruk, Okinawa, Omaha Beach, the Rápido River, and the Rhine. Vargas was proud that he had an inscribed photograph of every Mexican-American who had won a Medal of Honor—except, of course, those who had been awarded the medal posthumously.

As Vargas finished listing the complaints home buyers had lodged against the construction company, Miguel peered up at the autographed photos. The faces seemed a silent tribunal, which had unanimously voted for his conviction.

"—Even now, Miguel, many of the new foundations are sinking, tearing up sewage pipes, causing sanitation problems. Our people have been complaining to your company for weeks now, but nothing has been done. They have decided to go to the Federal Housing Authority, and I don't think I have to tell—"

"I know, the company will lose buyers, then its bank financing, finally its license." What Miguel thought but didn't say was that he and his brother Raúl would be back out on the street again, starting all over again—if they were fortunate enough to stay out of a federal prison.

The swarthy man leaned forward to lay a hand on Miguel's shoulder. "That does not have to happen. Señor Vargas wants us to give you the chance to straighten this out...and because of your war record, we have agreed to wait. But not for long."

Miguel nodded somberly. Already, he saw himself in another office, before another group of unfriendly faces. His silence seemed to unsettle Vargas. Pulling his chair closer, he said, "Look, Miguel, we all know that you had little knowledge of these problems. Whether you should have made it your business to find out how your own company was doing its business is another question. But now that you are aware of the situation, you must prove you are with us—or we will have to assume that you are against us. The choice is yours. But you must make it this very day."

Miguel had never been in the conference room before, a narrow room, oblong as a tomb, decorated with several stuffed animal heads; impressive evidence that Donahue usually caught whatever he stalked.

He was at the end of the table, standing near the head of a wild boar. Other executives, including Raúl, were seated around the table. Their expressions were almost as hostile looking as those of the animal heads hanging behind them.

The company's chief financial officer was concluding his analysis of the situation. "So you see, Salazar, several rather unfortunate things simply happened at the same time. But the odds of that occurring again are infinitesimal. Statistically speaking, of course."

"Look, Salazar, be reasonable," another man heatedly added. "We've already said that when our new line of bank credit kicks in, we'll try to straighten out this situation. What the hell else can we promise you?"

In the last half hour, Miguel had learned more about his company's finances than he had in the previous months. His long silence seemed to embolden Raúl. "And besides, the buyers themselves are partly to blame for all this. They expect a mansion for a measly ten thousand bucks! And hell, I don't care if they are war veterans, nobody can ask for more than what they pay for—"

"Oh, that's mierda, Raúl! A man buys a new house, he has a right to expect its roof to stay on, and foundations firm enough not to sink down into the sewer line! And it's this poor vet who has had to spend money he doesn't have to fix his house the way it should have been built!"

"In time, Miguel," Raúl stammered.

"What about the present danger to those families who cannot afford these repairs?"

Miguel waited for an answer he had decided would not be good enough. An older executives softly cleared his throat.

"Well now, any such repairs at the present time could stretch us past the breaking point."

"I understand that, Mr. Carson," Miguel replied. The elderly man was the only one who had seemed remorseful when Miguel had earlier checked off his long list of home buyer's complaints. "But I also know, sir, that if there is a federal investigation, or if any of these families get hurt and sue us, it will be many times more expensive."

"What about the financial danger to the company?" Raúl heatedly asked. "Do you not owe it a little loyalty?"

"Yes, Raúl. I owe it a great deal of loyalty. But I owe even more to the veterans who bought houses from us because they believed what I told them."

He turned to the other men. "Now I want you all to believe this—if by tomorrow morning we have not started to repair at least the more serious problems, I will quit this job and make public my reason for doing so."

Miguel held Donahue's stiff stare for a long moment, and then limped out the door. After he had gotten out of earshot, Raúl forced out what sounded like a laugh. "Ah, my brother has always been a great one for bluffing."

A ripple of nervous laughter went around the table but stopped when it got to Wade Donahue.

"No, Raúl, your brother wasn't bluffing at the Battle of the Rápido River, and he ain't bluffing now. But neither am I when I tell you that if you can't convince him to come around to our way of thinking, I'll find somebody who can—and I don't have to spell out what that'll do to your own position with this company."

With that, Donahue reopened a thick binder, and the meeting that had been interrupted by Miguel's surprise visit, resumed.

CHAPTER 34

As a boy, Miguel had been fascinated by a little puzzle his grandfather often made for him: a series of small boxes, each set inside the other. Each box was more difficult to open, but Miguel's persistence usually paid off. The last tiny box always contained a coin. Now, he felt he was playing a similar game. He had finally found out what his company had done—but still needed to learn *why*.

From the office, he went to the company's current construction site. The foreman was a long-jawed man who had lost the use of one arm in the war when he had courageously continued to weld on a control tower in the midst of a Japanese air attack.

But in broaching the subject of home buyer's complaints with the foreman, Miguel might as well have been Japanese himself. The man went silent as a stone. As Miguel was leaving, however, he was offered a curious parting remark.

"Good house is like a good pie," the foreman said, gazing out across the job site. "Poor ingredients can spoil it—but now these here seven little houses gonna come out real tasty."

As Miguel walked back to his cab, he knew that the first box of the puzzle had just been opened. The problem was not workmanship. The foreman, a Sea Bee during the war, would not allow that to happen. The problem had to be in the building materials. Miguel would have to search for the next clue at a housing site already completed. Three miles away, he found the second box.

He had walked from house to house. Most of the men were away at work, but their wives were willing, indeed anxious, to talk. He took down their names, listed their complaints, and saw for himself the great difference proper building materials could make.

Yet this second box only told him of the nature of the problem. He would have to open another one to learn the answer to a more important question: Why his company had allowed inferior materials to be used.

Late that afternoon, he found the third and final box at the last house in the tract. Jesse Figueroa had been with the famed 101st Airborne during the war. His outfit had parachuted behind German lines in the dark hours just before the dawn invasion at Normandy, the first American combat unit to fight on French soil.

Later, Figueroa won a Bronze Star for bravery. Finally returning home to El Paso, it seemed that most of his battles were finally behind him. He had gotten a job with Miguel's own company, then married his high school sweetheart and eventually bought a house from his own company. Then the dream went dark.

When Figueroa complained about the problems with his new house, he was fired. Now he worked as an all-night watchman in an old hotel, making less than half his former salary.

But why, Miguel persisted, had the company used such inferior building materials? The answer did not surprise him. It was for reasons common as commerce and almost as old as time.

The former paratrooper had opened the last box. There was no coin inside it—only another puzzle. Miguel was now aware of how difficult it would be to correct the problem. Yet his spirits suddenly quickened. He had found another cause.

CHAPTER 35

By the time Miguel got home, the barrio was cloaked in the soft red mantle of late afternoon, the time of day he liked best. People were having their supper, and the streets were quiet, almost deserted. But as he climbed out of the cab, he saw something that shattered his meditative mood. Raúl's new red convertible was parked in front of the apartment house.

It was Lorena, however, who was waiting for him in the apartment. She sat stiffly perched on the sofa, next to Graciela. José Luis stood over near the window. As Miguel walked into the living room, he thought to turn on a lamp. But when he saw the crushed expression on Lorena's face, instinct told him that what might follow next would be better said in less light.

"I have never been here before, Miguel, and I was not invited to come today," Lorena said in a lifeless voice. "But when Raúl told me what you told Donahue and —"

"Yeah, hey're all mad as hell at me," Miguel barked, flinging his coat across a chair. "I am also damn mad at me! Because just today did I finally find out what a fool they've been playing me for!"

"Miguel, calm yourself," José Luis ordered, pushing a chair forward. "And here, you probably have been on your feet all day."

Miguel ignored the chair and continued to pace around the room. "But they were anything but fools. They always built the first few houses in every tract real good, because those were the ones usually checked by the government inspectors. But later, when the company lost time because of bad weather, or their money got tight because they were over-building, that's when they got even smarter."

He was speaking directly to Lorena, as if he partially blamed her for what Raúl and the company had done. José Luis, however, had sensed the reason behind Miguel's resentment toward Lorena. His own contempt for his new daughter-in-law had not cooled, yet he suddenly felt compelled to intercede. "Now, be fair, Miguel! Surely you cannot believe that Raúl's wife had anything to do with this?"

Miguel flushed with embarrassment. The true cause for his hostility toward Lorena abruptly became apparent to him. His best cover was, he thought, to get angry all over again.

"And so the *smarter* they got, the more compromises they made. Stucco instead of plaster, half-gauge wire instead of full strength, just one goddamned cover up after another — and all in the holy name of saving money! But now we are starting to pay for it. A few days ago, a ceiling collapsed and killed somebody's dog! What's next, for God's sake?"

Miguel suddenly hated the dream that had first lured his family from Mexico and was now proving just how hollow it had always been. His father had never believed in the promise of *el norte*, always assuming the worst about the United States. Now his attitude made a subtle shift.

"But, Miguel, are there not agencies who check such things? After all, this is not Mexico where the average person has no protection!"

"Sure, but put a bribe into the right pocket, and it's back to business as usual!"

Until now, Lorena had sat silent. "Yes, what you say is true, Miguel. But Raúl swears that when the new bank loan comes in, the company will repair every single house. But they won't get the money unless they keep building. Raúl says this is how construction companies do business."

Miguel turned to Jose Luis. "You were absolutely right, Papá. There are some things about this lousy country that we will never understand!"

'You are wrong, Miguel," José Luis heatedly replied. "This country has the best laws in the world — so how can you hate it just because a few people choose to break them? Do you blame a beautiful statue because some vandal has been stupid enough to deface it?"

Miguel seemed dumbfounded. "Now it is you I do not understand! You have never had anything good to say about this country, till now that everything is falling apart."

José Luis could only muster a sheepish smile.

Miguel turned to Lorena. "Maybe what my father says is true. But you can still tell Raúl for me that if there is not a repair crew out by tomorrow, I will go to the authorities myself."

Lorena's eyes had filled with tears. Fumbling through her purse for a tissue, she took one, with a grateful nod, from Graciela. When she had cleared her eyes, she looked up at Miguel and with a rueful sting in her voice said, "I'll save you the trip. Raúl thinks there will be federal indictments coming out in the next few days."

Miguel suddenly felt dizzy. The others watched him as if waiting for an explosion. Then a curious thing happened. Now, knowing that the situation could no longer be saved, his mind began to move off toward a vaguely peaceful place, devoid of strife and suffering.

He had felt this way only once before—at the Rápido River. He had made it away from the German side of the river, but when he became too weak to control his raft, he gave himself up to a greater force: the will of God.

He had never been religious in any formal sense. His grandfather had told him too many stories about the priests in Chihuahua. Yet deep down, he still clung to a battered sort of belief. Now, he heard himself silently concede, Thy Will be done.

Turning toward the others, he suddenly felt flooded with compassion. They had foundered on the same shoal. The ship was going down with all hands on board.

"I'm sorry, Lorena," he said, touching her shoulder. "I know none of this was your fault. If I had not been so gutless, the whole thing might never have happened."

"Don't use that word, Miguel," Lorena softly said. "Cowards don't win the Medal of Honor."

"I was okay overseas, fighting the enemy. But I've never done very well here in the barrio. If anybody needs me, I'll be across the river. I seem to think better over there."

Taking up his cane, Miguel limped away. Watching him go, Lorena quietly began to cry. Graciela and José Luis glanced helplessly at each other, waiting for the other to say something encouraging to her. She had been a Salazar for only a few days, but already the family's wayward fortunes had engulfed her.

With a start, José Luis realized that the living room had grown so dark he could barely see the others. He rose and turned on a small lamp. "Listen, Lorena, would you like some tea?" he gently asked. "I have a special kind the old Indians used to drink when they were feeling sort of sad. What do you say we try some?"

Lorena made an effort to smile. Holding her grateful gaze for a moment, José Luis was struck with a thought: even with her green eyes clouded with tears and her nose red from crying, she was as pretty a sweet-faced young woman as he had ever seen.

In that fleeting second, José Luis decided that from now on he would try his best to care for her as if she were the daughter he had always wanted.

What Miguel liked most about the cantina was that almost nobody else knew about it; not many gringos, at least. It had no sign, only an unmarked door that led down a long flight of steps. He also liked the blind accordionist who sometimes played there. The sightless man seemed to go with a bar that had no sign or windows, and very few customers.

The musician had been playing for the past hour, but only now did he remember the request Miguel had made when he'd first come into the near-deserted club. The song had long been one of Miguel's favorites, because he was aware of the legend behind it.

His grandfather had once told him that "La Paloma" was very special to the Empress Carlota. After her husband Maximilian was deposed as monarch of Mexico, she had returned to France to spend the last years of her life in an insane asylum. But the haunting melody had made the long journey with her, and the story went that in later years, Carlota's nurses only had to hum its first few bars to becalm the former Empress.

Listening to that same piece now, Miguel experienced a similar feeling. What the hell, he thought. You shoot your best shot, and if it doesn't work out, you simply take your whipping like a man.

As if on cue, he saw the image of his brother reflected in the long mirror behind the bar. Raúl seemed half-drunk and in a dangerous mood.

"Man, I've been in every dive in Juárez looking for you. Never guessed you'd be drinking in a dump like this!"

"You could have found me at the apartment earlier, but instead you sent Lorena to do your dirty work."

"Sent her? Hell, I was mad as piss that she went," Raúl growled. "She probably just made things worse."

Miguel took a sip of tequila. 'You give her too much credit. Christ himself could not make things any worse."

The bartender ambled over to take Raúl's order.

"Double martini. The drier the better," Raúl ordered. The Mexican drifted off, looking confused.

"I don't think he gets too many orders for that drink," Miguel said, chuckling. Raúl grunted and turned back to the mirror. Miguel studied his brother's image for a long moment.

Beneath this bastard's bullshit, he's as scared as he was the night our truck ran off the road on the way to El Paso, Miguel said to himself.

"I don't know about Christ," Raúl was saying. "But I do know that you have made the situation worse yourself, most of all for Mister Donahue."

"Hey, I don't give a damn about him. It's everybody else I worry about—including that brand new wife of yours."

"But you personally don't have a worry in the world—the government might send Donahue and me away for five years, but they'll never send a war hero to prison for even five fucking minutes!"

"Don't be so sure of that. Anyway, there are worse places than prison."

"But, hell, Miguel, even if you do get sent away for a while, when you get out there'll be that army disability pension and your GI Bill just sitting there waiting for you, like a winning lottery ticket. But me, after I do my five years, I'm back on the street, hustling nickels and dimes and old women again."

"Oh, you'll claw your way back up, Raúl," Miguel said, casually running his hand across the sleeve of Raúl's expensive-looking sports coat. "Hell, you'll have half the clothing stores in El Paso rooting for you."

"Hey, don't try to hustle a hustler, okay?" Raúl snarled, pushing Miguel's hand away.

Miguel's expression went dark. He knew he was an inch away from socking Raúl. "Now you better go back across the river and hustle yourself up a good lawyer. But you'll be all right. You made your way out of the barrio once, you can always do it again."

Raúl snapped his finger at the bartender. The martini was still being mixed. He turned back to Miguel. "Let me tell you something everybody but you already seems to know, okay? Before I got this job with Donahue, I was just another guy going nowhere in one hell of a hurry. But I just happened to have a brother who came home a war hero—and without that medal of yours, I couldn't have got a job sweeping the floor of the toilets in Donahue's office. So don't give me this bullshit about getting another chance. I had mine. I blew it. Over and out, soldier. End of report!"

The bartender had finally arrived with the martini. Raúl sopped it up with a few quick swallows, then stared into his empty glass.

"How was it?" Miguel asked quietly. He wasn't mad at Raúl anymore.

"Just proves my point," Raúl said with a grim smile. "I'll never give this guy another chance to mess up a martini."

Miguel chuckled. "Yeah, but who knows, the next time he might not make the same mistake."

Catching the bartender's eye, Miguel flashed two fingers at him to indicate another round of the same.

"I'll pay for your drink if I'm wrong," Miguel said.

"You have always been the guy who paid, Miguel—even when you were right," Raúl said softly.

Miguel thought for a moment. If Raul had committed certain crimes, his own cowardice, he realized, had made him a co-conspirator.

"What's that old dicho about blood being thicker than water? What do you want me to do, Raúl?"

"Wait..." Raúl muttered before his emotions strangled the rest of his words. Composing himself, he said: "We're temporarily broke. But there is a lot of government money that's owed us for houses we've already built. The new bank loan from Dallas is tied to that money. But if you blow the whistle on us before we get that loan, we're finished. We might be, anyway. There could be federal indictments filed against us in the next few days."

"Lorena told me," Miguel said. He waited for Raúl to continue. He didn't seem so glib anymore.

"But, Miguel, if you just wait till we can get that loan, there's an outside chance we can pull out of all this—and you have my promise that on the day we get the money, we'll have repair crews out that same day. I myself will be riding in the first truck, dressed to go to work."

Miguel chuckled. His brother had grown accustomed to woolen blends, and he doubted Raúl could so easily make the transition to khaki. He also knew the promise had arrived too late. Yet for him to now voice more recriminations would be, he realized, little more than hollow displays of an integrity he no longer possessed.

"Okay, Raúl. I'll wait—and tell Donahue that I'll always be grateful to him for the chance he gave us," Miguel said with a wistful smile. "For a couple of boys from the barrio, we didn't do so badly there for a while, huh?"

Raúl seemed amused. "Thanks for trying to say thanks, Miguel. That's never come so easy for anybody in our family."

Miguel nodded and finally worked up to the question he had wanted to ask Raúl for the last few days. "Hey, you don't love Lorena Calderón. Why did you marry her?"

Raúl was momentarily stumped. "Maybe like that old joke, 'seemed like a good idea at the time,'" he muttered. "I know you still love her. Shame she doesn't have a twin sister. But even if she did, they would both be better off if they never met us."

Raúl smiled sadly and started away. Watching him go, Miguel drained his drink and hoisted his glass toward the bartender, and limped over to press five one-dollar bills into the blind musician's palm.

"*La Paloma, otra vez, por favor.*"

CHAPTER 36

It was the only park in the barrio. Walled in on three sides by decaying structures, it was called "The Cemetery" by the younger residents of the Second Ward who avoided it as if it were an actual graveyard.

For the past few years Santiago had walked past this park every morning on his way to school, usually pausing to peer at the old men morosely moving their domino pieces around and around, as other old men read their tattered Mexican newspapers. Even older men stood still as sentries, simply staring at the walls of crumbling brick.

The sight reminded Santiago of pictures he had seen of elephant graveyards in Africa. But on this particular morning, he did not stop, nor even pause, at the narrow entryway to the tiny park.

At about this same moment, back at the apartment, Miguel was on the phone. His mother stood nearby, waiting to hear the latest news before she left for work. He had called to confirm with Wade Donahue the agreement he had made the night before with Raúl. But both Donahue and Raúl were out of the office. He was about to hang up when Donahue's private secretary casually mentioned something that made his knuckles go white.

"No, I had not heard about that. Please tell Mister Donahue when he comes in that I'm on my way over there right now," Miguel exclaimed, slamming down the phone.

"What is it, Miguel?" José Luis asked.

"Another accident at one of the houses."

His parents seemed stunned. "Well, I am not going to work until you call us back to tell us exactly what has happened," Graciela said, getting out of her coat.

Moments later, Miguel was out the front door. Graciela carefully hung up her coat and drifted over toward José Luis. Taking each other's hand, they peered toward the door which Miguel had failed to close.

The headline read CEILING COLLAPSES IN VET HOUSING TRACT; and beneath, the sub-heading "Child Seriously Injured — Investigation Pending."

Reading it, Miguel felt his right knee buckle. His throat went dry and for a few seconds the air left his lungs. Finally, handing the vendor a coin, he folded the newspaper into something resembling a club and stalked into a building.

Inside the company's main office, he noticed that most of its former staff were now gone; those still there seemed as solemn as attendants at a funeral. He nodded to the wary-looking blonde woman behind the reception desk.

"Good morning." His greeting sounded more like an accusation.

"Is it?" the middle-aged, lantern-jawed receptionist frostily replied.

"Where is everybody?"

The woman peered at the papers on her desk. "Well, you'll be happy to know that we've had some temporary layoffs."

Miguel's grip on his cane tightened. "And Donahue, has he also been laid off?"

"Hardly. He just called from the airport. He's flying to Dallas this morning."

Miguel suddenly slapped his newspaper down across the woman's desk and smiled. "Maybe we should all get out of town."

The blonde nervously gathered papers off her desk. Crossing over to a cabinet, she began to file them away. "It's a free country. You can think whatever you wish."

"Why not give me a straight answer, Miss Burgess?"

The woman continued to make a show of being busy. "Mister Donahue's gone to speed up the new bank loan—though it probably doesn't matter to you if this company sinks or swims, does it?"

"I'd watch your mouth, if I were you, lady." Miguel's voice had gone ominously soft.

"Now that's just a rumor I've heard around the office, but you know how fast the truth can sometimes travel."

"If that's what they really believe, let them drown in their stupidity, including my brother."

"Your brother has gone to Dallas with Mister Donahue and a few of the others who are still fighting to keep this company afloat," the blonde said with a self-righteous smirk. She sat back down. "Is there anything else I can do for you?"

Shaking his head, Miguel walked back to the door, where he stood gazing at the motto painted on its glazed-glass surface. *Veterans Helping Veterans.*

Then, with the swiftness of a spasm, emotions that had lain repressed for many months suddenly exploded. His cane went smashing into the door. Glass flew wildly in every direction, but he did not stop swinging until the last shard had been beaten from the door frame.

Breathing heavily, Miguel looked back. Several people were staring at him, disbelief written across their startled faces. He smiled. He had not caught anyone's attention so completely in a long time.

"Yeah, Miss Burgess, there is one more thing you can do for me. When you order the new door, tell them to leave off the slogan."

Miguel's parents had waited an hour before José Luis had gone to buy a newspaper, thinking it might contain some information about the company. She was translating its front-page article for him when Miguel walked into the apartment.

"Yeah, I read it," he exclaimed. "I found out more from that newspaper than I did at the office."

"But what does your brother say about this?" Graciela inquired hopefully. "Surely he can fix this problem, no?"

Miguel's expression went dead. His mother, like most Mexican mothers, believed there was *nothing* their eldest sons could not set straight.

Laying aside his cane, Miguel limped into the bedroom he had shared for the past year with his brother, Santiago.

"Raúl went to Dallas with Donahue to see about the loan from the bank," Miguel called back.

"Well, it was not wise of your brother to leave in the middle of all this trouble," Graciela exclaimed.

Miguel chuckled. "No, Mamá. Like always, Raúl did the most convenient thing — now, I think it would also be smart if I got out of El Paso myself."

He had hauled out an army duffel bag from a closet still crammed with hand-me-downs he had inherited from Raúl, and began to pack his newer clothing into the bag. After he had done so, he peered around the room and suddenly realized that every picture, poster, book and plant there belonged to his younger brother. It seemed that from the beginning, he had never wanted to make the room his own. He had always felt the same way about the United States.

His parents were standing in the doorway.

"Where are you going, Miguel?" José Luis asked, his eyes fastened on the bag.

Miguel walked to the window to stare out at the purple mountains that sat south of the river. "We have waited a long time to return to Mexico. This seems like a pretty good time for us to go."

A light came into José Luis's eyes, but his smile stopped in midjourney and the light abruptly went dim.

"That is true," José Luis said. "But perhaps we should wait a little longer."

Miguel turned from the window and took hold of his duffel bag. "We still don't have the five-thousand dollars my grandfather said we should have saved before we went home. But I think he would understand that if we don't go now..."

"Miguel, be reasonable," Graciela exclaimed. "It will take us time to make all the arrangements."

"Then you and Papá will have to make them. I will wait for you at the San Antonio Hotel over in Juárez."

"No! It is not right to leave under such circumstances, like thieves in the middle of the night. This is not the way your grandfather would want us to return home!"

Miguel gently cradled his mother's face with his hands. "But not all of us have the courage of my grandfather—and if I don't get across the border now, I'll soon be in the El Paso jail, with federal charges hanging over my head. Do the best you can, Mamá."

They suddenly turned away. Someone was coming into the apartment. A moment later, Santiago walked into the bedroom.

"Why are you home from school so early?" José Luis asked with a vacant frown.

"All the kids are talking about the accident at the housing tract. I came home to see if I could help."

"You should have stayed to defend your brothers," José Luis proclaimed. "Now go, get back to school!"

"Wait, Santiago," Miguel said, taking a wad of money from his pocket. "You want to help, take this money to the parents of the little girl who got hurt."

Santiago smiled. "Oh, hey, on my way home, I heard that the little Ramirez girl is going to be okay."

Something resembling a grateful smile shot across Miguel's face. "Thank God for that. Now get going!"

Santiago, starting out of the room, abruptly stopped. "I don't even know where she lives—"

Miguel's face twisted with fury. "Listen, don't go stupid on me! How many Ramirez families can be living in a six-house tract?"

Santiago quickly walked away without saying another word. Miguel moved back to the closet to see if he had forgotten anything. His medal-clustered service jacket still hung in the closet.

"You are not taking your uniform?" Graciela asked.

"No, let's leave the memories behind us when we go."

The remark triggered something in José Luis. Placing his good arm around Miguel, he quietly said, "You know, one part of me wants to say to hell with everything, let's go home. Another voice tells me to wait, that things are not so simple…you see, my son, I now have to confess something I have never admitted before…the United States has been very good to this family. We should take our leave of it in a more respectful way."

"I have already paid my respects to this country, Papá. I'll wait for you over across the river."

Hugging his mother, Miguel grabbed his duffel bag, took up his cane and limped out of the apartment. Graciela followed him up to the door and then drifted to the front window. She and José Luis watched Miguel cross the street and start toward the bridge. Her words, when they came, seemed like escaped thoughts.

"We return to Mexico with things as they are now, it will cripple Miguel worse than anything that happened to him in the war."

"But even worse to go to prison for something he knew nothing about," José Luis said, shuddering slightly. He could almost hear the prison gates slamming shut behind Miguel.

CHAPTER 37

Late that afternoon, a strong wind came snarling out of the mountains, stripping the last leaves from the scrawny sapling trees that lined the tiny park. The mid-October air had abruptly turned bitter, and the old men still in the park reluctantly started for home.

At the deepest end of the park, José Luis shifted his weight once more, trying to find a comfortable spot on the wooden bench. He wondered if the pews and kneelers in the old church where Graciela had gone to pray were any friendlier to the human body.

She had implored him to go with her, but José Luis had gently refused, reminding her that guidance could be found anywhere. He peered around for a moment; yes, even here, in this pathetic excuse for a park, where many a hope had already withered and died.

Across the river, in a hotel that once served as the headquarters for the Revolution's famed Army of the North, Miguel was thinking about another dream that had died. He was seated on the balcony of his room, massaging his lame leg as he studied the lights on the other side of the Rio Grande. There was a knock at his door.

Miguel rose and started toward it; probably a U.S. Marshal, he thought, here to serve him with a federal subpoena. He wondered whether the service would be valid if made in a foreign country. But then the gringos were rarely restrained by such technicalities.

"Lorena," he exclaimed, smiling for the first time in what seemed like several days.

"Hello, Miguel," Lorena muttered. She was in the hallway, directly beneath a light bulb. In the harsh glare her face looked drawn and gaunt. Her pageboy hung limply on her head like a loose- fitting helmet.

"Your father said I could find you here."

She paused to inhale deeply, as if gathering strength from some badly depleted source. "He wanted me to tell you that federal subpoenas were issued late this afternoon for you and Raúl."

Miguel's expression remained fixed. 'You should have just called. You look sick…"

"I'm all right." Lorena mildly protested. "Anyway, there is another reason why I came to see you."

Miguel's smile was expectant. "I'll bet you haven't eaten anything all day." He reached back into his room, grabbed his key and shut the door. "Come on, I'll buy you dinner. I owe you one. Remember?"

Lorena mustered a wan smile and fell in step with his halting gait. They started down the long, dimly lit corridor.

The dining room, like the old hotel itself, had a faded elegance about it. A high ceiling, potted palms and murals with a tropical motif gave the room a sadly dated look.

An elderly pianist in a frayed tuxedo had expertly played one piece after another for a crowd of no more than a half-dozen people. Most of them scarcely seemed to know he was in the room.

Miguel and Lorena had worked their way through a a couple of broiled steaks, and were now finishing off with cinnamon-flavored coffee. They had spent the last hour dodging around each other, smart prizefighters who knew enough to stay out of a clinch.

"You were right. I hadn't eaten all day."

"You looked like you hadn't eaten in a week," Miguel murmured, wondering when she would get around to whatever had brought her to his hotel.

"But this dinner was worth the wait," she said, dabbing at her mouth with a napkin. "Let's see, just how long ago was it that we made that Saturday night date?"

Miguel remembered the exact date, yet instinct kept him from admitting it. It would place him at a disadvantage too early in whatever game Lorena was playing with him. "I am more interested in why you came here tonight."

Lorena went to her purse. Taking an envelope from it, she handed it to him.

"Ah, so you're serving me with the federal subpoena yourself, eh?" he said, flipping the envelope to one side.

His bantering tone annoyed Lorena. "There is seven hundred dollars in that envelope. All the money I've ever been able to save. Use it to help you and your father get a fresh start down in Chihuahua."

Miguel wasn't sure whether to feel insulted or gratified. "What makes you so certain we're going back to Mexico?"

Lorena leaned across the table and placed her hand on his arm. "Because I know that's what your father wants more than anything else in—"

"There are other lives to consider."

"Yes, like your own. Miguel, listen to me. You will probably be arrested the second you cross back over that river!"

"The same thing will happen to Raúl when he gets back from Dallas—so save this money to defend your husband. Don't worry about me."

"Why are you making this so difficult for me?"

Poetic justice, Miguel thought. She had always made things so hard for him.

Across the room, the pianist was playing *Solamente Una Vez*. Miguel remembered that it was the same song he had heard in the placita the night Lorena failed to show up for their date, the evening he had decided to enlist in the army.

"Besides, Raúl's defense is all taken care of," Lorena was saying. "He called me from Dallas this afternoon. Mister Donahue has hired both of them a very good lawyer."

"They'll need one," Miguel muttered.

"And if you go back, you might need a better one!"

Miguel turned to face her. "You better save your concern for Raúl—and for yourself, as well."

Lorena smiled ruefully. "We'll slide through all this somehow. We're the same slippery kind, Raúl and I...and it's too late for us to become anything else."

"Maybe it's also too late for me."

"Only you still have the courage to start all over again. I wish I did."

Miguel sat studying her. "Maybe you have more courage than you think," he said quietly, taking her hand in his. "Hey, do you know that song?" he asked, glancing toward the pianist.

Lorena seemed annoyed. 'Yes, of course. It is—"

"I once read something interesting about the man who wrote it. He was, as you probably also know, a rather homely little man who was married to a very beautiful movie star—and somebody once asked her how she could be married to such a homely man—"

"Miguel, shouldn't we be talking about—?"

"The movie star answered that the person had seen only the man's face, but not his soul."

"But you are not homely, and you certainly aren't little."

Miguel seemed unsure of what she was trying to tell him. "I know how you still feel about me. I also know you would have never said a word if you thought there was any love left between me and your brother."

A shadow seemed to fall across Miguel's face. "And is there any love in this brand-new marriage of yours?"

Lorena peered out across the near-deserted room. "It's funny, but until all this trouble started, I didn't realize that I loved Raúl. What's sad is that I don't think I'll ever be able to convince him of that."

"Have you tried?" Miguel heard himself say.

"I'm working on it, but I don't know Raúl very well...in the last few days I've realized that your brother doesn't like himself very much, so maybe he'll never believe that anyone could love him. But yes, I do love him."

Miguel felt strangely relieved. If he couldn't have her himself, at least his brother was better than a stranger.

She had stood up to buckle the full-length leather coat that Raúl had given her as a wedding present.

Handing her back the envelope, Miguel said, "I'll walk out to get you a cab."

"It's freezing outside. Be bad for your leg. But you think about what I said, *hermanito*. The seven hundred dollars will be waiting for you the day you decide to go back to Mexico."

Miguel nodded gratefully. Lorena suddenly felt a great surge of affection for him. Leaning over, she kissed him on the cheek.

Their eyes held for a moment, and then she was gone.

She had truly been, he realized, just another one of his illusions.

A short while later, he experienced what seemed another such illusion. Standing out on the balcony of his hotel room, Miguel suddenly felt that he was not alone. A wave of warmth coursed through his body, though by now the night had turned well below freezing. He had rarely believed in anything he could not prove

214

with his five senses. Yet now, surely as he knew his own name, he was certain that he felt the presence of his grandfather.

Sebastián Salazar had managed the miracle of covering a distance of two-hundred and thirty miles and four full years back in time, and was now standing alongside him, silently offering his strength and support as he had done so often throughout Miguel's first sixteen years.

CHAPTER 38

For most Mexicans Saturday meant only a half-day of work, more than ample reason to celebrate. By one o'clock that afternoon, the large park that sat in the center of Juárez was already filled with people. On a bandstand an orchestra comprised of teenagers were tuning up under the baleful eye of their elderly conductor.

The tall trees that shielded the square had grown sparse, and the bench Miguel sat on was littered with leaves. He had barely slept the night before and fatigue had caught up with him. He had just closed his eyes when he heard someone call his name. His father and younger brother were approaching from the far end of the park.

"Hola," Miguel yelled out, putting a cheerful smile on his face. He felt he owed them some sign of cordiality after his sour display of the day before.

José Luis raised his good arm and fashioned an extravagant wave. Miguel had often noted that his father always seemed livelier on the south side of the river. But he sensed there was something more than mere geography behind his father's manner.

Miguel embraced his father, and playfully mussed the wave in Santiago's hair. "So how goes the battle, little brother?"

Santiago carefully smoothed back his hair. "I found the Ramirez family and gave them the money. The little girl's mother said she knew you had nothing to do with the bad thing that happened. She said she would pray for you."

Miguel flinched, as if ducking a blow that had come so fast the others had not even seen it. Then, he put his arm around Santiago.

"Forgive me for the way I spoke to you. But everything had just piled up and—"

Santiago smiled, showed the thick set of braces Miguel had bought for him.

"Hey, you don't have to explain something so obvious. It's not like I'm a kid or something."

Miguel clapped a chastened expression on his face and turned to notice that his father was intently looking toward the bandstand, appraising the proceedings as if he hadn't a more serious thought on his mind.

"Okay, Papá, let's have it," Miguel muttered with a knowing smile. "You didn't come all the way over here just to listen to music."

"I went to the GI Forum this morning to see Antonio Vargas," José Luis said, still staring away. "Señor Vargas says that everybody in the barrio is still behind you."

It took Miguel a moment to figure out what his father was suggesting. "You want me to go back and stand trial?"

"Señor Vargas thinks you have a good chance."

"Listen, Papá, Antonio Vargas is many good things, but he is not the federal judge who will hear my case. Vargas may think I have a good chance, but there is an even better chance that if I go back to El Paso, you will have to return to Chihuahua without me."

José Luis made no immediate response. The orchestra had begun to play a polka. A wistful smile came over his face, and for a moment, he lost himself in the music.

Miguel sat down next to him and waited for his father to finally say what he had crossed the river to tell him. When José Luis finally spoke, his voice seemed soft as a distant memory.

"This is the Mexico I remember, Miguel, the music of my childhood...of a time when all things seemed possible. But as a man grows older, his dreams finally become those of his children."

"What about your dream, Papá? The dream of someday going home to Mexico."

Turning to study the earnest faces of his two sons, José Luis chuckled. "That was my dream. But in truth, none of my sons ever really shared it with me. Raúl was born wanting to leave Mexico. Santiago now has his friends and his future on the other side of the river."

José Luis paused to smile fondly at Santiago. The boy seemed happily surprised by what his father had said. José Luis turned to Miguel. "And you, Miguel, who fought so bravely in a great war, you have truly earned your place in the United States. And if it does not turn out like we hoped, not yet at least, well, very little in life ever does…but that should not keep us from trying as hard as we can."

José Luis looked toward the bandstand. The young musicians were still playing the polka. Miguel sat watching them and marveled at how gracefully his father had accepted the death of his dream.

Noting his expression, José Luis smiled and softly shook Miguel's shoulder. "Don't look so sad.Worse things could happen to us than having to stay in the United States," he said brightly, though when he rose to his feet, Miguel noticed that his father's eyes, as if pulled by a magnet, slowly turned southward.

"I know what it has cost you, Papá, to come and tell me this," Miguel muttered, walking around to face his father. "But the decision to go back across the river must be my own. Can you understand that?"

José Luis appeared bemused. "Understand it? I insist on it! Now I can return to your mother with a clear conscience. But you must let us know of your decision as soon as possible, so we can make the arrangements."

Miguel smiled and leaned down slightly so that his father could kiss him on the forehead, something he had not done for many years. José Luis seemed touched by the gesture.

Santiago, having listened respectfully to all that had been said, remembered something. Reaching into his pocket, he said, "Oh, hey, I almost forgot! Here, I brought these over for you. I thought they might help you make the right decision."

Miguel peered down at the war medals and service ribbons in his brother's hand. Each one carried with it an indelible memory. "Thank you, Santiago," Miguel quietly said, taking the medals and battle ribbons. Then he turned back to his father.

"I'll let you know soon as I decide. And tell my mother not to worry, eh? Like you said, things could be worse."

CHAPTER 39

Miguel had never been inside his favorite bar in the middle of the day. In the harsh light streaming in from the open door, it looked tawdry and rather filthy, reeking of strong disinfectant. Ordering a drink at the bar, he was wondering what had attracted him to such a place when he noticed a small group of men coming down the steps.

He turned away, not having come into the cantina looking for company. But one of the men already had recognized him. Breaking away from his companions, who were settling into a booth near the steps, the man walked toward the bar.

"Hello, soldier!"

Sliding onto a stool next to Miguel, Casillas loudly called out to the bartender. "Hey, wake up and pour me a double Scotch." Then, with a sardonic smile, he turned to Miguel. "I'm celebrating. I just joined the unemployed this morning—and if you think it was easy to get fired from that junkyard where I was working, you know nothing about the jalopy business!"

The bartender arrived with the Scotch, which Casillas promptly threw down. Then, noticing Miguel's cane, he asked, "Say, how good can you walk without that thing? Better, I hope, than I can flag down a baseball with my right hand, eh?"

Miguel thought for a moment, giving the question more importance than it deserved. He was trying to slow Casillas down. "Captain, you are the first person who has asked me that since I got home from the war."

"What the hell did you expect, soldier?" Casillas barked back. "We're the only ones who remember what it cost us to win that war!"

Miguel looked away. Once before, when he had run into Casillas at the homecoming banquet, their conversation had left Miguel feeling like a total stranger to his old comrade-in-arms. Now, thinking this might be another such occasion, he drew back into the illusory safety of silence.

Casillas was not so drunk he didn't notice Miguel's sudden coolness. "There I go again, old Charley One-Note, huh?" he said with a lame smile. "Hey, I read about your troubles in the newspaper. If there is anything I can do for you, it will soon be the time to ask. You see, I never say no to anything or anybody while in a state of inebriation. Don't bother looking it up. It means dead drunk."

"I would like to get your advice, Captain," Miguel said finally. "What do you think I ought to do?"

Casillas glanced over at the bartender, indicating that he wanted his drink done again. "Forget what you ought to do. What do you want to do?"

Miguel tried to mask his disappointment. His query had been answered by another question.

"I'm still not sure. Thinking about going back to Chihuahua; maybe start a little business with my father."

"Mexico! That's where I ought to go myself. Maybe down there they still know how to treat a professional soldier."

The bartender reappeared. Casillas gulped down his drink, and then banged the heavy glass on the bar. The bartender chuckled, this time at the ready with another load.

Watching Casillas drowning himself in alcohol, Miguel was growing sick of the stench of Casillas's self-pity.

"I took your advice, Captain, about not testifying before that army board of inquiry."

"Good," Casillas boomed. "You think our own people would like hearing how we were treated? That we were as expendable as a load of garbage—the poor brown little soldiers nobody else in the entire fucking American army cared about losing. Hell, maybe that's what the 'E' in E Company stood for—the Expendables—because that's all we were!"

Casillas had flung forth his words in a flurry of bursts and now stepped back, like a fighter who has thrown everything he has and waits for his opponent to fall.

But Miguel did not fall, though he was aware there was some truth in what Casillas had said. Yet he also knew that what had been done to his rifle company at the Rápido River was not enough to condemn the entire American army. It was still a young army and a young country, and both could change for the better.

Casillas, of course, would think such a feeling naive. But Miguel now remembered something he had read in an army hospital: 'A cynic knows the price of everything, and the value of nothing.'

"Captain, if the American army is so rotten, why are you trying so hard to stay in it?"

The question caught Casillas flatfooted. When he finally responded, his voice had a more respectful tone. "Why? Because a soldier can at least fight back against something. But as civilians, who the hell can we fight?"

Miguel nodded. He had often experienced the same feeling. "So what's the answer," he softly asked. "Where's the best place for a couple of old 'expendables' like us to go?"

Finishing off his drink, Casillas stared out across the dusty, light-dappled cantina, toward where his friends were sitting. "We found it, soldier," he quietly said.

Turning away, Miguel saw that Casillas's friends were still happily chattering away about their wartime heroics. Yet they were, he thought, a rather somber sight; though most of the men were still rather young, the best time of their lives seemed to already have passed them by.

Now they would probably spend the remainder of their days trying to recapture those shining moments in one dimly lit bar after another.

"I better get going, Captain."

Casillas spun around, a subtle urgency shadowing his smile. "No, come on, stick around! I know my pals over there would be real pleased to meet you."

Glancing back at the veterans, Miguel drew forth a wad of bills from his pocket. "Some other time. But tell your friends their next round is on me."

Half-saluting his former commander, Miguel started for the steps that led up to the street. Casillas glumly watched him go and then noticed that Miguel had left a few small army medals amongst the money he had laid on the bar.

"Private Salazar," Casillas called out. "You left some of your medals back here."

Miguel looked back. He seemed to be weighing some unseen substance. "My mother still has the big one in a little box at home. Those others...I think I'll try to make it without them for a while. Good luck, Captain."

Saying that, Miguel struggled up the steps and out into the glaring sunlight. Casillas sat staring at the discarded medals. Finally picking them up, he wove over to his friends, who were still proudly recounting their wartime experiences.

It was about noon when Miguel came out of the hotel. Shouldering his army duffel bag, he started for the river. At the bridge, almost all the pedestrian traffic was moving south, people returning home after having worked the previous week in El Paso. High above the long span of steel and concrete, the flags of Mexico and the United States flapped briskly in the wind.

Nearing the far end of the bridge, Miguel glanced back for a moment, and saw the young coin catcher watching him from the south bank of the river. Miguel waved to him, and wondered if the boy was hoping he might return to Juárez that night. Miguel had always tossed him at least fifty cents; most tourists never dropped him more than a few pennies.

He felt a sudden concern for the boy, and for that he was grateful. For a fleeting moment, he could forget his own troubles. He glanced up to see that the sky was growing darker. Rain was death for the tourist trade, but if the clouds stayed to the north, it might yet be a profitable night for his young coin-catching friend.

Coming to the far end of the bridge, Miguel stopped at the U.S. Customs booth. An officer stepped out and curtly asked him to declare his citizenship, something Miguel had been asked every time he had crossed back to his barrio in El Paso.

This time it seemed as if he had never been asked the question. The officer stood waiting for Miguel's answer, and seemed anxious to get back to the football game being broadcast over a small radio in the customs booth.

"Citizenship?" he brusquely repeated.

In the next few seconds, four years filled with people, places and passions flashed through Miguel's mind. Then, with just a trace of a rueful smile, he quietly answered.

"American."

PART TWO

CHAPTER 1

Francisco Salazar had found his rightful time and place in the Rio Grande Valley of south Texas. His son was not so fortunate. In 1950, Alejandro Salazar had roamed as far from the rich, red soil of the valley as the Korean War could take him. Now, he was reluctantly returning because he had found no other place he could call home. The word home once meant a great deal to him, but he now regard-ed it just another four-letter word. He felt he had not had a real home since his family left Chihuahua City that cold December morning in 1941.

As his bus went thumping down the tar-streaked, two-lane blacktop, he remembered another long bus journey, the arduous trek he and his father and mother had taken in the hope of soon being reunited with the rest of the family in El Paso.

Had it really been little more than ten years ago? It felt more like fifty! Or maybe that was simply how many different places he had lived in since that day he waved goodbye to his Uncle José Luis and the rest of the family. But a misunderstanding had taken him and his family in the one direction, his uncle's family in another; a mistake that had deeply mauled the last ten years of his life. The journey had started in a village whose name he could no longer remember and ended in a town whose name he would never forget. There his mother had died, and there he had come to hate his father.

The battered old bus came whining off the highway and, shuddering into a lower gear, went groaning past the ten blocks that comprised the downtown part of Mission, Texas. Alejandro rose from his seat. Tugging tight the tunic of his Marine Corps uniform, he grabbed his sea bag.

At the far end of the tiny town was the one-pump gas station that doubled as the local bus depot. Alejandro had left from this same station the day he went off to enlist in the Marines. He was returning at almost the same time of late afternoon.

The station was as he remembered it — the same young, rather slow-witted attendant, still sucking on a Coca-Cola, the same small cluster of sour-faced old men sitting in their unraveling wicker chairs, waiting for something that might break the monotony of their afternoon.

Not much of a homecoming, he mused. But then he had not expected a brass band. How different this welcoming committee was from the one that had greeted his cousin Miguel in El Paso. Some seven years earlier, Santiago had written him about it in great detail. Alejandro had cherished that letter. But now, making his way toward the door of the bus, he wished he had never received it.

Miguel had returned from a war that ended with the blare of victorious trumpets; Alejandro's war had faded away to the muted strings of a stalemate. Miguel had come home to a tumultuous welcome, and even though serious charges later had been leveled against him, his good fortune had held steady. He had been acquitted, and now co-owned a successful gasoline station and auto repair shop in the south side of El Paso.

How much good luck could any one Mexican have? Alejandro wondered. There was only so much of it, and perhaps his cousin had already been given the family's entire quota.

As the bus limped to a stop under the station's tattered canopy, the old men craned their necks to see who might be disembarking. They seemed disappointed that only a single passenger, a stranger at that, had come off the bus. Alejandro stood looking around in the vague hope of spotting a familiar face. Nobody was waiting for him.

Noddeding politely to the old men, he shouldered his sea bag and started off toward a nearby migrant worker camp. He had wired his Uncle Pedro from San Antonio that he would be arriving in Mission that afternoon, but knew that there were few more efficient ways of wasting money than to try and reach a farm worker by telegram.

He had not bothered to advise his father of his arrival, nor had he written him a single letter in the two years he was away. He still remembered the deep chasm that had existed between them, a breach born by the death of his mother.

But as he came around the station, his frown gave way to a surprised smile. His Uncle Pedro, looking half asleep, sat perched up on a dilapidated contraption that vaguely resembled a car. Rousing himself to disentangle his body from the machine, he smiled. In the two years since Alejandro had last seen him, his uncle's hair had gone completely white, though Pedro was still in his mid-forties.

The two men silently embraced. Pedro, too overcome with emotion to speak, took Alejandro's bag and laid it in the car's rumble seat, and then hauled forth a piece of plywood, which he placed over the exposed springs on the far side of the front seat.

"Got a new old car, eh?" Alejandro asked as he warily eased himself onto the makeshift cushion.

"All mine when I make the last three-dollar payment," Pedro replied as he began to hand-crank the motor.

After several cranks, the engine started. A small flame instantly burst up from the manifold. The car had no hood, and the sight of the engine catching fire startled Alejandro.

"No, don't worry, only a little leak from the carburetor. It bums off quick," Pedro muttered, climbing behind the wheel. Grinding the car into gear, he took it into a wide turn and down a dirt road that began to curve through country colorfully painted with ripe produce.

For the first few miles they drove along in silence. Alejandro, knowing that the subject of his father would eventually come up, finally asked, "Did he know I was coming home today?"

"I show him the telegram," Pedro exclaimed. "Your father wanted to come with me to meet the bus, but—"

"But then he heard about some farm worker who hadn't been paid, or been mistreated or whatever, and off he charged like old Don Quixote himself, eh?" Alejandro said, trying to smile. No sense, he thought, making his uncle any more uncomfortable, caught as he had been for the last several years, between his last two living relatives.

Pedro seemed relieved. "Your father is getting ready for a big meeting with the growers next week. Did you know he now speaks for many of the farm workers in the valley?"

"Including a woman I hear is more than twenty years younger than him."

Pedro seemed stuck for a reply. When he finally spoke, his voice gave hint of battles between his heart and his head. "It kills me to say it, but in many ways she is better for your father than was my own sister Juanita," Pedro muttered. "Yes, she is young. But she is also strong."

Alejandro frowned. "I don't give a damn if she's got a cast- iron crotch. My father has to live with her, not me."

"Before you decide to hate her, you should at least meet her," Pedro protested. "Did two years in the Marines not teach you to shoot only when you were sure of the target?"

"I don't plan to get close enough to shoot her."

"Oh, yes, you will, Pedro growled. "She and Francisco will be at your fiesta tonight at Mendoza Creek."

Alejandro flinched. "I don't think so, Uncle Pedro. I want to stop off now and see my mother. Then later, I have to go talk to the Señorita Devereaux. So better let me off here."

Up ahead, just beyond a large arbor pregnant with ripe peaches, a small patch of rickety crosses stretched toward the crest of a grassy hill. Pedro slowed the car down like a pilot nervously approaching a makeshift landing field.

"What business can you have with the Señorita Devereaux?" The query sounded more like an accusation.

"I have been waiting for that question for the last seven-thousand miles. But I didn't return from so far away just to go back to work in the fields. The day I left here, the Señorita said she would have a job waiting for me. Now, with your permission, I plan to take it."

Pedro brought the car to a stop below the graveyard. He sat gazing at it for a few moments. "Your mother always thought you were a very smart boy. But smart is not wise. And remember that old *dicho*: Be careful what you chase, because you might catch it."

Pedro found his smile again. "And here is a saying of my own: if you think you can get out of coming to your own homecoming fiesta—that I personally spent more than two weeks' worth of wages on—then you are not as smart as your mother thought."

Alejandro chuckled. Climbing down from the car, he stood looking toward the little pauper's plot where his mother was buried. He felt as if he were standing at the portals of a church he had not entered in too long a time.

"Okay, Uncle Pedro. I'll see you tonight."

Pedro grunted. Grinding into gear, he went clanking away. Alejandro waited until the machine disappeared and then started up the slope toward his mother's grave.

Its wooden cross had been repainted many times over the past ten years, and always the selection had depended on his mood. Now it was a fresh, forest green. His uncle had chosen a good color, he decided. Not overly bright, but better than the black he had used so many times.

Kneeling beside the grave, he was stirred by a sudden thought as he noticed an old newspaper blowing nearby: the thousands of newspapers, magazines and books he had read in the years since his mother had died. He hoped that she was somehow aware that he had managed to round out his meager formal education in a way that would have pleased her. He also recalled the dozens of grade schools he had attended in the valley, and the many Anglo teachers who had taken the time to give him additional instruction—kind people who had often gone out of their way to praise him in front of his mother.

Then Alejandro realized that he had forgotten to bring fresh flowers. For now, all he could place at the base of the wooden cross were the decorations on his uniform: the Bronze Star he had won for valor under fire and his battle ribbons from the Korean War. Together, they carried the history of much that had happened to him over the last two most dangerous years of his life.

By the time he got to the migrant camp, the sun had sunk from sight. Yet even in the soft reddish light, the settlement seemed as squalid as he had remembered it. The tar-paper hovels, home to more than a hundred people, looked much the same as the one in which his mother had died.

He had just walked into the camp when a little girl shyly approached him. Was he the soldier everyone was expecting? When he nodded, she gave him precise instructions on how to get to the site of the fiesta. Speaking rapidly, she ran her sentences together as if she had memorized the words. Alejandro smiled. His uncle was apparently taking no chances that he might not attend his own homecoming.

"Gracias, muchachita," Alejandro replied. "Pero mira, ¿no quieres ir conmigo? Pienso que van a tener muchas cosas sabrosas de comer."

He had invited the little girl to the fiesta, where there would probably be many delicious things to eat. The child hesitated for a moment. Then, in a voice so soft he could hardly hear her, she politely refused. There was, she murmured, a hot meal waiting for her at home.

But her eyes, made larger by the gauntness of her face, told him otherwise. He had often seen this strange streak of pride in migrant children, but knew that in another few years she would have it beaten out of her. Then, with childhood collapsing behind her, she would become like most other migrants—humbly grateful for a decent meal, and not overly concerned with whatever she'd had to sacrifice to get it.

As she walked away, Alejandro asked an old woman if the little girl might come with him to a fiesta. Where were her parents? Her father was dead, and the girl's mother was sick. The old woman was sure it would be alright if she was brought home right after she had eaten.

Alejandro quickly caught up with the little girl. Gently taking her hand, he coaxed her off in the direction of the fiesta. "¿Como te llamas?" he asked.

"Ilsita Villareal," she shyly murmured.

Alejandro smiled down at her and walked out of the camp as fast as her short strides could manage. He had, over the past two years, often dreamt about this same camp. Even now it seemed something out of a nightmare. Open sewage lines, leaky water pipes, and piles of rotting garbage had made the camp a rat-infested quagmire.

As he walked clear of the foul-smelling mud, he vowed that this camp, along with many others, would someday have to be drastically improved. His father had obviously failed, though more because of bad strategy, he thought, than for lack of good intentions. So the war would have to be fought not only against the growers who owned such squalid camps, but against his father, as well. Alejandro had been waiting to wage this battle since the night his mother had died.

CHAPTER 2

As he drew closer to a wooded patch that sloped down to the edge of a creek, Alejandro noticed a ragged strip of canvas hanging between some trees:

Welcome Home Lance Corporal Alejandro Salazar

With his young companion still in tow, he cautiously advanced. Several people began to applaud, as he slowly made his way forward, shaking hands with many of the men in the crowd. Old remembrances were exchanged until he reached the table of honor.

His father rose from the table. The crowd quieted down. The men stood studying each other. In the few years since they had seen each other, both had changed. Alejandro thought his father looked more impressive, his long, wavy hair now heavily flecked with gray, as was his thick mustache. But there was a stoop to his shoulders. He no longer looked as tall as he once had.

Francisco had noted some changes. Alejandro's body had filled out in the Marine Corps, but his five-foot, ten-inch frame didn't appear to carry so much as an ounce of fat. He had become better looking, Francisco decided — and his strong features and steady manner gave notice that he would not be an easy man to push around. His mother, Francisco thought, would be proud of him.

Like diplomats representing unfriendly nations, father and son warily shook hands. But Pedro had by now drunk enough beer to suddenly give vent to an urge he had long suppressed. Taking hold of both men with his powerful arms, he pulled them closer to each other. With no other recourse, they awkwardly embraced.

A cheer came from the crowd of some fifty people, as an old accordionist struck up a corrido. Women hurried forward with plates of steaming rice, beans, and the ribbons of beef which Pedro had been marinating for the past several hours.

"Alejandro, meet my woman, María Antón," Francisco abruptly announced, glancing toward the young woman at the other end of the table.

In the gauzed light coming from a kerosene lamp, Alejandro could see that she was about thirty, with lustrous black hair which fell to her shoulders. She had heavily lashed brown eyes, a ripe, plum-colored mouth, and teeth that were slightly oversized but brilliant and even. Among migrant workers, good-looking teeth were as rare as a three-figure bank account. María Antón was, Alejandro thought, one of the most striking-looking women he had ever seen. His past feelings toward his father suddenly were tinged with an unexpected emotion — envy.

"Welcome home, Corporal Salazar," María murmured, extending her hand. Shaking it, Alejandro coolly replied, "Thank you. But my home was in the Marine Corps. It feels good, though, to be back in the sunshine of Texas. It got a little cold over in Korea." He started to turn away, but María quickly reclaimed his attention. "Well, I feel I already know you," she exclaimed, smiling. "Your father has shown the newspaper clippings about your Marine division around so much, the paper is falling apart — "

"Ay, Maria, don't tell him that," Francisco grumbled. "He will think he's important as a general."

"The only important thing I did over in Korea was get out of there alive," Alejandro quietly replied.

His Uncle Pedro scoffed. "Hah, how did this Salazar get so humble? Not from his father, for sure!"

The crowd laughed. The first dangerous shoal had been safely traversed. Alejandro turned toward another table. His companion had already torn into her plate of food. Catching her eye, he winked. Ilsita Villareal smiled bashfully and went on eating.

Two hours later, most of the guests had taken their leave in that deeply polite manner poor people often have. Alejandro had shaken each and every hand. Now, grateful the evening was almost over, he sat down to listen to the plaintive sound of a guitar coming from along the edge of the creek.

At the other end of the table, his father looked rather drunk. He was showing a set of newspaper clippings to an old man who had joined the party late. Paquito had been one of Francisco's first organizers, and once served in the military of his adopted country. During the First World War, he fought in the Battle of the Argonne, returning home without a scratch. Ironically, soon after coming back to a farm worker job in Texas, he had fallen off a rickety ladder, fracturing his elbow. Too poor to pay for proper medical attention, he had permanently lost the use of his left arm.

Watching Paquito intently studying the clippings that everyone knew he couldn't read, Alejandro smiled. The night his mother had died, Paquito had stood praying just outside the shack. Alejandro still remembered the old man's kind and consoling words.

"Hey, look at this one here," Francisco was saying, displaying another tattered clipping. "This boy's outfit was the best. They didn't call it the First Marine Division for nothing, eh?"

Paquito seemed to smile, though it was hard to tell for sure. He had lost most of his teeth, and a bushy mustache covered much of his upper lip. "True, Don Francisco," he exclaimed, using the respectful form he sometimes employed when addressing him. "But what will this great warrior of yours do, now that he is home from the war?"

Alejandro winced. The question he hoped to avoid on this, his first night back, had finally been asked. Pedro saw the collision coming, and like a clown trying to divert an approaching bull, he began to wave his arms around.

"Hey, you people drunk or what?" Pedro protested. "The boy just finished fighting a war where he wins a medal for bravery and almost freezes to death. Now he is home for only a few hours and already everybody wants him out tomorrow picking peaches!"

Some people nearby laughed. But all those at his own table turned toward Alejandro. In the pale yellow light, their unblinking stare made them look, he thought, like large owls.

He took another sip of beer, and said, "I do plan to start work tomorrow morning—at a job that might someday make me enough money to get my own farm."

A silence fell over the table. "You plan to rob a bank, or what?" Francisco asked with icy politeness.

When Alejandro hesitated, his uncle again stepped into the breach. "That is a crazy," Pedro exclaimed. "Anyway, on this next harvest, we hope to get at least sixty-three cents an hour—"

"Yes, I know. Señorita Devereaux told me the growers were giving you all a raise," Alejandro murmured.

"Who told you?" Francisco barked, abruptly rising.

Alejandro ignored the question. "Tomorrow morning, I go to work full-time for the Devereaux farm."

The first blow had been struck. His father's counter punch, however, was freighted with more force. "What job can she offer to the son of a migrant worker, other than to betray his own people?" Francisco asked, slowly coming forward.

Alejandro rose and squared his shoulders. He knew that if his father tried to slap him, as he had done so often in the past, he would not only ward off the blow, but deliver one of his own. Two years in the Marine Corps had filed a hair-trigger on his reflexes.

"Señorita Devereaux told me times are changing. She wants to change with them. Now that the war is over, she hopes the growers can work with the migrants...make things better for everybody. My job will be to help the workers on her farm in any way I can. Labor-management relations, she calls it."

Francisco was now so close Alejandro could smell the beer on his breath. "So that's what she calls it, eh? I have another name for it. But whatever we call it, tomorrow morning you go give it back to her!"

In the silence that followed, everyone but Maria and Pedro quietly took their leave. Alejandro waited for his uncle to again intercede—and was surprised when it was María who came to his defense.

"Forgive me, Francisco, but the boy has just returned from fighting a great war. Who can blame him for thinking he has earned something better for himself?"

Alejandro frowned. It annoyed him that she had called him a boy. Turning back to his father, he said, "And I did not struggle through that war, Papá, just to come home to a sixty-three cent an hour job."

Francisco's expression slowly softened, though when he spoke, a sarcastic stain still stuck to his words. "Now we must say good night. We have to get up very early to go on earning the forty-eight cents an hour your new employer is still so generously paying us."

A wave of relief swept through Alejandro's body as he watched his father move off into the darkness. María Antón also seemed relieved. Firing a furtive smile in Alejandro's direction, she hurried on after his father.

Only Pedro lingered behind to issue a warning. Later, Alejandro would remember his exact words. But for now he smiled. His Uncle Pedro had done all he could to make the homecoming fiesta a festive occasion.

"Thank you, Uncle Pedro. It was a fine fiesta."

The compliment did not seem to register. "Alejandro, it is right that you come home expecting more than you had. But careful how you get it, so you do not lose something of yourself that you can never replace."

Their eyes held for a moment. Then, with a wry smile, Pedro gently cuffed Alejandro on the chin. "When you get sleepy, come to my shack. I make up a cot for you, eh?"

Alejandro nodded. But he had already vowed he would never again sleep in a migrant camp. Listening as his uncle's footsteps faded away, he thought of the three-mile trek he would have to make back into town to get a motel room for the night. But already he felt as tired as if he had walked home from the war. Fighting with his father had always left him feeling as if he had been physically beaten.

Removing the coat of his uniform, he looked around for something he might use for a pillow. His eye fell on the canvas banner. Taking it down, he rolled it up, and laid out on one of the wooden benches. What had his cousin's first night home from the war been like? He had always loved and admired Miguel and would forever remember that his cousin had once saved both him and his mother from a watery grave. If only Miguel were here now to lend him support and advice, Alejandro thought, realizing that though he had just returned from one war, another had already begun.

CHAPTER 3

Margaret's father had died recently, leaving her the stewardship of one of the largest farms in south Texas. The farm had first been established back around the turn of the century, rumor having it that Margaret's grandfather had won its initial five acres in a poker game.

Her father, François, had not been so lucky. His wife had died of a brain tumor when Margaret, their only child, was ten years old. Thereafter, the Frenchman raised his daughter like the male heir he would never sire. Later, he sent her to the University of Texas, where she became one of the first women to earn a degree in agronomy.

While she was away in college, Devereaux's benevolence— always part of his nature—grew. Despite a melancholy personality and the constant pressure brought upon him by his fellow growers, he was warmhearted toward the migrants who worked on his farm. His camp was the cleanest, the best-equipped of any in the entire valley. The other growers often came to complain that he was spoiling his farm workers. When they did, Devereaux would simply smile and retreat to his library without even saying goodbye. Margaret had inherited both her father's compassion for poor people and a profound contempt for the opinions of his peers.

The Devereaux place sat on a slight rise, dominating the view for many miles around. The main room of the house was the operations center. Erosion maps, weather charts, blight-testing devices, and numerous items of the sort—all part of Margaret's recent effort to modernize the organization—filled the room. But the past had not been forgotten. Hung high over a massive fireplace was an oil painting of her father.

Alejandro had never seen such a large room, not in a house at least. He was ushered into the room by a middle-aged, angular-faced black man—the farm's foreman in all but official title since the death of Margaret's father.

Years earlier, François Devereaux had removed Sam Winslow from the fields. The Frenchman had called it a "cultural experiment." He hired a tutor to give the young black what amounted to a high school education, all the while allowing the boy to learn as much as he could about farming without making a complete nuisance of himself. The experiment proved such a success that Margaret now relied on the soft-spoken Negro to a degree that had tarnished the relationship with her other employees, as well as with Sam's own people. Like many Mexicans, most blacks in the valley always assumed that if one of their own achieved success, it had to be at the expense of selling out their moral principles.

At the far end of the pine-floored room, Margaret was intently studying a map that indicated the exact number of fruit-bearing trees on her property. Standing behind her was a lean, hard-eyed man of about sixty; a good five inches over six feet, and completely bald, his presence was commanding if not downright threatening. Strother Finnegan carried the title of foreman; a title Sam Winslow had earned many times over but had never been given.

Margaret smiled, and beckoned Alejandro closer. She was now almost forty, but her blue eyes still shone brightly against her sunburned skin and closely cropped blonde hair. In the two years since Alejandro had last seen her, she had acquired the relaxed assurance common to self-made men, not surprising since her father had raised her to act like one.

He remembered that his own mother had always been fond of this tall, lanky woman who was invariably kind and helpful to the migrants who worked for her father.

"You're early, Alex. Thought it'd take you most of the day to get squared away," she said as a way of welcoming him.

"Didn't have that much to do. Got some civilian clothes, rented a room, and bought an old car."

"Hope it's reliable, you're gonna be racing around a lot."

"It got me here today. Now I'm ready to go to work. I like the idea of a job where I don't have to carry a rifle."

Margaret chuckled, and turned to the man standing behind her. "Let's hope you don't end up wishing you still had one. You know my foreman, don't you?"

"Hello, Señor Finnegan."

"Hello, Salazar," the foreman grunted. His handshake was gruff, as was the unspoken message that came with it. Margaret had hired Alejandro, but it would be him who would fire him.

Margaret caught the same message. With a mirthless laugh, she turned back to Alejandro. "Strother thinks I'm crazier than a Brahma bull for taking you on steady here."

Alejandro flinched. He already seemed in danger of losing his job before he'd even started it. Reading his expression, Margaret smiled ruefully. "But since I never make mistakes, little ones at least, you should work out fine." Margaret turned toward the black man. "But just to make sure, I want you to stick tighter than tar to Sam here. What he doesn't know about running this farm can be put on the head of a pin. Right, Sam?"

"You doing all the talking, Miss Margaret," Sam muttered, avoiding the foreman's eyes. Alejandro glanced over at Finnegan. Margaret's remark did not seem to have pleased him.

The migrants arriving for the upcoming harvest had brought with them a full load of problems: children sick with measles and mumps and riddled with rickets. Over the next few days, Alejandro spent most of his time driving into town for medicine and taking pregnant women to the local clinic. Margaret had empowered him to sign for all medical expenses, and he felt strangely proud in doing so. He also felt sad; ten years earlier, a single bottle of inexpensive medicine might have saved his mother's life; soul-satisfying work, and each evening he returned to his rented room exhausted but content. He was making three hundred dollars a month and meals, if he wanted them, in the kitchen of the Devereaux house. Within the next three or four years, he figured to be able to save enough money to make a down payment on a small farm of his own.

There was, however, another reason behind his sense of satisfaction. If Margaret's enlightened attitude proved contagious, it might spread to every farm in the valley, and hence do away with the need for a farm workers' union. Contented workers did not join labor causes, even those headed by men as respected as his father. Alejandro still believed that his father's obsession with the movement had claimed the life of his mother.

Returning from work one night, he wrote a long letter to his cousin Miguel. For years they had been writing each other. Miguel

241

had sent him a little money at least once a month. In every letter Alejandro ever wrote his cousin, he had always tried to stress the positive, though at times this had taxed his creative abilities, as well as sorely tested the truth.

This time, there was plenty of good news to report, and for a change it was all accurate.

CHAPTER 4

The lobby of the finest hotel in the Rio Grande Valley was so filled with flags, posters, and memorabilia related to Texas, it seemed to be in some sovereign country which had no connection with the United States. This chauvinistic motif was enhanced by the two-dozen Stetsons neatly placed on a table — and one battered, sweat-streaked straw hat.

Pedro Terán and María Antón stood nearby. Since coming into the hotel, they had uttered hardly a word. Now they furtively glanced toward a set of closed doors. Behind those large mahogany doors, the growers of south Texas were holding their quarterly business meeting.

They had first grouped together to present a unified front to the wholesale produce chains that for years had played them off one against another. It was an uneasy alliance, jackals banding to kill a lion, each yearning for the largest share of the spoils.

Over the course of their two-day meeting, they had agreed on new prices, transportation costs, candidates for political office, and, almost as an afterthought, the working conditions and wages for their workers. Now, moments before the meeting was to be adjourned, they had invited in Francisco Salazar.

This was the first time he had been asked to one of their meetings — finally having become an unavoidable nuisance. For Francisco, this meeting would be the initial step in a journey he had been waiting to make for the past ten years. Only a few moments before he was asked into the room, Margaret introduced Alejandro to the growers. He had been hired to do a job, she said, that was in the best interests of all concerned. Her approach was pragmatic: farm workers nagged by health problems and worried about the welfare of their families were simply not as productive.

Margaret's short speech was not well-received.

Francisco's speech met with the same reaction. He wanted a fifteen-cent an hour raise on the upcoming harvest, better sanitation facilities, fresh drinking water, and a far cheaper charge for the food the growers were to provide his workers. It galled the growers that he had mentioned these benefits as if they were the farm workers' God-given right.

A paunchy, white-haired man came to his feet. Bertram Agajanian was the most powerful grower in the valley — and looked it, with skin as coarse as a crocodile and shoulders that made him seem wide as a water buffalo. "Six cents, Salazar. Best we can do, all we can do. Take it or leave it."

The old grower was standing only a few feet away from Francisco. Alejandro, sitting near the rear of the room, girded himself. His father hated Agajanian, and over the years Alejandro had seen many of their discussions almost turn into physical brawls. But now his father simply smiled and shrugged, as if to say he'd tried his best and it hadn't been good enough. Alejandro knew him well enough to know that there was some danger lurking beneath his diffidence. Agajanian sensed the same thing.

"Now looky here, Francisco, I got some idea of what your workers have gone through," the grower murmured, changing tactics. "Hell, I was once dirt-poor myself, unlike some others here I could mention, but won't," he said, glancing in Margaret's direction. "But now we don't want to bring your folks along so fast we wreck the economy of this entire area, do we?"

Francisco, indicating the silver-inlaid boots the grower was wearing, he said, "My workers are doing so well now, they could buy a pair of boots like yours with only a half-year's worth of wages."

Margaret laughed. "I hope most migrants have enough good taste not to even want such a pair!"

Agajanian's heavily lidded eyes blinked a warning. It went ignored. Margaret did not know the elderly grower very well, but her father had detested him. Another grower rose slowly to his feet. Jake Hennessy was a dour, muscular man who only recently had been invited to join the growers' association, and had the fluttery look of a man whose status still seemed uncertain.

"But if Salazar keeps hitting us up for more money, I'm gonna have to hock my own boots," Hennessy said with a queasy smile, a remark rewarded by several sour frowns. Hennessy had made the mistake of dragging the issue down to a personal level.

Agajanian grimaced. Then, drawing forth a plug of chewing tobacco, he pulled up a chair and planted himself in front of Francisco. "Now listen, amigo, you go along with us on this upcoming harvest, and we might finally be able to give you that fifteen-cent-an-hour raise on the next one. Sound fair to you?"

"It sounds more like a broken phonograph record."

"You ain't being patriotic, friend," the old man purred, biting off a piece of chewing tobacco. "Ain't stopped to consider the welfare of the American consumer who—"

"Still the same old song, Señor," Francisco retorted.

Some of the other growers looked glum as pallbearers. They knew Francisco's nephew had won a Medal of Honor, and that his own son had been decorated for bravery in the more recent war. Patriotism was no longer a viable tactic, and most of the growers knew enough to keep the issue at half-mast.

The silence was broken by Jake Hennessy. "But, hell, Salazar, Miss Margaret here has already proved our good intentions by hiring on your boy full time."

Francisco twisted around in his chair to face his son. From a distance of fifty feet, the men studied each other. Alejandro was impressed with his father's calm yet gutsy manner, which reminded him of the skilled poker players he had known in the Marine Corps, men who had the ability to stay in a game, regardless of what weak hands they had been dealt.

"No, the thing it proves," Francisco finally said, "are the bad intentions of my son."

"You're right, amigo," Bert Agajanian quietly declared. "The only thing that ever proves anything is money." Taking up an empty liquor bottle, he began to stuff it with one hundred dollar bills. The grower knew enough, however, to beard the baldness of the bribe. "Now 'course this is strictly for the use of your workers. But maybe you could keep out just enough to buy yourself a new pair of work boots, huh?" Francisco smiled and looked down at his tattered boots.

The bottle kept moving, getting slightly heavier as it passed from hand to hand. But when it reached Margaret, the collection came to a momentary halt. "No, gentlemen, I didn't put young Salazar to work just so we could more easily buy off his father," she said, passing the bottle on to another contributor.

Agajanian's eyes narrowed. "Just like her Daddy, Miss Margaret does speak her mind," the crust-faced grower muttered with a slim smile. "But that didn't make either one of 'em always right."

The bottle, now crammed with money, passed back to Agajanian, who with a dramatic flourish, stuffed in another hundred-dollar bill. For most of the growers, carrying around a wad of such bills was a symbol of status, another way to prove to their peers that they were fully entitled to membership in the association.

Alejandro had intently watched as the bottle made its way around the room. Now he saw his father again turn back toward him.

"Well, my boy, if you are smart enough to advise the Señorita Devereaux on her labor problems, perhaps you can also tell me what to do about my own."

"Take the money, Papá," Alejandro quietly suggested. "Your workers can do a lot with twenty-seven hundred dollars."

Many of the growers smiled. Alejandro had seemed to have passed his first loyalty test. "Hey, if that don't beat all—he figured right down to the last dollar!" Hennessy exclaimed.

Francisco flashed a rueful grin. "My son has always been smart that way."

"Say, let's hope that there talent runs in the family," Agajanian smoothly murmured. 'Take the money, Frank. Hell, you've earned it."

Francisco slowly rose and stared at the elderly grower, who was wrapping the bottle with a newspaper. Alejandro waited for his father to finally explode. Instead Francisco took the bottle and said, "Well, maybe there are some things we don't always earn...but take them, anyway."

Agajanian emitted a satisfied snort and began to usher Francisco toward the door. "Sometimes we gotta go along to get along. But now you can prove your good intentions by getting all your folks signed up at the new six-cent rate and have 'em start off toward the harvest area. Okay, Frank?"

Nodding blankly, Francisco walked out the door.

A wave of satisfied smirks spread from grower to grower. He had just been bought off, they believed, with little more than pocket change and a pile of worthless promises. Alejandro knew, however, that their victory had come at too cheap a cost. Later, there might be a higher price to pay.

Back in the lobby of the hotel, Francisco's grimace gave way to a strange smile. He had gotten more than he'd hoped for. "A six-cent raise is all they claim they can afford," he said, as Pedro and María joined him.

"And you are smiling because they had you come all this way just to tell you again how poor they are, eh?" María asked. She sensed he was holding something back.

Francisco chuckled. "They also told me I should get a new pair of boots."

María and Pedro stood waiting for a punch line, but it never came. Instead, Francisco steered them toward the main door. "You drive back to the camp. I'll take a bus and be there in a few hours."

Reining back their curiosity, Pedro and María moved across the lobby, uncomfortably aware of the many frowns they were drawing from the hotel's well-dressed patrons. Waving them goodbye, Francisco ambled back to the long table to retrieve his straw hat.

Sam Winslow was standing next to it. "Say, maybe you ought to get a new sombreo to go along with the new boots, huh?"

The question sounded friendly. Francisco liked the black man, though he had always been on the wrong side. "Yes, my hat is almost as old as the last raise the growers gave us," Francisco said, fondly studying his battered straw hat. "Maybe I'll trade it in for one of these Stetsons."

"Whatever, careful it don't cost you more than you can afford to pay."

There seemed sincere concern in Sam's coffee-colored eyes, though why Francisco could not discern. Struck with a sudden impulse, he offered his hand to Sam. "Most honest talk I heard all morning."

A few moments later, as Francisco walked out into the daunting sunshine, he felt a great surge of relief. His long-awaited meeting with the growers had gone even better than he had hoped. He had not been given what he had secretly hoped not to get. But the twenty-seven hundred dollars was an unexpected bonus. Later, it might make the difference, he thought, between winning and losing.

CHAPTER 5

The old bus had stopped every few miles to take on passengers; now, fully loaded, it rolled steadily toward its final destination. Francisco sat looking out the window at the passing countryside. Every few miles there were concrete silos and cinder block warehouses, formidable as fortresses. Nearby, dozens of pieces of farm machinery seemed like a military motorized division, the pyramids of stacked produce its supply depot — symbols of the power held by an enemy he would soon be fighting.

The bus limped to its final stop. Passengers began to disembark. Yet for several seconds he made no move to follow them; his train of thought broken only when the bus driver irritably hit his air horn.

He had walked a mile down a dirt road when he came to a sign about half the size of a billboard. THE HENNESSY FARM "The Future Citrus King of the Rio Grande Valley." The ornate lettering set off by painted trumpets seemed an attempt to create the effect of a musical fanfare. Hennessy had been a fullback on his high school football team, but Francisco, along with a few growers themselves, thought he had played one game too many without his helmet. The man was about as stable as a runaway truck — and about as dangerous.

Arriving at the Hennessy camp, Francisco strode through an admiring throng of farm workers, and headed for the far end of the encampment — a distance of no more than a hundred yards, and usually taking no more a few minutes to cover. But on this day, he walked it more slowly than ever before. Sights he had once taken for granted suddenly seemed more hideous, perhaps because he now thought there might be a chance to finally correct some of them.

Mothers stood slack-shouldered under the shade of scrawny, blight-disfigured trees, holding the infants who were suckling from bottles of Coke. Old men, a few with cataracts so thick they could hardly see, were trying to repair shacks that mocked their efforts. Francisco knew that they were simply trying to remain useful, as were the old women who served as the water-bearers.

Pedro was working under an abandoned packing shed. He had laid out several tools borrowed from as many people and was starting to fix the carburetor on his Model-A when Francisco appeared on the other side of the car. He said nothing, simply smiled, but it was enough to alert Pedro that something was in the wind. Wrapping the tools up, Pedro laid them in the car's jump seat, as Francisco climbed aboard the plywood on the passenger's side.

Pedro started the engine. As usual, it burst into flames, a startling sight Francisco usually sardonically commented on, but this time he said nothing. Pedro knew now that his earlier premonition was correct.

Halfway out of the camp, they were flagged down by María Antón, her eyes blazing with expectancy—but seeing the rigid cast on his face, she silently climbed into the rear jump seat.

All the way to the main highway and for miles beyond it, Francisco did not utter a word. María was annoyed and bewildered but uncertain as to how best to pry open his thoughts, she remained quiet. A few hours earlier, María and Pedro had been stunned by his easy acceptance of the growers' token raise of six cents, an offer that had not included any provision for more sanitary camp facilities, better food or safer transportation—everything Francisco had fought for years to win.

Yet instinct told María that he had a plan. What now distressed her was that the man who was both her lover and her leader was not confiding in her.

Angry and confused, she silently listed all the reasons why his lack of confidence was unjustified. She was hardly a newcomer to the cause, but a seasoned soldier who had been battling the growers since she was old enough to work in their fields.

Years before, her parents had drowned when their overloaded migrant bus had plunged into an irrigation ditch. For a long time afterward, she had been passed like a keepsake from one poor family to another.

She had just turned twenty when she met Francisco, and from that moment on, she was his most ardent admirer and loyal lieutenant. But it had only been in the last year that her admiration had ripened into love. Now there was nothing she wouldn't do for him—except allow him to be less than the great man she thought he was. But though she loved him more than any man she had ever known, she would not allow him to deny her the important rank her experience had earned her.

Francisco now spoke for more than three hundred farm workers. In ten long years of struggle, he had created a loosely formed federation comprised of a sizable portion of the migrants in the valley. The workers attended the federation's monthly meetings, complained as much as they wanted, and went back to work the following day grumbling that things were not changing as fast as they should.

But for the few cents a week they paid in dues, the federation was a bargain—a way to renew old friendships and bask in the feeling that they were members of a community, rather than the homeless nomads they had become in order to stay alive. Among these workers, Francisco was greatly admired—more for his aspirations than for his achievements. But if he was their captain, there were other men who were the lieutenants, each holding as much power in his own camp as Francisco did over the organization. And these men rarely agreed on even the time of day.

Thus, to steer the leaders towards any specific goal was like fishing with a badly-frayed line; Francisco had to be careful not to put too much weight on it, lest it break into separate pieces, none strong enough to serve any useful purpose. Many a catch had been lost in just such a way, though the line had sometimes proved tough enough to pull in a few minor concessions from the growers.

Maria sensed that Francisco was about to test the line as it had never been tested before.

Late that afternoon, Pedro's car rolled past a small green and white sign: Devereaux Farm—Delivering Quality Produce for Three Generations. The truth, simply stated, apparently needed no trumpets.

Francisco, along with Pedro and María, had been to several other camps that afternoon, and compared to any of them, the Devereaux camp seemed a refuge. Though cheaply made, it was designed for people, rather than pigs, and rare was the migrant family that didn't feel fortunate to return to it.

Margaret was considered the most liberal grower in the valley. To Francisco, she was simply the smartest—a university-educated woman who knew that the agricultural business could not remain forever untouched by the labor movement. What made Margaret a formidable adversary was that she seemed keenly aware that the better she treated her workers, the longer it would take for a farmworker union to become a reality.

Francisco knew that she had inherited her father's compassion for poor people, but also realized that she, like her father before her, was of a breed that would gladly give a man a dollar before they would, under the threat of duress, loan him a dime. He felt the same way himself.

Hence he had always had a grudging admiration and even secret affection for her, though he would have much preferred to hate her, as he did all the other growers. Hate was a more useful emotion.

CHAPTER 6

On on an elevated railroad siding, a long-faced elderly man was encamped behind a table, several sheets of paper, a hand-cranking adding machine and a metal box at his side. The Devereaux paymaster spoke with a Germanic accent, betraying an origin that had made him unpopular during the Second World War. But the soft-spoken old man was more American than most of the people who had harassed him. His family had arrived in Texas during the last quarter of the previous century. Germans in that wave of immigrants had given names to towns like Schulenburg and New Braunfels, communities now among the most important in south Texas.

But nothing important had happened to the elderly paymaster. During the Depression, he had lost the farm, which had been in his family since 1896. After that, he was never again quite the same man. Finally putting away his ambitions like an old suit of clothes that no longer fit, he had gratefully gone to work for François Devereaux.

On this part of the huge farm, the end of the workweek had coincided with the end of the work itself. Miles away, a new harvest would soon commence, and the workers standing in line for their pay were anxious to get there. This last week had not been good for those working on a per-box basis. The crop had slowly played out till finally it was gone.

Up on the platform, the old German called out each worker's name, their hours worked or boxes filled, and cranked up their total wage. This he would take from the steel box and hand to a supervisor standing nearby whom in turn handed the money to the worker after the migrant signed his name or made his mark on the paymaster's receipt sheet.

The mood was relaxed, as it always was on payday, and as each man's output was announced, the workers called out good-natured insults. But the mood changed somewhat as they walked away from the paymaster toward a large concession stand where Ramón Rompego sat waiting for them in a tattered red-velvet chair. Ramón owned the concession stand, was a labor-contractor, and also Francisco's representative on the Devereaux farm; all conflicting positions that Ramón handled with the dexterity of a juggler.

Ramón usually made note of anything which had even the slightest connection with his well-being, but on this particular afternoon he failed to notice that Francisco had pulled into the camp. Ramón went on grabbing his ten-percent contracting fee from each man who had just been paid — in Ramon's mind just recompense for the effort he had made on behalf of those workers who labored on Margaret's farm.

He was the only man who charged such a fee, and most of the workers paying up were, as usual, grumbling about his commission, though with words too soft to hear. One worker, however, had recently arrived from Mexico, and not yet aware of Ramon's power, now made the mistake of openly challenging him. "You did not say nothing of this this commission when you hired me in Matamoros, Señor Rompego," the worker — a small, grizzled-faced man — exclaimed in clear and precise Spanish.

Hearing this, a barrel-chested man working inside the concession stand snapped his head up. He was stacking items on the counter, marking them at about twice their regular price. The worker had handed Ramón a fistful of fifty-cent pieces. Ramón counted the coins carefully and then stared balefully at the little worker.

"Forgive me, my friend. A mistake not to tell you. But still, you now make more times the money you were making in Mexico," Ramón said. "You are short here by a dollar and fifty cents."

The worker stared down at his shoes. Then Ramon's assistant, the big man behind the counter, saw that trouble was coming in the form of a wiry young Filipino.

Years before, the Filipino had re-christened himself "Juan Rizal," the great hero of his homeland, and though many migrants knew his real name, anyone calling him anything other than Juan was quickly given what the muscular Filipino called an "attitude adjustment."

"Hey, Rompego," the Filipino called from the crowd. "Sure the little guy gets paid more up here than down in Mexico. But you also charge us a lot more up here!"

Ramón nervously flashed his gold-capped teeth. The Filipino was just crazy enough to be dangerous. Ramón nodded slightly to the man behind the counter, then rose slowly from his red-velvet chair, and began to parade around, pulling at his clothing.

"Well, this silly fool has given me the chance to say it again. So I will," Ramón snarled. "Look, do I dress like a man making so much money? Why? Because I am always doing favors for people less fortunate than me."

Many of the men in the crowd, bemused by such a bald tactic, chuckled. But the little worker was not amused, for the big man was now struggling to pry loose his pay.

Seeing this, the Filipino rushed forward. But before he could even raise his hands, the big man hammered him hard with a massive fist.

Juan Rizal careened away like a car out of control, crashing back into a tall stack of empty soda bottles. Badly cut and dazed, he stumbled to his feet. He turned to glare at the gathering crowd of workers, his eyes blazing a clear signal: he neither wanted nor expected their help.

Up on the platform, the German paymaster continued to crank his figures, though out of the corner of his eye he had seen the fight unfolding. The Devereaux supervisors, lithe, hard-looking men dressed in tan from stem to stem, stood leaning against the wall of the shed, paying no more attention than they would to a couple of brawling mongrel dogs.

The Filipino went slashing back at the big man, firing his fist into the man's face; once, twice, both solid hits. The big man barely blinked. An eerie smile formed over his fat face. Juan Rizal suddenly realized this was one fight he could not win. He could only hope somebody would stop it before the big man killed him.

Juan glanced toward the crowd—and in that moment the big man sprang on him, pinning Juan to the trunk of a tree, where he began to savagely hammer him with ham-fisted blows. The Filipino dropped to his knees, and his attacker went at him with hob-nailed boots.

Francisco, along with María and Pedro, stood watching what was now a massacre. Yet Francisco made no effort to stop the fight, though he certainly looked as if he wished he could. Pedro shot him a glance, as did the old black man who had accompanied them to the Devereaux farm.

"Francisco, you don't stop that fight, the next time we see the Filipino will be at his funeral," Pedro muttered.

"This is Ramon's territory. I cannot interfere. Not now."

Pedro's disappointment took but a second to congeal into anger. Striding through the crowd, he clamped hold of the big man's bull-like neck, and hurled him headlong into a long row of garbage cans. The crowd stood stunned with disbelief. The only person smiling was the paymaster. For years, he had hated Ramon's bodyguard.

The big man finally sat up. Collecting what was left of his wits, he began to pick the garbage from his face. Then, with nothing short of murder on his mind, he glared at the crowd, searching for the fool who had been stupid enough to attack him. But when he realized it had been Pedro Terán, a sick smile swept across the man's refuse-stained face. With a loud sigh, he rolled back into the garbage. The fight was over.

Ramon's surprise now turned to humiliation. Pedro had helped the battered Filipino over to a water trough and then strode back to the little worker whose mild protest had prompted the fight. Taking up the scattered money that belonged to the man, Pedro poked it back into the man's shirt pocket. Seeing this, the crowd applauded.

Ramon's expression coiled with hatred. His face, even in repose, seemed something out of a comic book: black hair so slick it looked lacquered, large bushy eyebrows, flaring nostrils, and a mouthful of gold- capped teeth gave him a countenance perfectly suited to his character.

Noticing that the fracas had finally drawn the attention of several supervisors, Francisco tapped Ramón on the shoulder, and indicated that they should take a little walk. They started toward a sorting shed at the far end of the camp.

"Ramón," Francisco said quietly, "meet the man who helped us organize the camp over in Uvalde. This is Thomas Jefferson Jones. He has been with me almost from the beginning."

Jones had with the years since become more dignified-looking. Except for his tattered hat and overalls, the tall black man could have passed for a preacher. Jones was about seventy-five years old, but when he smiled, which was often, he seemed ten years younger. He was smiling now.

"Afternoon, sir," he said to Ramón.

Ramón's lips formed a blank smile. He was trying to gauge the influence Jones might have with the man walking between them.

"I have never seen you at our meetings, Señor Jones," Ramón muttered, hoping to put the black man on the defensive. But Ramón had forgotten about Pedro, who was walking just behind them.

"That is because you have not been to a meeting in a very long time," Pedro muttered ominously.

The black man stifled a smile. "Well, what counts now is not where we been, but where we going."

Ramón Rompego stopped short. Un-wrapping a fudge bar, he began biting little bits off it. "I knew you would not be unhappy with the six-cent raise," he said to Francisco. "But the raise we got is better than none at all. Everywhere the news is terrible. Half the world is unemployed!"

Pedro smiled. "And we have more terrible news for you."

"Really, my friend, what is that?"

"For us, things will soon get better."

CHAPTER 7

After they were all seated, Francisco cast aside his genial tone and manner like the mask it had been.

"A six-cent increase is all the growers have offered on the new harvest. Nothing else. The same spoiled water, foul food, and the high price for both of them." Francisco smiled. "Oh, yes, they did say things might be better on the next harvest."

Thomas Jefferson Jones went slack with disappointment. It was in his nature to be hopeful, though this trait had been trampled so often by reality some people now thought him a little touched in the head. Francisco was not of the same opinion. Indeed, it was the old black man's undying faith in the future that had first sealed their friendship.

"We was hoping for about three times that raise, and a few extras besides, wasn't we, Frank?"

Francisco smiled grimly as he took two envelopes from his pocket. "We will get it, Tom. But we have to do more than just hope for it." From the envelopes, Francisco took out a large wad of money, which he laid on the table. A strange quiet ensued. No one at the table had ever seen so much money in one place at the same time.

"Almost eight-thousand dollars, including the twenty-seven hundred dollars the growers tried to bribe me with this morning. The rest is the money we've been able to put together in ten years of filling fruit jars with fifty-cent pieces."

The money was a somber sight. Weighed against all the battles the federation had fought and the many sacrifices its members had made, the pile of cash seemed something of a joke.

Ramón Rompego was not laughing. He had already guessed what Francisco planned to do with the money.

"Not enough to win a war with the growers, my friend."

"That's true, Ramón," Francisco replied. "But enough to win the first battle, and with it the best wage we have ever seen."

Ramon's rubbery face twisted. "Francisco, you cannot be thinking of taking our workers into a strike!"

"That is exactly what I am thinking, Ramón," Francisco said, unfurling a map he had taken from his hip pocket. The others looked on with stunned expressions. They had reacted to the word 'strike' as if it were the name of a dreaded disease. They knew, of course, that a strike was the ultimate weapon of any labor group, but they were also aware that weapons could sometimes backfire.

"A fool's game you play, Francisco, because what will stop the growers from just using the scabs, or maybe even bring in a load of labor from below the border?"

"Bringing in that many workers from below the border will take the growers too much time," Francisco replied. "As for the scabs, by the time the growers can round them up, we will have the fields completely in our control."

Jones creased, haggard face looked as if he were in pain. "Whoa now, Frank. What's to keep the growers from just having us all arrested for trespass?"

Francisco turned the map so the black man could more easily read it and began tracing some of the lines on it with his finger.

"That's where we're lucky this time. I have checked all this out—this new harvest area is surrounded by county roads, roads we have as much right to as anyone else. Without this right, we have no chance. But with it...well, if we don't try it this time, we might never again get the chance."

Francisco felt beads of sweat on his forehead. When he had faced the growers earlier, he had come expecting very little and knew he would not be disappointed. Now, facing the men seated around the table, he hoped for much more, but was not at all sure they would give it to him.

María tossed out the first life preserver. Clearing her throat, she rose from the table. "Well, no one has asked me my opinion, but I think we should strike. The Virgin Mother herself knows that we have tried everything else."

Francisco smiled. But it appeared Maria's vote was the only one he had won. Ramon's floppy lips formed a sneer. "You sure anxious to throw away that eight-thousand dollars," he muttered, intently nibbling on his candy bar. "But would you be so quick if it is your own money? So let's put this crazy idea of a strike up to people who put up the money, eh? That's the way a real union works, don't it?"

This was the query Francisco dreaded, the question to which he had no ready answer. So simply sliding past it, he began to count some of the money, which he handed it to the black man.

"Tom, you buy the provisions," Francisco said. "Pedro and I will take care of everything else —"

Pedro heatedly interjected. "And when the growers open us up like cantaloupes? What then, Francisco?"

"We also know how to open up a cantaloupe."

Pedro's rock-hard fist slammed down on the table. "No! We hit back, we never win. Better when the growers start cracking heads, we have our people simply lay down across the roads so that —"

"To get tire tracks across their faces?" Francisco shot back.

Pedro marshaled his thoughts for a moment. "Maybe you are right. But a great man over in India once tried such a thing, and when the struggle was over, he had brought down an empire. 'Nonviolent intervention,' he called it."

Francisco turned to gauge the reaction of the others. Maria quickly looked away, knowing if he saw her eyes, he would know that she agreed with Pedro. But Francisco knew that, on this issue, his voice was one against four. These odds, however, did not bother him. He had always considered himself a majority of one.

"Well, brother," he finally said, smiling at the man who had become more of a brother to him than his own had ever been. "You and this great man from India can call it whatever you like. I call it suicide."

Ramón suddenly came to his feet. "Then let the workers vote on that, too! Let's find out what they call it. I mean, have we got a real union here, or just a one-man organization?"

A strange sound came from Francisco. To María and Pedro, who knew him so well, it seemed like a fire alarm. Francisco's oversized teeth were clacking together, a sure sign he had finally reached the limit of his patience. In ten years, this was the most explaining to anyone he had ever done.

Yet he knew that if he lost his temper now, his cause could go with it; even worse, his position of leadership might pass to another man. Probably Ramón Rompego, who controlled more than seventy-five workers, many of whom profited from the patronage he adroitly dispensed on the Devereaux farm, like the shrewd politician he was. Francisco needed those seventy-five workers in his fight against the growers. Without them, the battle might be lost before it had begun.

Bending low across the table, his voice bottomed out at a level even María had never heard before. "First, if this was a one-man organization, I would never have bothered to bring you all together." His eyes slowly scanned the faces around the table. "Second, I am not against giving our workers the chance to vote. They have done so before; they will again. They could do so now, if only we had a little more time. But when a man finally gets a chance to kill a mad dog, does he stop to take a vote?

The others sat chewing on this bitter bone of truth. Francisco slowly rose to his full height and awaited their verdict. But it was only after Ramón Rompego tossed away his half-eaten candy bar that Francisco realized that the tide had turned in his favor. Losing an argument was the one thing that could kill Ramon's appetite.

CHAPTER 8

One hundred yards away, Sam Winslow brought the Devereaux station wagon to a stop under a large tree. Margaret climbed out of the back seat of the car, closely followed by Jake Hennessy. Sam and Alejandro stayed in the car. Sam knew that every time he and Ramón Rompego came together, an ugly argument ensued. Alejandro's reason for remaining in the car was much the same, though it involved somebody else. He had already made note of the old Model-A sitting nearby.

"Wilhelm," Margaret shouted up at the paymaster. "Where's the little weasel hiding out?" 'The Weasel' had been her father's nickname for Ramón.

"Behind the sorting shed, counting all his money," the paymaster called back. "And I'm just about finished with my counting up here."

Margaret looked pleased. She liked the old gentleman, though he occasionally made mistakes on his tally sheet, which had cost her more than a few dollars.

"Good work, Wilhelm," Margaret yelled. "But now don't go funny with those figures again. We aren't running a philanthropic organization here."

The old man smiled and returned to his computations with renewed concentration. Margaret waved to a few of her supervisors and moved briskly toward the sorting shed, Jake Hennessy at her heels like a faithful retriever.

She walked with the long, sure stride of a trail boss, and it was all Hennessy could do to keep up with her.

"Good Lord, Miss Margaret," Hennessy gasped, "walk like a damned cowpoke hurrying off to the chuck wagon!"

Margaret slowed down. "Yeah, you're right, Jake. And the race doesn't always go to the swift, does it?"

"Anyway, like I was saying before, I'd sure sit down hard on the weasel's face if he ain't got all his folks signed up at the new wage, ready—"

"Jake, since my father died, I haven't needed anybody to tell me how to run my business," she said, frowning. "You tend to yours; I'll tend to mine."

"Miss Margaret, I hate to tell you this," Hennessy declared like a doctor delivering a dire diagnosis, "but you keep on doing a man's job and you're gonna finally be relieving your bladder just like one: standing up!"

Margaret snorted. "Jake, if that's by way of another proposal of marriage, I'll say this much for you: you have more approaches than a sidewinder snake."

Jake Hennessy squared his football-player shoulders just a bit and slowed down. It was downright unseemly, he believed, to be discussing such a serious subject while moving at this rate of speed.

Fifty yards up ahead, the migrant meeting had ended. Francisco carefully folded his map and tucked it back into his hip pocket.

"So what happens to us now?" Ramón asked forlornly, opening up another fudge bar.

Pedro Terán turned to him with a dangerous smile. "We will have it pretty hard for a while, but nothing like it would be for you if the strike does work, and you have not been with us."

"One thing I promise you, Ramón," Francisco added. "If we can hold our people together for just six days, our work will be done." Jones suddenly brightened. "Yeah, but on that seventh day, we gonna be ready to take us a break. Just like the Lord Almighty in the Good Book, huh?"

Francisco chuckled. "Tom, you would have made a good preacher." Jones rocked back on his heels in mock indignation. "I am a preacher, Frank. Just ain't got me no church or congregation or no collection box, that's all."

As they came through the side of the shed, Hennessy was waiting to ambush them. "Okay, Salazar," he said with a big smile. "Sure hope you got everybody all signed up and ready to hit that new harvest."

Francisco clapped on a hangdog smile. "To tell you the truth, Señor Hennessy, our people are not too happy with the new wage. I am doing what I can, but the workers are free to make their own choice."

Hennessy's expression went sour. He turned toward Margaret, as if to give her the first shot, but for a moment, she said nothing. Margaret was thinking again, as she had many times before, that Francisco would have made a masterful poker player. Finally turning away from him, she fastened her cool blue eyes on Ramón Rompego.

"What about your folks here, Ramón?"

Like a man standing barefoot in hot sand, he shifted from one foot to another. Out of the corner of his eye, he saw Pedro move slightly toward him.

"As Francisco say, the wage is a little problem."

Pivoting toward the station wagon, Margaret motioned for Sam and Alejandro to join her. They both alighted from the car and trudged forward.

Hennessy also moved forward. The upcoming harvest was the most important of his life — the one he thought sure would finally put him on equal par with his fellow growers. Yet some instinct kept him cautious. He looked like a man whose skin had broken out in a bad rash but knew to be careful exactly where he scratched.

"Thought we settled all this, Salazar," Hennessy said with a stuck-on smile. "Mighty poor form, you having to ask permission for something you already agreed to."

Before Francisco could reply, he saw Alejandro slowly approaching. Nodding politely to Margaret, he started away. She mulled the situation for a few seconds and hurried after him, Hennessy again at her heels.

"Okay, Frank, you win," Margaret muttered with some effort. "Six cents was the agreed wage raise, but we might be able to go nine, if we can get this signed and settled."

The offer caught Francisco by surprise. He wondered what prompted the new offer. How much did Margaret know or suspect about the impending strike? What he did know was that the other growers would never approve of the new increase. At least not yet, he mused with grim satisfaction.

"A very interesting offer, Señorita," Francisco said in the courteous tone he always used in her presence. "But of course the workers would still have to vote on it."

Hennessy's head snapped back as if he'd been grazed by a bullet. "Bullshit, Salazar! When was the last time you allowed them sheep of yours to vote on anything?"

This was no grazing shot. Francisco had taken a direct hit which might have staggered, perhaps felled, a lesser man. Starting toward his car, he called back, "Believe me, Señorita Devereaux, when the workers reach the new harvest, they will do the right thing."

Alejandro had caught the tail end of the conversation, but the expressions left in its wake told him there was big trouble ahead. Margaret turned to him. "Your father has always been stubborn, Alex, but now he's getting stupid. I just offered his folks another three cents, which he either didn't hear or didn't believe."

Margaret's tone seemed a subtle warning. "Now, you run over and tell him I'll do all I can to get the growers to go along with this additional raise. But I want his promise he won't do anything foolish till I get back to him. Day after tomorrow at the latest, and by then—"

Hennessy angrily interjected, "But now there's gonna be some folks who don't think it too smart to put out a fire by throwing more money at it!"

"Oh, they will," Margaret coolly retorted. "Once I show them the dollars and cents of it."

"Don't even bother," Hennessy exclaimed, stomping off toward Margaret's station wagon.

Alejandro started away. His father had climbed behind the wheel of the Model-A, and with María, Pedro and Jones aboard, he took it into a wide, bumpy turn. Alejandro broke into a trot, but tried not to run after the car. His father had never run after anything or anyone, and this was one thing about him that Alejandro admired.

But once his father saw him trailing after the car, he stopped. Francisco's sense of decorum obviously covered his son as well.

"Listen, Papá," Alejandro said, nodding to everyone in the car, "the Señorita will have an answer for you on that wage raise in another day or so. All she asks is that you wait till then."

Francisco saw that every eye in the camp was riveted in his direction, and for that reason he kept a smile stuck to his face. "So tell me," he coolly inquired, "exactly what is it you do for the Señorita, other than try to make your father look like a fool?"

With that, Francisco ground the old car into gear. Watching the battered jalopy pull away, Alejandro had the feeling it was taking his job with it. He started back toward where his employer stood waiting.

Margaret was framing the obvious question, but the expression on his face quickly killed it.

"Well then, what the hell do they want?" Margaret asked. Alejandro shook his head and looked back at the Model-A, which was now clearing the camp.

"I guess they want more money, Miss Devereaux. But my father has never learned the right way to ask for it. Now maybe they plan to..."

Alejandro had no exact idea of what his father planned to do but knew that a strike was one of his options, though in his mind, a disastrous one. Just now, he had avoided saying the word 'strike.' He had enough Indian blood to be somewhat superstitious. If something were said often enough, it sometimes materialized.

His father was also superstitious. A few hundred yards out of the camp, Francisco saw Juan Rizal walking in the direction of the highway. Earlier, he had admired the way the young Filipino had handled himself.

"Let's give that tough little guy a ride," he muttered, slowing the car. "We might be able to use him."

Pedro wondered if Francisco's sudden decision might be prompted by remorse over having allowed the fight in the camp to have gone on far too long. Pedro had always suspected that a sense of guilt often colored many of Francisco's decisions.

Guilt would play no part in another decision Francisco had already made. He had earlier concluded that the eight thousand dollars in union resources would probably not last long enough to carry his workers to victory. Another few thousand might mean the difference between winning and losing.

He knew that investing hard-earned money to finance a migrant strike would be considered by most people a form of fiscal suicide. There was, however, one person who might be willing and able to offer the money without any thought of financial return.

He was wrong. As luck would have, two people would soon offer to come to his aid. Like Francisco had felt long before he had come to Texas, they also had been waiting for a worthy cause.

CHAPTER 9

"Salazar-López Texaco," Alfonso grumbled, cradling the phone receiver next to his ear. He glanced at his watch. Already past six, and his wife invariably had their evening meal on the table at half past the hour. Josefina López was almost as chunky as Alfonso, loved to eat her own cooking, and was not a patient woman.

"Wait a sec, I'll go get him," Alfonso muttered, setting the phone down on the long, cluttered desk he shared with Miguel.

Walking out of the greasy little office, Alfonso started toward the repair shed behind the service station, putting on a baseball cap as he went. In the past seven years, Alfonso had lost almost all his hair and was wary about venturing outdoors without shielding his scalp. Miguel had once counted more than twenty caps and hats around the office and knew his little partner and oldest friend had many more at home.

"Hey, Miguel, somebody wants you on the phone!"

Miguel looked up from where he and the station's two mechanics were admiring the engine of an almost new 1952 Hudson Hornet that a customer had just left to be lubed. Miguel loved the lines of the car, and was seriously thinking about buying one himself.

"Who is it?" Miguel asked, wiping his hands clean.

"He didn't say," Alfonso called over. "But it sounds like he's standing in a hole somewhere far away." He had guessed right on both counts.

Alfonso's description had not narrowed the field by very much. Most of the people Miguel knew were in a hole of one kind or another. He took a last look at the car. The Hudson was equipped with Hydra-Matic drive, a recent development, and Miguel had only a few moments earlier discovered that with only two pedals to manipulate instead of three, he had been able to drive the car.

"That Hudson's a beauty," Miguel said, as he grabbed his cane and limped toward the office.

"Yeah, but first we better pay off our last bank loan," Alfonso groused. "And why are you keeping those two grease monkeys around here for so late? Hombre, you know they get time-and-a-half after six o'clock!"

Miguel laughed. "Go home, you get nervous when you're hungry." Alfonso frowned and followed Miguel into the office.

"Hello, Salazar speaking," Miguel said, brushing back his graying hair as he picked up the phone. "Uncle Francisco! Man, you sure take a long time between calls, don't you?" he exclaimed, beaming with pleasure. "Yeah, Santiago's fine. Remember, I wrote you a few years ago that he'd gotten a scholarship to Texas A&M? He's in his junior year there now, doing great… How's Alejandro? Yeah. Tell him I'm proud of what he did over in Korea…and how are things with you, Tio?

The question apparently was not so easy to answer. Miguel sat down, and for the next few minutes he said nothing, only nodding his head from time to time. Back near the door, Alfonso intently looked on. He could tell from Miguel's expression that something serious was being explained to him.

Finally, Miguel stood up and quietly said: "Yes, I understand perfect. It's a bad investment… yet I promise you, even if I have to walk through the barrio with a tin cup in my hand, you'll have the money by Monday morning."

A wistful look came into Miguel's eyes. "I'll tell you how you can repay me! You and Alejandro and my brother Santiago are the only family I have left. But except for your son, none of you are worth a damn at writing letters… okay, you promise, eh?"

Miguel smiled. "Good luck, Uncle. I'll be pulling for you. Let me know how it all comes out."

Softly hanging up the receiver, Miguel finally muttered, "Two thousand dollars."

"He's also thinking about buying a new car and wants you to loan him the money?"

Miguel seemed surprised that Alfonso was still in the room. "You don't know my uncle. He's lived like a beggar for the last ten years—but never would take a dime from either me or Raúl. Very proud man, my uncle."

"But now not so proud?"

"Go home, Alfonso," Miguel said, and drawing forth the stub of a pencil he had behind his ear, he began to sharpen it. "Maybe I'll stop by later. Ask Josefina to save me a taco." Miguel still had not gotten used to eating alone, though his parents had both been dead now for more than three years.

Alfonso changed into another baseball cap and left the office muttering about something. Miguel sat down and tried out the point of his pencil. Then, pulling the phone closer, he dialed a single digit. "Operator, how can I call information in Dallas?"

"The Grinberg residence. To whom do you wish to speak?"

The refined voice seemed that of a middle-aged black woman. Miguel was impressed. "Yes, can I talk to Mrs. Grinberg, please?" he said, making an effort to carefully enunciate his words.

Already he could feel the palms of his hands go moist. Lorena Calderón was like a virus he had never been able to shake. In the years that had passed, and after her unhappy marriage to Raúl, she had salvaged the shattered pieces of her life and was now the wife of a successful attorney in Dallas.

"Who may I say is calling?"

"Miguel Salazar, calling from El Paso."

"Thank you, Mister Salazar. One moment, please."

Lorena had just gotten home from shopping for a birthday present for her husband and was now upstairs changing clothes.

"Miguel, what a surprise," Lorena exclaimed, picking up the phone extension in her bedroom. Her voice still sounded like a symphony to him. "But how on earth did you get my phone number?"

"Well, there are not too many lawyers by the name of Nathan Grinberg living in Dallas," Miguel replied, trying to sound calm.

Lorena laughed uneasily. Carrying the phone with her, she walked over to a liquor cabinet to mix herself a drink. She had sensed she might need one. But for the next few minutes, their conversation stayed on safe ground. She seemed genuinely curious about what had happened to him in the seven years since they had last seen each other at the trial in El Paso, where the man who was now her husband had represented Wade Donahue and Raúl.

"Well, enough about the past," she finally said. "I know this call is costing you a lot of money, so why don't you tell me what's on your mind."

Miguel slowly came to his feet, and began to tell her why he had called, and was surprised the words came so easily. But he had always been better at championing causes other than his own.

" — It's the end of the road for my uncle's workers if he can't raise enough money to get them through the strike — and I guess he had nobody else to call but me, and I had nobody else to call but you."

Lorena made no immediate response. Miguel uttered a quiet curse. He had blown it, he thought. "I can't blame you if you turn me down. It's a lousy investment. My uncle has no sure way to ever pay you back. But I do — and I give you an oath on the grave of my parents, you will be paid back every cent of the money, with interest…even if it takes me five years to do it."

"No, this is exactly the type of investment I have been looking for. But I can only contribute a thousand dollars. The other thousand dollars you can pay back in whatever manner is most convenient — without a dime in interest." She mentioned her street address in Dallas.

Miguel quickly told her to whom and where the money should be wired. "Thank you, Lorena. But I'm curious about just one more thing."

"I have my own checking account, and my husband is very generous," she said.

"I just wondered why you're so willing to do this."

Lorena chuckled. "Because I'm famous for repaying my debts. If it hadn't been for you, I wouldn't have met Raúl, and if it hadn't been for him, God rest his slimy soul, I would never have met my husband. Simple, huh?"

Miguel did not think it was that simple. "You heard about Raúl?"

"A friend in El Paso sent me the newspaper clipping."

"The strange thing is that if only the judge had given him the full sentence, he would probably be alive today. He hadn't been out of prison for more than a month when he was killed. Your husband did too good a job defending Raúl at the trial."

"And I heard Raúl just barely knew the woman he was with that night over in Juárez."

"Her husband thought he was somebody else. For once Raúl was completely innocent. Sad and funny at the same time."

Lorena had drunk just enough to lower her guard.

"What's that old saying, 'Life is what happens to us while we're out making other plans.'"

Miguel remembered that his uncle had once told him the same thing.

"So tell me about you, Miguel, are you married?

"Hah, no such luck—if that's the word for it."

"And your father and mother, how are they doing?"

"She had heart trouble, and he had developed lung cancer. They died a few years ago, almost within a month of each other."

"They loved each other very much. You were lucky to have had them."

"How about you, Lorena? Have things worked out the way you planned? Are you happy?"

She paused to freshen up her drink. "That's a word I don't use so much anymore. I'm content and secure. Nate is a very good man. My only worry now is that his health is starting to fail. Still, I could have done a lot worse. Listen, I almost did!"

Miguel could almost see the wry smile on her face, but he said nothing.

"What are you thinking, Miguel? I can hear your gears grinding."

"Oh, I was just wondering how things might have been different for all of us, if only you and I had kept that Saturday night date."

"I have wondered about that myself."

Miguel glanced up at the clock on the wall of his office. Sweet Jesus, they had been talking for more than fifteen minutes. Alfonso would faint when he saw the phone bill.

"Lorena, I better let you go now. But thanks again, and I'll be sending you at least fifty dollars every month. Okay?"

"That'll be fine, Miguel…and now you have yourself a wonderful life. God knows you've earned it," she mur-mured before hanging up. Catching her image in a mirror, she dabbed at her eyes with a tissue. It wouldn't do to let her husband see she'd been crying. He already knew she drank.

Outside Miguel's office, the two mechanics now had the Hudson on the grease rack. Peering up at the car, Miguel smiled wistfully.

"I sure did like that car," he said to no one in particular. The call from his uncle had cost him the car. But it already had proved worth the price. He again felt close to his uncle, whom he had always admired. That helped, for the moment at least, to fill the hole that the death of his parents and of his brother had left in his life.

Even better, the call had prompted him to telephone Lorena, a call he would have otherwise never made. She had sounded if not happy at least grateful for the way her life had turned out—and for that he was happy. Best of all, she seemed to still care for him. He knew now that they would always be good friends, a consolation prize well worth fifty dollars a month.

CHAPTER 10

Inside the Hennessy camp, lame and ailing vehicles sat groaning underneath their loads. A long, badly mistreated bus droned in the tenuous dawn light as migrant families piled the belongings of a lifetime onto its crumpled roof. Cast aside was everything that could not be loaded. The wooden crucifixes that blessed their ramshackle huts would, however, be brought along, so as to perform the same service over the course of the short but arduous journey.

Pedro moved quietly through the camp, helping where he could. Many migrants were destined to reach the new harvest fields too late, bodies or vehicles too rundown to get them there on time. Yet these workers had packed up, just the same. To stay in an area where there was no more work was a shameful admission of defeat.

Inside Pedro's car, two young boys had already set off on an imaginary trip. The older boy was steering while the other lad sat studying a tattered road map. Neither boy would be making the trip.

From inside the shack next to the car, Francisco and María watched the boys making their way across their illusory terrain. Francisco was thinking about another trip he had made many years earlier; a journey that by a cruel twist had split him and his family off from that of his brother, José Luis. At the time, it had seemed a disaster. But perhaps, he mused, it had all been for the best. His older, more cautious brother, were he still alive, would never approve of what he now planned to do.

Inside the shack, Paquito stood ironing a badly worn khaki shirt. Thomas Jefferson Jones was looking at him in a troubled way. Paquito knew why, but neither man said a word until Pedro entered the shack and nodded his head, as if to indicate that all was ready.

Jones looked up from his breakfast of bread and cold coffee. "We're on our way to the Promised Land."

Paquito flashed a toothless smile, and handed the khaki shirt to Francisco. "So you look your best when we get there, eh?"

Putting on the shirt, Francisco studied Paquito. He was about the same age as his father, Sebastián, would have been; perhaps part of the reason there had always been such a strong bond between him and the old migrant worker. Neither of them fully understood this, yet both knew it could not be easily broken.

"Did you ever think that one day we would attempt something like this?" Francisco quietly asked.

Paquito had been told of the strike the night before, and afterward he'd been unable to sleep. Now he simply shrugged his shoulders. "A man lives long enough, he can see just about anything. Only hope I live through it to see what happens afterward."

Pedro finished his coffee. "Already we run a little late, so you make the speech to the workers a quick one."

"Hah, it will take me only two seconds to make that speech," Francisco muttered, starting for the door. In the light coming from a kerosene lamp, Pedro watched him go. Looking away, he saw that the black man was staring at him.

María joined Francisco at the doorway where they watched the workers moving through the streaked light, collecting small children, belongings, and coaxing their machines to life. In the dust and light-splintered darkness, it seemed a dream slowly taking shape. For many years, he had waited for this exact moment. The chance had finally come to test both his courage and cunning.

He felt a surge of warmth pass through his body and knew he was as ready as he would ever be. He turned and peered into María's eyes. His expression was one she had never seen before.

"If we win, María, maybe we can finally settle down. I yearn for one place, one job, and one woman. I don't want another wife of mine to die because I was too busy off someplace counting cantaloupes."

She chuckled. If what he had just said was a proposal of marriage, it was carefully couched. But she had long since realized that his eloquence was at the exclusive service of the cause. He was more at ease talking to fifty people than trying to converse with just one person—especially a woman. Yet, somehow, that had always made him even more special to her.

Taking his hand, María looked back toward the camp. Her words, when they came, were faintly self-mocking. He had always admired her ability to make fun of herself. He had never found the sublime strength to laugh at himself.

"Thirty is a terrible age for a woman," she said softly.

Yet it did not seem so for her. In the soft caress of a new day, her features seemed freshly cut from the smoothest of brown sandstone. "At thirty, we are too old to believe everything a man tells us but still young enough to want to."

Francisco smiled but before he could frame a reply, she stepped quickly out of the shack. He stood watching as she went over to the Model-A, where she offered the two young boys a few words of encouragement. Then she laid a laundry bag with everything she owned into the rumble seat of the car.

Francisco went to open up a cardboard suitcase that was only a little larger than a briefcase. Pedro cautiously approached him.

"Francisco, what you say a minute ago was a joke?"

"I made a joke?" Francisco asked.

"What speech has only two seconds in it?"

Francisco turned back from the door. "A speech that has only two words in it. 'Let's go.'"

"Better to tell our people now what it is you plan to do."

"So they can take the next two weeks to think about it? I will tell them when we get closer to the new harvest fields. Less time they have to think, the more they will be ready to fight."

Saying that, Francisco walked out of the shack. Pedro turned back. Both Paquito and Jones seemed shaken by what they had just heard. Pedro smiled with an assurance he did not feel. "But with the growers so wrong about everything, how can it be possible for Francisco not to be right about this?"

Thomas Jones rose from the orange crate he had been sitting on and turned off the kerosene lamp. "That's gonna be for you to finally figure out."

The three men moved out to meet the day that had finally come. Pedro paused for a moment at the door. He glanced back at a tattered photograph of Emiliano Zapata he had once stuck to the wall of the shack, back in the days when things had seemed a little less complicated.

A migrant caravan of impressive size was now poised to roll. Near the narrow gate that led out of the Hennessy camp, Francisco savored the moment for a few seconds and then waved the machines forward.

But as the dilapidated vehicles crept past him, the air was suddenly split with a wrenching sound; the grinding crunch of a transmission gear popping loose. The driver of the stalled truck hurriedly ground it into second gear, and the heavily freighted machine labored forward a few feet. The driver yelled out to Francisco that the truck had lost only its first gear. He needed but a good push to get it rolling again.

"You hear that, muchachos?" Francisco called to the men sitting on a horse-drawn wagon directly behind the stalled truck. "That big black cockroach needs a push!"

Several men came forward, and as they put their shoulders to the truck, one of them, prompted perhaps by the mention of the word "cockroach," began to sing. The song had become famous almost a half-century before, during the Mexican Revolution.

"La cucaracha, la cucaracha,

Ya no quiere caminar.

Porque le falta, porque le falta,

marihuana que fumar... "

Soon more than a hundred people were singing, something they had never done on their way to a new harvest.

Half an hour after the caravan had left the Hennessy camp it had not yet reached the main highway, which sat only a few miles away. Radiators overheated, bald tires blew out, baggage feel loose. And always when the procession halted, the few cans of clean drinking water were hurriedly passed around.

CHAPTER 11

Some hundred yards from the highway, Jake Hennessy sat behind the wheel of his new Buick convertible, watching the migrants approaching. Hennessy's foreman, Jess Ballard, stood on the far side of the car, leaning across its fender. Everything about Ballard seemed big. His large melancholy-looking eyes were framed by a long, leathery face that rested on a rangy six-foot frame.

As Ballard watched the caravan, he had one ear cocked, waiting for Hennessy's next emotional outburst. Already he had indulged in several temper tantrums. His confrontation with Margaret Devereaux the day before had left him in a vile mood and he had spewed his anger towards his other employees, six of whom were nervously standing around a pickup parked nearby. But Hennessy was giving Ballard a wide birth, having long since realized that his foreman was not an easy man to push around.

Jess Ballard was nobody's man but his own. His expertise was for hire, but nothing else came with it. He knew as much about farming as any man in the valley, yet had never been hable to own a farm of his own. Hence, beneath Ballard's wry manner, a simmering resentment lay like a depth charge. Now and again it exploded; nobody knew nor feared this more than Jake Hennessy.

But if Ballard was hired for his expertise and ability to defuse potential trouble, Maurice Ripps, the slope-shouldered man behind the wheel of the pickup truck, was employed by Hennessy for exactly the opposite reason.

Ripps was an irregular-shaped man whose shaggy hair and pointed features gave him the look of a jackal. He had spent easily half of his adult life in jails and prisons all over Texas, having learned little that might be of interest to the average grower. But he had the knack for frightening Mexican migrants, which had nothing to do with his physical strength. Something was missing from Ripps—and for many Mexicans, it was a soul. Whatever he was missing was the reason Hennessy had hired him.

As the caravan drew closer, Hennessy went rigid, like a hunting dog suddenly picking up a strange scent. He looked over at Ballard, but the older man's expression did not encourage idle conversation. Hennessy turned toward the truck. Inside it, Ripps was bobbing around in time to the honky-tonk music blaring from the truck's radio.

Climbing from his convertible, Hennessy strode over to the truck to crack his bamboo cane hard across the truck's front fender. Ripps's grin froze solid, and the radio went off almost as quickly. After a long moment, he and his fellow employees slowly spilled out of the truck, uncertain of exactly what they had done to anger their boss, yet well aware of how little it usually took.

The caravan had pulled even with them. From a small rise fifty yards from the dirt road, Hennessy and his men watched it creep closer to the highway.

"Hey, Mister Hennessy," Ripps ventured with a sly smile. "How come all them migrants who supposed to be so unhappy about the new wage sound like some damned bunch of parakeets?"

This question had already crossed Hennessy's mind. Jess Ballard offered his own opinion. "Maybe the migrants are singing because they're crazy," Ballard drawled. "Crazy enough to think things might be better for them on this new harvest."

Hennessy's forehead furled with irritation. He hated Ballard's way of making sarcastic comments in front of his other employees. Hennessy thought of again cracking his cane across the fender. Controlling himself, he instead turned back to Ripps.

"You the dumb ass who's chirping like a parakeet—them bastards out there look more like buzzards."

A superstitious man, Hennessy took the migrants singing on their way to a new harvest site as an unfavorable omen. In all his thirty-eight years it was something he had never seen before. He decided that the singing had to be stopped—even if it cost him money. Marching back to his convertible, he opened its trunk and took out a five-gallon can of gasoline.

"Well, one sure way to scare off scavengers is with a little display of fireworks, right, boys?" Hennessy said, handing the can to Ripps. Then he turned to Ballard. "And while Ripps and the boys are off playing with matches, you round up as many workers as you can that ain't part of Salazar's gang. Have 'em waiting at the new harvest site."

"Hey, just slow down there, Mister Hennessy," Ballard snorted, straightening up his hard-muscled body. The two men stood silently facing each other across the hood of the car. Several of the other men drew closer.

A fist-fight had been brewing between Hennessy and Ballard for as long as many of them could remember, and they knew this was one fight Jess Ballard would never lose, even if he had to settle it with a shovel.

"When in hell did you have that brilliant plan?" Ballard asked.

Hennessy smiled proudly. "Just now — while you all was sleeping, as usual."

"And what makes you think the other growers gonna go along with such silly shit? If you recall, this here upcoming harvest is a joint operation."

"Hell, they're gonna like it fine," Hennessy exclaimed. "And even if they don't, it's the gesture that counts, right?"

"Well, I ain't about to be a party to such horse shit," Ballard said, his voice steady and unbending. "Them scabs take twice as long to pick anything, including their teeth, and then they mash up the fruit so bad, you might as well go into the goddamned jelly and jam business!"

Hennessy's rigid expression shattered with relief. "Oh, hell, Jess, I ain't talking about actually using them morons! I just want 'em hanging around the harvest camp when Salazar's gang gets there. Give him something to think about!"

Considering the source, Ballard thought this was not a bad idea. "Still think it's a waste of both time and money. And it ain't just your money anymore, Jake. I got your promise of a piece of the profits on this one, remember?"

Hennessy had made the offer one night after he had guzzled down a pint of whiskey and was feeling pretty good about things in general and the upcoming harvest in particular. But his offer to Ballard had been made in private, and Hennessy later thought that if the harvest came in as big as expected, he could always duck behind a drunk plea and renegotiate the figure.

Ballard was, as usual, too fast for his flat-footed boss. What the foreman had in mind was a tradeoff, his agreement on the scab labor in return for Hennessy's open admission about the profit-sharing deal. Realizing this, Hennessy felt the skin on the back of his neck get hot. Ballard had done it to him again, trading, as it were, a penny for a quarter.

"Five percent of gross profit was what you offered, right?" Ballard asked. Hennessy stared glumly down at the ground.

"Right," he muttered, then suddenly released his pent-up fury on his favorite target.

"Ripps, you stupid asshole, move!" Hennessy roared.

The words withered the shaggy-haired man like a shotgun blast that had barely missed him. But all he could think to do was shift the gasoline can from one hand to another.

"Sure thing, Mister Hennessy—but exactly where to, if you don't mind me asking?"

The grower seemed ready to wring Ripps's neck. He turned to the other men and muttered between clenched teeth, "What I want to get across to Salazar's folks is that they best get signed up for the new camp—because there ain't gonna be an old one to come back to, not the west side anyway."

"And you want it done now, boss?" Ripps stammered.

Hennessy's features contorted. He whipped his cane against the fender of the truck—hard. The move seemed to mollify him, and his voice now became almost gentle, as if he were instructing a group of small children.

"Well now, Maurice, it wouldn't do us much good if Salazar's folks didn't see it, would it?"

Ripps knew enough about the law to know that he needed to cover himself with a direct order from his employer.

"But a number of folks could get a mite scorched," he said. "Besides, that west end of the camp ain't gonna be worth fifty cents wholesale after it's burnt."

"Hell, that entire camp ain't worth more fifty cents right now," Jess Ballard drawled. "And there's still some women and children over there, so less you boys are hankering to get Ripps's old room at the county jail, I'd be sure to give them migrants plenty of notice. Them folks ain't firewood."

"Yeah, old Jess here is right for a change," Hennessy admitted. "So you boys be careful, but be thorough. Get more gasoline over at the depot. Now move, before these other migrants get so far away they can't appreciate the entire point of the party."

The men climbed back onto the truck. Ripps quickly slipped behind the wheel. Revving the engine, he gave Hennessy a thumbs-up signal and went barreling toward the migrant camp. The sound of honky-tonk music again came blaring from the truck.

Hennessy watched the truck disappear in a billowing trail of dust. "Idiots. I am surrounded by fucking idiots."

Ballard nodded in agreement, but said nothing.

"And a foreman who knows a lot more about produce than he does about people," Hennessy exclaimed.

Ballard simply smiled. Hennessy snorted with disgust. They turned to stare at the passing caravan of migrants.

As the caravan crawled along, Ballard thought about the people who might still be in the camp, the old workers too feeble to make the journey and the women who would not leave their side.

Ballard's own parents had been migrants. He had grown up in camps even worse than the one now about to be torched. For much of his life, he had lived on the barren outskirts of society — and better than most men, he knew how years of grinding poverty could turn a migrant worker sick inside his soul — and perhaps desperate enough to go on strike.

For years he had felt that a farm-worker strike might eventually happen, and on the day he first met Francisco Salazar, he realized it was inevitable. Now, Ballard sensed that a strike was definitely in the wind and knew that if it succeeded, it would cost him a sizable amount of money. Probably even his job. Hennessy would have to find a scapegoat, and none of his other employees had stuck their necks out on behalf of the migrants like his own foreman. Thus, it made little sense for Ballard to feel any sympathy for the workers. Yet, in the deepest reaches of his heart, he knew that to try to kill off such a feeling would be no easier than to attempt to forget his own parents.

CHAPTER 12

The fire started on the west side of the camp. Hennessy's men, remembering Ballard's warning, had told the few people remaining in that section to evacuate immediately. But inside the first torched shack, somebody had left a few gallons of heating oil. The ensuing explosion sent burning shards flying.

A few seconds after the explosion, Francisco heard a weak scream and saw an old woman run from one of the dwellings, beating frantically at the hem of her burning dress. When Francisco first heard the explosion, he thought it had been the backfire of a car—and started off toward where he knew a young Oklahoman migrant was still trying to start his car. But hearing the old woman scream, he turned back.

Pedro had already reached her. The old woman, now hysterical, careened around in fiery circles. Grabbing hold of her arms, Pedro took her gently to the ground and quickly tried to tear away the lower part of her dress. Moments later, Juan Rizal ran up with a horse blanket. In another fifteen seconds, they had choked out the fire. The old woman lay gasping prayerful thanks that she had not been more severely burned.

But the fire was far from finished. Beyond a long narrow row of dwellings the blue and red flames shot fifty feet up from the west side of the camp, the fire making a snarling sound as it consumed everything in its path. The tar paper shacks caught fire so fast that flames were spreading almost as rapidly as a man could run.

Then came a second scream, more frightening than the first, for it was from a child. Fifty yards away, the flaming destruction had danced across a divide and now crackled over the roofs of the nearest shacks. Sitting between two shacks which lay directly in the path of the fire was the car belonging to the young Oklahoman. The scream had come from one of his children.

Atop the old car sat a small wooden doghouse and cardboard luggage. Francisco knew the material would ignite the moment the flames came close enough. He started for the car, and as he did, María hurriedly moved the old woman further away from the fire. This freed Pedro and Juan Rizal to sprint for the car — a race between them and the roaring fire. They had almost reached the stalled vehicle when from around the far corner of the muddy street came six men carrying torches.

Hennessy's men suddenly stopped, stunned that the fire had spread so far so fast. Dropping their torches, they came running forward.

Francisco saw them coming, his expression hardening with hatred. Had he been able to see past the swirling smoke and the shimmering haze that the intense heat had created, he would have seen that the men wanted only to help. What he did see clearly was the loping figure of Ripps, moving toward the stalled car, a flaming torch in one hand, a sawed-off shotgun in the other. Francisco quickly angled toward him.

Somewhere near the middle of the quagmire, the men collided, the impact sending Ripps ricocheting across the mud. He had barely come to a full stop when Francisco heard another scream. The shack nearest the Oklahoman's car had caught fire. Flames licked hungrily around the top of the vehicle.

In that moment, Pedro and Juan reached the car, only to see that its back doors were tied with rope, the young Oklahoman still desperately grinding the starter. Pedro began to untie the rope as Juan put his back to the rear bumper, trying to push the car away from the burning shack. But even the cries of the three children in the back seat could not infuse him with the strength to move the car even a foot across the deep mud.

Francisco reached the car and began to rip loose the luggage from the top, which had already caught fire. Then suddenly, Hennessy's men were helping to push the car. Within another agonizing minute, it finally rolled free of the roaring flames. Only then, with the young farm worker, his wife, their three little girls and the family's cocker spaniel safely out of the car, did Francisco look back toward the man he had sent sprawling across the mud.

Moments before, Ripps had been mad enough to murder him, but the barrels of his shotgun had clogged with mud. Now, he burned with righteous outrage. He had wanted only to help the migrants trapped in the car. Glaring at Francisco, he slowly smiled. The Mexican had finally given him all the justification he would ever need to kill him someday.

Francisco had just returned from making arrangements for the old woman to be taken to an emergency clinic when he saw Pedro approaching through the thick swirls of black smoke, which still sat over the camp like a funeral wreath. Paquito and María were with Pedro. The old man, dazed by the disaster, spoke first.

"The growers know you plan to strike, Francisco," Paquito murmured. "They do not bum a camp down for nothing."

Francisco waited for a thick gust of smoke to pass. "If they know of our plan, it was Alejandro who told them," Francisco grimly muttered. "He guessed yesterday and went to them with his suspicions."

Pedro's expression went as black as the smoke still sweeping around them. "Don't be stupid, Francisco!"

Pedro had never called Francisco such a word before. He had been unable to channel his anger until he heard Francisco's accusation. "Tinging told the growers. It was your fault," Pedro harshly barked. "You should have told the workers what you plan to do. It was not only their future at stake, but as we now see, even their lives."

Francisco knew Pedro had spoken the truth, but he also knew that if a similar circumstance ever arose again, his decision would be no different. He stood glaring down at the ground, and only then did he realize that his hands were burnt. A strange sense of relief came over him. The injury gave him reason to walk away before Pedro could say any more.

A few miles away, the migrant caravan had almost reached the highway when the workers noticed the black smoke rising from back at the Hennessy camp; it took only a few seconds for the meaning of the smoke to become clear. When it did, the singing stopped. When the caravan started forward, what previously had seemed a parade now looked like a funeral procession.

CHAPTER 13

By nightfall, as his father's workers bivouacked some five miles from the new harvest site, Alejandro sat studying the the stars from the window of his small, sparsely furnished room, seriously thinking of re-enlisting in the Marine Corps. He had come home from the Korean War hoping to earn the friendship and respect of his people. He had earned both in the mountains of Korea, but here, in the fertile flatland of the Rio Grande Valley, respect and friendship were proving tougher to achieve. By now, he had realized that he was distrusted and disliked by many of the very people he was hired to help.

It was the old story about the crabs in a barrel, each clawing toward the top, yet all equally determined to keep any of their fellow crabs from climbing out. Most Mexicans migrants thought there were only so many available opportunities, and each time one was taken, their own chance for success diminished.

Alejandro had made it—for the moment at least—out of the barrel. One more place at the table of respectable society had been taken. But the notion that he might help make room at that same table for another Mexican simply never occurred to most migrants. They were wrong to reject such an idea, he thought. A man was not a crab, though many men often behaved as if they were.

That night, walking along Mission's main street, he decided to kill a few hours inside the town's only theatre. The film playing that evening managed to deepen his desire of rejoining the Marine Corps. The picture was a saga set in Hawaii just prior to the Japanese attack on Pearl Harbor.

Alejandro remembered how the infamous attack had been the cause of his grandfather's deathbed command, the order that triggered the family's exodus to the United States. But what struck him the hardest as he watched the powerful film unfold, was the comradeship that existed among the men—soldiers sticking together under the cruelest of circumstances. That had been his experience with his fellow Marines in Korea. He had been liked and admired as a warrior. Now, he was mistrusted and almost friendless. Even the once unbreakable bond between him and his Uncle Pedro seemed strained.

Early the following morning, Alejandro walked into the Devereaux house from its rear door, and went quietly to the huge room that served as the farm's operations center, expecting to find it filled with people. But the room was deserted.

In the stillness, he studied the trappings of wealth that were everywhere in the oversized chamber, his gaze caming to rest on the portrait of Margaret's father over the massive stone hearth. Something in the old Frenchman's expression reminded him of his grandfather; each had the dauntless look of men who had lived by a code loftier than any imposed by law. A welcome thought flashed through his mind: both men, he thought, had they been birds, would have been eagles.

He was dwelling on this notion when Sam Winslow came into the room. Alejandro smiled uncertainly in the direction of the Margaret's black retainer. Like most migrants, he had been brought up to smile at anyone in a position of authority.

"I did not think anybody was up yet," he said, holding his grin in place.

Winslow picked up a stack of mail off Margaret's desk. Glancing through it, he tossed several pieces into a wastebasket with the assurance of a man who knew Margaret's business as well as she did.

"This is a farm operation, Salazar," Sam muttered. "Not some country club."

The black man's tone slowed Alejandro's response. "I guess you heard the news about the fire at the Hennessy camp, and him rounding up all the scabs?"

Sam's expression clouded with contempt. "That man's been shooting himself in the foot for so long now, it's a wonder he can still walk."

"There will be trouble when my father arrives at the new camp," Alejandro declared quietly. Such trouble, he thought, could well cost him his job.

"Tell me something I don't know, Salazar."

Alejandro shrugged. "I ought to be there when my father arrives. I might be able to help."

Sam wheeled around. "Only way you can help is to stay as far away from that camp as you can."

Alejandro stood frozen by the hearth while the black man continued sorting through the mail. Neither was aware that Margaret was listening to their conversation as she sat inside her father's library, going over a stack of pricing sheets. She had been working at her father's old desk since before dawn, not realizing anyone was in the house until she heard Alejandro and Sam's voices coming from the main room.

An undercurrent of hostility still existed between them, and Alejandro impulsively decided to force Sam's feelings out into the open. He could deal with the unmasked malice of an Anglo better than with the black man's muted animosity.

"You don't like me working here, do you?"

Sam appeared surprised the question had to be asked. "Thought I'd made that petty obvious."

"What have I done to you that you should hate me?"

Sam's face contorted, sending askew features that were usually frozen in a blank mask. "Hey, best get something straight," Sam muttered with a quiet menace in his voice. "I can't afford to hate nobody. All I can do is handle other people's hate."

In the library adjacent to the larger room, Margaret looked up from her pricing sheets. She took off her reading glasses and waited.

Sam quietly continued. "Like most of the white folks in this valley who hate the idea that a black man pretty much runs this farm, though it'll freeze in hell before I ever get the title of foreman that goes with the job."

Sam paused, as if waiting for a painful cramp to pass. "Then there's my own folks, black people who hate me just because it was me and not them that Miss Margaret's father brought out of the fields. He could have picked anybody, but for some reason he chose a black orphan boy who'd been running scared for most of his life. I was lucky, that's all. Some have it, some don't. But what was I supposed to do, throw away my luck because there wasn't enough of it to go around?"

Alejandro stood silent for a long moment. "Why are you telling me this?"

Sam's expression knotted with irritation. "Because I see you falling into the same hole I'm in. Listen, you want to make a new life for yourself, go do it some place where people don't remember your old one."

"Maybe I got lucky, too," Alejandro said, carefully measuring his words. "But does that make it wrong for us to take advantage of our own good fortune?"

With a withering smile, Sam tossed aside the stack of mail still in his hand and started out of the room. "Not wrong, boy, just dangerous," Sam said, walking away. "Because whatever you get, you gonna have to pay for—and maybe with something you can't replace."

Sam's comment unsettled Alejandro. It was the same warning his Uncle Pedro had given him the first night he had gotten home from the war.

In the adjacent room, Margaret sat very still for a long moment. Alejandro's remarks surprised her, but Sam's comments saddened her. She had known him all her life, yet now realized that she had never truly understood him. She had been with him around other members of his own race but had never bothered to notice how they reacted to him, had spoken with him almost every day for the past several years, yet never once asked him a personal question.

For the first time, she wondered what his life was really like. Friendless, she realized. The few distant relatives he occasionally spoke about lived up around San Antonio. He almost never went out. Maybe, on occasion, to a picture show in McAllen that catered to Negroes. He did enjoy reading, and often late at night, she would hear him moving about in the library her father had so carefully filled. Sam seemed especially fond of the French classics.

Not much of a life, she thought. Maybe Sam had come to live vicariously through the stirring sagas of Dumas, Zola and Hugo, because certainly, there was little drama or romance in his own life. For Sam, his existence seemed synonymous with his work.

Margaret smiled ruefully. She and Sam had that in common.

CHAPTER 14

Maurice Alpert Ripps could sense impending violence as surely as a mongrel dog can smell out raw meat. He had sat alone the previous night, carefully cleaning and oiling his sawed-off shotgun with the care one might show a favored child. Now, standing on the small rise overlooking the new harvest site, he slid two shells into the twin barrels of his shotgun, ready for whatever pleasures the hot, humid first day of the harvest might bring.

Glaring out across an engorged orchard, he grinned. Down below, the camp was crawling with indigents—the men Jess Ballard's men had rounded up from bars, bus stations and public parks. Their efforts had not improved Jake Hennessy's disposition.

Ripps glanced across the hood of Hennessy's convertible and wondered if he would ever catch its owner looking happy about anything. A sour expression creased Hennessy's face like a permanent scar. Hennessy had watched Ripps load the shotgun, but thought it pru-dent to make no comment. Should the ex-convict later use it and the results prove troublesome, Hennessy would claim he had never even seen the weapon.

Allowing himself a small smile, Hennessy opened a can of beer and waited. Down below, migrant caravans were approaching the camp from three different directions.

Inside, the grower's men stalked through the mob, making certain all was ready with their welcoming committee. Ballard's men had rounded up a hundred men, but at best they were a mixed bag: ex-jailbirds, winos, misfits, even a few laggards who had sometimes tried to legitimize their sloth by calling themselves communists. The common denominator was a deep and sincere hatred for hard work—especially the type they had been hired to pretend they were about to do.

In the distance, a large group of farm workers were approaching along the wide county road that ran adjacent to the harvest fields. The camp sat some five hundred yards in from the main highway, at the crossroads of two other county roads.

A hundred yards from the entrance to the camp, Jess Ballard sat peering out from inside his pickup truck. The first migrant vehicle had come into sight. Warily, Ballard watched the big bus loom closer, and he hurried his truck into a turn and raised dust in the direction of the camp.

Behind the bus, dozens of vehicles of all descriptions, most of them loaded well beyond good judgment, a few, even beyond belief, slowly chugged forward. Through the dust and disarray it was hard to tell which had been wilted worse by the journey, the machines or the men, women and children.

Inside the bus, past windows caked with twenty miles of grime, the workers' destination came into view. Hauling themselves to their feet, several migrants made for the door, thinking they would have their pick of the few hundred little shacks inside the fenced-in camp. They were glad to be the first of Francisco's workers to arrive.

Moments later, the scheme born in Hennessy's mind took on human sinew. Men from every corner of the camp raced toward the main gate. Several vehicles were quickly pushed in front of the camp's main entryway.

As the bus neared the gate, the stocky black woman driving it saw the commotion up ahead. She cautiously geared down and finally stopped. Several workers began to bang on the doors, yelling for her to open up. But the black woman calmly held her ground, one hand clamped tightly to the door-release handle. She had been assigned the duty of safely delivering the largest single load of workers, a responsibility she obviously took seriously.

But the migrants behind the bus were beyond her power to control. Now they began barging out. Up ahead, several club-wielding guards rapidly formed a line across the entrance. The number of migrants at the gate doubled, then tripled, and angrily began to push aside the vehicles that cordoned off the entryway. Shouting erupted into shoving, as at last the guards pulled away from the gate. They were being paid enough to referee a slugging match but not to participate in one.

Then, as if following a precise command, a horde of indigents came roaring into the gap left by the departing guards. What started as a skirmish instantly escalated into a war.

Many indigents seemed surprised. They had been told that their presence alone would suffice for the purpose the growers had in mind. But now, as the battle broke out into club-swinging chaos, the indigents' own frustration fueled the fight like gasoline being poured over a fire.

Inside the bus, the black woman honked the horn, and opened the doors to finally let loose her reinforcements. The first person out of the bus was a frail-looking little man, but he had no sooner reached the gate than he was knocked to the ground, his glasses falling from his face. Unable to discern friend from foe, he started to search for the spectacles, inching through the mayhem on his hands and knees.

On a rise a hundred yards away, Jake Hennessy could not believe what he was seeing through his high-powered binoculars. He had not expected the migrants to fight back. Having seen enough, he slung his beer can in Ripps's direction and quickly slid behind the wheel of his convertible.

"Come on, you idiot," he yelled at Ripps. "Let's get down there before they all kill each other off!"

Ripps looked confused as to the exact nature of the problem. "Hell, don't seem so terrible, just one mongrel dog chewing up another one—"

"You stupid bastard! To harvest that crop, we're gonna need somebody who's still alive!" Hennessy exclaimed, stripping the car into gear. Several other men had piled into the car and appeared amused that Ripps had just dug himself into another hole.

With a jackal-like bark, Ripps abruptly turned to the men in the back seat. "Hey, so I overlooked something—don't mean you pussies can split a gut about it!"

"Fuck you, jailbird," one of the men snorted.

Hennessy had to smile. Picking on Ripps was about the only thing he ever did that always had the full approval of his other employees.

The battle was still raging as Hennessy maneuvered his Buick through the mob. Off to one side the guards and supervisors watched the fight like amused spectators at a sporting event. Already two workers lay crumpled on the ground.

Noticing them, Hennessy blasted his horn. The noise only seemed to further spur the fighting. Hennessy, voice rent with rage, then screamed something that only Ripps seemed to hear.

Drawing forth his shotgun, he pointed it straight up and fired off both barrels. Instantly, the crowd quieted. Then, as if by magnetic force, their attention slowly focused on the convertible. Hennessy was now standing on its running board.

Moments before, the old worker who had lost his eye glasses had finally found them, undamaged—but the twin blasts from the shotgun badly startled him, and he had dropped the glasses again. This time they shattered.

In the uneasy silence that followed the blast, Hennessy ambled through the crowd, his personal militia right at his heels. Migrants and indigents began to draw away from each other, instinct telling them that the previous battle was only a prelude to something much worse.

As they separated, Hennessy cautiously approached the two felled migrants. The workers still lay face down in the dirt, their heads framed by pools of blood. Both men were unconscious. Hennessy's expression was a curious blend of contempt and compassion. Looking up, his eye fell on an indigent lurking nearby, a longhaired man with the build of a blacksmith. The bloody club he had used to bash the two workers still hung from his hand. He looked as if he was half-expecting Hennessy to congratulate him.

The grower stood pondering the situation. If either of the two workers died, the police investigation might prove troublesome, but not necessarily incriminating. Hennessy knew most of the local law-enforcement officers, and those he didn't, his ally Bert Agajanian controlled.

No, Hennessy thought, the biggest danger would come not from the police, but from the leader of the farm workers. A commotion suddenly stirred the crowd. When Hennessy saw what had caused it, he flinched. Francisco Salazar had finally arrived.

For a long moment, no one in the large crowd moved or spoke. Spotting the injured workers, Francisco silently strode across what was now neutral territory. He knelt down next to the men to more closely ascertain how severely they were injured. Then he rose to his feet slowly. He had seen the man with the bloody club in his hand. They stared at each other for a few seconds before the burly indigent finally let the club slide from his grasp. Francisco's expression curled with bemused contempt. He walked forward to pick up the club. The indigent's belated attempt to disavow responsibility for the brutal assault had struck him as almost comical.

Hennessy saw his chance. Striding up to the indigent, he swung at him with the swiftness of a rattlesnake. The sound of cracking bone broke the silence like a rifle shot. Blood spurted from the man's nose, and he fell away yelping like a badly mauled dog. Wiping the blood from his fist, Hennessy turned toward the workers, and pointed at the two migrants still lying on the ground.

"Let's get them two workingmen to the hospital quick as we can," Hennessy commanded. Jess Ballard sprang into action. Summoning forth a few of his supervisors, he eased the injured workers toward his truck. Hennessy watched as the unconscious men were gently laid onto the rear of the truck, then bellowed out a final command, "And tell them doctors to give those two boys the best treatment they got available. I'll personally stand good the medical bill. But you also tell the white coats that if those two boys don't pull through, they'll play hell collecting their fee."

Keenly aware that every eye in the camp was on him, Hennessy announced, "Hell, wasn't so long ago I was also picking produce. I know what it is to work for a living—unlike some goddamned growers I could mention."

Hennessy turned to peer at the burly indigent who lay groaning a few feet away. Digging into his pocket, Hennessy took out a silver dollar and tossed it to the man. "But about all I'm gonna do for this here bastard is buy him a bottle of Mercurochrome."

Several migrants nodded with unbridled approval. Hennessy was playing the part of the protective patrón, a role Mexicans appreciated more than most. Many had worked under the old 'hacienda' system in Mexico, as had their fathers and grandfathers before them. To a poor Mexican there was nothing better than working for a man who was smart in the head and soft in the heart.

Sensing a breakthrough, Hennessy beckoned the workers forward. "Come on," he boomed, waving the migrants into the camp. "We have plenty of hot food and clean water for all of you, just quick as you sign up at the new wage and are ready to go to work."

Hot food and clean water seemed too good to be true, and indeed it was. What was waiting inside the camp were baloney sandwiches and water mixed with Kool-Aid to disguise its fetid taste. Most of the workers were not, however, in the mood to split hairs. Bone-tired, hungry, thirsty and still shaken by their initial reception, several migrants started into the camp.

Watching them come forward, the indigents sullenly sauntered away. They had more than earned their meager pay that day. But the workers' migration into the camp stopped a moment later. Francisco had taken up the discarded club. With a sudden gesture, he raised it above his head; a reminder to his workers of something they should not forget so soon.

Having reclaimed their attention, he began to speak in a voice freighted with fury. "Listen to me, you men," he commanded. He waited for silence, and then continued. "Two of our people were badly injured here today. No one can deny it is a fine thing Mister Hennessy did sending them to a hospital, even agreeing to pay the medical expense out of his own pocket. But it might be too late for anybody but God himself to save them now."

As Francisco spoke, several migrants continued to slip into the camp, their eyes cast shamefully downward. But these men had families to feed. What they needed now was food and work, not speeches.

Noticing the defections, he continued. "I remember that not too many years ago, when my wife Juanita used to get sick, some of the other growers were not so interested in getting her to a hospital, let alone in paying her doctor bills."

Tossing aside the club, Francisco now held out his right hand. The joints and knuckles on it were tangled with knots, a sobering sight that drew the interest of even the indigents. "Many of you already know, it was only when I broke a finger or caught my hand in a machine that I could get the growers' attention. A worker who cannot use his hands is of little use to them."

Francisco lowered his hand. "So this interest in the welfare of our two injured friends comes a little late. Ten years too late."

The history lesson was over, but its moral hung in the noonday heat: those who forget the past are doomed to repeat its mistakes. It was a moral the migrant workers understood.

Hennessy's eyes hardened. "Well, it's a smart man who knows when he's finally whipped," he announced with a reluctant smile. "So how does two cents an hour up and above the last wage offer sound to you boys?"

Francisco's response came quickly. "That also sounds ten years too late."

A quiver shot through many of the migrants grouped closest to the confrontation. They seemed proud that he had spoken as an equal to Hennessy, but waited to see how long this circumstance could last.

Paquito and Pedro, who had arrived with Francisco, had climbed onto the back of a truck to better assess the situation. From there, they saw the two remaining columns of migrant workers, coming from opposite directions, fast approaching the junction.

Hennessy, not having made note of this, reluctantly turned back to Francisco. "Now, amigo, I do wish you'd try to be more reasonable," Hennessy murmured with a sly smile. "After all, like they say in the Good Book, 'blessed are the peacemakers.'"

"The part I remember is that 'the meek shall inherit the earth,'" Francisco replied, vaguely amused that he and the grower were jabbing at each other with little more than quotations from the Bible.

Hennessy's composure suddenly shattered into flying shards. "Oh, hell, Salazar, let's stop this silly horse shit and get down to business," he bellowed. "Now just how long do you think this sad sack of shit you call a labor union is gonna be able to hold out against me and some of the most powerful growers in this valley?"

Francisco's gaze swept slowly over a sea of somber faces before riveting back on the man who had finally asked the question he had been asking himself for the past ten years.

"We are prepared, Mister Hennessy, to hold out for as long as it takes you and the other growers to finally treat us like human beings and not animals."

The words came in an understated way but seemed to carry with them the full force of a movement whose time had arrived. Pedro, still standing on the truck, looked over at Paquito and smiled. For years, they had heard Francisco deliver speeches but never had they seen such a reaction.

Many workers now had firm expressions on their sun-punished faces. Aware that something unprecedented was taking place, they looked proud to be a part of it.

"Look, Paquito," Pedro murmured. "Francisco only had to tell our people what he wanted from them."

Paquito's toothless smile went slack. "If only the two injured workers had known of his plan a little sooner."

Pedro, somewhat daunted, turned toward the crowd. Hennessy had began to wade through the migrants. His supervisors trailed behind him, brandishing long pick handles.

"Enjoy yourself while you can," Hennessy roared. "Because by tomorrow morning, we're gonna have us rounded up enough scabs to kick you sad sacks of shit plumb outta here!"

But the crowd's attention had already gravitated toward one of the approaching columns. At the head of one caravan, Thomas Jefferson Jones was standing on the running board of the lead vehicle. As the old black man waved, the migrants let out a cheer. They knew that whatever battles might lie ahead, they would be fought with at least some of their compatriots at their side.

Francisco was not a man who smiled easily. Earlier that morning he had gone to the local Western Union office, half-expecting to find a telegram from his nephew Miguel explaining why he had been unable to raise the money. Instead, two-thousand dollars were there waiting for him. As always, Miguel had delivered on his promise.

Remembering this, Francisco happily called out, "Well, Hennessy, it looks like we are getting a little less sad."

"Yeah," Hennessy boomed back, "but no matter how many folks you got, they still gonna get damned thirsty and plenty hungry before this is over"

Hennessy's reply trailed off, for as the newly arrived caravan had drawn closer, some of the men aboard its largest vehicle began to strip the covers from dozens of hundred-pound sacks of rice and beans. This was, Francisco thought, one of those rare moments in life when everything seemed perfectly measured and timed. He was, after all, the same man who once dreamed of fighting the bravest bulls before the biggest crowds in all of Mexico.

"Well, as you can see, Hennessy," Francisco declared, nodding in the direction of the heavily loaded trucks, "I found something else to spend the growers' money on, instead of that new pair of boots."

Hennessy was out of rebuttals. Snatching the attention of his supervisors, he pointed vaguely in the direction of the camp's gateway, and fired off one last shot at Francisco. "Yeah, but all the food in the world ain't gonna change this mob into men, which for your sake they best be when me and mine get back here tomorrow morning!"

Another roar came from the crowd, and for a moment he thought it was in response to his parting declaration. But his grin lasted only until he realized that they were greeting another arriving contingent of workers.

"Hey," Francisco yelled, waiting for the grower to turn back toward him. "You better bring a lot of people with you!"

Hennessy spun hard on the heels of his expensive boots and plowed toward his convertible, his full corps of supervisors close behind him. Noticing this, he abruptly wheeled around, causing a slight pile up. "Now what the hell is all this? Rats coming off a sinking ship? But this here ship ain't sinking, and you boys ain't leaving! I want you all to stick around to keep them other rats," and here he pointed accusingly toward the migrants, "from crawling into the camp. That there camp is private property. Let them migrants roost on the road like the goddamned gutless chickens they are."

The supervisors looked less than enthralled with the command but finally shuffled back toward the camp. Watching them go, Hennessy eased into his convertible. This time, Ripps was seated inside. Hennessy jammed the machine into gear and, furiously honking his horn, eased his way through the crowd.

Francisco watched the convertible pull away before he allowed his attention to swing back to the newly arrived group of farm workers.

María Antón was standing on the truck that led the caravan, her face smeared with dirt and grime from the long journey. But her eyes were glowing with pride. Francisco had entrusted her with delivering safely a large group of workers, and like his nephew Miguel, she had kept her promise to him. Their gaze held for a moment.

Then her eyes went toward the county road that led back to the highway. Sheriff's vehicles, sirens screaming and red lights flashing, were racing closer; behind them was a large panel truck bearing the call letters of the most influential radio station in the valley. Watching the truck barrel closer, María frowned. The arch-conservative radio station had always been one of Francisco's worst enemies.

CHAPTER 15

The large map on the wall was covered with a sheet of clear plastic over which several parcels of land were outlined with coloring pencils—the areas of the Devereaux farm and of a few other growers that were soon to be harvested as a joint operation. Numbers over some of the sections indicated the optimum amount of workers and harvesting supplies needed to bring in the produce most efficiently—a vital decision, as crucial to the effective harvesting of ripe crops as the equipment and troop emplacement to an army in time of war. Peaches were especially delicate—a miscalculation of forty-eight hours could result in the loss of tens of thousands of dollars.

Margaret, along with many of her top employees, had been juggling these figures since seven o'clock that morning. It was now well past noon. Alejandro had stood quietly in the background, listening and watching. He no longer had any doubts that Sam Winslow was the true foreman of Devereaux farm. Over the preceding five hours, Sam had cleverly controlled the meeting, quietly interceding time and again to measure with amazing perception the actual requirements of each harvesting area, even while beating back the self-serving demands of the section supervisors. Margaret had sided with him on every issue.

This had embarrassed Strother Finnegan, the putative foreman. Vaguely liberal in his attitude toward blacks and Mexicans, he was now goaded by what he considered a galling setback at the hands of a black man with twenty years less experience. His benign attitude towards blacks in general, and Sam Winslow in particular, had begun to erode. The telephone rang, for what seemed the fifteenth time that morning. Sam answered it in a voice that belied the calm manner he had managed to maintain for the last several hours.

"What the hell is it now?" he asked of the caller at the other end of the line. He paused, cupped the receiver, and said to Margaret, "It's Hennessy. Sounding even louder than usual." Margaret groaned. The difficulties she was encountering reminded her of another morning—five months before—when she sat alone making her father's funeral arrangements. Then as now, she felt overwhelmed by both his death and the awesome responsibility she had inherited.

"Oh, sweet Jesus," Margaret muttered to Sam. "Tell Jake I have laryngitis, or something."

Sam grinned and turned back to the receiver. "Miss Margaret can't talk right now. Says she's got laryngitis, or something."

A commotion came over the line. Sam held the receiver at arm's length. "Wish Mister Hennessy would develop himself a permanent case of that disease," he muttered. Margaret reluctantly reached for the receiver.

"You catch me at a rather bad moment. Can I call you back in a couple of hours?"

The racket on the line grew louder. Margaret's tired-looking eyes went darker. She listened for another few moments, and then turned to Alejandro, who was standing near a radio. Twisting her fingers in the direction of the radio, she indicated that she wanted him to turn it on. But the only thing that came on was a snappy jingle for Campbell's tomato soup.

"Come on, Jake, the news can't be that bad. All I hear are soup commercials," Margaret responded. "I think you just tied on another drunk last night, and your brain turned to molasses this morning." But at just that moment an announcer's voice came over the radio. Sam, along with Margaret's foreman and one of her supervisors, who was still awaiting a final determination on his harvest area, drifted toward the radio.

"Hang on, Jake," Margaret said. "Something's coming on now."

A newscaster was hammering hard on what obviously sounded like a major news event.

—Now apparent that the migrant workers plan to lock off the entire harvest area, which will almost certainly lead to more of the violence that took place this morning, when two migrants were badly beaten in a savage brawl. But if this unprecedented labor dispute is not resolved very soon, there could be another casualty — a large peach crop worth better than a quarter million dollars, which within another week will reach spoilage state —

As the broadcast continued, Margaret returned to the telephone. Hennessy's voice was still coming from the end of the line. It took her a moment to break through his monologue. "Hey, listen to me, dammit! You were right. Does look pretty serious," she said. "But I still don't want to hear about any more workers getting beaten up. You feel the urge coming on again, just remember one thing: that crop of peaches can't be picked by people who are in a hospital."

As Hennessy's reply boomed over the receiver, Margaret hung up the telephone and walked toward the center of the room. As instinctively as the others had gravitated toward the radio, she moved closer to the portrait of her father over the stone hearth.

The broadcast ended. Its message, however, lay over the room like a funeral wreath. Margaret's foreman was the first to speak, his face flushed with anger. "First thing we oughta do when we get on top of this mess is shovel back to Mexico every ungrateful greaser in this valley," Finnegan exclaimed, using his bulky arm as the bulldozer he would employ in such an effort.

Margaret frowned. Noting her expression, Finnegan paused, and smiled in Alejandro's direction, as if to grant him a dispensation. "Except the good ones, of course," the foreman murmured. "Ones who have proven themselves fine, decent and patriotic Americans."

'My father thought that included a lot of Mexicans," Margaret quietly observed. "He used to say that without them, we would have had a tougher time ten years ago winning the big war."

"Besides," Sam added, "many of them now naturalized American citizens, anyway."

The foreman turned away to light a cigar. Alejandro stood waiting for something to happen. The news of the strike unnerved him more than he let on. His first reaction to the broadcast had been to put as much distance as he could between himself and the radio. Dammit, Miss Margaret," the supervisor said, "oughta be something we can do."

Margaret turned to her father's portrait, something she rarely did in front of other people, fearful it might make her appear even less authoritative than her foreman had always thought her to be. "Yeah, but Dad used to say that sometimes what helps the most are the things we choose not to do."

305

Ramón Rompego knew that the first contingent of workers to arrive at the harvest site would bear the initial brunt of the trouble. Further, he realized that by delaying the arrival of his own workers, most of the major issues might be resolved by the time his caravan got into camp. If he waited, a confrontation with Margaret and Sam, which might cost him his powerful position on the Devereaux farm, could be avoided.

Several migrants had contested Ramon's stalling tactic. The most outspoken was the Filipino, Juan Rizal. Francisco had charged him with the responsibility of moving those workers into place, knowing Ramon would find any excuse to drag his feet. But Rizal's efforts to speed the caravan up were checked by Ramón's bulky bodyguard; the bully still harbored a smoldering resentment over the humiliation he had suffered a few days before.

Early that afternoon Margaret spotted Ramon's caravan nestled under some large shade trees a hundred yards off the main highway. Along with Sam and Alejandro she had gone first to the harvest site and, seeing that Ramon's workers had not yet arrived, doubled back along the highway looking for them.

By the time the station wagon pulled up to the caravan Ramon's seventy-five migrant workers had reached the breaking point— hungry, tired, and disgusted that it would be nightfall before they made it to the camp.

Margaret wasted no time in asking Ramon and his workers not continue on to the campsite. She first wanted to meet with the other growers to see if they could reach a settlement with Francisco Salazar.

This was, of course, Ramon's intention. But he now quickly realized it might work to his personal advantage to pretend otherwise. His face wrinkled with feigned worry as he began to protest loudly.

Following the conversation from a short distance away, Juan Rizal had the feeling that Ramón and Margaret were dancing around each other, she urgently requesting of him something he already intended to do, he demanding the right to move on, something he had no intention of doing.

"But Ramón, if your workers join up with Salazar before I've had a chance to iron all this out, it's not going to work to anybody's benefit, including your own!"

Ramón smiled. She had finally mentioned the one thing that interested him. "But after my workers are in the camp, there will be plenty of time to reach agreement that—"

"Ramón," Margaret interjected. "We're running out of time—and have you ever tried telling produce ready for picking to be a little more patient?" The real reason she wanted to stall Ramon's progress was that if his workers were at the camp before an agreement had been reached, Francisco would have his full force in place, ensuring that the bargaining was in his favor.

Breaking out a Hershey bar from his cache, Ramón slowly chewed it as he pondered Margaret's question. She seemed to have run out of arguments. Margaret and Sam had discussed this possibility on the way over, and Sam had recommended that any final gesture be made by Francisco Salazar's son.

They were aware that the migrants had not accepted Alejandro. An announcement of a wage raise coming directly from him might help change their minds, making him a more efficient employee. She disliked anything that was not productive, and people were no exception.

But Margaret had not discussed with the other growers, nor had they approved, the wage raise. She turned back to Ramón with one last entreaty. "Well, you stay stupid like this, and you're going to end up with blood all over your hands."

Ramón angled toward Alejandro. "Yes, but if Francisco Salazar think I go back on my word of honor—which everybody know is my proud possession—the blood on my hands will be my own!" Ramón's declaration seemed to please him.

Margaret studied the workers clustered around the battered vehicles that had miraculously brought them this far. With visible reluctance, she nodded to Alejandro. This was the moment he had been waiting for since the first hour he had gone to work for the Devereaux farm: his chance to prove himself a true friend to the farm workers.

Reaching into Margaret's station wagon, he drew forth a battery-powered bullhorn. "Listen to me," he called out in Spanish. Then, noting that the long caravan contained more than a sprinkling of blacks, he reverted to English. "Now we know you are anxious to get to the new camp. But it is a dangerous place right now. Already two of your fellow workers have been badly injured—so until this trouble can be settled, Miss Devereaux wants you to stay away from the camp—and as a sign of her good intentions, she now offers you a three-cent raise over the wage that was offered only a few days ago."

A mild cheer came from the crowd. But as the applause abated, a question came from the rear of the caravan. "So meantime, Salazar, we sit here listening to the growling of our empty stomachs?" queried a black man dressed in tattered overalls, and a gaunt-looking child in his arms.

Alejandro had no answer. Both Margaret and Sam had, however, already given the matter some thought. She muttered a few words to Alejandro, who now turned back to the crowd. "Your stomachs will not remain empty. For as long as you stay here, you will eat as the guests of the Devereaux farm. Food will be brought to you. That is a promise from the Señorita herself."

From a bus crammed beyond capacity with sweltering passengers, a Mexican leaned out the window and yelled, "Hey, what good are these promises, Salazar? I heard better promises than that over at the fucking Salvation Army!"

Alejandro's eyes hardened. "Take the garbage out of your mouth and hear me again! You have the word of the Señorita herself—and who here can remember her ever going back on a promise?"

None of the migrants, it seemed, could recall such an instance. Yet their final response came slowly, like in a rural election, one vote at a time. Several workers slowly began to climb down off their vehicles, smiling shyly in Alejandro's direction. More than his words, his display of temper had convinced them of his sincerity. In their world anger was a reliable indicator of anyone's true intentions.

Ramón appraised Alejandro with the expression of an actor who has just seen his understudy deliver a matchless performance. Ramón was himself not as good an actor. His hostility hung over him like a billboard.

"Okay, Salazar," he murmured, "I do what the Señorita wants—but only on the condition you do something for me."

Alejandro waited to hear this condition. He hoped it would not completely unravel the agreement.

"I want you to be telling," Ramón continued, "to both your father and your uncle that while they were getting people's heads bashed up, I was getting the raise they wanted!"

Ramon's caveat could be easily granted and might even work toward a larger purpose, Alejandro thought. He took Ramon's hand, and said, "You have my word — and by tomorrow morning, it will be my father himself shaking your hand."

"Or wringing his neck! Having gotten that off his chest, Juan Rizal angrily shouldered his duffel bag and started away on foot toward the highway. But Ramon's elation was not to be squelched by a single defection. Raising his arms, he clasped his hands over his head like a prize-fighter. The response from his workers was less than rousing. They knew that Ramón could turn almost anything into a self-serving celebration.

Margaret, more adroitly gauging the workers' mood, now decided to make her own departure, having already realized her purpose. Sam and Alejandro were inside the station wagon when she climbed into the back seat.

As Sam took the car toward the highway, Margaret leaned forward to lay a hand on Alejandro's shoulder. This surprised her almost as much as it did the two men in the front seat. She was not given to such physical gestures.

"Alex, I hope to do as well with the growers as you just did with the workers."

He did not know that the compliment was prompted by a rush of guilt; a feeling Margaret could not quite account for, yet one she knew was connected in some way with her new-found admiration for the son of her most implacable enemy.

CHAPTER 16

That same afternoon, a corps of sheriff's deputies tried to arrest Francisco's workers for breaking the county's trespass statutes. But to their teeth-grinding chagrin, they found that the migrant leader had the law on his side. Some few weeks earlier, Francisco had gone to the county seat, where he had sought out an elderly lawyer, one of the town's few civil libertarians. The old gentleman, Francisco had heard, had recently taken on the Senate Committee on Un-American Activities. Publicly, he had branded the politicians who were the driving force behind the hearings as the "most un-American men in America." The old lawyer's statement had not played well in south Texas—but for Francisco, it was all the recommendation he needed.

After first researching the law and the county records, the lawyer delivered a favorable opinion. Still, Francisco had insisted on reading the applicable statutes for himself. This so impressed the lawyer that he had contributed his fee to what he guessed was Francisco's cause. Then he took him to the best restaurant in town and bought him the most expensive meal on the menu. Francisco had eaten his food in silence, aware of the stares boring into him from every corner of the large room.

But leaving the county seat, he was in buoyant spirits—knowing now that his workers had as much right to the rural roads and the fifteen feet of county easement alongside them as anybody else. These narrow strips of land would afford the beachhead from which he could wage his war against the growers.

On the easement to the county road leading down from the main highway on which Francisco and his workers were now bivouacked, small campfires lined both sides of the road for hundred yards. The song Las Mananitas could be heard over the stillness. Sung in Mexico to young people on the morning of their birthday, it had come several hours too late today. Still, nobody had expected this moment of celebration. But Francisco was good about remembering birthdays and had even sent someone into town to buy a cake. María was accompanying the song on her guitar, her eyes on Ilsita Villareal, the little girl whose birthday it was.

A few yards away, Francisco stood with Pedro, Paquito and Thomas Jones, watching. They had each contributed a few coins to the modest collection María had taken up for the child. Yet Ilsita's eyes seemed to be searching for someone who was not there. She had eaten very well this evening, almost as well as she had on another special occasion many nights before. Peering around, she looked again for the young man in the strange uniform who had been her benefactor that night, the evening he had first returned from a place her mother told her later was very far away.

As the singing continued, some half-dozen cattle trucks rumbled by on their way to the camp another few hundred yards down the road. The trucks were loaded with indigents like those who had been brought in the day before. But after the brawl with the workers, many of them had scattered like lint blown by the wind.

Paquito heaved a sigh. "By the morning there will be enough people in that camp to pick the peaches."

Pedro flashed a hollow smile. "But if Ramón and his workers ever get here, we will have enough men to keep them from getting their hands dirty."

However, both Pedro and Francisco had already given up on Ramón. If he had not arrived by now, they knew he wouldn't be coming until their dispute with the growers was settled. The war with the growers would have to be waged with some thirty percent fewer men than Francisco had counted on—a serious setback, but one that he had been curiously reluctant to discuss.

As the last truck had rolled by the encampment, Pedro decided to finally open up the matter. But in turning back toward Francisco, he was stymied by the expression on his leader's face. Francisco was intently looking at the little girl whose birthday they were celebrating, but seemed to be seeing someone else. He was remembering other birthdays celebrated alongside the rural roads of south Texas. But his little boy had never seemed to mind, for back in those distant days, he had loved everything his father ever did or said.

By the following morning, thousands of residents of the Rio Grande Valley had heard about the strike, and many had summoned forth a wave of wrath the force of which they had not felt in more than ten years, not since the Japanese sneak attack on Pearl Harbor. Some hundred vehicles now sat alongside the edge of the harvest site as several state troopers—and at least a half-dozen reporters—warily prowled the perimeters of the workers' makeshift camp.

Several reporters walked past the long line of workers to inspect the situation inside the indigent camp. The vagrants were provided hot food from two large portable kitchens, yet despite food and shelter better than most had ever enjoyed, they seemed apprehensive.

After the roundup of a few days before, their numbers had grown far fewer. Of the several truckloads that hauled them in the night before, about half had sneaked out of the camp, once they ate as much food as they could hold. Most of these luckless vagrants, it seemed, had no stomach for anything else.

The most archconservative radio station in the valley had sent Larry Edwards, its best reporter, to cover this story about striking farm workers. Edwards figured it would be one of the toughest assignments in his ten-year career—one that had included on-site broadcasts from burning buildings and police shoot-outs. The danger, as Edwards saw it, was not to his physical person but to his sense of professionalism. He already sensed that any fair, objective reporting of the strike would create a clash with the county's established power structure, as well as with his own bosses at the radio station.

The star radio reporter had once attended the same small teachers' college as Lyndon B. Johnson. By this time, Johnson was one of the most powerful members of the United States Senate. Many Texans liked to boast that he might someday become the first Texan to occupy the White House.

Edwards often dwelt on the career of his school's most famous graduate. He envied the Senator's rare knack for helping poor people even while drawing support from the rich. Few people in the entire country had ever mastered the trick—and none probably in Texas. Larry Edwards knew that he was not among them. He would pay the consequences if he tried to follow the dictates of fair play.

Getting a signal from his chief technician, the reporter took a deep breath and began to speak into a microphone that had been set up outside the camp. "Good morning. Larry Edwards speaking." The voice was surprisingly resonant, coming as it did from such a slender man. But Edwards' professional role model for many years had been the famed newscaster Edward R. Murrow, a fact now apparent in the Texan's clipped, portentous style. Edwards had learned from a legend that a newscaster's voice could lend weight to even the lightest of topics. He now spoke with a quiet yet hard-punched urgency that would have done justice to the Battle of Britain.

"I'm standing here alongside a little country road just outside the town of Mission, where one of the biggest battles to ever hit the Rio Grande Valley might soon be decided. The migrant worker strike, the first ever in this entire region, if not in the entire country, I believe—which I initially reported upon yesterday—now seems like nothing short of a brush war. But to this observer, it looks like one the migrant workers cannot win. At this moment the growers are making an all-out effort to round up enough outsiders to harvest this peach crop themselves."

As Edwards summarized the situation, his voice was being heard over many thousands of radios in the valley. One of those radios belonged to Pedro Terán; a tiny model he had wired into the electrical system of his car. As he listened, Pedro was driving slowly along the county road that led back to the highway. Moments earlier, he had driven Francisco and Tom Jones down to the camp to get a current count on the number of indigents still remaining. Returning to their own settlement, the voice on the radio narrated what they had seen.

"Meantime, the growers are providing hot food and soft drinks for those in the camp, and, I might add, have promised to do so for anybody else who wants to go to work."

Pedro flinched. This offer would be very tempting to the two hundred workers whose own food supply would be exhausted in another forty-eight hours. Then, he caught sight of a solitary figure approaching from the highway. If it was who he thought it was, the news would soon get worse.

Edwards paused for a commercial, and in the interim, one of his assistants came out of the control truck to hand him a note. Reading it, the newsman lit a cigarette, took a couple of puffs, and turned back to the microphone.

"Welcome back, folks, to our on-site broadcast of the migrant worker strike. Only moments ago, we received word that the workers from the Devereaux farm, under the leadership of someone named Ramón Rompego, have agreed to settle for a tentative wage-offer of some two cents an hour above the raise first offered several days ago. We will try to confirm this report with other sources—but if our information is correct, this shall surely force the other leaders of this strike to seriously reconsider their position—an uncomfortable spot that to this reporter would now seem to rest between the old proverbial rock and a hard place."

Thomas Jones, riding in the front seat of Pedro's car, cut off the radio. "Don't rightly think that to be the case," Jones angrily exclaimed. "Wouldn't be the first time them radio folks twisted the truth around for—"

"It is true," Pedro said, recognizing the approaching figure. "I had the feeling Ramón would do this."

Jones's haggard features hardened. "But the man done give us his word," Jones exclaimed. In the simple world of the migrant worker, there was no more binding form of contract.

"Yes," Pedro replied with a parched smile, "that was when I first know we were in trouble."

Jones started to retort, then swallowed his sentiments. He knew he had a tendency to sermonize.

Francisco had said nothing, still half-hoping that the radio report was only another ploy. But when he looked up ahead and saw Rizal trudging toward the encampment, his hopes flickered out like a candle caught in a sudden draft.

Francisco turned back to the workers, who having seen him approach, had gathered along the edge of the road. He knew most of them by name, knew their histories, how many children they had, and which of those kids had ever been seriously ill, even knew where most of these workers had originally come from. But now, for the first time, he was no longer certain of where they were going—nor if they had the courage to get there, wherever it was. They had responded well the morning before, but that had been easy enough. His speech had dwelt mainly on reclaiming their sense of pride, rather than on the sacrifices entailed in the effort.

Francisco remembered how during the early months of the Korean War, many an outraged patriot had turned pacifist with the arrival of his draft notice.

Voices came from the front seat, but they sounded to him like the mutterings from a distant daydream.

"—Still think Ramón will be too scared to take them folks of his into the fields alongside them scabs."

"Yes, he does not have the courage to be a rat. Only a mouse," another voice replied.

"But if the growers don't know that, they're gonna think they don't have to negotiate with us now. What we oughta do is get back in touch with them, see if this thing can still be settled."

Francisco's eyes snapped into focus. "It is the only thing we can do," he said aloud. He knew what he had to do. Reality had ruined his other options. "Stop the car."

Pedro and Jones, thinking that he had decided to try and settle the strike, exchanged a surprised smile. But it lasted only until Francisco jumped from the car with a bullhorn in his hand. Facing the line of workers closest to him, he called out to them over the bullhorn, his voice an amplified whisper.

"Amigos, we have lost the support of Ramón Rompego. Like the scared mouse he is, he has made his own deal with the growers. But our struggle can still be won. Ramón and the scabs cannot pick the peaches if they cannot reach them. The growers with all their power cannot provide them with arms that long—but now it will probably get worse for us before it gets better."

He paused to catch María's eye. She was standing some fifty yards away with a group of migrant children.

"But it will get better if you can do one thing," he slowly continued. "You have to believe...not in me, but in yourselves and in your children and in our cause. If you can do this, not all the growers or the police, or all the politicians in this valley can stop you."

A smattering of applause came from the workers, but Francisco was already assigning people to various harvest fields. Watching him move through the large throng of farm workers, María trembled. He was sending unarmed migrants off to war; yet they were moving briskly and in exact accord with his commands.

In that moment, María felt she no longer knew the man she loved. Yet, she sensed now that her destiny was so entwined with his, nothing short of death would ever separate them.

Then she caught a glimpse of something that brought a sudden rush of tears to her eyes: a vision of a man who had struggled for many years to build a refuge for himself and his friends — but as his shelter was nearing completion, he would realize that there was no room for him in the very structure he had built. He was standing at its door but somehow could not move into it.

Confused and distraught by this strange image flashing through her mind, she made no real effort to understand its meaning. There were other things to worry about now — like the small children still standing by her side, silent and wide-eyed with apprehension.

For the past fifteen minutes, the somber-sounding voice on the radio had summarized what had transpired at the harvest site over the last several hours. It was late afternoon, and the dark, heavy curtains in Margaret's office had been drawn, giving it the look of a sitting room in a mortuary.

Indeed, the twenty two men gathered at the Devereaux house that afternoon seemed mourners at a funeral. Only five of them, however, would be immediately affected if the news got no better: the five growers whose acreage was directly involved with the strike. Yet this made the predicament no less important to the other growers, foremen, and supervisors whom Margaret had brought together. All would feel the severe aftershock of a successful labor strike, an unnatural event many of them thought tantamount to an earthquake.

Apparently Francisco Salazar was going forward with the strike. Earlier, the growers had expected him to arrive, hat in hand, to make whatever deal he could. Now it seemed obvious that he would not be coming at all, hat in hand, or otherwise. There was no use in denying the authenticity of the newscast. Larry Edwards's professional integrity was an accepted fact. If Edwards said something over the air, you could, to use the local vernacular, take it to the bank — a place now much on the minds of several of the growers in the room.

For every hour the strike continued, the cost of settling it would go higher, and if it could not be resolved before spoilage set in, their loss would be disastrous.

Margaret had been unusually quiet throughout the afternoon, trying to figure out how her father might have handled the situation. She remembered his skill at settling disputes, his manner of always approaching a problem from the direction of his opponent. She alone of all the growers had tried to comprehend what had motivated Francisco to bring the battle to such an explosive level. She was fated to fail in this effort; for to her way of thinking, the issue still seemed one of money—a battle between those who wanted more and those committed to keeping what they had.

In reality, it was a clash between cultures. Margaret could not understand Francisco's complex nature nor see that behind the mask he almost always wore was a three-thousand-year old heritage which revered not success, but honor. The raise she had offered Ramón Rompego might have been enough to settle the strike, but she had made the offer to the wrong man.

Inadvertently, she had placed Francisco in a position where he would have to refuse any offer that breached a protocol he had spent ten years in protecting—and if prolonging the strike cost him his life, it would be of no great consequence. To him, dishonor was far worse than death.

CHAPTER 17

Alejandro had been standing off in the far shadows of the room all afternoon, some instinct having prompted him to remain as unnoticed as possible. As twilight settled in, Margaret walked around the room, turning on a few lamps. She had not paid much attention that afternoon to either Alejandro or Jake Hennessy, who also had sought out some form of protection.

Encamped behind the bar, Hennessy was now less than sober, but far from drunk. As Margaret moved past him, he lurched up to his full height, much like a schoolboy straightening up as his teacher passes by his desk.

"Hell," Hennessy said in a sodden voice, "we oughta just let the state troopers haul all that trespassing trash off to the garbage dump for about thirty days."

Margaret did not bother to turn back. She no longer had time for irrelevant issues or non-productive opinions.

"Oh, sure, people," Margaret muttered, "and let that sad bunch of scabs kick all the profit out of our produce."

Bert Agajanian looked up sharply. "Jake, you're still chewing on the wrong bone. Salazar was smart enough to get his folks camped on county roads. So best pull yourself together—because if you can't be part of the solution, we're gonna have to regard you as part of the problem."

Hennessy grinned at the crusty old grower and made a show of setting aside his bottle. Pouring himself a Dr. Pepper, he gulped it down like it was the first thing he had to drink in several days.

Sol Medak, another one of the growers, had been uncommonly quiet that afternoon. He was a grizzled-jawed old Armenian whose family, like Margaret's, had first settled in the valley more than fifty years earlier. He was a man who, on principle, disliked no one, except, of course, the Turks, who had once almost destroyed his homeland. Most of the migrants who worked for the

Armenian thought him a good employer. Neither his station in life nor theirs had ever gotten in the way. But Medak's hard-earned security was about to be seriously threatened by the strike, and like many another good man before him, the old Armenian was suddenly finding it difficult to make the payments on his moral principles.

"Okay, Maggie, you may be right," the Armenian said, "maybe another ten cents more an hour might settle this strike. But what will it take to settle the next one, and the one after that? I go no further, because by that time I will probably be working for the migrants myself!"

Margaret liked and respected the old man, though at times she thought he could be a little dense. "Sol, don't you see? If we can't get this current harvest in, there might not be another harvest for some of the growers in this room."

Several growers glanced furtively in each other's direction, none seemingly anxious to be placed in such a tenuous category, where a single disastrous harvest might permanently put them out of business. Proud men, they wore their financial independence like a favorite suit of clothes, though many among them now stood to have it severely curtailed if the strike continued— especially Jake Hennessy.

He had brought his foreman, Jess Ballard, and Maurice Ripps to the meeting. Neither had said a word for hours, though by now each had his own notion of how the strike might be settled. Ballard leaned toward Margaret's idea that another ten-cent raise might be enough to turn the tide, though this solution would surely cut into his own profits. Yet he also knew that if the strike continued, there would be more casualties like those he had taken to the hospital the previous morning.

Ripps thought the stand-off could be solved with far less monetary sacrifice. All he needed was a couple of crop-dusting planes and Salazar would stagger back to his senses. The ex-convict was hoping someone would ask him his opinion. Mauling migrants was something he did well, and like most men, he welcomed any opportunity to show off his expertise.

Agajanian had already arrived at the same solution. Swiveling around in his chair, he suddenly fired off a question that sounded more like an insult. "Hennessy! How many them sorry scabs you been able to round up?" the crusty-skinned old grower demanded.

Caught off guard, Jake Hennessy spilled a bit of his Dr. Pepper over the front of his shirt. He waved a finger in the direction of his foreman. "Well, I can't say for sure, sir. My foreman's been doing the head counting."

Every eye in the room turned toward Ballard. Most of the men knew him and were aware that without his expert guidance, Hennessy would never have lasted a year in what they liked to call the "big leagues." They also knew that Jess Ballard was an ill-tempered man who had never managed to own a farm of his own. Hence, in their eyes, his opinions were tainted by both his personality and unsuccessful past.

Ballard slowly strode to the center of the room. "With all due respect, Mister Agajanian, I don't think it matters a hoot and a holler how many scabs we got—"

"Just say your piece, get done with it," the old grower growled.

Ballard smiled. "Assuming you boys can stomach some truth for a change, it's like this," he drawled, pleased that many of the growers were already frowning.

"Half them scabs that came didn't stay past the few first times they got their nose into the feedbag—and them still there, ain't none that look much interested in putting out an honest day's worth of work."

Ballard aimed his words directly at Agajanian. "Now you keep bitching about paying out more money to Salazar's farm workers—but you already spent half a ton of dollar bills on a sad bunch of scabs who think hard work is something that oughta be outlawed."

Ballard paused to gauge whether he had made the slightest dent, then quickly continued. What it comes down to, once all the horse manure has been scraped off, is this: even allowing for another ten-cent raise, them farm workers, some with twenty-years' experience, are still gonna be making less than some damned dishwasher on his first day on the job. So I think you boys need to get with the program. We're in the middle of the twentieth century, in case nobody's checked a calendar lately."

From across the room, Alejandro winced. There was a fine line between courage and foolhardiness, and Ballard had not only crossed it, he had trampled on it. He had long been fascinated by Ballard, considering him as an outsider in spite of his position and power—a man deeply imbued with that reckless form of courage that sometimes comes to a man who no longer expects anything but the worse. Alejandro had seen that hopeless sense of valor in the desolate mountains of Korea.

Something strange then happened. Every eye in the room swung away from Ballard as half-a-dozen conversations burst forth. It seemed as if Hennessy's foreman had never opened his mouth, indeed had never even been in the room.

"Yeah, but if we could just get enough of them scabs into the fields, that might stampede some sense into that damned Salazar," came one suggestion from the center of the room.

The old Armenian bolted to his feet. "Listen, I am sick of such stupid talk! Let's do now what we should have done yesterday. Make Salazar this one last offer and leave all this silly stampede stuff to the cattle business."

Margaret looked as if she had just been thrown a life preserver. "And let's do it now, before there's even more bad blood between us and the workers."

"Oh, hell, we got more'n enough bad blood now to last us a life-time," Hennessy muttered from his command post behind the bar. "What we need is a bit more pride, some-thing Miss Margaret apparently don't think so precious no more."

Before Margaret could react to this surprise attack, coming as it did from a source she had thought totally immobilized, Sam ambled to the center of the room.

"Pardon me, but I'd like to relate some news that's come in over the last few hours," he said in a cool, deferential way. The growers peered at Sam for a long moment, and then nodded grudgingly, granting him access to their undivided attention. But it was only a temporary visa and revocable at a moment's notice. The growers were not in the mood for another scolding.

Gauging the prevailing mood, Sam continued. "What we've heard is this: with the radio broadcasts and all, the wholesale buyers now know the trouble we're in—and they are out looking for another source of peaches. So if we don't get this strike settled mighty soon, they're gonna get one, even if they have to go all the way to Georgia to find it. Now, with every due respect, all the pride in Texas ain't gonna replace spoiled produce, nor lost markets neither."

Sam's mention of the possible loss of wholesale buyers made an impression on the growers. Harvests came and went, but big markets, once lost, tended to stay that way.

Margaret's eyes swept across the room as the growers, one by one, reluctantly nodded, finally approving her proposed wage hike, though in their eyes, it offered a solution almost as repugnant as the strike itself.

Having won the fight, Margaret decided to do some-thing she had been considering since the day before. She had been impressed with the way Alejandro had handled Ramón Rompego; so impressed she had decided to fire him. She realized it was a mistake, given the present predicament, to keep him on her payroll. It could only turn him and his father into bitter enemies. She thought herself stupid and callous for ever having hired him.

Her words came so soft that standing on the other side of the room, he had to strain to hear them. "Okay, Alex. Go tell your father it's sixteen cents an hour more. And when you go, you might as well stay. Your folks have greater need of you now than we do."

Noting his stunned expression, Margaret forced herself to finish off the job. Hell, even crippled animals were usually put out of their misery with a single shot. "I really decided yesterday, Alex, to let you go, when I realized that you're too fine a young man to get caught in the middle of all this."

Alejandro felt he'd just been kicked in the stomach but still had no idea why. "Excuse me, Señorita, but I don't understand —"

"Well, maybe one day you will," Margaret said, looking rather confused. "But by way of partially making it up to you, my book-keeper'll strike you off a severance check for three months' pay." There seemed nothing more to say. Alejandro nodded curtly and strode off toward the front door.

He had not felt so humiliated since the time many years before when his father had slapped him in front of several people. Yet this seemed worse, for it had come with no warning and less reason.

The growers watched him make the long walk across the huge room. No sooner had he walked out of the room, however, than they began to converse as if nothing out of the ordinary had happened. What to him was a tidal wave had struck the growers as little more than a pebble hitting a stream, making a ripple, and then quickly disappearing beneath the surface.

Sam Winslow stood waiting at the front door. He was not at all sorry to see Alejandro depart, but the swiftness of the dismissal had shaken him. Sam knew that for a black man or a Mexican living in south Texas, the trip from the penthouse back to the outhouse often could come with the abruptness of a summer storm.

"I'll have that check delivered to your boarding house," Sam said. "No sense you coming back here just to get caught again in a buzz saw. Good luck, Alex. If it means anything to you, I think you did a helluva good job for us," Sam muttered with a pained smile, stretching out his hand.

After shaking hands with him, Alejandro hurried out of the house and started down a sloping lawn toward the circular drive where his coupe was parked. Reaching the driveway, he paused to look at the other vehicles parked nearby — all far newer than his own.

He noted the make and color of each car and pickup truck. This information, he thought, might later come in handy. Already a plan was forming. If he could not retrieve the irreplaceable, his sense of honor, he had decided to do the next best thing: wreak revenge on those who had so unjustly robbed him of it. In this, he was very much like his father.

Half an hour later, Jake Hennessy came out of the Devereaux house to find Bert Agajanian sitting inside Hennessy's open convertible. "Jake, I sent my driver on ahead," he declared, leaning across the front seat to open Hennessy's door for him. "I'll hitch a ride with you, if it ain't too much bother."

"Oh, be a privilege," Hennessy purred, sliding behind the wheel.

The two men rode for several miles in silence before Agajanian observed aloud that Hennessy certainly owned a fine automobile. Beaming, the younger grower thumped his steering wheel.

"Yes, sir, she is indeed!" Hennessy exclaimed. "But if you'll forgive me, I don't think you came along with me just to see how my new car runs."

The old man shifted his granite-like features into a more pleasing arrangement. "What I like about you, Jake. Quick on the uptake — and I got me a plan that's gonna require some folks with both brains and brawn. That's where you come in, young fella."

Jake Hennessy suddenly was sorry he had sent Ballard and Ripps back to his farm with somebody else. He would have liked both men to have heard him praised by the most successful grower in the valley.

"You see, Jake," Agajanian continued, "I figure that while Miss Margaret is out playing the great philanthropist with our money, somebody oughta see to it that this strike is settled for a price we can all afford to pay. Follow me?"

Hennessy had no idea what he meant, but already knew that there was no way in hell he would refuse to go along with it. He had spent most of his adult life trying to win Agajanian's respect. Now his chance had come.

Alejandro had also formulated a plan. If it worked, the scheme would force the growers to settle the strike on the worker's terms, as well as provide him with more than enough money to make a fresh start somewhere else. The idea, he thought, was nothing short of perfect. It was also illegal, dangerous, and completely immoral. Driving back toward Mission, he grew uneasy.

He decided to make one stop before going on to see his father. This time he remembered to bring flowers. Standing next to his mother's grave, he recited the Lord's Prayer she had once taught him. He had come to seek her benediction—but the more he tried to justify his plan, the more stone-like the silence.

Like many Mexicans, he thought death as nothing more than the physical absence of the deceased, and over the past ten years he'd had countless conversations with his mother. Never once had he left her grave without feeling replenished in both heart and soul. But on this late, windy afternoon, he felt strangely vacant. For the first time since his mother had died, he felt she was truly dead.

Rising slowly to his feet, Alejandro noticed that the medals he had left behind the week before were now almost covered by the bluebonnets that grew wild over the graveyard. Had it been but a week, he mused, since he had first returned from the war? It felt more like a year.

A few hours earlier, Margaret Devereaux had told him that perhaps someday he would understand why she had fired him. Maybe, he thought, someday his mother would understand why he now had to avenge himself.

CHAPTER 18

The sun had fallen by the time he arrived at the migrant encampment. The workers had bunched together for their supper, the air sweet with the smell of pork beans, peppers, and corn tortillas.

He found his father near one of the many small fires that lined the settlement like crude streetlights. Maria stood nearby, cooking for Francisco and the little group of men gathered around the fire: Pedro, Paquito, Tom Jones, and Juan Rizal, the Filipino who had walked several miles the day before to bring them the news of Rompego's defection.

Alejandro quickly relayed the growers' final offer to his father, and a long moment he held his breath, fearful that his father might accept the offer. When it was refused, he quietly laid out his plan, mentioning first that he had been fired that afternoon.

"So I was right," Francisco said. "I told your Uncle Pedro the growers were just using you to bring pressure against your own people. When they realized you could not help them settle the strike, they threw you away like an old newspaper."

Alejandro had not come to that same conclusion, but he knew that arguing about it now would only confuse the larger issue. Peering into the fire, he said, "I know how to settle the strike...but in a way the growers are not going to like."

Francisco rose from his haunches and walked slowly around the fire. "But can you be sure that the growers will try to bring workers up from Mexico?" he quietly asked.

"Once the growers realize you have refused their final offer, they will be desperate for manpower. They know Ramón's workers will not cross your picket line. They also know the scabs cannot harvest the crop, and for sure not in the short time left before the peaches start to spoil."

Alejandro gazed directly into his father's eyes. "The growers will have to bring in at least two hundred men from below the border. Men desperate enough for work to cross your picket line. And the moment your own workers resist, the police will haul them away on an assault charge. Work will began, and then the pressure on you from your own people to settle the strike will be very strong. The growers will be back in control."

Alejandro paused, as if to allow his father to fully digest all he had said. "One thing more. The growers have brought workers up from Mexico before, with bribes at the border and money to the contractor who rounds up the men and trucks them across the river. There is only one road they can use, and they will come to-morrow night or never."

Alejandro turned to face the others, as if squaring off to hit any objection head-on. None was forthcoming, though Pedro's eyes were hanging on him like grappling hooks.

Francisco stretched his crippled hands over the fire and at last broke the silence. "And what if these workers never make it past the border guards at the river?"

Alejandro grinned. He had thought out his plan well and was prepared for questions tougher than this one. "If that happens, Papá, all we really lose is the money for the few supplies we will need, and those I will pay out of my own pocket. But if the work-ers do get across the river, and we have done nothing to stop them, the cost will be far greater."

The others were standing on a small rise that led up to the road. From where Alejandro knelt near the fire, they loomed above him like a jury in a trial of sorts, his father the judge.

Tom Jones had said nothing throughout the discussion. Now climbing to the edge of the road, he stared off to the south, as if already envisioning the convoy coming from Mexico. "You talk-ing trash," he said softly to Alejandro. "It'd take a miracle to stop that convoy of trucks."

"To stop them, yes," Alejandro replied. "But nothing more than a couple of good men to turn them in the wrong direction."

Hearing this, Pedro lurched down toward Alejandro. "You told us that," Pedro said, drawing ominously closer. "What I want to know is why you tell us all this."

Alejandro warily came to his feet. "If they bring in two hundred workers," he said, "the growers will have to pay the contractor maybe ten dollars for each man—two thousand dollars. My father and I, who will be taking most of the risk, will each take a fourth of the money. Your workers keep the rest for food. It could be the difference in winning or losing."

Pedro had already surmised such a motive. His voice went husky with contempt. "So, after we break the law by sending the contractor in the wrong direction, we break it again by stealing the money that was waiting for him!"

Alejandro had never stolen anything in his life, and his uncle's words burned him like a hot iron. "Call it what you want. But the growers and the contractor, who will also be breaking the law, will not lose too much sleep over it. Besides, I'm going after the money alone. If I am lucky, all of you win. If I fail, the rest of you lose nothing."

Pedro's weathered features tightened. "But if you do not make it back safely, your father will lose a son, and I a nephew."

Pedro heaved a sigh and drifted away. Alejandro went to squat next to his father, who was warming his mangled hands over the fire. For a while both men simply stared into the flame.

"For ten years now, you have been struggling here in this valley, yet you've never saved enough money to even buy yourself a decent coat. So, for once, get something for yourself. Remember what we lost because you could not afford a five-dollar bottle of medicine."

That was something Francisco would never forget. But the memory did not motivate him as Alejandro had hoped. His father rose abruptly to his feet. "Your Uncle Pedro speaks the truth. This plan is not legal. Even worse, it is not right. It is also dangerous, you going after the money alone. Do you think I have so many sons I can lose one to such a crazy idea?"

The decision seemed inexplicable, yet his father's eyes told him that it was final. Francisco started toward the trucks parked at the far end of the encampment, going to check on the amount of food that was still left, something he had done several times over the past few days. Each successive trip had been harder than the last. His feet dragged as he trudged past the long line of migrant workers whom he would no longer be able to feed in another thirty-six hours.

Watching his father walk away, Alejandro angled up the incline. His ambitious plan had given way to a more modest one; as of now, he was just another poor Mexican looking for a job.

His next letter to his cousin Miguel would not be so optimistic.

CHAPTER 19

Miguel Salazar's body was like a badly battered old car that needed to be warmed up for several minutes before it could be put in gear. Mornings made him feel old. His routine never varied. First he would sit on the edge of his bed and massage his lame leg; then, when it seemed to be was working, he would limp across the living room of his small apartment into a tiny kitchen and put on a fresh pot of coffee.

After that, he would shower and shave. Never having grown to like his looks, he had perfected the trick of shaving without looking at himself full-face in the mirror. When he had dressed, the coffee was usually ready. Next he would go to the front door and pick up the newspaper, and only then would he start to make his breakfast, always the same thing. His friend Alfonso joked that Miguel ate cornflakes so often, he made a crunching sound when he walked.

By now, the street had come alive with the racket of people going off to work. It was the noisiest street in the barrio, and Alfonso had often urged Miguel to find a better neighborhood. He could afford a much nicer apartment, but he had lived in this same area since he first came with his family from Chihuahua City, and it gave him a sense of continuity to remain there. Almost everything else in his life had drastically changed. His parents and older brother were now gone, and his younger brother, Santiago, was away in college.

Munching his cornflakes, Miguel studied the sports section of the paper. He had become an avid fan of the New York Yankees. Alfonso had once asked him why, of all the teams in the major leagues, he had pledged such undying loyalty to the Yanks—an easy question to answer. Though they were a team comprised mainly of cripples and castoffs, they still possessed the character to win the most important games.

It was now half-past seven. Leafing through the paper one last time, Miguel searched for news about a migrant worker strike in south Texas. There was nothing in the El Paso Times about it.

"I hope you make it," Miguel said aloud, thinking about his Uncle Francisco. Talking to himself was a habit he had fallen into soon after Santiago had left for college. Some people teased him about it, but he had made no effort to curb the habit. Somehow it made him feel less lonely.

He had just started away from the apartment house when he thought to check his mailbox; an easy thing to forget since he rarely received any mail. But his good spirits lasted only as long as it took him to read Alejandro's letter, the first his cousin had written since returning from Korea. Crossing the crowded street, he called Alfonso from a pay phone to say he would be a little late for work.

Though Miguel hadn't been there in several years, it was exactly as he remembered it. The little park was still frequented mainly by old men. Standing at the gate, he watched them as they stood or sat, seemingly frozen in their tracks. His brother Santiago had been right when he once likened the park to an elephant graveyard.

Finding an empty bench, he sat down and carefully reread Alejandro's letter. He had rarely received such an optimistic report from his cousin. Yet the more he read, the more somber he became. He was, however, happy that Alejandro was so pleased with his new job, proud of the effort he was making on behalf of the farm workers entrusted to his care. It sounded like soul-satisfying work. Alejandro had found a cause. Carefully refolding the letter, Miguel put it back inside the envelope and tucked it in the breast pocket of his army jacket.

An old man now sat down next to him. Taking a small thermos from a burlap sack, he turned to Miguel, and with a toothless smile and a feeble gesture, offered him some coffee.

"No, pero muchas gracias, Señor" Miguel muttered, turning away. His eyes slowly swept across the park. He thought again about the letter he had just read. Never before had he felt envious of Alejandro. But now he did. His own existence, by comparison, suddenly seemed dull and pointless.

He hated feeling sorry for himself, and now made a mental checklist of all the reasons why he shouldn't. After all, he had a fairly successful business, was in pretty good health, had a few fun-loving friends, and enjoyed the fights and baseball. Oh, sure, he would have liked to have had a houseful of kids, but he had never found but two women he wanted to marry. But hell, he thought, a man can't have everything.

"Stop whining, you silly bastard," he said out loud.

Hearing that, the old man next to him smiled nervously. Embarrassed, Miguel rose and started back toward the gate. His checklist had failed to console him. What was missing in his life was exactly that which had once, while in the army, given it some sense of purpose. His more recent goal of making a comfortable living had been a poor substitute.

Walking toward the gate, he nodded politely to a few of the sad-eyed old men. They were wearing military-style shirts that seemed left over from the First World War. His own wartime experiences flashed through his mind. Perhaps in a curious way, they were the answer to his dilemma.

He started downtown. But he had walked only a few blocks when he stopped to hail a cab. His lame leg had told him in the unmistakable language of pain that it had gone far enough.

Climbing into the cab, he asked the crusty-looking Anglo driver, "You know the GI Forum?"

"Never heard of it, pal," the driver grunted, flipping on his meter.

"It's up on Kansas Street." Miguel said, settling back for the short ride into downtown El Paso.

He had not been inside the offices of the GI Forum since a morning seven years earlier, when he had learned the full extent of the trouble both he and his construction company were in. Much had changed since then.

The GI Forum was the largest Hispanic organization in the United States. The chapter in El Paso chapter had been remodeled, substantially enlarged, and now employed a dozen people. When Miguel was first there, only Antonio Vargas and an elderly secretary staffed the office. The local Forum office was still named, however, after Miguel's former commander, Major Gabriel Navarrete.

Vargas was still there, though arthritis had recently forced him into a wheelchair, the disease severely hitting his already crippled limbs. He could, however, still hold a pencil in his hand and a phone to his ear, all he apparently needed to keep doing his job.

There was another man in Vargas's office that morning, and he too was in a wheelchair. Miguel had the feeling he had seen him somewhere before, but couldn't quite recall the occasion.

"Don't remember me, do you, Miguel?" the slight, frail-looking man asked with a friendly smile.

"You look familiar, but—"

"I was the bastard who gave you such a bum time that night you were the guest of honor at the GI Forum banquet," said Jorge Cantú. "But then, that was a long time ago."

"Hey, now I remember," Miguel said. "You were the guy who asked me how the hell I had gotten such a good job when I didn't know my ass from my elbow."

They both chuckled at the memory.

"Anyway, I never got the chance to apologize to you," Cantú said, extending his hand to Miguel.

"You kidding?" Miguel laughed, shaking hands. "If it hadn't been for you, I'd probably still be up there trying to explain how the hell I had gotten that job."

"Jorge now works with us here at the Forum," Vargas said. "Doing real good, too."

Miguel turned to look around the office. The walls, with their fresh coat of paint, had weathered the years better than Vargas and were still graced with the autographed photos of winners of important medals from the Second World War, though the collection now featured many of the heroes of the more recent war. Places like the Nantong River, Inchon, and the Chosen Reservoir had joined the list of locations where Mexican-American servicemen had distinguished themselves in battle.

Studying the photos, Miguel noted that Alejandro's former outfit was well-represented. It had been, even before the Korean War, a unit steeped in history. The First Marine Division had fought at Chateau Thierry during World War I, and later, during the Second World War, it had heroically brought the battle in the South Pacific to Japan's front door as the Marines had hammered their way across islands such as Iwo Jima and Guadalcanal, names indelibly associated with great moments in Marine history.

"Well, Miguel, you didn't come here after all these years just to look at the pictures on my walls," Vargas said with an inquisitive smile.

"I just wanted to see how things were going. Besides, I never thanked you for your help back during the time of my troubles."

Vargas sighed and lit his pipe. "I wish the story had ended on a happier note. I was sorry about your brother Raúl."

"Yeah, but in a way, it was a miracle he lasted as long as he did. Raúl liked to live close to the flame. Anyway, how are things going these days with you and the Forum?"

"Better in some ways, worse in others. The guys coming back from the Korean War are not welcomed like we were. Nobody cares much for a war that ended in a tie. The government has cut way back on veteran's benefits."

"What's the good news?" Miguel quietly asked.

"The Forum is much stronger now than it was in the beginning. We are in a better position to help our people receive what they already earned for themselves over in Korea."

"Yeah, maybe so. But I think your battle position here is slightly undermanned."

Vargas smiled. He had just guessed Miguel's reason for having come to see him. "What remedial measures would you recommend, Private Salazar?"

"You could use another volunteer."

"He'd have to be either real dedicated or real dumb. The pay for volunteers is not even as good as it used to be. Have anybody in mind?"

"I don't know how dedicated this guy is...and he's also a bit slow on his feet. But even a wheelchair doesn't seem to have slowed down you or Jorge, has it?"

Vargas extended his hand across the desk. "Welcome back, Miguel. Maybe General McArthur was wrong when he said old soldiers just fade away, eh?"

CHAPTER 20

Early that following morning, it was discovered that highly favorable weather conditions had momentarily stalled the crop spoilage. In any labor strike, time could determine the outcome, and Francisco's workers had just been dealt a major setback. Yet as he walked out of an orchard that morning he felt strangely relieved that the peach crop had held firm.

His concern for the crop was as natural to him as the color of his eyes. He had worked in harvest fields most of his life, first on his father's tiny farm in Chihuahua City, later on dozens of farms in south Texas.

He had always felt good whenever he walked alone through an orchard ripe with the first crop of a new season. The earth had again yielded forth its bounty, and in moments like these, he could almost forget how much he disliked the grower who owned the land.

Walking through an orchard ready for harvesting, he sometimes had the feeling the land truly belonged only to the people who loved it, those who knew and appreciated its miraculous capacity to survive neglect and regenerate time and again. He had spoken of this for many years, but it was a fanciful notion that had yet to make him a dollar richer. Now he had other things on his mind.

It was barely eight o'clock in the morning, but already the harvest area was jammed with state troopers, news reporters and a small army of onlookers. They sensed that the workers' struggle could not go on much longer, and like a crowd at a bullfight, they wanted to be there for the kill.

Trudging toward the migrant encampment, Francisco was unaware that Larry Edwards had seen him. Saying nothing to the many other reporters standing nearby, the newsman angled toward Francisco. Edwards was the only reporter who had recognized the approaching figure in the wrinkled khaki pants and tattered coat as being the man whose photograph had been in some of the local newspapers.

"Morning, Salazar," Edwards said, a faint hint of friendliness in his voice. Francisco nodded, but did not slow his step. Edwards grimaced. Interviewing him would not be as easy as he had thought.

"Like to ask you a couple of questions, don't mind."

"If I do mind?" Francisco asked, staring straight ahead.

The newsman cleared his throat and quickened his step. "My name's Larry Edwards. News broadcasting is my game—"

"I know who you are, Señor. I am not so sure what your game is."

Edwards let loose a feeble laugh, then turned back to see if any of the other reporters had picked up Francisco's scent. Satisfied they hadn't, he hurried after him.

"Anyway, if you'd answer only a few questions, it might help balance our coverage just a bit."

Francisco's attention had gone to a group of migrants. Watching him approach, their expressions brightened.

"No, better ask your questions to somebody who still has some answers," Francisco replied, his eyes fastened on the workers.

The newsman twitched slightly. He was not accustomed to getting turned down. Yet his instincts warned him not to immediately press the issue. They walked in silence for some time before Edwards reframed his request.

"I think those folks of yours might see some advantage if their side of the story was told, for a change."

Francisco continued walking, though the novelty of such an idea became more attractive with every step he took. Finally, he stopped and turned to the newsman for the first time.

"Let's go someplace else. I don't want to be looking at all these poor people while I'm talking about them."

Edwards broke out his second smile of the morning.

"Got my station wagon just down the road, if you want to take a ride."

Francisco went on walking. Several migrants waved in his direction. Forcing up a smile, he solemnly returned their salute. Noting this exchange, Edwards said, "I think those folks know you're doing the best you can. Your problem, if I can interject a personal opinion, is in trying to do the right thing in the wrong place. Still, you've made one hell of an impression on a lot of people who don't impress that easily."

Francisco arched an eyebrow and chuckled. "Hey, if you're not careful, you're going to cheer me up."

"I've been careful all my life. That's my problem."

"Well, I tell you this, Mister Edwards. Right now, I would trade you even, my problem for yours."

Edwards smiled again—his third smile this morning—and for a second, he wondered what his broadcasting idol might say about that. Edward R. Murrow probably never smiled that much in an entire month.

Half an hour later, María was on her knees, washing some clothes alongside the bank of a small creek, a few hundred yards from the migrant camp. Bent over the water scrubbing clean the spare pair of khaki pants and shirt she had taken from Francisco's suitcase, she did not see the man approach. The creek, bordered by tall willow reeds, sat some ten feet down from a dirt road. It was cool and peaceful alongside the edge of the water, a welcome contrast to the heat and tumult back at the encampment.

A reflection appeared in the water of someone standing up on the rim of the road. Shading her eyes, she peered up toward the figure. Recognizing it, Maria shuddered.

An ominous smile slid across the face of Maurice Ripps. He stood still as a sentry, and snapped his fingers. Another man came into view—one of Hennessy's supervisors.

"Hi, Mary Guadaloop," Ripps called down pleasantly, greeting María with the pair of names he used with all Mexican women. "If you're taking in laundry now, I got a pile of clothes that could do with a scrub, if the price is right."

María turned back to her wash, hoping he had not seen the fear in her eyes. His reputation for violence was known throughout the valley, and unlike so many other things of his, it had been justly earned.

"What is it you want, Señor?" she quietly asked.

Ripps chuckled as if he had been asked a very stupid question. Signaling the supervisor to follow him, he started down the steep embankment, saying, "Oh, nothing much, just a little powwow with your boyfriend is all."

"Go talk to him," María exclaimed, hoping that would be the end of the conversation, yet knowing it wasn't. She went back to her scrubbing, eyes still fixed on his shifting reflection in the water.

"In private," the supervisor finally said in a thin voice that be-lied his bulk. The big man looked somewhat pained for having said this and wouldn't have if Ripps had not prompted him with a poke in the ribs.

María looked up and, disarmed by the supervisor's awkward demeanor, asked, "Why would Francisco want to see you in private?"

In spite of another poke in the ribs, the large man did not reply. Ripps's pointed features fell into a pout. "We come down here with the latest wage offer," he replied. "But was ordered to pre-sent it to Francisco off to one side, away from all them reporters. Growers think they'll lose face if everybody knows how many concessions they're making to get this strike settled."

"And the growers sent you to make this offer?" María asked, unable to strip the sarcasm from her voice. She flinched at having made such a mistake. Ripps had broken many a bone with less provocation.

But he simply smiled and said, "I guess the growers figured Francisco would appreciate it more if I was the one carrying the offer, eating humble pie every mile of the way."

The idea seemed ridiculous to her, though it matched much that had happened before. The growers had not been right about any-thing yet.

"All I know, Señor Ripps, is that Francisco went off in a station wagon a little while ago," she softly said, and instantly wondered whether she had revealed too much.

Standing across the stream, his voice was as soothing as the rip-pling water. "He's sure gonna like the news I'm carrying... so why don't we go find him?"

María knew this was not a request, but a command. Keeping her head low, she glanced around. The entire area was deserted. "Sure," she said, "let me get these clothes back to the camp, and we can go, eh?"

Ripps lost his smile. Easing down to the stream, he tramped over the shallow water to clamp hold of María's basket of wash and started to toss the clothes out across the water.

"But now," he muttered, "with that new wage and all, you folks gonna be able to buy some brand-new clothes."

Half an hour later, they still had seen no trace of the station wagon. Ripps had driven up and down dusty dirt roads for two miles in every direction from the encampment and even passed it a few times, hoping to catch a glimpse of the migrant leader. María had thought of jumping from the truck, but she was wedged between Ripps, who was driving, and the big supervisor, whose bulk closed off her only other avenue of escape. By now, Ripps had sunk into a sullen silence as his frustration slowly built into fury. María did not dare look directly at him, yet she could almost feel the heat coming from his coiled, hard-muscled body.

Several thoughts had dropped into his mind like bricks on his head, especially the fire at the camp, and how he had been knocked into the mud by Francisco Salazar.

Recalling this, he rubbed his bruised shoulder. The plan Hennessy had detailed to him the night before called only for Francisco's temporary detainment; but now Ripps had decided on a few more dramatic possibilities.

Sitting behind a thicket of orange trees, the abandoned chicken coop was impossible to see from the road. One had to know it was there. Easing his pickup truck past the full-blooming trees, he stopped in front of the long, low, foul-smelling coop. Several seconds passed, but neither he nor anyone else said a word.

Then, with what she hoped sounded like a laugh, María finally said, "You think he is hiding in a chicken coop?"

Ripps's ferret-like features formed a smile. Casually coming out of the truck, he paused, and then clamped hold of María's arm. In another few seconds, he jerked her clear of the cab and manhandled her to the door of the chicken coop. The supervisor sat watching with a tentative frown. He had no idea of Ripps's intent but would have wagered a week's salary it was anything but honorable. Heaving a sigh, he climbed from the truck and trudged toward the coop, looking like a child going off to take a whipping.

Ripps had just pushed her past the front door when he backhanded her across the mouth, sending her crashing across a long table which was strewn with excrement and feathers. Coiling his hand for another strike, he saw that the big man now standing just inside the door. Ripps sheepishly dropped his arm, but when the supervisor made no immediate comment, he grinned. The big man, he assumed, had just declared his disinterest.

"Well, Mary Guadaloop," he purred, jerking María to her feet. "If you just tell us where your old man really is, Big John will go fetch him so's we can start the party."

María could smell the foul odor of chewing tobacco on Ripps's breath. She tried to retreat a step or two, but his hold contained little slack.

"I told you the truth, Señor, Francisco went somewhere in a station wagon. But even if you find him, do you think he will come back here to see you?"

In an instant, Ripps tore off the tiny locket Maria wore around her neck, and tossed it to the supervisor.

"Sure, if he thinks you're here waiting for him—and I reckon this little trinket should convince the bastard," he replied, looking pleased with himself. "Now where is the motherfucker?"

When María remained silent, his fist struck again. She tumbled back into a pile of mildewing straw, sending the frightened chickens in every direction. He waited for the shrieking to die away, and then advanced toward her.

"You worthless bitch," he muttered, his breath coming in short, heavy strokes. "I tried treating you like a white woman. Now I'm gonna try something else."

Leaning down, he took Maria by the wrist. This time, however, she was able to break free. But after scrambling no more than ten feet away, she realized she was out of room to run.

Ripps smiled and unzipped his fly.

Maria's expression hardened, her eyes a blazing black against the sudden paleness of her skin. Her fear then gave way to rage, and for that she was grateful. Anger would serve her better than fright. Her breath came in short spurts, and it took her a few seconds to issue a final warning. "This will not be free. One way or another, you will have to pay for it."

Ripps laughed and reached into his pants pocket. "Oh, suits me fine—and Big John there can be my witness that this was nothing more'n a little business transaction. So don't you later go to yelling rape, hear me?"

Taking out a few dollar bills from his pocket, he tossed them down to her—and almost in the same moment, his fist came crashing into her face. The bone-crunching blow knocked her past a tall stack of crates. Lying crumpled on the ground, she had just caught her breath when she looked up. Ripps was standing just beyond her legs.

Back at the door, the supervisor puffed at a cigarette as the sound of slapping and muffled cries suddenly filled the fetid air. Then another sound rent the quiet like a scream, the sound of clothing being ripped.

"Come on, Ripps," the supervisor exclaimed. "Getting a little too tough for my taste, man."

From behind the fallen crates, Ripps's voice barked back. "And it's gonna get a lot tougher. So if you ain't up to watching, best wait for me back in the truck."

Vaguely relieved, the supervisor walked out the door. But he had gone only a few feet from the coop when his stride first slowed, then stopped. He clenched his large, raw-boned hands. He was a family man—this stump of a Swede—and the thought of his wife had crossed his mind. The big man realized that if it were his wife whom Ripps had cornered back in the chicken coop, he would have killed him with his bare hands.

But he had been instructed by Hennessy to cut Ripps as much slack as possible. The Swede had, however, gone a little fuzzy about where his boss's plan ended and Ripps's personal program began. He looked back toward the coop, his face furrowed with doubt.

Rips had tom Maria's gingham shirt to pieces, and would have done the same with her blue-jeans, if he'd had the strength. Instead, he jerked them off her body, and ripped away her panties. She felt her body go rigid with fury. She had reconciled herself to the worst, but had silently vowed not to give him the satisfaction of seeing her look humiliated.

Ripps hovered over her for several moments before she realized what was happening. Looking up, she saw that his hairy face was bathed with sweat, and there was a strange, almost anguished gleam in his eyes.

She realized that beyond all his bluster, he had been unable to muster the one thing he needed to complete his conquest. A faint smile swept across her battered lips, a look of triumph and relief. Ripps saw the smile and knew his defeat was final.

He had just arched himself upright when he saw the supervisor. The scorn in his eyes smacked Ripps like a slap across the face.

For a moment he seemed dazed by his defeat. Then, getting to his feet, he zipped up his fly.

"You are luckier than you think," María murmured. "If you had raped me, Francisco would have killed you—if I had not done it first."

The supervisor smiled. The little Mexican gal has grit, he said to himself, and her courage now spurred his own. "Come on, stud," he said quietly, basting his words with scorn. "This little gal was way too much woman for you anyway."

Ripps nodded blankly and backed toward the door. The Swede held his ground for a moment, and reached into his shirt pocket. Taking out Maria's locket, he gently handed it to her. With a grateful nod, she reached up, and suddenly realized that she was nearly nude. Flushing with embarrassment, she quickly covered herself with her tattered shirt. The big man looked away.

Taking off his windbreaker, he tossed it back in her direction. He was halfway to the door before María could stammer out her thanks.

Turning around, the Swede seemed to want to leave her with something more than just his jacket. He wanted to apologize, most of all for his own craven behavior that had allowed the situation to sink to such a brutish level. His guilt was, however, a little too heavy, so all he said was, "Been looking for a good excuse anyway to buy me a new jacket." He smiled and walked out the door.

Several long seconds passed before Maria heard the truck pull away. As the tenseness slowly drained from her battered body, she leaned back to take her first deep breath in more than an hour. For several seconds, she sat listening to the welcome sound of complete stillness.

She felt cut off from all sense of time and space, in a faraway place where there was no past, no future, only the painful present. She had not felt so utterly alone since the morning she had learned that her parents had drowned. Then she became aware that she had something clenched in her fist: the locket the supervisor had handed back to her. Francisco had given it to her the night they had celebrated her last birthday. Staring down at the heart-shaped locket, María's eyes finally filled with tears.

CHAPTER 21

Francisco had driven into town with Larry Edwards who had invited him to breakfast. But over two cups of coffee, he had been unable to change the newscaster's opinion about the efficacy of the strike. Edwards still thought it had come at the wrong time and in the wrong place. Francisco had, however, made the newsman see the human side of the struggle.

Edwards had never interviewed a farm worker before.

Like most Americans, he was unaware of what went into making the United States the best-fed country in the world.

An hour later, as they returned along the highway, a truck raced past them, in the opposite direction. Francisco thought he recognized the truck, but didn't get a good look at its occupants.

Ripps had recognized Francisco. Slamming his brakes hard, he sent the truck into a dusty slide along the shoulder of the road. Not quite coming to a full stop, he craned his neck around. "There goes the bastard. That's him in that station wagon!"

The Swede frowned. "So the Mexican gal was telling you the truth all along about the station wagon, huh?"

Ripps ground his truck into gear. "What he's gonna wish he was in now is a fucking tank."

The truck screeched through a turn and quickly closed to within three or four car lengths of the station wagon. Ripps began to blast his horn as he pulled abreast of it.

Inside the station wagon, Edwards looked over. He had no idea what was happening, but already suspected it wasn't anything good. Ripps was shouting and waving wildly for him to pull over. Edwards had just decided to do so when he glanced back. Ripps was waving a pistol.

Edwards had served in the army during the war and prided himself on the risks he had taken in the jungles of the South Pacific. But he was no fool. He could recognize stacked odds when he saw them. Mashing down on his accelerator, he had sensed that the men in the truck were hell-bent on killing the man sitting beside him and knew that if he witnessed the murder, his own life might be next.

The vehicles raced down the highway for another half-mile. Then the truck eased back. Edwards and Francisco had just exchanged a look of relief when the sound of gunfire jarred the air like a cannon blast. Ripps's third shot found its mark. The station wagon went wobbling off the road, one tire blown to shreds.

Francisco quickly realized that by remaining in the car, he was needlessly endangering the newsman's life. Over the noise and tumult, he yelled for Edwards to slow down so that he could jump from the car. But Edwards now seemed as if he had accidentally grasped a live wire and couldn't let go. His hands clamped in a death grip on the steering wheel. Stomping the gas pedal to the floor, he took the car careening off toward a cornfield.

The air shuddered again with the thick thud of gunfire Ripps, surprised by the car's sudden turn, whipped his truck into a tight arc, and got off another shot before taking up the chase. The Swede glanced at the handle to his door, waiting for his own chance to jump. He knew that under the calmest of circumstances, Ripps was a highly dangerous man. Now, maddened beyond all measure and wildly waving a pistol, he was no safer than the whirling blade of a buzz saw. But for now, the big Swede could do nothing more than just hang on. He was on a roller coaster, and there probably would be no getting off until the end of the ride.

As Ripps slowed to reload his .38, the station wagon charged into a cornfield, the six-foot stalks enveloping the car like a shroud. In the brief lull, Francisco got set to jump from the car — until he suddenly realized that Ripps had no idea that the man driving the station wagon was Larry Edwards; and that once he discovered it, he could not afford to leave such a witness alive.

He had believed he could save the newsman's life by breaking away from the ex-convict. Now he knew that this would only leave Edwards at the mercy of a man who had never shown much of it. Francisco, like the Swede back in the truck, was strapped in for the rest of the ride.

The station wagon cleared the cornfield, and for a split second, Francisco thought they had lost their pursuers. Then he saw that Ripps was waiting for them alongside the far edge of the field.

The only open land was in front of them. Edwards, badly startled, jammed into second gear, and raced toward a slight rise. Beyond, lie a narrow bridge that crossed over a wide irrigation ditch.

The station wagon had stumbled over the rise when Edwards saw a small tractor coming right at him. A heavy-set man was driving it, and when he saw the onrushing car, he jerked to his feet, poised to jump clear. Edwards hit his brakes, skidding to a stop some twenty feet from the tractor's front end. Slamming his car into reverse, Edwards turned his head back and let out a loud curse. The truck was now right behind him.

Ripps leaned out his window, shrieking hysterically, but his words were buried by the roar of gunfire. His first round was followed by a second explosion. He had shot out the car's other rear tire. An instant later, the truck's big wooden bumper slammed into the station wagon and began pushing it toward the tractor.

The farmer, recovering quickly from his initial shock, ground the tractor into reverse gear and began to back off the bridge. Clearing it, the farmer, shaking with rage, bolted to his feet. He waved his fist as the two other vehicles rumbled past him, then aimed his own machine in the direction of a farmhouse about a hundred yards away.

Francisco saw him heading for the house and hoped he had gone to call the state police. But the old farmer was not in the habit of calling for help. He had gone to fetch his shotgun.

Edwards headed for a heavily furrowed field, thinking that with two flat tires, he might be able to move across it better than the truck. But within moments, the truck caught up with the car. Howling with glee, Ripps fumbled through his shirt pocket for more ammunition. Up ahead, the station wagon, badly battered and with both rear tires blown, seemed as easy a target as a wounded, cornered animal.

Ripps's smile froze. He was out of ammunition. Tossing the pistol aside, he gunned his engine and began to ram the truck into the rear of the car again. The violent impact instantly revived his enthusiasm. The Swede's spirits also lifted, for a different reason. He had noted that Ripps had exhausted his supply of shells. The ride was finally coming to an end.

Up ahead, the field had been recently irrigated and the ground was soggy. Long, lean pieces of pipe ran along the base of each furrow, and in one such shallow depression, the truck suddenly got stuck. Ripps slammed the machine into reverse gear, then back into first, trying to rock it out of the rut. But the more his tires spun, the deeper down the truck sank.

Finally, he could only sit watching the station wagon slowly bounce away, its flattened rear tires riding wide and sure over the rich wet earth. Looking like a leftover from a demolition derby, the station wagon clanked off toward the highway.

Drowning in frustration, Ripps jammed his transmission in and out of gear, sending the truck's tires cutting into the ground like jackhammers, until the tires bit into something solid—and at that moment, the Swede sprang from the truck and went stumbling across the muddy furrows, never once looking back. Had he done so, he would have seen that one of the truck tires had bitten into a water-valve, instantly triggering a sprinkler system. Water came pouring over the stalled truck like a tropical rainstorm.

For a fleeting second, Ripps thought of abandoning the truck. Then the full consequence of such an action came crashing down on him: losing both the battle, as well as a late-model truck, would be far more than Jake Hennessy, would be able to bear. "No fucking way," Ripps muttered to himself. So he remained seated inside the truck, sullen and brooding, like the last passenger on a slowly sinking ship. Then he saw the farmer striding down one of the long furrows that led directly toward the pickup—and in his brawny arms he carried a ten-gauge shotgun.

At the sheriff's station in Mission, both Francisco and Larry Edwards signed their names to a criminal complaint of assault and battery. Edwards first tried to charge Ripps with attempted murder, but the deputies were unable to find any bullet holes in his station wagon, and the charge was reduced to the lesser felony. Francisco had patiently given his version of the story to the investigating officers, though he felt it was a waste of time. Never had he seen the local police take sides against a prominent grower and rarely against anyone who worked for one.

When the ordeal was over, Francisco and Edwards parted company. The newsman had to get back to the radio station for his noontime program. Outside the police department, they shook hands, made a few remarks about what they had been through, and walked away from each other as casually as if they had just met. But both knew they were forever bound by an experience neither would ever forget.

Walking away from the police station, Francisco found himself moving in the direction of his son's boarding house. He had never been there, but the place had been described to him, and in a town the size of Mission, that was all he needed to know.

He was not sure why he was going to see his son, and a little later, when he had not found him at home, he was equally uncertain why he felt relieved. He did not know that Alejandro had left town to look for work.

CHAPTER 22

Alejandro had driven first to McAllen, then all the way to Brownsville, where he checked out some employment ads and left an application with several small companies. He did not make a favorable impression on any of the men who interviewed him. He seemed bored and distracted. In reality, Alejandro had spent the morning just biding his time before re-enlisting in the Marine Corps.

At the recruiting office, he was welcomed for the first time that day as a man of honorable achievement—and not merely another Mexican looking for a job. The recruiting sergeant had served in Korea, and for the better part of a half hour he and Alejandro swapped stories about the war. The sergeant had been stationed not far from the Chosen Reservoir the morning the Chinese had poured across the Yalu River in howling waves of hundreds of thousands of men, to quickly mire the war in a stalemate. In a way, it had been worse than losing. Remembering, Alejandro and the sergeant had run out of memories. Then the sergeant abruptly pulled them from the past.

Outlining the opportunities awaiting Alejandro—if he chose to rejoin the Corps—the stench of the Korean War was soon buried. It all made for a heady brew, and leaving the office with the re-enlistment forms, he promised to return as soon as he settled his personal affairs. The sergeant seemed disappointed that he had not signed the papers before leaving the office.

But he was waiting for something to happen, though he was as yet uncertain what its final form would be. What he did know was that until it occurred, he would not be free to leave the valley for good.

Driving back to Mission, he heard the broadcast over his car radio. The newscast lasted fifteen minutes, all of it devoted to the events of that morning that had involved the newscaster himself. In a voice charged with contempt, Larry Edwards reported the details of what he was still calling a murder attempt on the lives of both himself and Francisco. Edwards closed his broadcast with a comment that soon unleash an unexpected reaction.

"But beyond how any of us might personally feel about this farm worker strike,'" Edwards concluded, "'there is a far greater issue at stake here, and one that should deeply concern every citizen in Texas. It's this idea called democracy, what this great land of ours is all about. It's why men have been willing to go to war and even die for this country for the last one-hundred-and-seventy years. Now, I may think this labor strike is very ill-advised and even counterproductive, but the farm-workers' right to strike and my right to report it are protected by two precious pieces of paper called the Constitution of the United States and the Bill of Rights—and any man who wants to change them is going to have to do it in the halls of Congress, and not out on some rural road with a gun in his hand. We Texans haven't fought and died in three wars in this century alone to tolerate that kind of twisting of the law, and I pray to God that we never will...'"

Five miles away, Edwards signed off and looking up from his microphone past a panel of glass, he saw that his engineer's booth was crammed with fellow employees. A few wore proud expressions, but all seemed stunned by the nature of the broadcast. Edwards had surprised even himself, for until the last moment, he had not decided to make any editorial comment. He had known such a gesture might cost him his job, and was sure of it a moment later when his telephone rang.

Hanging up the phone, Edwards walked out of the booth, a curious spryness in his step. The worst the station manager could do was fire him, and Edwards had already decided that was better than being fired at.

"I'd just about given up believing in miracles," the old black man said softly.

Thomas Jones and Pedro Terán were standing along-side their encampment, watching as dozens of buckets of hot soup were unloaded from several cars and trucks. A stout, handsome little woman with short-cropped gray hair had organized the food collection and was supervising its disbursement. Nearly a hundred migrant workers had gathered around the vehicles; they too seemed astounded by the sight before them. Once the workers realized that the convoy had come bearing free food, they had felt like cheering. But something about the little woman's matter-of-fact manner had dissuaded them. She had quickly made clear that what prompted the food collection was not sympathy, but principle.

" — When we heard that radio report," the woman said to Pedro, "about what that ex-convict had tried to do to one of your folks, we just couldn't turn the other way."

Pedro started to reply, but the little woman didn't seem to think her remark required an answer. "But now that don't mean that many of us have changed our mind about this strike, because we haven't. The only time to strike is when you got a chance to win...and the most I'd bet on your chances here is half a jar of marmalade."

Pedro smiled. "I would not even bet that much, Señora. But if all the growers were like you, we would never have any reason to strike." The little woman, who had been widowed for many years, stared sternly into Pedro's eyes, and suddenly blushed. Annoyed with herself, she grunted and strode off toward where the last of the 'miracle' was being unloaded.

An hour later, Francisco took Pedro, Jones and María to a deserted railroad siding about a half-mile away from the encampment. He wanted to tell them what had happened earlier with the newsman and, not knowing if Ripps might still be prowling around, had decided to take them away from the camp. At the railroad siding, Francisco learned that María also had come in for her share of Ripps's attention that morning.

She told the story sparingly, but her badly bruised face spoke with more eloquence. Francisco's mood slowly went as black as the sling he now wore around his arm. He had sprained his shoulder in his own encounter with Ripps, but the pain he felt at this moment had nothing to do with the injury.

He had returned from the police station in Mission with his mind almost made up. Now, learning of the attack on Maria, his decision became final. He would act on his son's plan.

Hearing this, Pedro and Jones exchanged a mournful look. Pedro rose to his feet to make a final plea. Francisco was seated up on the siding, and as Pedro moved around below him, he seemed a petitioner pacing before a tribunal.

"Yes, I too am filled with anger," Pedro haltingly proclaimed. "But remember that it was the work of only one man. But the good thing that happened an hour ago at the camp with the food was the work of many people. So do we forget the good to remember only the bad? Do we fight to get what is fairly coming to us, or are we now to steal from the growers, like nothing more than thieves in the night?"

Not a loquacious man, Pedro seemed surprised that he had spoken at such length. But perhaps all argument was futile anyway. Pedro had never really believed they could win their fight against some of the most powerful growers in the Rio Grande Valley.

For him, and from the beginning, the cause had served a different need: the opportunity to feel appreciated, to belong to something and somebody, a chance he thought he had lost forever the night his sister Juanita died. Yet Pedro knew that there was a fine line beyond which most courageous men cannot be shoved—and that Francisco had finally reached it.

Thomas Jones had come to the same conclusion. His clouded eyes fastened on Francisco for a while before he finally spoke. "Frank, you once said we could never really bargain with the growers unless we had time on our side. Well, about an hour ago, a lot of white folks gave us a little more time...so now don't you think it's about time we settled this strike, forget this fool business?"

The two men studied each other. Whatever they were searching for, neither found. Jones shrugged his stooped shoulders and quietly said, "Well, I was praying to the Good Lord you would change your mind, 'cause I knew I couldn't change mine."

Francisco smiled. He and Jones had been friends for many years, and the old black man's decision would not mar their friendship; indeed, it had deepened it. Francisco knew that Jones was right. Recognizing the truth, however, was not the same as accepting it.

The black man came forward to shake Francisco's hand solemnly, as if he never expected to see his friend alive again, and then walked toward Pedro's car. But halfway there, he turned back with a question that was not as casual as it sounded. "I can just walk on back, Pedro, if you planning to stay."

Pedro's moment had come. It had been ten years in the making, and would be the first time that he had ever broken away from the man he respected and loved like the older brother he never had.

He stood staring down the railroad track that no longer went anywhere and thought of those ten years.

"When you first told us about the strike," Pedro said, his voice soft as a distant memory, "you said that when a mad dog comes at a man, he does not stop to take a vote.... All I know is that if I go with you now, brother, I am no better than this same mad dog."

Pedro suddenly was embarrassed. The moment had called, he thought, for a stirring summation of his most deeply held principles, yet all he had managed to mention was a rabid dog. Shrugging his shoulders, he walked rapidly toward the car.

Watching the old car disappear, Francisco lingered on something Pedro had said. He had called him 'brother,' a word he had never used before. Francisco thought of his real brother. He had not written to José Luis for many years; there had never been much to write about. Now that there was, his older brother was no longer alive to hear the news. Just as well, he thought. José Luis wouldn't have liked it anyway.

Francisco suddenly felt exhausted. Pulling up a piece of cardboard, he lay back on it and placed his straw hat over his face. A moment later, María came to stretch out beside him. Then they did something they had never done in daylight. They fell asleep, their bruised arms entwined around each other.

An hour later, Maria awoke and as if she had been dreaming about it in her sleep, said, "I don't like the idea of what you plan to do to the growers."

Pulling his hat to one side, Francisco stared up into the bright, cloudless sky. "Is it any worse than what they did to us this morning?"

María sat up and rubbed the painful ache in her hip. The bruises all over her body were themselves an answer to his question. But her conscience and the lingering memory of Pedro's words were saying something else. "Still, Pedro is right about the money. If we steal it, we are no better than the growers who have been cheating us out of our rightful wage for all these years," she said with a dark frown.

Francisco slowly sat up and looked at her. He had seen that grim, clenched expression on her face a few times before, and he knew it meant what it had always meant: she was disappointed in him and would remain so until he started acting again like the great man she thought he was. He despised many things, but none more than that clenched expression on María's face.

Climbing slowly to his feet, he set his sweat-streaked hat firmly in place and started toward the encampment. "Yeah, okay. I'll talk to Pedro again," he muttered. "Both of us cannot be right, that's for damned sure."

María slowly followed him. As she trudged along she reached into the pocket of the baggy jacket and took out her tiny locket. Clasping it tightly, she smiled.

CHAPTER 23

As Francisco and María tramped back toward the encampment, Margaret and Sam Winslow were heading for the same destination. As they drove along the highway, they noticed several dozen vehicles moving in the opposite direction, an occurrence that Sam laconically noted.

Margaret made no comment. She had been quiet for the past fifteen minutes. Her silence bothered Sam. He wondered if he had done something wrong. Ordinarily, Sam could gauge her mood, but not this time. A few notions crossed his mind. But even his best guess had not come close.

Margaret, for one of the few times in her life, was feeling sorry for herself. Sick at heart over the strike she had been unable to settle, she was questioning her ability to run the huge farm—or even if she wanted to spend the rest of her life saddled with such a responsibility. She could, of course, sell the place, and then live comfortably anywhere she wanted for as long as she wanted. But where would she go? And what would she do there, and with whom would she do it? She needed a man by her side, the right man.

For many years, Margaret's sex life had been the subject of much speculation. Most people knew that she occasionally went out with Jake Hennessy. But they also knew he had never taken her to bed, for if he had, he surely would have plastered the news all over the valley. Some folks thought Margaret was simply asexual. Others had come to a stranger conclusion: she was, they thought, probably one of those un-American types who favored her own sex, a theory lent further credence by her masculine attire and manner.

Both conclusions only proved that she had covered her tracks. The truth would have scandalized these same people almost as much as their overheated speculations.

Margaret was still seeing a man she had fallen in love with while in college—now a failed actor married to a socialite. They had wanted to get married right after graduation. But soon, his ambitions had pulled him in one direction; Margaret's obligations to her father in another.

For the past decade, however, she had met her married lover in San Antonio for the yearly stock show. Taking a suite at a discreet hotel, she and the man she once almost married would live as a married couple for several days. But for the last few years, his passion had been dimmed by both guilt and alcohol. All that now remained between them was a fragile friendship held together by little more than wistful memories.

Seeing the migrant encampment in the distance, she wondered again what her life might have been like if circumstances had not forced her into being something other than simply a woman.

Up on a rise, Hennessy had positioned himself across the high-way from the farm-worker encampment. There he and his corps of supervisors could more covertly observe the next part of his plan unfold. Ripps's bungling still banged against brain, making him more cautious. Ripps had not only failed; he had hauled the re-sponsibility for his actions like a dead skunk to Hennessy's doorstep.

Only an hour earlier, several deputies had come to his home with a warrant for Ripps's arrest on an assault-and-battery charge. They had grilled Hennessy in a hostile manner that surprised him. With a start, he realized that the lawmen liked him far less than they feared the valley's most prominent newsman.

Talking to the officers, he silently marveled that Ripps had failed to recognize a face as well known as that of Larry Edwards'. It was a blunder big enough, he thought, to send Ripps back to jail for the next several years.

But Hennessy would need Ripps that night for the third and fi-nal phase of Agajanian's plan. Afterwards, he would discard the ex-convict like any other piece of machinery that had outlived its usefulness.

Now, the plan was back on schedule. Hennessy had cleared the camp site of everyone but the migrant workers. He checked his watch once more. "The party should be starting in another few minutes," he said to a supervisor standing nearby. "Now you sure all them news reporters have gone for the day, huh?"

"Counted every one of their pointy little heads as they left," the supervisor said and turned toward the Swede. "We sure don't need any more of them broadcasts."

The grower's attention swung to the Swede. Hennessy had castigated him for his part in the morning's fiasco, but had been careful not to humble him. Hennessy didn't need another hostile employee who might later testify to his own complicity in the matter.

"I knew Ripps was a moron," Hennessy muttered. "But I didn't think they made even idiots that stupid."

The Swede had heard about the warrant for Ripps's arrest, and dreaded going home that night, certain a similar summons would be waiting for him. He did not know that the official complaint made no reference to his own involvement. Neither Edwards nor Francisco had ever mentioned a second man in Ripps's truck. They had noted the stricken expression on the Swede's face—and concluded that he was also an unwilling a participant in the morning's mayhem.

Hennessy's attention swung back toward the migrant encampment. He was waiting for something to materialize on the far horizon.

Down below, the encampment sat sweltering in the late afternoon heat. Pedro and Jones had returned from the railroad siding more than an hour earlier and were now supervising the allotment of fresh drinking water. When the last can had been dispatched, Pedro saw that their water supply was almost gone.

"Almost no more water. I have to talk Francisco out of that crazy idea. This must be settled now."

Jones nodded his gray, grizzled head in agreement. "Hallelujah, brother. There is a season for all things, and this one done come to its end."

Jones followed Pedro over to a bucket of water where the Mexican began to wash the grime from his face and hands. The black man's short sermon had stiffened Pedro's resolve. He would convince Francisco to settle the strike that very afternoon, even if he had to carry him to the negotiations.

It would not be as far a trip as he had envisioned. Margaret's car had stopped no more than seventy-five feet away. The grower had come to make one last attempt to settle the strike, and had decided to make it directly to Francisco Salazar. Sam had suggested the tactic to her, remembering how her father often succeeded by making small but symbolic sacrifices — gestures that his fellow-growers thought unimportant.

His daughter was now about to sacrifice her pride. The owner of one of the most successful produce farms in south Texas had come to call on a penniless migrant worker.

It was not a gesture that came easily, and for a long moment, she remained inside the protective cocoon of her car. When she finally spoke, there was a note of relief in her voice. "I don't see him standing around here, do you, Sam? Suppose he's off counting all the money he's gonna cost us."

Sam's expression abruptly brightened. "There's Pedro Terán. He'll know where we can find Salazar."

Climbing out of the car, Sam started down an incline, and suddenly looked back toward the car, thinking he had left its engine running. Sam yelled to Margaret to cut off the motor, before realizing it was something else he heard.

The crop-dusting planes were flying in low, streaking toward the migrant encampment. Sam froze, startled for a moment. Then his eyes met those of the one person he had hoped not to see that afternoon.

The old man had known and worked with Sam's father, and from the time Sam had first been freed from the fields, he had watched him like a hawk. The black man was Sam's conscience, and because Sam knew this, he hated and feared and loved Thomas Jefferson Jones more than any other man in the valley.

The two black men, without saying a word, had eloquently communicated with each other. Sam nodded in the direction of Margaret's car, indicating that she had come to make whatever peace was still possible. In turn, the old man had implied his approval, tapped Pedro on the shoulder and pointed toward the Devereaux station wagon. For several seconds, the moment was pregnant with promise, but would quickly abort.

The approaching planes suddenly swooped lower to unleash their weapons. Streams of pesticide bombarded the encampment. Men, women and children scurried for cover. There wasn't any. Pedro and Jones stood transfixed, watching the workers scatter. They knew there was no way of avoiding the noxious fumes. Better to simply stand still and not waste the pure air still in their lungs.

Sam hurried back to the station wagon. Rolling up its windows, he climbed inside where he and Margaret watched the unfolding spectacle in stunned silence.

Half a mile away, the fleeing farm workers seemed no larger than ants. Hennessy, looking well satisfied with the situation, turned to his supervisors. "Now them bums in the camp know to wait until the final wave of pesticide comes down, huh?"

"You kidding?" the supervisor said, handing Hennessy back his binoculars. "Them scabs ain't gonna move their dead butts into the fields till the air is completely clear—and even then, they're gonna have to be bulldozed away from the feedbag."

Frowning, Hennessy brought the binoculars up to his eyes. He could no longer see the indigents because of the contaminated air, but knew that in the drama unfolding below, the scabs were now little more than bit players. The spraying of the insecticide was the important thing. The pestilence had the power to dispossess Francisco's workers of the strip of public land they tenuously held.

As the second wave of fumes came down, many of the workers linked hands, making desperate movements look a little like a children's game. The pesticide struck like a nerve gas, inflaming eyes, lungs and even skin, hitting hardest the old and the children. Elderly workers were dropping by the droves, and children began vomiting all over themselves as they wheeled around and around in the furious grasp of parents too scared to stop. Up above the tumult, the planes made a tight circle and came sputtering back over the encampment, spewing the last of their pestiferous load.

For several minutes, little could be seen of the entire settlement, and all that could be heard was the sputtering crop dusters and the screams of more than two-hundred frantic farm workers. Paquito had been among the first to go down. His lungs had been in bad shape since he had taken a dose of mustard gas during the First World War. Combined with thirty years of working around heavily sprayed produce had already taken a fearsome toll.

Carrying the old man under a makeshift tent, Pedro left him in the care of a few younger workers, and began to organize the hauling of water from a nearby irrigation ditch. With the supply of fresh water now exhausted, the water from the ditch, though badly fouled, could at least be used to wash the burning pesticide from the skin.

Francisco and María had been about a hundred yards away when they first saw the crop dusters angling in the direction of the encampment. Without saying a word they started to run toward it, praying that what they thought was about to happen could somehow be stopped. They reached the edge of the encampment just as the first blanket of smothering pesticide came over it. For the next several frantic moments, Francisco and María helped get many of the old people and children to the irrigation ditch.

Francisco was down in the ditch washing the pesticide from the face of a small, nearly unconscious boy. Gently passing the little boy over to his dazed parents, he scrambled back to the crest of the ditch, and there beheld something he thought he would never see.

The fumes had finally lifted. The workers, arms still locked together, had held their precious strip of county-owned land, and despite parched throats and through blistered lips, they quietly began to sing.

Francisco stood listening, but made no effort to draw any closer to his workers. As the full import of what he was witnessing slowly washed over him, his eyes filled with tears. For ten punishing years he had organized the farm workers of south Texas; he alone had been responsible for starting the fight—but now finally knew that the workers themselves were someday going to finish it, a humbling yet exhilarating thought.

Inside the camp, Hennessy's supervisors had prodded the indigents to move beyond the line of workers and into the fields. Slowly moving forward, the indigents seemed awed by what they had witnessed. As they came abreast of the long, thin line of workers, many of the indigents did a remarkable thing.

They began shaking hands with the workers, a gesture that started with one man and quickly spread. Watching from a safe distance, the supervisors stood staring at the spectacle, and knew the battle was lost. The indigents had silently joined ranks with the farm workers.

Up on a rise a half-mile away, Jake Hennessy felt the bile swirl in his throat. He had just been dealt another defeat, and his day was not yet over. He still had to report back to Bert Agajanian, a task he dreaded but dared not fulfill. Earlier, Hennessy had thought of telephoning the old grower with the news of the Larry Edwards debacle. He had decided to wait, hoping the successful outcome of the second phase of Agajanian's plan might mitigate the previous defeat. Now he would have to report a double disaster. Shuddering as he strode to his car, he wondered what the foul-tempered old grower would say and do to him.

Down near the fields, the singing continued. Pedro had made his way back to Paquito, who still lay inside the tent. Two old women were gently cleaning the pesticide from his arms and face. He seemed to have aged greatly in the last few minutes, and Pedro realized how frail his friend must have always been. The old man made a brave effort to smile. "Don't worry, Pedro. I am better than I look. The children got it the worst."

Paquito's comment about what had been done to the migrant children brought back images still brutally vivid in Pedro's mind. He waited a long moment before trying to speak. When he did, his words were a declaration of war. "Francisco was right. It was stupid to think we could talk to the kind of people who would do such a thing to our children."

For a long moment, Paquito searched Pedro's eyes for some sign of accommodation, but he knew that reality had now ruined every recourse other than all-out war. Sensing this, Paquito's own eyes slowly filled with tears.

Margaret also was in tears. When the fumes first lifted from the fields, she and Sam had left their car to help the stricken migrants. Sam hauled water from the ditch while Margaret wiped the pesticide from the faces of several terrified children, their fright made worse because they had no understanding why such a thing had been done to them.

She had watched the catastrophe unfold with the expression of someone witnessing the eruption of a volcano. But by the time it subsided, she had made several important decisions. Sam returned from the ditch with another can of water. She ran a rag through it and went on wiping a little girl's face. "When all this is over," Margaret murmured, her eyes on the girl lying in her arms, "I want these people to have immediate use of the camp. That means clean water and decent food, and I don't care how much the other growers squawk about the cost. These folks are going to be made to look like human beings again, even if it's the last thing I ever do for them."

Margaret's remark struck Sam as rather odd. He was about to comment when his eyes were drawn elsewhere. In the distance Paquito was being helped toward a car, his arms draped around Pedro's broad shoulders. Then Jones gave the driver money to insure Paquito's admittance into a hospital. Migrants without money had occasionally been left to die just outside the hospital's front door.

Sam turned back to Margaret and nodded in the direction of Pedro and the black man. "Them two there at the car are part of the bunch you're gonna have to deal with, Miss Margaret—and they're gonna be tough now. But they're both good men and I think they'll try to be fair."

Margaret studied the two workers standing near the old Model-A. She knew both men by face and name, but somehow it seemed as if she were really seeing them for the first time. "For your sake, Sam, I hope you're right," she said. "Because you'll be doing the negotiating for the Devereaux farm."

Her earlier remark, the one that had hit Sam from an odd angle, now came back to him. "And just where you gonna be, Miss Margaret?" he cautiously asked.

A half-hearted smile came over her face; uncanny, she mused, how Sam could sometimes stumble onto her most furtive thoughts. "Oh, I'll be around, Sam. Least for a while yet," she said, handing the little girl to her parents who had just returned from the irrigation ditch. "If the other growers are smart, they'll also let their foremen do the negotiating. After what's just happened here, Francisco Salazar will probably retch at the sight of a roomful of growers.?"

Sam's expression clouded. Her tone of voice seemed too casual for what he thought she was telling him. "Yeah, that makes sense—but what about your own foreman?"

Margaret turned and studied the strong, honest face of the black man kneeling beside her. She was looking at Sam Winslow but was thinking about her father. She wondered whether he would approve of what she was about to say and finally decided it didn't matter.

"Sam, you're the foreman on this outfit now," Margaret softly said, and suddenly chuckled. "But before you go to pieces, just remember that it took me nearly forever to come to this decision."

The black man blinked with disbelief. He rose slowly to his feet. He too was thinking about the man who had first brought him out of the fields so many years before. Sam had at last realized his dream. But now, amidst the human wreckage still all around him, it seemed obscene to fully taste his triumph. A sour expression seemed more suitable to his surroundings.

"Well, do we sit around here congratulating each other for the next half hour, or do we start getting that camp in shape?"

Margaret semed relieved that his blunt manner had not changed. She had noticed before how other men's demeanor grew more pompous with every promotion. Sam was a welcome sign that the best people changed only for the better.

CHAPTER 24

A couple of hundred feet away, Thomas Jones was saying good-bye to Pedro. They had shook hands, but only after Pedro hand-cranked his car and climbed behind its wheel did the black man show his emotions.

"Brother, I sure hate to see you go," Jones said, pawing the ground with his well-worn high-top shoes. "Though after all that's happened, can't rightly say I blame you. But now you be mighty careful. I'm gonna take it as a personal insult if you don't get back here all in one piece."

Pedro smiled and took the car back toward the railroad siding where he had last seen Francisco. But Pedro had driven only as far as the edge of the encampment when he saw Francisco and María walking toward him. He pulled over sharply. When they approached, Pedro nodded back in the direction of several people who still lay on the ground. "The growers finally came to negotiate with us," he murmured, his voice solemn as a sacrament.

"We got back just when it started." Francisco's manner seemed surprisingly controlled. Pedro was relieved that they had witnessed the catastrophe himself, for he knew he could never have adequately described it. "Then you know that the workers are still with you."

Francisco and María exchanged a glance. Pedro had just told them, without saying so, that he was coming with them. A smile slipped past her bruised features. "That is funny, Pedro," she said, "We had decided we could not go without you."

"Yeah, that's true, brother," Francisco said with a worn chuckle. "Hardly any of the rest of us has a car."

Dwelling on the miles that lay ahead, Francisco took the sling from his shoulder and tossed it into a nearby fire. Then he and María climbed into the car. But they had gone no more than a hundred yards when they were waved to a stop. The Filipino strode boldly toward them. Peering at Francisco, Juan Rizal finally said, "After what happened here today, I hope you have decided to go through with your son's plan." Francisco nodded, but said nothing. He could certainly use another good man. But drafting the Filipino for such a mission was out of the question. If Rizal wanted to go, he would have to enlist, which is exactly what he now did.

"You know by now that you can count on me."

Francisco remembered the first time he had seen the young Filipino in action. It had been at the Devereaux farm only a few days earlier, the afternoon Juan Rizal had gotten into the brawl with Ramon's bodyguard. Rizal lost the fight, but had won Francisco's admiration. He had also, since rejoining the workers at the camp, been the first to volunteer for whatever dirty job had come along.

Alejandro's landlady had told him of his visitor that morning, a caller he assumed had been his Uncle Pedro. Now, when she advised him that he had another visitor, he assumed the same thing. This time he was right. Setting aside the Marine Corps material he was reading, he started down a creaking flight of steps.

Pedro stood waiting on the front porch of the house. Alejandro, struck by the defeated smile on his uncle's face, knew instantly why he had come. The two men silently embraced, then strode briskly toward Pedro's car.

The late afternoon sun had left the tree-lined street cool and peacefully patterned. Francisco, María and Juan Rizal were waiting in the car. Alejandro listened quietly as his father recounted the troubles that had transpired over the last few hours. Although he had already heard everything but the rape attempt on María, he did not interrupt his father, sensing that he was not merely imparting informa-tion but attempting to justify his change of heart.

Asking them to follow him, Alejandro walked over to his own car and opened its trunk. Earlier, he had stored inside it all the equipment he thought they might need to implement his plan. The two older men grimaced as he uncovered a snub-nosed .38 pistol.

"The gun is insurance. If we're lucky, we won't need it. If we're not, it might be all that gets us out alive."

Pedro drew a deep breath. "I don't like it."

"I don't like it, either," Alejandro said, smiling. "But I'm not going without it."

Pedro and Francisco exchanged an agitated glance. Then, with a resigned look, Francisco nodded. He had, in effect, just vacated his position of leadership. Alejandro was now in command. This should have brought him some satisfaction, but another emotion suddenly shouldered all else aside. What he felt was fear, though not for him. He had faced far graver danger in the killing fields of Korea. He was thinking about his father and uncle. He was about to take the two men he loved most into a situation they might not survive. Shoving aside his concern, he said, "Go get the others. We're taking my car."

Pedro's expression hardened. "The growers know your car. Be the same as leaving your fingerprints. If we have to abandon our car, better it is mine, which needs to rest anyway."

Good arguments, Alejandro decided, though deferring to his uncle only made him feel worse. The possible loss of Pedro's car had just been laid like another log on top of Alejandro's shoulders. The load soon became heavier. Transferring the equipment from his car to Pedro's, Alejandro remembered María Antón.

He stood pondering his next move. María would be, he thought, of little help in carrying out his plan. She might even be a detriment—another person he would have to protect. He thought she should stay behind but decided not to press the issue. The temporary armistice between him and his father still seemed too tenuous.

He was glad, however, that Juan Rizal had come along. He liked the grim, resolute look in Rizal's eyes and the way his muscular body already seemed poised for action. The Marine Corps had taught him how to quickly measure a man, and the young Filipino, without having said a word, had instantly passed his test.

An hour later, they stopped at a roadside diner where Alejandro offered to buy them all a good meal. Probably their last supper, Pedro joked. The near-deserted diner was on the highway that led to the Mexican border town of Reynosa, the only town large enough, Alejandro figured, where the growers could recruit two hundred workers on short notice.

Coming out of the restaurant, he raised the tattered top over Pedro's Model-A. The top would offer little protection against the weather, but might help keep them from being so easily recognized. He made no mention of this to the others. Except for Juan Rizal, they already looked like convicted felons on their way to prison.

The trouble started early. The radiator was leaking, causing the car to continually overheat. Several times they were forced to stop and refill the radiator. Alejandro thought of going back for his own car, but by now it was too late. The convoy could come at any moment, though chances were it would come later when the highway was almost deserted. But this he did not know for sure.

Within the next thirty minutes, they found what he thought was a suitable location for the initial phase of his plan—and there they began their final preparations.

The site was a long row of abandoned fruit stands alongside the highway, shielded on each side by several tall trees. Behind one of the trees, Alejandro and Juan Rizal quickly changed into khaki pants and caps. The clothing was Marine-issue, and though not perfect for their purpose, it gave the men a semi-official appearance.

In the all-enveloping darkness, Alejandro asked, "How do the pants fit, Juan?"

"Close, but no cigar," Rizal said, grinning as he rolled up his cuffs. Alejandro thought the Filipino would have made a good Marine.

While Alejandro and Rizal changed clothes, Pedro and Francisco found some broken-down wooden supports. On these they nailed the sign which Alejandro earlier had taken from the trunk of his car. Then they quickly climbed into the Model-A to go wheeling again in the direction of the border. When they had gone some few miles, they were forced to pull over once more to attend to the ailing radiator. Then they sat waiting in the darkness for the lights of the convoy to finally appear.

An hour crawled by, and in the silence and absolute darkness, some of them wondered what they were doing out on this cold black night, huddled off in the middle of nowhere, waiting for a convoy which might have been nothing more than a figment of Alejandro's imagination.

María thought the situation absurd. Like a movie in which migrant workers were masquerading as mobsters. But if it was, they were all actors shoved into extremely difficult roles with little or no training. Alejandro seemed the sole exception. María was impressed by the way he had handled himself, with what he had said, and even more what he had chosen to leave unsaid. He seemed as calm as if they were sitting at a drive-in theatre, patiently waiting for the movie to commence.

It was nearly midnight when he finally decided that the convoy wasn't coming, or perhaps had taken a different route. Rousing the others from their sleep, he climbed out of the car to pour more water into its radiator. The trip back to Mission would be a long one.

Inside the car, Pedro cleared the sleep from his eyes, peered through the darkness toward the highway, and suddenly laughed. The dreaded danger had failed to materialize. But Francisco felt disappointed, though he did not know exactly why. If the growers had failed to recruit a convoy of Mexican workers, they probably would now have to settle the strike on whatever terms they could get. For all Francisco knew, he might have already won the biggest fight of his life, and yet, he suddenly felt inexplicably sad.

Only when he caught his son's eye did he realize the reason for this reaction. In the murky light, each man's expression reflected the same feeling. They had lost out on the money that would have been collected. But neither had really counted on that; seizing the money had simply been one more way of settling their score with the growers.

What they truly missed was the chance to settle the score, to square at last their own account so that they could start their relationship anew. The hope for this chance, Alejandro now realized, was what had kept him from signing his Marine Corps re-enlistment papers.

Suddenly, while he lingered on this thought, he turned and saw, knifing through the darkness, a long bank of lights. There were eight large trucks in the convoy, each covered with a heavy tarpaulin. The trucks angled slowly around a slight curve, then gained speed as they came roaring closer. In another few seconds, they were rumbling past Pedro's car, their lights hitting it with a strobe effect.

Alejandro counted the trucks. After the last one had passed, he turned to his father. "Eight trucks, probably twenty-five men in each one. Two hundred workers. Just about what we and the growers were hoping for, eh?"

Smiling, he climbed back into the car, and a moment later, Pedro took it into a tight turn. Knowing what was coming next, María began to silently pray.

The next fifteen minutes seemed like an hour as Pedro punished his old machine, as he had never done before. The car, laboring to pass one truck after another, began to shake as if caught in a violent windstorm. The Model-A whined in protest, but only after it had passed the lead truck did Pedro ease up on the gas pedal.

Now the toughest test: they would have to reach the fruit stand several minutes ahead of the convoy in order to put the next phase of the plan into action. But they were luckier than they thought. The trucks were moving slowly.

Alejandro did not know that Hennessy had repeatedly stressed to the Mexican contractor that once the convoy crossed the border, it adhere rigidly to the posted speed limit. He had managed to bribe everyone but the Texas Highway Patrol, and there could be real trouble if the convoy were stopped for whatever reason.

Half an hour later, Pedro brought the weary Model-A to a shuddering halt behind the fruit stand. Alejandro checked his watch. They were five minutes ahead of the lead truck, he figured. Getting out of the car, he ran down the highway. Fifty yards away from the stand, he laid out his first flare. Then, moving back toward the stand, he spaced several more.

Francisco and Pedro hurried past Alejandro carrying a sign that they placed near the first flare. They placed a second wooden support directly in the middle of the road, twenty yards out in front of the stand. They had finished setting up this last roadblock when they noticed a long string of lights breaking through the darkness, glaring like an apparition in the heavy mist. The final bit of business was at hand. Taking out his pistol, Alejandro checked again to see that it was fully loaded.

CHAPTER 25

Inside the cab of the lead truck were three Mexicans. The driver, a muscular-looking man with a face cratered with smallpox scars, chomped nervously on a dead cigar. The busy-eyed man in the middle crouched forward, as if expecting trouble around every bend in the road. The leader of the convoy was the contractor with whom Hennessy had made the deal. He sat hunched next to the window, his ponderous jowls hanging under keen, suspicious eyes. Tossing his spent cigarette away, he took down a map from above his visor. The map was heavily lined with crayon, and as the leader traced their present course with his finger, he noted that an upcoming junction was not very far ahead. Grunting something in Spanish to the driver, he placed the map back over the visor. Then he saw the sparkling flares.

The leader let loose a curse and drew forth from the glove compartment a pistol, which he jammed inside his boot. As the truck came closer to the burning flares, he leaned back and twisted the edge of his wispy mustache; he had seen the sign, which bore a familiar, reassuring name: Hennessy. The leader also noted that the two men standing behind the sign did not appear to be Texas highway patrolmen, but rather, local police.

Remembering that Hennessy had assured him that the venture would be well greased with bribes, the leader turned to the driver and said in Spanish, "It's all right. Probably some police who work for Hennessy. Maybe there has been a change in the plan."

As the driver geared the big truck down, the convoy leader flashed a tobacco-stained smile. Perhaps this was as far as he would have to transport his human cargo, he thought. If so, he was moments away from collecting the last half of the money he had been promised. Hennessy had already advanced him a thousand dollars, but the contractor had spent some of the money on the rental of the trucks. The other two men had demanded their pay in advance, a sum commensurate with the risk they were taking.

With the workers themselves the contractor was more fortunate. Hennessy had allocated ten dollars for each man, this apart from what they might later earn in the harvest fields. Enough, Hennessy thought, to prove honest intent on the part of the growers.

The contractor thought differently. He had paid each worker only five dollars. They had made it safely past the Border Patrol. The trip looked downhill the rest of the way for them.

The driver began braking to a stop, easing his truck onto the narrow shoulder of the highway. Behind him, the seven other drivers slowed to do the same. Then, as the lead truck came to a full halt some few feet away from the first barrier, Alejandro and Juan Rizal stepped out from behind it and strode toward the cab of the truck.

Alejandro knew the next few seconds were critical. He would have to gain their confidence quickly, and he knew the best way would be to place them on the defensive.

Marching to the cab, he shined his flashlight directly into the leader's face. Then, employing the manner of a Marine Corps drill-sergeant, he barked, "Well, you sure took your sweet fucking time!" He swept his light across the three rather startled men in the cab.

It took the leader a few seconds to regain his compo-sure, and when he replied in Spanish, his voice was livid with suppressed anger. "Speak in English," Alejandro curtly interjected. "You're in the United States now!"

The leader's words came in a mangled combination. "Si, señor, pero salimos de Reynosa a little late, mucho trouble getting the last fifty workers, so we run un poco tarde —"

"Yeah, you people do everything a little late, don't you?" Alejandro snarled. "Okay, how is everything else? No trouble at the border?"

The leader frowned. He had just about exhausted his English and deeply resented that he was being forced to speak in a foreign tongue. Then he remembered the money. If this arrogant young man shining the light in his eyes was holding the money for him, it would be best to endure his insults, at least until the money safely changed hands.

"The border cross is fine," the man muttered.

"Good," Alejandro said, feigning relief. "But there's been a little trouble up this way. Hennessy wants you to deliver the workers to another location. It will be safer for you...and not as far. Now, bring your truck around that shed. I'll show you on my map how to get there."

The leader glanced over at his two companions, but both had vapid expressions on their faces. The contractor sat weighing the situation; something did not appear right to him. The moment seemed trapped in time. Alejandro abruptly stepped back from the truck. "I'm not going to stand around here waiting for the Texas Highway Patrol. You want the rest of your money, move your truck!"

The leader flushed up a queasy smile, then turned to lash out an instruction to his driver. The big truck lurched forward. Watching it slowly rumble away, Alejandro gave Juan Rizal a terse instruction. "Hold the next truck in place—even if you have to throw yourself in front of its wheels."

Alejandro hurried after the first truck as the Filipino started toward the convoy. It would be Juan's job to explain the delay to the driver of the second truck so as to freeze the convoy until Alejandro had dealt with its leader.

The first truck had barely come to a stop behind the fruit shed when Alejandro jumped on its running board and clapped his pistol to the contractor's head.

"Get out of the truck, all of you," Alejandro muttered, now speaking in Spanish. He jerked open the door. When the leader still hesitated, Alejandro grabbed him by the leg and spun the man violently around. The leader's head went clanking past the running board and he fell heavily to the ground.

Stunned, he slowly got back to his feet and was quickly joined by the man who had been sitting next to him. The driver, however, now thought of bolting from his side of the truck. But when he turned to do so, there was another man standing next to his door. The expression on Pedro's face was enough to make the driver meekly follow after his two companions.

As soon as all three men were out of the truck, Alejandro, herding them before the headlights, nodded to his uncle. Pedro trotted to the edge of the shed and waved to Juan Rizal who was still standing fifty yards away, next to the second truck.

Muted, confused voices now came from the rear of the first truck. Alejandro, his pistol still trained on the leader, walked to the back of the truck where he made sure the tarpaulin was secured from the outside. The soft sounds coming from inside the truck seemed like the soft bleating of sheep.

His grim expression went slack. He knew that the men bunched in the back of the truck had braved the border crossing with only the intention of finding honest work, and in this they were doing nothing more than following in the footsteps of his own family. Yet a cruel circumstance had made them his enemy. He whispered an encouraging word to the men he could hear just on the other side of the tarp. The delay was temporary, he said. They would all soon be safely on their way again. He did not mention in which direction.

In the darkness, Francisco and Maria were intently watching him from inside Pedro's car. Staring out toward the truck, Francisco experienced the strange sensation of being a spectator watching events completely alien to his nature. Something precious, he thought, was being lost, though he was not certain of exactly what it was.

He was aware, however, that what was now unfolding before his eyes bore little connection to the dream he had harbored in his heart for more than ten years. He looked over at Maria with what he hoped was a reassuring smile. It was not enough to sway her. She continued to quietly pray.

The second truck now came lumbering around the shed with Juan Rizal trotting alongside it. As it came to a full stop, he opened the door and hauled the driver out, then hurried him toward the front of the first truck where the leader and the two other Mexicans were still standing. In the glare of the headlights, the men seemed suspects in a police line-up.

Shoving the leader off to one side, Alejandro turned to the three other men. "Start walking," he said in Spanish.

The driver of the second truck, dazed by this sudden sweep of events, nervously fingered the ring on his hand.

"¿A dónde, señor?" he asked in a quavering voice.

"Home," Alejandro grimly replied. "Start out across that field. Keep off the highway, but stay close to it. The road will take you back to the Rio Grande."

His voice was stern, but his eyes betrayed him. The driver of the second truck was a young man of his own age, with a slender body and eyes which seemed haunted by deprivation. Alejandro noticed the man's wedding band, and he wondered how many children the man might have and whether he had always been able to feed them.

"All three of you, get moving—and consider yourselves lucky. You will not have to walk as far as the others," he said, steering the three men with his pistol toward an open field. Looking utterly defeated, they began to trot away into the darkness.

Now he waited until they had gone more than fifty yards, then turned and nodded to Pedro and Juan Rizal. The Filipino jumped into the cab of the second truck as Pedro hurried back toward his car. Seconds later, the Model-A went rolling to the highway and turned in the direction of Mission. Once the car disappeared, Juan took the truck out from behind the shed. Flashing his lights and sounding his horn, he signaled for the convoy to follow after him. The lights of the truck next in line snapped on, and a moment later, the entire convoy was again moving. Juan Rizal saw it coming in his rearview mirror. Grinning, he ground his machine into gear and started away, now at the head of the convoy.

There remained one large and immediate problem: Alejandro had to find out where the convoy was originally headed, for it probably was there that the remainder of the contractor's money would be waiting. He would have to either coax the convoy leader into cooperating or try to beat the information out of him. Judging by the man's size, that could turn into an all-night chore.

When he could no longer hear the guttural roar of the convoy, he motioned the contractor back behind the steering wheel of the truck. Climbing in on the other side, Alejandro indicated that they should move off in the same direction the trucks had taken. The vehicle groaned through a turn and lumbered back toward the highway. As he framed his first question, a thought stopped him cold. It was obvious that the convoy leader must have been ordered to deliver his workers to some secluded spot, which meant the convoy would have had to move over back roads and through little-known areas to a place the contractor might never have seen before. Somewhere in his truck there had to be a map.

In the glove compartment he found nothing but a few Mexican comic books and a half-empty bottle of tequila. Then his eye caught something stuck above the visor. Holding the piece of paper to the dashboard light, he smiled. The map was conveniently marked. A large X indicated the final destination of the convoy.

Turning to the driver, he lowered his pistol slightly in a gesture of vague goodwill. "You just saved us both a lot of bumps and bruises." The man flashed an uncertain smile.

A light rain had started to fall, and in the heavy mist of the moonless night, Alejandro almost missed the next junction on the highway. 'There, turn to the right," he suddenly barked. "And then stop and cut off your lights."

The convoy leader grunted a prayer, thinking his final hour had arrived. The truck came to a stop some fifty feet behind another vehicle. Then the lights of the truck snapped off. Alejandro saw someone approaching in the darkness. Leaning over to take the truck's keys from the ignition, he climbed out and walked back to the rear of the truck where he stood whispering with the four people who had just joined him.

"Everything okay, Juan?"

Rizal's grin broke through the darkness. "I took the trucks off to the west about five-hundred yards past the junction. Then I stopped, got out and walked around in circles, just like you told me, before I came back here to meet your father."

Alejandro reached through the shadows to pat the Filipino on the shoulder. "The other trucks followed you okay?"

Juan Rizal could not resist a satisfied chuckle. "Like elephants in a circus."

The Filipino's mood seemed contagious. Alejandro turned to his father, a subtle hint of pride in his voice. "Well, that's some two hundred workers we don't have to worry about anymore."

Francisco nodded somberly. Pedro, accurately sensing his feelings, whispered, "We have been lucky, Francisco. We should stop now, while we still win."

Francisco could not see the faces of Pedro or María clearly, though he could almost feel the grim expression in their eyes — but knew he had already gone beyond the point of no return.

"I made a promise to my son," Francisco murmured to Pedro. "And you know how few times I have been able to help him."

Pedro shrugged. It was too capricious to comprehend. In the minds of the two men he loved most, an illegal and dangerous course of action seemed their only way toward reconciliation.

"María and I meet you at the tower in about an hour?" Pedro murmured.

Francisco pulled Pedro and María closer to him. "But if we are not at the tower in one hour, we probably ran into trouble. So get away from there fast. Tomorrow morning, Pedro, you do what I should have done several days ago. Settle the strike the best way you can."

Pedro and María recoiled slightly. Francisco had finally admitted his error, but he seemed wistful than remorseful.

"If I liked better what we do," Pedro said, "I would pray for divine help."

Francisco chuckled. "Even with your crazy driving, it got us this far."

María spun abruptly and started back to the car. She had wanted to send Francisco off with an encouraging word, but his bantering remark cut her to the bone. Pedro turned to Francisco, shook his head sadly, and headed back to the car himself.

Alejandro found the key to the lock that secured the truck's rear tarp. Opening it, he helped his father into the hold. Past the covering, frightened Mexicans anxiously peered out from the shadows. He muttered something to them in Spanish. The man who had just climbed into the truck, he explained, was only another worker belatedly joining the convoy. Francisco turned back to Alejandro. There seemed nothing more to say, so he simply shook hands. It was the first time they had shaken hands since even before the night Juanita Salazar died.

CHAPTER 26

Half an hour later, the big truck roared around a sharp bend in the highway, onto a dirt road, and past the large billboard that sat on the edge of the Hennessy farm. Alejandro nodded to Juan Rizal, who was sitting next to the window. They had earlier discarded the stiff-billed khaki hats and now wore battered snap-brim models, which they had pulled down low over their faces. They were still fifteen minutes away from their final destination, but were now in enemy territory.

At a clearing less than three miles away, Hennessy and his men were making ready for the arrival of the convoy. The area, about an acre in size, was enclosed by a chain-link fence. Only one gate led into the enclosure, and over it hung an old railroad lamp, its green light blinking through the blackened mist. Directly under the lamp and next to the gate, a supervisor stood guard, a ten-gauge shotgun cradled in his stumpy arms.

Inside the enclosure, under an overhanging tin roof, Hennessy sat counting out several stacks of money. The bills were all in ten and twenty dollar denominations. The Mexican labor contractor had warned him that larger bills would draw unwanted attention on the workers back on the south side of the Rio Grande River.

As Hennessy counted out separate stacks of one hundred dollars each, Jess Ballard wrapped them with a rubber band and tucked the money into a small canvas mailbag. Several supervisors huddled nearby around a little coffee urn that was no longer working. The men seemed disgruntled at being out on such a cold, rainy night. Earlier, Hennessy had made the night more frigid by announcing that they would not be paid for this extra service.

Now he paused in the count to bring his fingers to his mouth. A disgusted frown formed on his haggard features. Twice he had told Ripps to turn down the volume on the radio and, though the sound was now quite low, it still rasped on Hennessy's nerves.

Ripps sat perched on the seat of a tractor where he could hear all that was being said yet was high enough so Hennessy could not reach him with his bamboo cane.

The money held Ripps's eyes like a magnet. Hennessy had already warned him that by daybreak of the following morning, he wanted him out of the valley. Ripps had decided to go to California. It was also filled with Mexican migrants, and the growers there could probably use a man who knew how to keep their workers in line. But he would money to make such a long trip.

Hennessy was also thinking about money. Jerking his thumb in Ripps's direction, he said, "Shit, I oughta make that moron with the music box pay all this outa his own pocket, since he caused about ninety-eight percent of all our fucking problems. See how he'd like that music."

Ballard snorted. "Ripps never learned that tune—most likely the main reason he's had to spend so much time at the Huntsville Hotel."

Hennessy wet his fingers and started to count again. "Yeah, and if he ain't real careful, the stupid bastard's gonna get to sing the jail-house blues one more time."

Ripps barely heard the threat. He had noted that with the last stack of bills, there was now three thousand dollars in the sack. That much money was enough for the moment to keep his mind off murder.

For several miles now, Francisco Salazar had listened to the muted voices coming from every corner of the rear of the truck. He wondered what the faces that went with the voices were like. Most sounded young in years but old because of the things they said; below the border, there was sickness and disease and very little work. There were more than twenty men crammed into the back of the truck, and the smell was acrid. It was not the smell of filth, for these men came from a culture that prized personal cleanliness. Rather, it was the sad smell of poverty, of clothing that had been worn too long, of breath that hinted of food that was meager and not healthy enough. It was also the smell, if such a thing was possible, of utter desperation.

Francisco remembered another journey, one which also had ended near the little town of Mission but had begun much farther to the south. He and his wife and son had made that trip almost ten years before, but in a vehicle that had smelled much better. In some ways, he thought, his life seemed to be going backwards.

A sharp sound startled him. Alejandro, having seen the blinking green light up ahead, had tapped the rear panel of the truck cab with the snout of his pistol, then quickly had jabbed it into the driver's ribs. The labor contractor began to gear down. By now, he had realized that his convoy of workers had been diverted. There would be little chance of collecting his last three thousand dollars. The truck ground to a stop at the gate. The supervisor warily came forward, his shotgun poised for action. He scanned the faces of the men in the cab.

"Where the hell's the other trucks?" the supervisor demanded to know, walking up to the driver's window.

The contractor felt the gun in his ribs again. Alejandro then spoke, though he was careful not to lean too far forward.

"The others are a couple of minutes behind us, Señor. We came ahead to make sure everything was okay."

This seemed a reasonable precaution. Nodding, the supervisor unlatched the gate and pulled it open. The truck rumbled slowly into the compound.

Alejandro saw several men standing under a long, low-slung shed which sat on the driver's side of the truck. A string of bare light bulbs ran the length of the shed, but some of them had gotten wet and were sputtering on and off.

As the truck came to a stop some fifty feet from the shed, a half-dozen of Hennessy's men came out from under the shed and started toward truck. Watching them approach, the contractor's hand went toward his boot. But the pistol pressed to his side changed his mind. He twisted back toward Alejandro and whispered, "I have to open up the back for them."

Alejandro took the keys from the ignition, and passed them to a supervisor who had just come up to the window.

"The little silver key, Señor."

The man nodded and ambled toward the rear of the truck.

"Where's the rest of 'em, Rodriguez?"

Again, the Mexican felt a sharp stab of pain in his side.

"Two minutes away, Señor Hennessy!" the driver called out with a strained smile.

The tarp had been unlocked, and the men inside the truck began to cautiously climb out. Hennessy started toward the truck.

"So how many folks you get for me, Rodriguez?" Hennessy asked, expecting a song and dance as to why the final figure had not come up to the agreed-upon number. The Mexican contractor hesitated for a moment. His truck was now surrounded by armed supervisors. Then, in his rearview mirror, he saw that the gate had been reclosed, still guarded by the man with the shotgun.

"Well, maybe a few more than we count on," he finally replied.

Hennessy nodded in the direction of his foreman. Ballard cinched tight the canvas bag and sauntered from the shed to hand over the final payment. The contractor mumbled his thanks.

"All right, Rodriguez," Hennessy commanded. "You can make your turn around that lower shed...and then don't stop rolling till you get back across the river. Some Texas lawman catches you with that much money, he's gonna think sure you stole it—and I ain't gonna tell him no different."

The big man nodded solemnly. The grower had dealt fairly with him, and for a second he experienced a mild attack of remorse. He waved and made a wide turn and headed back toward the gate. The truck had not traveled more than twenty feet, however, when Alejandro grabbed the canvas sack. Handing it to Juan Rizal, he turned to crack the rear panel with his pistol again, this time twice.

In the hold of the truck Francisco heard the sound and knew it meant his son now had the money. Stumbling to the rear of the truck, Francisco peered past the flapping tarp. They were now only moments away from being clear of the enclosure. Then Francisco heard a sound. From the darkest corner of the truck, two Mexican workers had just roused themselves. The younger seemed drunk; the older man, apparently overcome by the congestion and foul smell, had obviously lapsed into semiconsciousness.

Now, as the truck rumbled toward the gate, both men stumbled to the rear and called out for the truck to stop. It was nearing the exit when Hennessy saw the two men.

"Hey, stop the truck," Hennessy boomed out. "We didn't get all the grease unloaded!"

A few of Hennessy's men trotted from under the shed, annoyed at having to go out into the rain again. In the cab of the truck, the contractor heard the command to stop. He had just barely brushed his brake pedal, when he suddenly felt himself flying out the vehicle. In the moment he had turned back in the direction of the shed, Alejandro had leaned over, opened the door, and shoved him hard. The driver hit the ground and rolled heavily over himself before coming to a stop in a sitting position.

But he had barely stopped moving when he began to bellow at the man guarding the gate. The supervisor had no idea what was happening, but something about it seemed comical. The Mexican, still sitting on his rear, looked as foolish as someone trying to command troops from a toilet seat.

Alejandro had slid behind the steering wheel, which now twisted crazily, as if with a mind of its own. For several harrowing seconds, he fought to tame the wildly spinning wheel.

Up ahead, the supervisor quickly closed and latched the gate. The two-ton truck hit the wire meshing at an angle, but the size and speed of the machine made it no contest. Hauling half the gate across his front bumper, Alejandro took the truck hurtling down the dirt road. The concussive sound of shotgun blasts came from inside the enclosure. Several of Hennessy's supervisors, standing where the gate had been, were furiously firing. But their target had become nothing more than a faint speck of red light.

As the firing continued, the labor contractor tried to explain to Hennessy what had happened. But every other word out of the Mexican's mouth was a curse word in Spanish. It took the grower several seconds to piece together the story. When he had done so, Hennessy screamed for Ripps to bring around his fastest vehicle.

Alejandro had sped some two hundred yards away from the enclosure before he turned on his headlights. But being able to see the road did nothing to improve it. As he struggled to avoid the worst of the ruts ahead of him, he did not notice the set of lights behind him, now knifing away at the distance that separated the two vehicles. From the rear of the truck, Francisco yelled out a warning. But it made no difference; the truck could go no faster.

Up ahead was the narrow, short-spanned bridge that they had crossed on their way to the compound. Alejandro realized that with half the gate still hooked to his front bumper, he might not be able to make it across the bridge.

At the mouth of the bridge, he brought the truck to a full stop. He had driven past several turns in the road and could no longer see the lights of the pickup. But he knew it was only seconds behind him. As the big truck stopped, Francisco and Juan Rizal jumped out and tried to pull the gate from the bumper. Alejandro gunned his motor furiously, but he had bullied the truck only a few feet across the bridge when the machine stopped cold.

Francisco shouted out a command. "Come on! We can swim faster than this!" he yelled, and taking the canvas sack from the truck's floorboard, he tossed the money to Alejandro, who for a split second hesitated, then flung himself toward the door just as the truck shuddered under the brunt of a shotgun blast.

Startled, they saw that the blazing lights of the pickup were now less than fifty yards away. In another moment, the three men leaped from the bridge.

The water was less than four feet, and hitting bottom they sank deep into the mud below the water. They had just surfaced when they heard the sound of a splash. Then, almost immediately came a second one. Alejandro held the canvas bag up with one hand; his pistol poised high in the other.

Then, with a slurping sound, two men came bobbing to the top of the water: the Mexicans who had been left in the back of the truck. For a fleeting second, the five men stared dumbly at each other. Finally, three of them broke into a strangled laugh.

Jess Ballard had the eyes of a hawk, and, as the lights of the pickup truck had snared the three men on the bridge for a split second, he had recognized them. But for the moment, he decided to keep this information to himself.

As the pickup snarled to a stop behind the convoy truck, Hennessy began screaming in every direction. Three of his supervisors bolted from the back of the pickup and went sliding down the steep bank of the ditch, and after the five men.

Alejandro was moving in a southeasterly direction. He had learned in the Marine Corps how to steer a course by the stars. But on this rain-swollen night, there were no celestial lights to guide him. He and the others had gone some hundred yards through an orchard thick with apricot trees when a road materialized. They stopped, undecided about which way to run. Then, hearing a sound behind them, Alejandro whirled his pistol around. But it was only the two Mexican workers. The five men stood looking at one another. Then they saw that back in the orchard, several lights had come into view, dancing about like fireflies.

Turning back to the Mexicans, who looked like half-drowned dogs, Alejandro explained that if they continued to follow him, their lives would be in serious danger. The two men nodded — but when he and the others darted across the road and into another orchard, the Mexicans hurried haplessly after them.

He had just stopped to warn them once again when his father heatedly interrupted him. "Save your breath. These poor hermanos see better than they hear — and we are not the ones shooting at them."

CHAPTER 27

Pedro took out his pocket watch again. It had been almost two hours since he had left the others back at the junction. Now, sitting in the dark, his car next to the water tower that was to have been their rendezvous point, Pedro made a decision. He would wait till daybreak. If Francisco and Alejandro had not returned by then, he would go look for them.

Francisco had ordered him to wait no more than an hour, but all that mattered to Pedro now was that what remained of his family appeared to be in deep trouble. For the past hour, he and María had barely spoken to each other, both too troubled to make an attempt at conversation. But in the first hour, with still in a hopeful mood, they had broken through the barrier that had always separated them.

It had been surprisingly easy. They were committed to the same cause and the same man, a firm foundation for a friendship, they realized, they could have formed years before.

The rain had slackened to only a light drizzle now, but the night was still black and starless. Climbing out of his car, Pedro stood listening to the eerie quiet. He was almost directly under the water tower, yet in the all-enveloping darkness, he had to squint to see it. His shoulders sagged with dismay. If he, standing only a few yards from the tower could barely see it, what hope did the others have to spot it from a distance? Leaning into his car, he clicked the lights on and off.

From a distance, the weak little lights looked as forlorn as a dim beacon coming from a deserted lighthouse.

The five men had stumbled through one orchard after another, but in exactly which direction Alejandro did not know. Pushing through low-hanging branches, he had cut his face and hands. He and the others now came out of an orchard and started across a large tomato field. Ahead, in the moonlight that had finally broken through the swollen sky, he saw what seemed a graveyard for discarded farm machinery. Pointing toward it, he led the others forward.

They had stumbled over several deep furrows when they saw the lights coming from the orchard behind them. A moment later, the air shuddered with the twin charge of a shotgun. Alejandro instinctively ducked, then pointed toward the machinery. "There, it's our only cover."

Still clinging tightly to the canvas sack, he broke into a run. His father and Juan Rizal started after him, but then something stopped Francisco short. A few yards behind him, the two Mexicans had come to a halt, seemingly at last resigned to the inevitable.

They had made the long journey from the border, hoping to find no more than decent work. Instead they had found something as incomprehensible as a nightmare. What they did understand was that they could run no farther. Slowly sinking to the ground like exhausted animals, they looked dazed with despair.

Glancing back at the approaching lights, Francisco could do no more than silently salute the two Mexican. Then, catching up with the Filipino, he noticed that the area up ahead was enclosed.

It had two gates, one at either end, and in the moonlight the machinery inside seemed strangely forbidding. Crossing through the enclosure, Francisco, Alejandro and Juan Rizal came within twenty yards of the front gate when they saw the road just beyond it suddenly bathed with light.

The pickup truck was moving very slowly, and as it neared the front gate, Alejandro recognized it. Turning to his father, he gestured in the direction of the rear gate. The three men started for it. But as they darted from one machine to another, the stillness was suddenly shattered, making the metal directly above them shiver..Alejandro hit the ground instantly, and peered toward the rear gate. Three of Hennessy's men were moving warily into the enclosure, the moonlight glinting off the barrels of their shotguns.

Inside the enclosure, Alejandro crawled back to where his father and the Filipino were crouched and laid aside the canvas sack to take out his pistol. The silence split once again with the deep growl of shotgun fire. The sheet metal above them shook with a loud whining sound.

Alejandro took hold of his father's arm. "You and Juan go for the front gate. I'll cover you from here and catch up with you in that orchard on the other side."

"No. I got you into this. It's for me to get you out," Francisco replied, voice cold with conviction. "Now, before the truck comes back," he added, grabbing the gun and box of shells.

"No, this was my idea that—"

"But the strike was my responsibility. Go!"

It took Alejandro a few seconds to decide. Then he suddenly clapped the Filipino on the shoulder, and in the next instant both men broke for the front gate.

A heavy volley of shotgun blasts came at them from near the rear gate. Francisco twisted around and fired back. He aimed high, but the sound of his return fire was enough to momentarily silence the shotguns.

In that split-second lull, Alejandro and Rizal bolted out the front gate and across the road into the darkness of the orchard. Moments later, Alejandro realized with a start that he had left behind the canvas sack. His father, however, had not forgotten it. Pistol in one hand, the growers' money in the other, he took a deep breath and bolted for the gate. But just as he reached it, the area was suddenly showered with light. The night exploded with gunfire.

Francisco froze for just a second, snared like a startled animal by the blinding glare coming from the lights of the pickup. In that moment a ten-gauge shotgun blast grazed his shoulder. His body spun wildly around and he dropped heavily to the ground.

From across the road, Alejandro saw his father fall. In that instant, he lost all track of time. The present suddenly became the past, the future too unbearable to even contemplate. He could feel Juan Rizal tugging at his arm, trying to tell him something. But all he could hear were the words that had blistered his ears the night his mother had died.

He had held his father partially responsible for his mother's death. Now he knew he would forever hold himself accountable for the death of his father. The cycle was complete.

Francisco had managed to scramble back inside the enclosure where he took cover behind a cultivating machine just beyond the gate. There, in the darkness, he sat catching his breath, pondering his next move.

He began to reload his pistol, not an easy thing to do now as his left arm was lifeless. Then he realized that he had lost more than just the feeling in his arm. He turned back toward the gate. There, by the edge of the road, lit up like a statue, was the canvas money sack.

Three figures were slowly approaching it, moving along the shadowy edge of the fence. From where Francisco sat, he had an unobstructed view of the area around the gate. The sack was only some twenty yards away from him. Gazing at it Francisco suddenly hated what it represented, hated that part of himself he knew he had lost in going after it. Yet the money still meant something to him, so he casually fired off another round. The bullet kicked up the dust a few feet away from the sack. Sufficient warning, Francisco thought.

The night went ominously quiet. As Francisco waited for whatever was coming next, long-forgotten things came softly tramping through his thoughts. It had been more than forty years since he had last fired a gun. It was 1910, the beginning of the Mexican Revolution. The shooting around Chihuahua City had spread like a deadly virus. Francisco's father, Sebastián, forced to buy a rifle, had taken his two young sons out into a field to show them how to use the weapon.

They had spent an hour firing at bottles and tin cans that Sebastián had given the names of the worst enemies of the Revolution. None of the names had meant anything to Francisco. But pleasing his father had, and he had tried to shoot well. Remembering that morning of so many years before, a smile formed over his haggard features. Strange thoughts, he mused, for him to have now that his life might not last out the night.

CHAPTER 28

Alejandro and the Filipino had just made it to the edge of the orchard when they heard the gunfire. Whirling around, he had seen his father stagger and fall. His right hand instinctively opened as he cursed himself for not having brought along a second gun. Several agonizing seconds would pass before he realized that his father was not dead. Francisco was crawling back toward the enclosure. Then Alejandro noticed that his father had left behind the canvas sack.

Ballard peered again at the sack. He didn't much care who ended up with the money, as long as it wasn't the man crouched next to him. Earlier, Ballard had noted the gleam in Ripps's eyes as the money was being counted. Now, he sensed that the ex-jailbird was only waiting for the right moment to stake his claim.

Ballard had earlier returned from the adjoining arbor where he'd been sent to ascertain whether the two men who had raced across the road were still in the immediate area. But he figured he wasn't making nearly enough money to get shot at, and so had made only a cursory inspection of the orchard.

"Well, shit, did you at least get a good gander at the guy we hit?" Hennessy growled.

Ballard shook his head and casually lit a cigarette. "Didn't see the two others, neither. Probably halfway to hell by now."

Hennessy, straining to control himself, turned to the other men. "Then that bastard inside the gate is the only one left," he said, "So you three guys rush him. I'll be right behind you to pick up the money."

None of the supervisors moved a muscle. Then one of them let loose a short stream of tobacco juice—which seemed to summarize the general reaction to Hennessy's command.

"Come on now, boys, show some balls," Hennessy hissed. "That son of a bitch is all shot up, probably even out of ammunition. Hell, maybe even dead—"

In that moment came the percussive sound of another blast. The men instinctively ducked down.

"Aw, shit, you boys so fucking stupid you can't tell a pistol from a shotgun?" Hennessy snarled. "That there blast came from the far side… from my other collection of idiots!"

Ballard, down on his haunches, looked up and smiled. "Yeah, but that don't mean the guy at the gate is outa powder. 'Course we could call over and ask him how his ammo is holding out."

Hennessy's face began to twitch. "Telling ya, outa ammunition, sure as shit, anyway gotta be dead by now, goddamn idiots—"

Ballard softly interjected, "We might be morons, but we're still smart enough to know we ain't making enough wage to get killed trying to save somebody else's money."

Ballard took another long drag off his cigarette. "But, hey, why don't you rush the guy? Hell, like you said, he's probably out of ammunition and dead by now anyway."

Hennessy glared at his foreman, then turned to the supervisors and suddenly gave them a strange, stunted smile.

"All right, boys," Hennessy murmured, "I'll rush the bastard myself. You men circle around back and tell the others that when they hear me yell, I want 'em to really let loose their cannons."

The three supervisors nodded uncertainly, thinking there was some catch to Hennessy's innocuous command, but then hurried off into the darkness. Ballard wearily flipped away his cigarette and started after them. Hennessy quickly grabbed him by the arm.

"Forget it, Ballard. No need for you to go anywhere but home."

Jess Ballard had not been surprised by much in a long time, but there was now genuine amazement in his pale-blue eyes.

"You saying I ain't your foreman no more?"

Hennessy grinned. "Hey, forget that foreman shit. You ain't even employed anymore. I just finally figured out that I can run things without you."

Ballard chewed on this for a moment. He rather liked the taste of it. "Well, okay. But just remember, I still got me a good chunk of money coming from the harvest."

"I'd get me a real sharp lawyer if I was you."

Ballard chuckled softly. "No, Jake. I've never had to rely on some shyster to get what was rightfully coming to me."

Hennessy abruptly turned away. Ripps, grinning, crawled closer to them, but said nothing.

"Think I'll follow those boys around back," Ballard said, "just to see they don't get lost. Oh, one final piece of professional advice, Jake: I'd watch this ex-con of yours real close. The men we been chasing ain't the only ones got their eye on that sack of money."

Ballard started away. As Ripps watched him move into the darkness, his jackal-like features went wide with relief. His competition had just narrowed. Like most dishonest men, Ripps had always imputed his own motives to everyone else. Now there was only Hennessy standing between him and a winner's trophy worth three thousand dollars.

His appraisal was not entirely correct. While Hennessy had been berating Ballard, Alejandro and Juan Rizal had found a hole in the enclosure some fifty yards away.

Francisco was still in the same spot as they cautiously came up along the fence. Hearing a slight sound, he slowly leveled his pistol and waited. He wondered who might be approaching and what he would do when they arrived. His son and the Filipino, he thought, were now safely away. So why not simply surrender? Far better than shooting, perhaps even killing, someone to protect money which had never rightfully been his. Then he saw that the sound had been made by his son. Alejandro knelt down next to him, relieved to see that his father was still alive, yet struck silent by the severity of his wound. Juan Rizal gently took the pistol from Francisco, then positioned himself where he might best protect their exposed flank.

Alejandro took off his denim coat and tucked it in Francisco's leather jacket next to his father's bloody shoulder. This done, he turned to face the Filipino. Yet for a long moment, Alejandro said nothing. He wondered why Rizal had chosen to come with them. Alejandro could understand his father's motive—but Rizal, it seemed, had come simply because he believed in something larger than either money or revenge. The thought humbled Alejandro.

"Juan, can you get my father out the other way by yourself?"

Rizal nodded, his eyes uncertain. "But what about you?"

Alejandro twisted around to get a better view of the front gate. "When you get into the orchard, go straight for about fifty yards, then to the right for another fifty yards. I'll catch up with you there."

Francisco's eyes narrowed with disbelief. "What good is the money to you if you are dead?" Alejandro gently took his father's hand in his. "If I can still get it, might do your workers some good. I owe it to you for getting you into all this—and for never being the son I should have been."

It was the first time in many years he had heard Alejandro speak to him in such a manner. He felt himself growing stronger, and for a moment the searing pain in his shoulder left him entirely.

Juan Rizal quietly broke the spell. "We better get going now."

Fifty yards away, Ballard arrived at the rear gate of the enclosure. Kneeling down behind some machinery, he lit another cigarette. Only a few minutes before, the other supervisors had reached the rear gate to join forces with the three men already there. Now the six men stared intently at Ballard, awaiting his command.

But Ballard simply shook his head and turned away. He looked out across the enclosure. The canvas sack still sat bathed in light at the lip of the front gate.

Less than thirty feet inside the gate, Alejandro poised himself to move. He had waited until he felt sure his father and Juan Rizal had made it safely out of the side of the enclosure and into the orchard. He had let the Filipino take the pistol, which left him with but three remaining weapons: surprise, agility and speed.

He took a deep breath and bolted toward the light.

The stillness shattered almost instantly. Racing for the gate, Alejandro could feel and hear the metal around him shuddering and whining. He had just reached the inner edge of the gateway when he stumbled and careened to the ground, still some five yards shy of the sack.

As the first shotgun blasts sounded, Hennessy darted up behind Ripps. "Now, rush him, you bastard! He gets the money into that orchard, it's gone!"

The gate was being blistered with buckshot, and Ripps seemed disinclined to expose himself to such a barrage.

Suddenly, he was violently shoved forward, and went tumbling to the dirt several feet past the front fender of the truck. But almost instantly he came crawling back, his face twisted with fury. "Bastard," Ripps howled, "you want the money that bad, you fucking go get it!"

These words had barely spewed from Ripps's mouth when Hennessy smashed his fist into his face. Then he grabbed the smaller man by the neck and slammed him hard to the ground.

It was the respite Alejandro needed to crawl the last few yards to the money sack. Taking hold of it, he went stumbling across the road and into the adjoining arbor.

Watching him, Hennessy's last vestige of self-control splintered into flying shards. He began to pummel Ripps with his fists and hobnailed boots, kicking him again and again in the face and kidneys. Then, finally spent, he stumbled toward the front gate.

But he had gone only a few feet when he felt the heavy twin barrel of Ripps's shotgun slam into the base of his neck. The blow sent Hennessy sprawling to the ground. Struggling to remain conscious, he rolled over on his back and tried to breathe as deeply as he could. Then he heard a voice from somewhere above him.

"Mister, you done whipped me for the last time."

Hennessy heard the sound of a motor starting up. Turning, he tried to clear his eyes. The truck slowly moved toward him, and from where he lay, it looked big as a house. The truck's twin spots slowly passed over him, big as search-lights, and then the oversized tires. Hennessy heard the sound of his bones breaking. The truck's front wheels rolled past his body and the long undercarriage inched past his face as the rear wheels came closer—and again the sound of squashed flesh and splintering bones.

The rear of the truck rolled past him and stopped. He heard the truck's transmission clunk into reverse gear, and then knew that Ripps was hell-bent on grinding him into hamburger.

Hennessy tried to roll to one side, but his feeble effort only made him a larger target. The lower part of his body seemed caught in quicksand. The rear wheels of the truck were just crunching toward him when Hennessy heard the shot that saved his life.

The truck shuddered to an instant halt.

Ballard lowered his shotgun. The blast had shattered the entire right side of the windshield of the truck. Inside the cab, Ripps sat frozen with fright, staring straight ahead with the unblinking eyes of a reptile.

"Get that snake out of the truck," Ballard muttered to the other men as he moved back to where Hennessy still lay crumpled only a foot away from the truck's rear tires.

Ballard knelt down and tried to ascertain the extent of the injury. While he did so, two of the supervisors opened the door of the truck and jerked Ripps out from behind the steering wheel. Hitting the ground hard, the ex-convict was starting to get to his feet when he looked up into the twin barrels of four shotguns. With a defeated moan, he sank back to the dirt.

Hennessy's eyes focused, and the first face he saw was Ballard's. Reaching up, he weakly pulled him closer.

"Kill him, Jess," Hennessy murmured. "Kill him like he was gonna kill me... let that be the last thing I see."

"Getting a bit dramatic, ain't you, Jake?" Ballard asked with an unconvincing smile. "Hell, you should know by now that Ripps can't do anything right."

Pulling himself free of the grower's grasp, Ballard said, "Besides, I'm on my own time now."

Getting to his feet, Ballard motioned forward a few of the supervisors and together they lifted Hennessy toward the bed of the truck. "Careful, boys," Ballard muttered as the men took hold of their boss's mangled body. "He's got one hip and half the ribs he owns broke real bad." After they had laid Hennessy onto the truck bed, Ballard peered down at him. Strange how tough it was, he thought, to still hate a man you thought you'd never see alive again.

"Jake, first off, we're gonna get you to a hospital. Then we're gonna take this..." and here Ballard jerked his thumb back in Ripps's direction, "this animal off to the zoo. Me and the boys here just witnessed a case of attempted murder, which should be enough to keep him locked up in the Huntsville Hotel for the rest of his life."

Hennessy nodded gratefully, then said in a suddenly corrosive voice: "But it was that Salazar kid must have started this mess. Saw him clear, Jess, no mistake."

Ballard grimaced. "I'd leave well enough alone for now, if I was you...though if it'll make you feel any better, after we get you to the hospital, I'll see if I can still track him down."

A faint smile came over Hennessy's pale face. "Gonna make this up to you, Jess."

"No need to do that, Jake," Ballard snorted. "Firing me was more than good enough."

CHAPTER 29

It was nearly dawn. Pedro and María had lapsed into a painful silence that held them mute for the past half hour. During that time, María had decided that the rendezvous point which Alejandro had mentioned was not the water tower, but rather a large barn less than half a mile away. Pedro thought she was grasping for straws, and said he would stay and wait a little while longer.

Within twenty minutes, María reached the barn only to find it deserted. Yet instinct told her to stay. Sitting down inside the door, she fastened her eyes on the darkness outside and began to pray.

A sliver of light had broken over the horizon, and the mist had begun to rise from the ground. In the soft, smoky light, the three men emerged like figures out of a dream. She saw them just as they came clear of a thicket of tall brush.

She ran out toward them, but her smile failed when she saw their faces, and vanished when she noticed that the left side of Francisco's body was drenched with blood. Taking off her coat, she draped it around him then turned to Alejandro and Juan Rizal. They did not look much better. They had been half-carrying Francisco for the last few miles and had gone about as far as they could. Getting him into the barn, they laid him on a pile of straw. María began to inspect his wound.

As Alejandro stood over his father, his body leaned at a strange angle. He seemed on the verge of falling.

"Pedro, at the water tower?"

"Yes," María muttered, her eyes on Francisco. "I came here thinking this was the place you said for us to meet. I guess I made a mistake."

"Good mistake," Francisco murmured. "We could not have gone much farther." Turning toward Alejandro, he said, "Go get your uncle…and take your money with you."

Alejandro weighed the request for a moment. "Let me stay with you. Juan can go, okay?"

A smile crept across Francisco's face. He reached up toward his son. Alejandro sank to his knees and took his father's hand in his. Both seemed aware that something important had changed between them, yet inexperienced at expressing their deepest feelings toward each other, their words came hard and only a few at a time. María watched as they struggled to say what had always been buried in their hearts.

"Besides, it is your money. Yours and the workers. All of you earned it, not me."

Francisco's expression crumpled with guilt. "Still, it is time I help you get something for yourself, make up a little for all the times I did nothing.

Alejandro stared at the worn knots on his father's hand; the history of his long struggle had been written on those gnarled hands. "There were always others that needed your help more than I did."

"What I think now is...you should get away from here with that money. Will you do that, just as a favor to me?"

The request was put in such a way that Alejandro could not refuse it. Stumbling to his feet, he looped the canvas bag over his shoulder. "Keep him warm, María. I'll be back as soon as I can."

María nodded but did not look up. Her eyes were brimming with tears she wanted neither Alejandro nor the Filipino to see. As Alejandro set off into the half-light of early morning, Juan closed the door and took up watch just inside the barn.

María turned to Francisco. Forcing a fragile smile, she said, "You have won. The growers will have to make their peace with us now."

His reply came slowly, as if he were still painfully building the ideas behind it. "It is the workers who have finally won. Now I have to get out of their way...so they can go on from here."

María suddenly remembered the vision she had had a few days earlier; the one in which a man had realized there was no place for him in the very thing he had built. Looking intently into Francisco's eyes, she sensed that her premonition was soon to become reality.

"But can you walk away from what you have worked so hard for all these years?" she softly asked, already aware that the man she loved was on the verge of making the most painful decision of his life.

"No, querida," he murmured, his voice now little more than a whisper. "The cause is walking away from me…and that is good. A man fights for something, hoping it will grow strong to go on without him… but now maybe I am like the soldier who does not know what to do when the fighting is finished."

Gazing into his eyes, María gently kissed him.

CHAPTER 30

Alejandro was stumbling across the furrows of an open field, the small canvas bag tied to his belt, swinging from side to side.

Finally stopping to catch his breath, he saw beyond a thick clump of trees what he had been hoping to see for the last several hours. Summoning up his strength, he started toward the tower, as yet unaware that a hundred yards behind him and closing fast was a Hennessy pickup truck.

Reaching a wide irrigation ditch choked with brush, he looked for another way to get to the tower, but the ditch seemed to run for several hundred yards. Hacking his way through the thick brush, he fell twice on his way down the steep incline. When he reached the water, it came well above his waist.

Fifty yards away, a figure suddenly appeared. The man was standing at the top of the ditch. But even if Alejandro had thought to look up, it would have been difficult to recognize the man. The sun was shining directly behind him, but what would have been obvious was that he was carrying a weapon.

Ballard intently watched as Alejandro thrashed through the water. The brush on the far side of the ditch was dense, and he had to wade against the tide, searching for a spot where he could climb from the water.

Hennessy's foreman had recognized him and had also seen the canvas bag floating beside him. He stood frozen at the crest of the ditch; his first impulse was to fire off a round. But then what? Should he manhandle young Salazar at gunpoint back to the sheriff's station? And what charge would he make against him? True, he had stolen three thousand dollars—but he had taken the money from men who were engaged in the commission of a crime.

The larger question in Ballard's mind was to whom he owed allegiance. Certainly not Hennessy, who had been underpaying him for years and would surely try to cheat him out of his rightful six percent share of Hennessy's upcoming profits. Nor did he feel he owed anything to the other growers, who, except for Margaret Devereaux, had always treated him like dirt under the heels of their expensive boots.

Slowly lowering his shotgun, he watched Alejandro come out of the water and struggle up the steep incline on the other side of the ditch. Moments later, reaching its crest, he quickly disappeared into an adjoining thicket.

As Ballard started to move back toward the pickup, something caught his eye. He stopped and peered down at the water slowly drifting toward him. Laying aside his shotgun, he started down to the base of the ditch. He had reached the edge of the water when the canvas bag came floating closer. Then, as if managed by some mysterious force, the bag snagged on a branch no more than a few feet away from him.

Crouching at the edge of the water, Ballard reached out and grabbed the bag. The money was very wet, but it looked as if it were all still there. Cinching the bag tight again, he stood still for a long moment, and then started up toward the crest of the ditch, where he saw that the morning had brightened. The mist had burned away, and the clear air smelled as good to him as fresh-cut grass.

In his youth, Pedro Terán had heard a story about a noble horse that had brought its rider a very long way to deliver a most important message. The townspeople had hailed the man as the hero. But when he tried to turn their praise in the proper direction, he saw that the real hero lay dead at his feet. Pedro was thinking about that story as he tried to start his old Model-A, so harshly punished the night before. Twice on the way to the water tower, the car had stalled; now it would not start. Knowing little about the mysteries of a car motor, Pedro began to make a personal plea to the car, quietly speaking to it as if it were an old friend.

Sitting next to him, Alejandro wondered whether the events of the previous evening had stretched Pedro's senses further than they had been designed to withstand. The moment might have been comical, yet given the circumstances chewing at its edges, Alejandro could only look on with a dismayed expression.

Thirty seconds passed as Pedro continued his quiet exhortation to the exhausted engine. Then he paused and tried the starter again. For a moment the car shuddered in protest, and then came alive. Alejandro shook his head in disbelief. He had long suspected that his uncle possessed special powers. Now he was certain.

Five minutes later, the old Ford pulled up in front of the barn. Jumping from the car, Pedro hurriedly made his way inside. Pausing only long enough to warmly shake hands with Juan, he knelt down next to Francisco to inspect his wound. The others withdrew a few feet away and awaited Pedro's diagnosis.

Pedro came to his feet, a small smile edging the fatigue from his face.

"I told them myself," Francisco murmured to Pedro, "the wound is not as bad as it looks."

Pedro turned to the others. "Well, do we get him to a hospital, or wait for him to get as bad as he looks?" Rizal quickly came forward and helped Pedro get Francisco to his feet.

"Everything will be okay, Pedro," Francisco muttered as they started him slowly toward the door.

"Don't talk," Pedro warned. "Save your strength for the growers."

"That's what...I am talking about. Time is running out for that peach harvest...and they will be depending on us, now that they got nobody else."

Pedro chuckled. In more than ten years, he had never heard Francisco express concern for anybody who was not a farm worker or a member of his own family.

María sensed Pedro's confusion. "Francisco wants you to go settle the strike...as the new leader of the workers."

Pedro stopped abruptly. "Hah," he muttered, "he must be hurt worse than we think!"

The morning had broken bright and clear. Francisco paused to savor the sunshine for a brief moment. "A fine day for a harvest, eh, Pedro?" he asked.

A simple question, yet Pedro could not answer it. His head and heart brimmed with thoughts so tangled they had completely silenced him. But of one thing he was sure; Francisco was about to walk away from the farm-worker federation he had founded and leave it in his hands.

Pedro felt like a man who had been an assistant for many years to a matador, and then had been abruptly beckoned out into the bullring itself. Ten years earlier, he had embraced the farm-worker movement only for the companionship it offered him. Since he was a rather lonely man, the cause had helped fill a void more fortunate men usually did with a family. Hence, of all the farm workers in the valley, he considered himself the least qualified to assume leadership of their federation.

"But why me?" Pedro asked in a tremulous voice. Francisco smiled. "For a very good reason, brother... because you earned it."

Pedro flinched. "But what about everything you have done for so many years to—"

"No, I only fought for it. There is a difference. Now the fighting is over...and Alejandro's former commander in Korea has told us what happens to old soldiers."

Pedro turned to Alejandro and was dismayed to see that he was wearing an approving smile. Alejandro looked at his father. He knew what the decision had cost him, and in this moment he was prouder of him than ever before.

After they eased Francisco into the back seat of the car the silence was broken by a question.

"Where is the money?" Juan Rizal asked.

Alejandro glanced down, then around where he was standing, and finally back toward the barn, his eyes wide with disbelief, yet curiously devoid of dismay.

"I must have lost it running to get my uncle."

The others fell silent for a moment, each digesting the revelation. Francisco was the first to speak. "You made a good trade."

His reaction enveloped the others. They sensed that in some mysterious manner the cause of justice had been served, though none were aware of just how equitably it had been rendered.

After they had climbed into the car, Pedro crossed his fingers and tried the starter. The engine, as if aware that its mission was not quite over, instantly sputtered to life.

They had gone no more than half a mile when Juan Rizal asked the question still on everybody's mind.

"What happens to you now, Mister Salazar?"

Francisco had always been a meticulous man with a plan for every contingency; yet beyond his decision to turn the leadership of the federation over to Pedro, he had made no other.

"I don't know," Francisco said to the young Filipino who had helped save his life. "But one thing sure...María and I will look for a place where the people don't need to be taking votes all the time." María turned, as if to caution him to save his strength. But his expression told her that he needed to get something else off his chest.

"The truth is...I never really listened to the voice of our people. The only one I heard was my own...and now it tells me I have come to the end of the road."

This was the saddest thing they had ever heard him say. Yet there was a smile on his face, which gave hint of a serenity that had taken him a lifetime to find. He had sensed that his son had finally forgiven him for the death of his mother, and this had freed Francisco to forgive both himself as well as the growers, whom he had always partially blamed for the death of his wife.

There was no one left to blame, nobody left to hate.

CHAPTER 31

The leadership of the migrant workers had already passed, if only temporarily, to an old black man who now made what he thought would be his final decision on behalf of the men, women and children entrusted to his care. Jones ordered that a broth be made from their last hundred pounds of potatoes—all that remained of the migrant food supply. "Potato broth for breakfast, and then we'll just have to let the Good Lord Himself handle lunch," Thomas Jones quietly intoned to Paquito.

Paquito had returned from a clinic in Mission, where the money Pedro had given him barely paid his bill. The young doctor had recommended that Paquito remain at the clinic for a few days, even offering the old Mexican the opportunity of paying off the bill in low monthly payments. But Paquito had never accepted anything on credit and thought it a litte late in his life to begin. He also believed it was a little late for his lungs as well.

Back at the harvest site, several large trucks bearing the Devereaux name were alongside the encampment. Margaret and Sam had arrived early that morning to make certain the regular camp had been properly cleaned and well stocked for the farm workers.

She and Sam had just completed their inspection when a Cadillac snaked its way through the congestion. Several men sat inside the car, and as it stopped alongside her, one of them poked his head out.

"Great day in the morning, Miss Margaret, I been looking everywhere for you," Agajanian said with a long-toothed smile.

"Been getting that camp cleaned and stocked. Want to give Salazar's folks a chance to rest and clean up, that's assuming we get this strike settled today."

"Oh, settling the strike should be no problem now," the old grower happily observed. "Guess you heard that Salazar is in the county hospital. Gonna be laid up for a while."

Margaret nodded blankly. She waited to see how much more information Agajanian might volunteer, though there was very little she didn't know about what had transpired the night before.

He had decided to tell Margaret only whatever might serve his purpose. But her cold expression now prompted him to turn up another card.

"Even heard that silly bastard Hennessy got all his own bones broke...and by one of his own goddamned men!"

Earlier, when she had first heard about the convoy of Mexican workers, she was infuriated that such a move had been launched without her approval. But for now, she still needed the old man's cooperation, so she remained silent. Sam, however, felt no such compunction.

"Yeah, but if Hennessy hadn't been trying to sneak in all them illegals from down south, he'd probably still be in one piece."

"Yeah, stupid son of a bitch sure snake-bit, ain't he?" Agajanian said, grinning. "First he's dumb enough to try and bring in that load of grease, then he lets 'em get taken around in circles for half the goddamned night! Gotta make you wonder if Jake's been playing with a full deck all along, don't it?"

Agajanian paused to run a hand through his mane of white hair. Sam stared at the old grower, thinking how incredibly transparent he was.

"Yeah, I never thought Mister Jake was real swift...but whoever first proposed that plan to him is even slower."

The lizard-skinned grower was wearing his reflector-style sunglasses, which now concealed the contempt in his eyes. Agajanian had never liked Sam Winslow any better than he had cared for the Frenchman who first brought Sam out of the fields.

The grower turned to Margaret. "Well, your boy here ain't thinking straight himself," he suggested. "Because with Salazar holed up in a hospital, his workers gonna be about as easy to lead as a thirsty horse to water."

Margaret and Sam had turned away, their gaze riveted on an old Ford that had pulled to a stop a few hundred feet away. Several workers started toward the car. The last time they had seen the old car, Francisco had been inside it. A murmur rose from the crowd. His absence seemed a troubling omen.

Climbing out, Pedro hurried toward where Paquito and Jones were ladling out the potato broth. Alejandro and Juan Rizal had also alighted from the car, but did not seem anxious to follow after Pedro. It was his job to explain the situation.

Moments later, almost two-hundred migrant workers had surrounded Pedro, and it took Sam Winslow longer to make his way through the crowd than it did to deliver his message. He had come to propose that Pedro meet that morning with the growers and foremen at the Devereaux home. In the meantime, the workers could rest in the adjoining camp where sandwiches and fresh water were waiting for them. The offer was graciously made and politely accepted. Watching Sam start back through the crowd, Tom Jones smiled. He admired the dignified and courteous manner in which he had made the offer.

"Well, now what you got to do," Jones said, turning back to Pedro, "is explain everything to the workers."

Pedro stared out at what seemed a sea of expectant-looking faces. "How does one talk to so many people?" he asked of no one in particular.

"Like you talking to an old friend," Jones said, smiling gently. "But you best get up where they can see you."

Climbing up onto the bed of a flatbed truck, he finally said, "Francisco Salazar should be making this speech, not me...but he was in a little accident and will not be back with us for awhile."

Pedro paused to clear his throat, which felt as if it were stuffed with cotton. He did not know what to say next, only that he had to continue speaking. The large crowd stirred restlessly. Standing at the edge of the truck bed, Paquito and Jones exchanged a worried glance.

Margaret and Sam also noticed that the workers were sodden and unresponsive. Agajanian saw the same thing. Grinning, he climbed out from his Cadillac to get a better look.

Pedro began to speak again. "So Francisco asked me, along with our good friend Tom Jones, to settle the strike the best way we can. Meanwhile, the Señorita Devereaux offers us the use of the camp. There you can rest for a few hours, and maybe by noon today, we start to bring in the harvest. So let's load into the trucks, eh? They will take you the rest of the way."

Pedro pointed toward the trucks. But the camp, which sat no more than three hundred yards away, might as well have been a hundred miles farther down the road. No one made any effort to move toward the trucks.

The sentiment of the crowd could have been expressed in the single sentence Sam muttered to Margaret. "They don't cotton to getting their orders from anybody but Francisco Salazar."

"Good Lord," Margaret said. "We couldn't get along with him; now seems nobody else can get along without him."

A few hundred feet away, Pedro started to alight from the truck when a question came from a little man in the crowd. He had asked if he might be permitted a question. Pedro, still standing on the truck, nodded. "Okay, Lidio. But make it an easy one."

Nodding, the little migrant worker snatched the hat from his head and stood fingering its tattered brim. Pedro, seeing how anxious the worker was, gently added, "And you take your hat off in church, not out in the hot sun."

The little man grinned sheepishly and put his hat back on. Then, taking a deep breath, he began to speak in so rapid a manner, Pedro could barely make out his question. "Okay, Pedro, I also wait long time, is okay, I like to wait it gives me time to think and what I think about is what can we expect now to happen thank you very much!"

A wave of relief swept across the little worker's face. His speech had seemed a perilous flight, and only now did he feel he had landed safely back. But his question had relaxed the crowd. Several people were smiling, amused by the manner in which the question had been posed and grateful somebody had found the nerve to ask it.

The moment had calmed Pedro down somewhat. As he now went about answering the question, his voice took on a strength that surprised no one more than him.

"What I think is this," he said, his eyes slowly scanning the crowd. "We have won nothing more than one small battle. The next one could be different. What I know is that we must try to deal fair. But they must understand this is part of what we were fighting for, the right to be given the chance to be fair. Now, with the little we have won, we see how well we use it. You will be the judge of that, not me. But for now, let's get on the trucks!"

414

His ordeal over, Pedro started for the edge of the truck, as some two hundred men, women and children began to move. Hurriedly, they wrapped together their meager belongings and started to climb on the Devereaux trucks that would carry them a distance of no more than a few hundred yards—but for the older workers, it seemed a destination they had been trying to reach for many years.

"Well, Pedro, with all due respect to Francisco, I ain't heard nobody talk no better to an old friend in all my life," Thomas Jones quietly said, putting his arm around him.

Alejandro was about to say much the same when his attention was abruptly drawn away. The farm workers had begun to softly sing the same song they had sung the day before, just after the crop dusters had blackened the sky with insecticide.

Agajanian stood mute for a moment. Then, grunting an obscenity, he climbed into the rear of his car and began to roll up the window. Margaret watched with a disdainful eye.

"Well, Bert, so much for your thirsty horses and water-trough theory, huh?"

Agajanian leaned forward to poke his driver. The black Cadillac made a short turn and began its retreat back toward the main highway, as several fully loaded trucks began to rumble by in the opposite direction.

"I wish Francisco was here to see this," Pedro said.

Thomas Jones nodded. "Yeah, I know, brother. But the man done all for us it was in him to do. The rest gonna be up to us." They strode silently toward Pedro's car. When they had reached it, Jones opened the passenger door for Pedro.

"Now, if you ain't of a mind to care, I'd like the honor of driving us over to the Devereaux house myself."

Pedro smiled ruefully. "You also don't like the way I drive, eh?"

Tom Jones laughed and got in behind the wheel. "Let's just say that years from now, I'd like folks to think I made some contribution to all this, even if it was nothing more'n getting us safely to the meeting this morning."

Pedro peered past the people still standing around the encampment, until he found the face he was searching for. Alejandro was standing alone, just across the road. Pedro motioned him forward, as if inviting him to come along to the meeting with the growers. Alejandro smiled. He could think of only one good rea-

415

son to go with his uncle: he had no other place to go. Pedro knew what he was thinking but still hoped that he would elect to stay by his side. He hated losing more than one Salazar at a time and was now on the verge of losing both of them in a single morning.

"Well, someday better men than me will come along behind us.... They will know what to do with what little we have won here."

Thomas started the car back toward the highway. As the Model-A passed by Alejandro, he gave them a wave that looked more like a salute.

The encampment was now almost deserted as the last truck prepared to pull away. Margaret and Sam were heading for their own machine when they saw Alejandro standing alone by the side of the road. For a moment Margaret considered the idea of asking him to come back to work for her. Then, remembering all the reasons why hiring him in the first place had never been a good idea, she reluctantly cast aside the thought.

Everybody was going somewhere—except Alejandro. He still had no idea where to go or what to do when he got there. He had always liked the idea of seeing California someday. Then again, he hated the thought of leaving his father and uncle behind. His head pulled him in one direction, his heart tugged him in another. Then he saw something that in an instant made him decide which of the two he would follow.

As the last truck slowly pulled past him, he caught a fleeting glimpse of a little girl. She was crunched in amongst the migrant workers up on the last truck but had managed to poke her arm through the side railing and was waving to him.

She was the little girl he had met the afternoon he had returned from the Korean War. He had invited her to his homecoming party. Now he felt strangely gratified that she had not forgotten him.

He found himself running along behind the last truck. When he reached it, several farm workers leaned down to help him aboard, then entwined their arms with his so that he wouldn't fall.

As the truck rumbled on toward the camp, he stood staring across what seemed a sea of trees passing below him. An image came to his mind. He was remembering the Pacific Ocean, a body of water he had twice crossed on his way to and from the Korean War—and he was thinking that like that immense ocean, perhaps the land now passing below him would always belong in some strange sense only to the men who truly loved it.

This had always been one of his father's favorite notions. Maybe, Alejandro mused, he was becoming more like his father than either of them had dreamed possible.

—THE END—

—EPILOGUE—

Pedro Teran had known that only one small battle had been won. What he could not foresee was that the winds of history would soon render it the last victory the farm workers of the Rio Grande Valley would win for another two decades.

In 1954, the United States implemented a program called Operation Wetback, and in its wake, hundreds of thousands of Mexicans from every part of the Southwest were deported, including many who had entered the U.S. legally under the Bracero Program in the 1940's.

Pedro, along with Francisco Salazar and Maria Anton, were among those deported. Only Alejandro Salazar, because he had served in the Armed Forces of his adopted country, managed to avoid the sweeping deportation order. That official mandate would vanquish a labor movement that several of the most powerful growers in south Texas had been unable to defeat.

But Pedro was right when he had said that better men would someday raise higher the farm workers' tattered banner, though in the decade that followed, their cause would lay fallow. But not forgotten.

Then, in the late 60's, it suddenly arose again, this time erupting with the force of a seismic tremor. The movement commenced in the San Joaquin Valley of central California, now led by a man who had himself once worked the harvests across the southern part of Arizona. This time, the cause would not fail.

For some of the Salazar family, the years that followed would not be so kind. Soon after returning to Mexico, Pedro was killed in an automobile accident. Francisco Salazar died in 1972, never having re-gained the use of his left arm. His wife, Maria, farmed the small piece of land they had managed to buy until her death in 1980.

Alejandro Salazar remained in Texas until the deportation order had taken away almost the last of the migrant workers Later, he wandered west, settling in Los Angeles. There, he worked at one meaningless job after another until 1960, when a chance encounter brought purpose back into his life.

After meeting Cesar Chavez at a rally in East Los Angeles, he quit his job the very next day to re-enlist in the farm worker cause. A few months later, in a farm worker field office, he noticed a young woman who looked familiar. Years earlier, Ilsita Villareal had been the little girl whom he had taken to the fiesta the night he had come home from the Korean War. Ilsita had been born in Texas, which made her an American citizen and hence able to avoid the deportation order.

Now, she was a pretty, sweet-faced woman of nineteen. Six months later, she and Alejandro were married in a meadow attended by several hundred farm workers.

Later, he was present when the first major farm-labor contract in American history was finally signed.

Alejandro's favorite cousin, war hero Miguel Salazar, eventually was elected to the National Board of Directors of the GI Forum, and proudly served in that position until almost the day he died. Frank Casillas, Miguel's former commander, passed away in 1953, at the age of forty-four. The professional soldier who had earned many medals for bravery had finally lost his long battle with alcoholism. Miguel delivered the eulogy at Casillas' funeral.

Years later Miguel was buried with full military honors, including a 21-gun salute at a military cemetery. He had left instructions that he wished to be laid to rest close to Captain Casillas, the soldier he had most admired.

As for Miguel's older brother, Raul, he was still in federal prison when he and Lorena Calderón were divorced. She would later marry the middle-age lawyer who had represented Raul at his trial. But the lawyer could not protect Raul from his own reputation, and soon after he was released, Raul was killed by a jealous husband outside a bar over in Juárez, in what was a classic case of mistaken identity. For one of the few times in his life, Raul had been innocent. After her elderly husband died, Lorena would remain in Dallas, and over the years would become admired for her many charitable activities.

Of Jose Luis's three sons, only the youngest, Santiago, would realize the dream of reaching his full potential. Graduating with top honors from Texas A&M in 1953, he later fought in the Vietnam War, rising to the rank of major. Afterward, he joined the faculty of his alma mater. Upon retirement, Professor Emeritus Santiago Salazar and his wife lived near the A&M campus in College Station, only a few hundred miles from the little town of Mission, where so many years earlier, another Salazar had once made a dream of his own come true.

Another dream came true many years later, when Alejandro Salazar and his wife, Ilsita, were at a ceremony as their daughter, Juanita—having attended Stanford University on a scholarship—graduated with a degree in Political Science.

Ten years later, Juanita—whom Alejandro had named after his mother, who had died in a tar paper shack on the edge of a migrant worker camp—was sworn in as one of the youngest representatives from the Delano area of the San Joaquín Valley to ever win office. The granddaughter of penniless migrant workers had been elected to represent a California district that contained some of the largest agricultural combines in the United States.

Fifty years earlier, her great grandfather, Sebastian Salazar, had sent the family to the United States in the hope it could someday make a better life for itself in *El Norte.* That hope had finally been fully realized.

ABOUT THE AUTHOR

Alejandro Grattan-Dominguez was born in El Paso, Texas, the oldest son of an Irish father and a Mexican mother. After flunking out of college twice, he finally made good at Texas A& M, before going on to SMU, (a transfer he likens as going from a concentration camp to a luxury resort) where he earned a BA in English Literature.

Relocating to Los Angeles, he worked as a claims adjuster, and amused by the fact that so many claimants experienced miraculous recoveries after receiving a settlement check, he wrote up a short synopsis—which somehow found its way to the famed director, Alfred Hitchcock, who over a very brief telephone call, encouraged Grattan to make a movie based on the story. After two long years, he had done exactly that—and thus his career in the movie business was born.

That career reached its zenith in 1979, when the filmmaker wrote, directed and co-produced the first major movie about the Mexican-American experience. The film, *Only Once in a Lifetime*, was invited to premier at the Kennedy Center, and later selected as one of a few films to represent the United States at the Deauville Film Festival in France.

Thereafter, Grattan's luck soured, as in his words, he developed a "reverse case of the Midas Touch." Finally, figuring that if he could not change his luck, he would at least change his location, he moved in 1987 to Mexico.

In 1988, he founded the Ajijic Writers' Group (which still exists today), and began writing novels. The next several years saw the publication of seven novels, (most of which are on amazon). The screenplays he adapted from some of his books have won several awards at film/script competitions in Mexico and the United States. In 2007, he was selected for inclusion in *Who's Who in Mexico*.

For the past 17 years, Grattan has been the Editor-in-Chief of *El Ojo del Lago* (Chapala.com), the most widely-read English-language magazine in Mexico.

His mother's country has proved lucky for him.

—THE LEGACY SERIES—

This book is part of the EgretBooks.com Legacy Series that comprises literary works conveying a broader awareness of cultural heritage.

Initial funding for the Legacy Series came from the estate of Helen May Miller, a native of the Missouri Ozarks, who sampled diverse cultures in her travels of more than sixty years across the USA, Canada, Mexico, and in Europe and Asia.

Ms. Miller began her career in the 1940's working at a succession of libraries in Arkansas, Maryland, Missouri, and on military bases in Germany and England. After returning to the United States in 1957 she pursued her career at state libraries in West Virginia and Idaho, serving almost nineteen years as the Idaho State Librarian before retiring in 1980.

A memoriam about her dedication to making books available to the public is on the Internet at
http://www.idaholibraries.org/idlibrarian/index.php/
idaho-librarian/article/viewFile/67/202

~ Mikel Miller, Managing Editor, EgretBooks.com

24096767R00256

Made in the USA
Charleston, SC
12 November 2013